TOGGENBURG – BOOK 4
Autumn Crocus

Michaela Francis

TOGGENBURG – BOOK 4
Autumn Crocus

ISBN: 978-1-78695-185-4

Published 2018
Fiction4All

Chapter One

Sarah was excited, although, if she was honest with herself, few people would have shared her excitement at that moment or even fully comprehended her reasons for being so. Of course, anybody not dead to the pleasures of natural beauty and perfect weather, would have empathised with her delight on this day, for the autumn sun shone in glory over the flat plane of the Rhine Delta, along the banks of Lake Constance, the surrounding peaks of Austria's Voralpberg to the east and the flanks of the Swiss mountains to the west. It was the first day of October and one of those days on which to savour the gift of life, with the leaves of the trees turning to gold, the Autumn Crocuses blooming in pale lilac amidst the marshy meadows and the sparkling crests of newly fallen snow whitening the tips of the peaks to the south. There was barely a breath of wind to stir the huge reed beds that lined the lake shores and Sarah had discarded her jacket long before as the warmer months granted this last benediction of autumnal benevolence before the onset of winter. Yet these factors were not the reason for Sarah's sudden excitement. She was, it is true, happy and the lovely day in the huge nature reserve of the Rhine Delta was just one more day of joy in a life that, over the past months, had become one of such fulfilment and content. Sarah was in love.

Yet even her new found love, so precariously won over the troubles of the past summer, did not explain her excitement. That particular source of excitement was flitting among some stubble and short grass a couple of hundred metres away from the little restaurant and camping site set deep within the Rhine Delta. It was a bird and, if truth be told, not a particularly spectacular one from the aesthetic point of view. The uninformed observer would have remarked that it was rather a drab small bird, lacking much in the way of flamboyant colouring. Sarah had once read that American birdwatchers had a term to describe such, not particularly eye-catching, small birds. They called them LBJs, which was not a reference to a past American president but an acronym for "Little Brown Jobs". The bird that was so exciting Sarah was the consummate LBJ but it was a Little Brown Job that she had never seen before.

Of course if you wanted to see birds then the Rhine Delta was definitely a place to visit. It was a great flat plain of arable land and marshy meadows intersected by numerous small drains, ponds and lagoons between the older winding course of the river Rhine that formed the border between Switzerland and Austria and the newer canalised river bed to the east in Austria where the two joined Lake Constance, at the south eastern tip of that vast body of fresh water. It had an enormous diversity of habitats within it; great reed beds along the lake sides, big open lagoons that filled with water fowl in the winter months, patches of woodland and alder carrs, sand and gravel banks, slow moving river backwaters, fast gravelly river courses, marshes, open fields and meadows, enticing little pools and drains, orchards and gardens, old gravel works and pumping stations and the boundless expanse of the open lake beyond.

Lake Constance itself is no ordinary lake for it is one of the largest bodies of fresh water in Western Europe and second only to Lake Geneva in the impressive array of large lakes that lay, at least partially, within Switzerland. From here, on the eastern banks, you could not see the western end of the lake for it was over the horizon some sixty three kilometres away. The lake covers some five hundred and seventy square kilometres; a huge basin carved from the lowlands, abutting the Alps, by the Rhine glacier in the ice ages. This enormous expanse of water is a magnetic attraction for water birds in the winter months and hundreds of thousands of ducks winter on the lake.

Sarah today had already seen evidence of the winter influx today; great flocks of Tufted Ducks and Pochards, the lovely Goldeneyes, flocks of Goosanders, Mallards, Shovellers, Teal, Gadwall and Red Crested Pochards. There'd been a small group of Black Necked Grebes in the little harbour at Altenrhein competing with the Little Grebes and a much rarer Red Necked Grebe on the Old Rhine at Rheineck. She'd seen big rafts of Great Crested Grebes out on the lake and a flock of coots she'd conservatively estimated at five thousand plus. The traditional flock of Wigeon were back in their favourite place at the pumping station and she'd counted forty plus Whooper Swans in a flock out in the fields, loving their evocative honking notes. In a little side lagoon near the New Rhine she'd been thrilled by the sight of a perfect little drake Smew; in her opinion, one of the prettiest of all ducks; handsome in its white and black plumage.

There'd been wading birds too. Flocks of Curlews seemed to be everywhere. Over a thousand of them spent the winter each year in the Rhine Delta. Then there'd been a small flock of Dunlin by the Old Rhine, a couple of Sanderling, a party of Ruff, one or two Redshanks, some Common Sandpipers on the new river and the odd Ringed Plover. She'd flushed two or three Snipe from under her feet and, best of all, there'd been a Little Stint on the sandbanks near the Seerestaurant Glashaus.

There were birds of prey to be seen as well. The Delta was filling up with Buzzards; many of them large pale birds from Scandinavia arriving to winter in the milder climes of the south. There were Kestrels and a couple of late Red Kites drifting lazily away southwards. As winter approached the big Goshawks left their fastnesses in the mountain forests to hunt the influx of waterfowl along the lake edges and Sarah had spotted one making a foray from a belt of woodland. A Peregrine Falcon had been perched on a telegraph pole; another bird that took advantage of the increased prey among the water birds in the winter months. She'd seen the first Hen Harrier of the winter quartering the marshes and reed beds and a little falcon she'd spied at some distance might just have been a Merlin. Sarah loved them all.

It was the smaller birds which really held her interest today though. The Rhine Delta was an important focal point for migrating passerine birds in the autumn; a sort of last stop refuelling point for birds following the easily navigable route of the Rhine southwards over the high alpine passes. On a good day, tens of thousands of birds grounded in their migration in the Rhine Delta. This was a good day! The sheer number of larks, pipits, Wheatears, wagtails, warblers, starlings, shrikes and others were just overwhelming and they were complimented by the already impressive number of resident species within the Delta. Sarah had had thrills in plenty. She'd never recorded so many Yellow Wagtails and Wheatears in a single day before here and there'd been thousands of Pipits. She'd seen a Lesser Spotted Woodpecker in the Alder carrs and a small flock of Penduline tits in the reed beds. She'd noted at least six Red Backed Shrikes in her diary, an early Great Grey Shrike had been hunting from a low tree and the reed beds and the low bushes along the river banks had been full of warblers including one she was almost sure was an immature Barred Warbler. The Delta was full of birds.

And there were not only birds either. There were Roe deer out in the fields, late butterflies on the wing, dragonflies for which the Delta was noted and the autumn crocuses growing in the damp meadows. Sarah was fascinated by all of them. She was an unrepentant nature lover. Everything that grew, flew, crawled, swam, walked or otherwise lived in the world about her was grist to her mill. Sarah adored the natural world about her; revelled in it, studied it avidly and never tired of its rich diversity. She was just twenty two years old but she had devoted years of her short life to the study of the natural world. Even at such a young age she was recognised as a local authority on the flora and fauna of her beloved Toggenburg; the beautiful valley nestling in the mountains of Eastern Switzerland which was her home. Even as a small child she had been the same; driving her long suffering mother to distraction by wandering off into the countryside to bring home every little bug or other creature she could catch. Her mother had despaired of her ever displaying interests more suitable to a little girl; had tried in vain to cajole her into wearing nice clothes and not regard her pretty summer dresses as suitable receptacles for carrying live toads in. It had been a losing battle. Sarah had never lost her sense of wonder for the natural world; had stubbornly refused to change and even three years studying history at the university in Bern had not dimmed her joy in the natural world.

Sarah had known and loved the Rhine Delta since she'd been a young child when her father and elder brother had brought her here for the bird watching and she'd been a regular visitor ever since. It was not far from the Toggenburg valley and she'd made a point of getting down to the Delta several times a year to record the movement and frequency of the creatures within it. She especially made it a regular place to visit during those months when snow on the mountains precluded her from her dearest passion of hiking up into the high places and over the years she had accumulated volumes of diaries recording her observations. Nowhere, however, within those volumes or among all her familiar favourites, was the little bird, she was now excitedly observing, to be found.

She had been returning to the restaurant with a mind to have a last drink before departing for home when she sighted it. She'd been at the Delta for most of the day. There was some sadness in that. It had not been merely enthusiasm that had driven her out of the house and the valley today. The person with whom she was in love with was away and had been for several days. It was the longest separation they had been forced to endure ever since Sarah had broken off her engagement to her boyfriend at her parents' house in southern Switzerland in midsummer and fled home under a cloud of parental disapproval to her Danny, her lover's, arms. Since then they had been inseparable and they'd pined for each other even if compelled to spend a few hours apart. But Danny had obligations that both of them knew would separate them on occasion, eventually. Sarah had been resigned to that fact from the beginning and had accepted that it was liable to be a not uncommon drawback in the new life they were forging together. Nevertheless, it had been hard for the first time. After a few days the house had just seemed so unbearably empty and lonely that Sarah had decided to try and raise her spirits with this excursion to the Delta.

She was being well rewarded for that decision now. On her way back to the restaurant the little bird stepping jauntily through the grass had caught her eye. She'd turned her binoculars on it and her excitement had grown. Finally she'd erected her telescope and subjected the bird to the most thorough examination she could devise, jotting notes feverishly in her diary as she did so. She noted its pale lores, its prominent malar stripe, its overall size and structure, the pattern of spotting on its breast and upper parts, the heavy almost thrush like bill, the pink legs and white edges to the tail. In the strong sunshine the bird showed up admirably in the telescope and, at last, she was satisfied. She pushed a strand of her long chestnut hair from her face and grinned in pleasure. "And that," she said aloud to herself, "Is a Richard's Pipit!" It was no common sighting. Richard's Pipit's were very rare autumn vagrants to this part of the world. It was the first that Sarah had ever seen. She could go home tonight and mark a little cross next to its name in her field guide.

Sarah's satisfied vocalisation must have startled the bird for it flew away with a curiously wagtail like undulating flight and a loud, harsh rasping call. Sarah didn't mind however. She had seen all she needed to and it was time to be making her way back in any case. She had time for a quiet drink and then she'd have to be getting back to the Toggenburg. She needed to be home in good time this evening for Nicole, her best friend, was coming up to the house for dinner and to keep her company. It promised to be an interesting evening. She had electrifying news for Nicole.

In deep satisfaction, she brushed a little spot of dirt from her telescope and stroked it fondly. It was a new acquisition this telescope. Previously she'd made do with a rather battered old Japanese scope that was showing the years of wear after being lugged around the mountainsides. This instrument was spanking new however. It was a Swarowski HD STM 80 that had cost some three thousand Euros when they had bought it during a magical sojourn on the North Sea island of Helgoland in the summer that Sarah had spent with Danny. It had been a blissful two weeks and the telescope brought the memories flooding back in fondness. It was just one of the many ways her life had become enriched since her fateful decision to throw caution aside and declare her love unconditionally to Danny, to her parents' unmitigated horror.

It had been the right decision. She could not now imagine how she ever could have thought otherwise or hesitated so long and agonisingly about it. In the last months she had found a joyous happiness she had never thought possible before and not even the unresolved alienation from her father and mother could take that happiness from her although it nevertheless still hurt her that they were so resolutely opposed to her new life and refused to speak to her.

Sarah shouldered her telescope on its tripod and retraced her steps to the little restaurant. It was only a matter of a couple of hundred metres and she was thankful of that for she was quite tired now after walking around the Delta for most of the day and she was thirsty too. It was a Saturday and the restaurant was full with day trippers and people from the camp site next door. The restaurant was popular with trippers to the Rhine Delta nature reserve for it had a pleasant aspect by a large bay of the lake with a little sandy beach in front of it. The bay was shallow and held extensive sandbanks when the lake level was low, which were good places to find roosting wildfowl and waders.

Sarah found a table free outside on the veranda overlooking the lake and set her telescope down. She hesitated for a moment before leaving it to go inside and order a drink. It was a very valuable piece of optical equipment and, with its fond memories for her, she was frightened of having it stolen. Actually it was the sentimental value that was the most concern to her for she had gone to the trouble of insuring it. She hadn't dared tell Danny that she'd insured the telescope. Danny would have laughed uproariously at that. Danny was so rich that the loss of a three thousand Euro telescope would have been an insignificant pinprick but all Danny's wealth had failed to ameliorate Sarah's inbred caution and frugality. She considered it criminal to possess such a valuable instrument and not have the basic sense to insure its value. She'd covertly insured it therefore and omitted to mention the fact. Even now she was reluctant to let it out of her sight without taking the precaution of asking a young couple at a nearby table to keep an eye on it for her while she walked inside to order her drink.

Inside the restaurant, Sarah rummaged through the pockets of her jeans looking for money. This was a

12

complicated business because she was carrying two types of currency on her. Naturally she had plenty of Swiss francs on her but this part of the Rhine Delta was over the border in Austria and the currency here was in Euros. She could still have paid with Swiss francs since they were close enough to the border for the two currencies to be interchangeable but that necessitated tedious consultations of the current exchange rate and the likely possibility of coming out of the exchange unfavourably. She still had Euros left over from the holiday in Helgoland however. She'd not converted them back to Swiss francs since she'd known it was likely that she'd be crossing the border at some future date and that they'd come in handy. The Toggenburg was, after all, only a few kilometres from Austria and not that far from Germany either.

She ordered a half litre of Radler, which was the German name for a shandy although, when they'd been on holiday in Northern Germany, she had discovered it was called an Alsterwasser there, presumably named after the lake, the Alster, in Hamburg. She remembered to speak high German to the serving girl. It wasn't the dialect in this part of Austria but at least it was more comprehensible to the locals than Swiss German. Sarah spoke perfectly good high German as well as Swiss German, French, some Italian and her native English which was her mother's tongue. Sarah had been born in England and raised in an English speaking family although she had lived most of her life in Switzerland. Nicole was English too and Danny was part English, part American and part Swiss. Sarah was easy in a multi-lingual culture.

Back at her table, with a foaming tankard of shandy in front of her, Sarah took out her mobile phone and keyed Nicole's number. Her ebullient former house mate had recognised her number on her mobile instantly for she boomed out. "Hi Foxy." Foxy was Nicole's pet name for Sarah, derived from the fact that her family name was Fuchs, the German for Fox.

"Hi Nicky. Finished work then?"

"Yeah I only had lunch to do and I'm free tonight and tomorrow. I can't think of the last time I got nearly a whole weekend off." It was normal, thought Sarah. Nicole was a waitress in a hotel restaurant in the Toggenburg and weekends were usually the busiest days of the week. The summer season was coming to a close now though and most establishments were cutting back on staff. Sarah grimaced at the thought. It was likely that Nicole would be facing a few weeks of unemployment shortly.

"Well that's good. Are you still coming up this evening?"

"Hell yes. Danny still away then?"

"Yes until Monday."

"Where have you been all day then? I tried calling your house but your housekeeper answered and said you'd buggered off for the day. I tried you on your mobile but that was futile too. I wish I could break your bloody anti-social habit of switching your phone off for protracted periods while you go swanning off on your jack."

"I went down to the Rhine Delta to do a bit of bird watching. I'm still there."

"Oh I see. Presumably you thought that the chiming of your phone was going to scare the little dicky birds away."

"Actually Nicky I didn't realise my phone was switched off until now. I hope Danny hasn't been trying to call me."

"Your arse will be toast if so. So how was it?"

"How was what?"

"Your bloody bird watching you muppet."

"Oh brilliant. I've seen loads of birds and I saw a Richard's Pipit."

"Was this Richard put out by you ogling his pipit, Sarah, or was he flattered by the attention?"

"It's a sort of bird you one-tracked moron. It's a really rare bird."

"God! What does Danny see in a geek like you?"

"Never you mind. Listen.... what do you want for dinner tonight?"

"How about your Spaghetti Bolognaise?"

"Oh for God's sake Nicky. Don't you ever eat anything else?"

"Not when you're making it I don't. Come on Foxy I haven't tasted your Spaghetti Bolognaise since you moved out of the house and in with Danny. I miss it."

"All right then, Sodding spaghetti it is."

"You're a sweetheart. Shall I bring a few DVDs along?"

"Good God no. We've got bloody hundreds of DVDs at home and perfectly good Wi-Fi. I'm sure we won't go short of something to watch on the telly."

"Ok. When are you going to get back?"

"I'm just having a quick drink and then I'm setting off home. I'll have to call in at the shops in Buchs on my way home though. I don't think we've got mince in the house. I'll pick up a couple of bottles of plonk while I'm at it."

"Whoa Sarah. Steady on honey. Don't be getting me too plastered. I was going to drive up to your place. I'm buggered if I'm going to walk all the way over to Oberdorf."

"What's the problem? If you're not working tomorrow you can stay the night."

Nicole hesitated. "Er are you sure Danny won't mind."

"Of course not. Don't be daft. We can have a girly night in like we used to."

"Sounds great. I'm looking forward to it. I hardly ever see you these days."

"Don't exaggerate Nicky. We spent all of Wednesday together."

"It's not the same as it used to be though Sarah. I used to see you every day when we shared the house together. Now you live miles away."

"Good God Nicky. We're not *that* far apart. I only live on the other side of the valley not the other side of the world. There's nothing to stop you popping up whenever you want, apart from laziness."

"Well I'm always a bit worried about disturbing your privacy now you're living with Danny."

"Don't be ridiculous Nicky. You're always welcome. I've told you that a hundred times. I'd love you to come around more often; we both would. Anyway Danny's been away all week and I could have done with the company."

"I've been working Sarah."

"You weren't working yesterday and I was at home all day."

Nicole paused guiltily. "I told you I had... things to do yesterday."

Sarah grinned evilly to herself. "Oh yes? Did you er manage to get through to Winterthur after all then?"

"Yes I did go through... just to do some business and what have you." Nicole's air of studied nonchalance was entirely unconvincing.

Sarah rolled her tongue in her cheek and grinned again. "Oh good. Did you... er happen to bump into Charlie when you were through then?"

Sarah could almost hear Nicole swallowing hastily on the other end of the line. "Oh er... yes just briefly. We had a quick drink together."

"Oh that must have been nice." Sarah struggled to keep the mirth out of her voice. Nicole had first met Charlie at Sarah's graduation party in Bern back in august and she'd been a little reticent about the relationship ever since, insisting that Charlie was just a

16

friend. The developing situation had been the source of much amused speculation between Sarah and Danny ever since.

"Anyway must go now Sarah." Nicole announced, obviously not wishing any further elaboration on this subject. "I'll see you tonight. About sevenish ok?"

"Yes fine. I'll be back long before then. Until tonight then."

As Sarah put her phone away, she became aware of the young man. He was a tall handsome boy sat a couple of tables away, perhaps in his early twenties with short dark hair and a look of quiet confidence about him. He was also staring at Sarah with frankly open admiration. Few people could have begrudged him that admiration for Sarah was a warm beauty that would have stopped most warm blooded men in their steps. Even dressed in her old jeans and checked shirt she was well worth looking at with her long chestnut hair, her lovely face with the soulful brown eyes and her admirably slim yet well-muscled and proportionate figure.

Sarah had never been a vain girl. Indeed she had always thought herself rather plain and ordinary and it had come as somewhat of a shock to realise that people regarded her as truly beautiful. In fact not until she had met Danny had she come to be aware of her own radiance; as if she had seen herself for the first time through somebody else's eyes. In the last couple of months she had become acutely conscious of the way other people saw her and it never ceased to surprise her. Before she had met Danny she had almost been notorious for her ability to sit around in public places blissfully ignorant of the admiration she attracted. It had taken Danny's uninhibited delight in her beauty to awaken her consciousness of her appearance.

The young man smiled at her and, out of politeness she smiled back. It was a mistake she saw. She was pretty sure that she'd seen him earlier on the camp site as she walked past so presumably he was camping here. Perhaps he thought that she was camping too. Whatever his thoughts, he evidently took her courteousness as an invitation to try his luck for he displayed every sign of intention to come over and talk to her. Sarah averted her eyes quickly. "Oh God!" she thought to herself. "I hope he isn't going to try and hit on me."

That appeared to be precisely his purpose for he rose to his feet and walked across with a slight swagger, bordering on arrogance. Sarah sighed and took a deep breath. This sort of thing was happening more and more recently. She wondered if there was some sort of twisted reverse psychology in that. Surely she had never had so many men try to pick her up since she had known Danny. What had happened to her in these past months that had made her doubly attractive to men? Fortunately she had a devastating riposte to any clumsy pick up line.

"Hello there."

Sarah raised her head. "Hello." She responded warmly. There was no need for incivility even when you were about to dash somebody's hopes.

"I was just wondering. Are you staying on the camp site as well?"

"Oh no. I'm just down here for the day. It's a bit late in the season to be sleeping under canvas for me I'm afraid."

The young man grinned. "Oh yes it does get a bit cold in the night when you're alone in a tent." He certainly fancied his chances here Sarah thought. The poor sap couldn't have called this one more wrong if he'd tried.

"Really?" replied Sarah. "Perhaps you ought to have brought extra blankets or a hot water bottle. Have you tried thermal underwear?"

"I can think of more pleasant ways of keeping warm by night. Can't you?"

"Yes I stay at home where I've got central heating."

"That's not very romantic."

"I'm a very practical sort of person."

"Really? Well how about you let me buy you another drink and we get to know each other a little more."

"I'm afraid you'd be wasting your time. I'm afraid I don't accept drinks from strange gentlemen."

"Why ever not?"

Sarah raised her face and looked him straight in the eye. "Because I'm gay. I'm afraid young men don't interest me."

The young man staggered as if he'd stepped on a rake. "You're joking!"

"Not at all, I'm quite serious."

"You can't be gay."

"I don't see why not. A sizeable percentage of the population manages to be."

"You're too beautiful."

"Well thank you for the compliment but I'm sure attractive looks don't preclude a person from being gay."

"But it's a god-damned waste."

"Really? I'm inclined to think that my girlfriend would disagree with you." Sarah finished the last of her shandy and rose easily to her feet. "I'm sorry if you've wasted your time. I'm sure there must be some nice straight girls on that camp site somewhere. Now if you'll excuse me I must be going."

Chapter Two

Sarah shouldered her telescope and tripod and walked away; crossing the car park and smiling to herself. Part of her had enjoyed the little encounter. The boy's face when she'd told him she was gay had been a picture. Certainly he hadn't believed her. She could hardly blame him. Until just a few short months ago she had had a hard enough time believing it herself. Now she accepted it. Now it was a part of her life and she no longer felt ashamed or frightened by it. How could she? She was living with the most beautiful woman she had ever known and she loved her. What was there to be ashamed about in that?

It wasn't that Sarah had enjoyed destroying the poor young man's clumsy approach. Sarah was not by nature vindictive or cruel. She hadn't even been particularly annoyed by his crude efforts. She'd been mildly amused if anything. There was even a part of her that considered, dispassionately, that it was no bad thing that young men approached young women. There'd be a marked decline in the population figures if they didn't, she supposed. No the thing that had afforded her pleasure was something rather more complex. It concerned her own personal feelings about her recently discovered sexuality and her growing confidence and acceptance of it. She had been able to look a complete stranger in the face and tell them that she was gay. A few months ago that would have been unthinkable. She felt quite proud of herself.

In the dusty car park there was more pride for Sarah. This bit she really enjoyed. Previously whenever she had visited the Rhine Delta she had had to take the Post bus out of the Toggenburg to Buchs and, from there, the regional train to Rheineck from where she would have walked across the border into the delta or perhaps have hired a bicycle from the railway station for the day. Not anymore! She fumbled in her jeans pocket for her keys.

On her key ring there was a remote entry key fob. Sarah pointed the device and the big, dark blue automobile across the car park chirped loudly and there was a clunk of unlocking doors. The big car was brand new and it was hers. Even weeks after she had come into its possession she still felt a thrill every time she looked at it. It was a big BMW four wheel drive, sports utility vehicle; the new X5. It was the first car she had ever personally owned. Her father had half promised to buy her a little car on her graduation from university but that plan had collapsed the day that Sarah had rejected her parents' choice of husband for her and run away from her own engagement party weekend to start a new life with a woman instead. The breakdown in relations with her parents had been so complete that they hadn't even attended her graduation. Daniela had bought her the car as a graduation present and it hadn't been cheap. Daniela had paid something over seventy thousand Swiss francs for the thing. It was already starting to justify its existence however. Their other household car was Daniela's Ferrari convertible. It was fast, sleek and loads of fun but hardly practical for day to day use. Already they were using Sarah's BMW for most daily purposes. The Ferrari had been relegated to the role of recreational vehicle for the days when they just fancied a spin in the countryside with the wind in their hair. It wasn't a car to go shopping with.

It was not as though Sarah's BMW was a little town runabout however. It was a serious, big and powerful car with over two hundred and eighty horse power in its diesel engine, capable of doing over two hundred kilometres an hour with ease on the open autobahn with the wind under its bonnet. It was just the thing for the rough tracks and roads around the Rhine Delta as well, with its off road four wheel drive and it handled the steep hills and country lanes of the Toggenburg with alacrity. There was nothing girly or feminine about it. It was aggressively butch and macho. Sarah ran a hand lovingly over the bodywork, warm from the afternoon sun. She was by no means a masculine sort of girl but there was some kernel of masculinity deep inside her that this car spoke to intimately. She loved her new car.

In deep satisfaction she carefully stowed her telescope away in the enormous boot and climbed in behind the wheel. As always she took a few seconds to just enjoy sitting in the car and running her hands over the dashboard in pleasure. The first time she had sat at the wheel of this car she had been terrified of it. She'd had a good driving coach however. Simon, the boyfriend of her life time friend Peter, was a racing driver and, under his tuition, she had rapidly gained confidence with the big machine. Simon's coaching had not stopped there either. Over the last few weeks he had also been teaching her how to drive Daniela's Ferrari as well and it was a standing joke by now that Sarah was a good deal more comfortable at the wheel of that car than Daniela, who had always viewed her own car with a trepidation bordering on timidity. Now if they took the Ferrari out for a spin it was as likely to be Sarah in control as Daniela.

Sarah turned the ignition and the big engine under the hood growled into life with a satisfyingly bass roar. She reached down and turned the stereo on. There was a new offering in the stereo; Daniela's new CD. It was a demo version. The finished product wasn't even in the shops yet and wouldn't be for a couple of months. Daniela had a new mini tour coming up to promote the CD and she was already playing a lot of the material from the CD in her live performances. Sarah loved the new album. It was as good if not better than the last one and that was still solidly in the charts and selling phenomenally internationally. They were predicting that the new album was going to be an even greater hit. It was going to be huge.

Sarah shook her head in wonder at the thought. She could never quite shake off the feeling of unreality that this remarkable person, loved by millions and universally acclaimed as a musical genius was the woman that loved her. Loved her! Loved simple Sarah; an unknown country girl from the Toggenburg. Sarah wondered how long her anonymity could last. So far they had been incredibly lucky. Although they were living quite openly if privately together the press hadn't cottoned on to the fact that Switzerland's hottest female star had a new girlfriend. Daniela had been protective of Sarah and had refused to comment on her private life in public. Although their friendship was pretty much common knowledge in the Toggenburg and a greater intimacy at least suspected, the depth of their commitment to each other was still only known to a handful of close friends and unknown beyond the confines of the valley. Even Sarah's parents didn't know the full truth. It had been bad enough that she had told them that she was gay and living with another woman but she could imagine their horror if they knew that her girlfriend was an internationally famous celebrity. They were bound to find out sooner or later of course. Sarah dreaded that day.

She eased the car out of the car park and steered along the little back roads towards Rheineck humming to the music on the stereo. As she approached the bridge over the old course of the Rhine, she reached into the glove compartment for her passport. The customs officials on the bridge didn't seem interested however and they waved her through. It had been different when she'd arrived this morning. She was after all driving an expensive new car with Swiss plates and the Austrian customs had stopped her and demanded to see her documentation. Apparently there was somewhat of a traffic in stolen luxury cars out of Switzerland.

Crossing the bridge Sarah regarded an old barge moored on the Austrian side of the river, that seemed to have developed a slight list to starboard, with regret. The barge had been there for years. It wasn't a working barge anymore. It was converted to a Chinese restaurant. Chinese restaurants were uncommon in Switzerland and, had she not been obliged to cook dinner for Nicole this evening, Sarah would have been tempted to have stopped for dinner there. It was an old favourite of hers and it was charming in the old boat. Sarah adored Chinese food although she rarely got the chance to eat it. Recently she and Daniela had experimented with it, buying a couple of cookery books specialising in Chinese cuisine and they'd even gone to the trouble of buying a wok. So far they'd had mixed results but they were improving. The most intractable problem had been in cooking rice. You might have thought that boiling rice was a pretty straightforward operation but to produce rice with just the right amount of dry fluffiness was proving to be an art form. Sarah had looked up the problem on-line however and found some useful tips. When Danny returned on Monday she determined to cook her a Chinese meal.

At Rheineck Sarah pulled onto the south bound motorway. She resisted the temptation to let the big car have its head on the main road. The motorway running north to south along the Rhine valley was one of the most notorious stretches of road in all Switzerland for accidents. It was a very busy road and Sarah treated it with the utmost of respect. The road followed the wide broad valley of the River Rhine, which formed the border between Switzerland and Austria. It was a classic glacial valley with a flat bottom and steep sides, flanked on either side by towering mountains. At the little town of Buchs Sarah pulled off the main road. Buchs itself was a small, fairly functional town just off the banks of the Rhine. On the eastern side of the river, facing Buchs, was the tiny little country of Lichtenstein sandwiched between Switzerland and Austria. The fact that you could drive in three separate countries in the space of ten minutes gave this little corner of the world a peculiarly local internationalism.

Sarah called in for provisions in Buchs. The shops in the town afforded her rather more choice than the local supermarket up in Wildhaus. As she was loading her bags into the car her telephone sounded once more. It was Daniela. That was hardly unusual. Danny called her every day; sometimes several times a day. Sarah lit up in pleasure and answered her call. "Hi darling!"

"Hello sweetheart. I called home. You weren't in."

"I went off for the day to the Rhine Delta bird watching."

"Hmmph! Don't be watching the birds too closely. I know what you're like as soon as you slip the leash."

"What do you mean by that?"

"Well you're forever picking up stray women. I can't take my eyes off you for a second."

"I do not! That's a monstrous accusation."

"Oh yes? You picked up Charmaine in Winterthur."

"She picked me up."

"And then there was Rozella in Ticino."

"Rozella's an act of God. She'd hunt down anybody who had XX chromosomes and a body temperature of over thirty seven degrees Celsius. Anyway my behaviour was impeccable on both counts."

"Yes well the sooner I get home to keep an eye on you the better."

"How's Berlin?"

"Bloody awful! God what a pig ugly town. I know that the city's had a few issues historically but it surely doesn't still have to look like a bloody bomb site."

"Don't let your Berlin fan base hear you saying

that."

"Well maybe I'm doing the place an injustice. I haven't got out of the hotel much to be truthful and the hotel is one of those places you'd like to get out of if you could. I told the manager not to book us into a Holiday Inn if he could avoid it. Bloody frightful characterless dumps. I can't wait to get home."

"Are you in the hotel now?"

"No I'm at the concert hall standing around like a spare fanny while the sound engineer tries to repair the PA system which has suddenly decided to go tits up on us four hours before the bloody concert's due to start."

"Oh dear. Bad day at the office huh?"

"Tell me about it. Roll on Monday when I can go home."

"Why can't you come back tomorrow? Surely once you've finished the concert they don't need you around anymore."

"I wish I could sweetheart but I've got two television interviews tomorrow."

"Oh! You're going to be on the telly?"

"Yes. One's an afternoon broadcast with the RBB which is the local ARD station and then in the evening I'm on live on a chat show on the main ARD network."

"Oh we can get ARD here. I'll have to watch it. What's the show?"

"It's the Sabrina Handelmeyer show at eight o'clock."

"Wait a minute isn't Sabrina Handelmeyer..."

"Yes she is. It could be an interesting interview."

"So when are you coming back?"

"Still on for Monday. I've a flight scheduled for Monday morning into Kloten."

"Do you want me to come pick you up at the airport?"

"No darling you don't need to pick me up."

"I wouldn't mind honey honest."

"Sweetheart, I'm just returning from a well-publicised three concert mini tour and several television appearances. That airport could be crawling with paparazzi. We don't want to be giving them fodder for the scandal sheets."

"Oh! I see."

"It's ok honey. I've got a car picking me up in any case. What are you doing tonight?"

"I've got Nicky coming around for dinner."

"I told you I couldn't take my eyes off you."

"Stop it Danny. You were the one that said I ought to spend more time with Nicky while you were away!"

"I'm just teasing you darling. Of course you should spend more time with her. She's probably pining alone in that house with you gone."

"Do I tell her about the house tonight or do you want me to wait until you get home?"

"Go ahead and tell her darling. I know you're dying to."

"Hey listen…. Nicky went to Winterthur again yesterday."

"Oh yes? Do tell all."

"Well she admitted under duress that she met up with Charmaine for a drink. She said it was just for a quick drink when I phoned her this afternoon but you could hear the guilt seeping down the phone. I definitely think there's something going on there."

"It's about time. They've been fannying about long enough. Did they meet up in the Planet?"

"I don't know. She didn't say. I bet it was though. The Planet's Charlie's usual afternoon hang out."

"Well, well, well. This could be interesting. It reminds me though. I have to see Charlie myself. If she's going to be filling in on bass for the tour in December we're really going to have to get her into the practice studio and start polishing her up."

"Have you definitely decided to take her for the tour

27

then?"

"Oh yes. She's a fantastic bass guitarist. Once she's up to speed on our stuff she'll be brilliant."

"Oh I'm pleased. It couldn't happen to a nicer girl. Can I tell Nicky that?"

"Yes you may regard it as official. It'll be interesting to see Nicky's reaction."

"Fantastic. That's two pieces of good news I've got for Nicky tonight then."

"God I'm missing you Sarah."

"I'm missing you too Danny. It's going to seem an age until Monday."

"I know. Still I should have a few weeks free after that. Maybe we can get in a couple of days hiking when I get back."

"It's getting a bit late for the high altitude stuff Danny. We've already got new snow on the mountain tops. Still we could do something at lower altitude or maybe we could get out for a bit of bird watching; go down to the Rhine Delta or even over to Fanel or somewhere."

"I look forward to it. You got any more work in the hotel?"

"No. Elke's pretty quiet for the moment. I did help out on Thursday but that was because she had a birthday party in. I guess that there'll not be much doing before the winter season starts. I've promised her that I'll help out as much as I can over the winter."

"You don't have to work honey. It's not as if we need the money."

"I like working at Elke's hotel Danny and I like bringing in at least some money. You know I don't feel comfortable always living on your money. Anyway Elke has been a good friend to us and I owe her that much."

"Ok darling. But it's *our* money all right; not mine."

"I'm not doing anything to earn it Danny."

"Yes you are. More than you know. By the way

have you looked over those enrolment forms for the university yet?"

"Yes I've had a look at them. They're pretty intimidating."

"Well we'll have to sit down and hammer them out if we want to get you all signed up for next year. Oh Christ!"

"What's up?"

"It looks like the roadies have got the system up and running again. I'm going to have to go and do a sound check darling. Look I'll catch you later ok."

"Yes sure. I love you."

"I love you too. I can't wait to be home. Talk to you later."

Sarah put her phone away with the aching yearning that any termination of a long distance call with Daniela always left her. She sighed heavily and eased her bags onto the back passenger seats. She climbed into the driving seat and slapped a hand against the steering wheel petulantly. She supposed she couldn't with justification feel put out by Daniela's absence. She'd known it was coming after all. She'd entered into the relationship under no illusions. It had been understood from the beginning that Daniela's career would mean protracted absences from home. It would get worse too. Daniela had commitments in November, a three week tour in December and an even bigger tour in the New Year. In January she could be away for as long as two months. Sarah felt wretched about it. She'd expected it to be tough but she hadn't quite foreseen just how gut wrenchingly lonely it would be without Danny there.

She wondered if it would get easier over time. Somehow she knew that it wouldn't. A childish part of her wanted to say "why does she need to take on so many tours and gigs; so many television appearances and recording contracts. Surely she's got enough money by now." But it wasn't about money any more, if indeed it ever had been. Daniela was casual about her wealth. She didn't live ostentatiously or throw her money about frivolously. Her house was large and comfortable but by no means the sort of place you would have associated with a multi-millionairess pop star. When not on the road working she lived quietly at home eschewing the trappings of fame and wealth. Even her one excessively visible status symbol, her Ferrari, had been a gift from her band members whom she had made rich. She didn't even like it very much and would have been perfectly content with something smaller and less noticeable. Money was not the driving force behind Daniela's career. It was more her own creative drive and the obligations she felt towards her fans. You sometimes felt as if she'd become rich almost by accident and not quite knowing how it had happened. Of course she managed the business side of her career astutely but she was not avaricious and she often yearned to be able to turn the clock back, live somewhere in a little bedsitter with her beloved Sarah and start all over again.

Putting her anxieties aside, Sarah restarted the car engine and drove out of the supermarket car park. The traffic was busy in Buchs but once away from the town it thinned and soon she was weaving across the flat river plain of the Rhine valley through the adjoining villages of Werdenberg and Grabs. Beyond Grabs the road rose steeply, climbing in a series of doglegs into the mountains, becoming narrower and finally climbing into thick forest high above the Rhine valley below. This was the eastern portal to the Upper Toggenburg, Sarah's domain. As Sarah emerged from the forest she was very nearly in Wildhaus which lay at the upper end of the valley of the Toggenburg.

She had markedly risen in altitude. Buchs, on the floor of the Rhine valley, lay at an elevation of 448 metres above sea level. Wildhaus by contrast was nearly eleven hundred metres high and beyond it stretching away to the west was the glorious Toggenburg. As Sarah rounded the bend into Wildhaus the view of her valley opened in a panoramic vista before her. Bordering the valley to the south were the chain of mountains, like a row of teeth, called the Churfirsten rising up to just over two thousand three hundred metres whilst looming over Wildhaus itself was the bulk of the Schaffberg, another towering peak and just the most southerly extension of the Alpstein; the great group of mountains that included the Santis massif and all the associated peaks. Sandwiched between these two mountain ranges was the rural, tranquil valley of the Toggenburg; a peaceful enclave, hidden within the mountains. The main road ran down the valley through the villages of Wildhaus, Lisighaus, Unterwasser, Alt St Johann and Steig. On the hanging sides above the valley floor were smaller settlements such as Schwendi, where Sarah's friend ran the Hotel Toggenburg and where Sarah still worked, Oberdorf, where Sarah lived with Daniela, and the little hanging side valley known locally as the Alpli where, until the fateful events of the summer, Sarah had shared a little cottage with Nicole.

Most of Sarah's life had been confined to this beautiful hidden valley and the sight of it never failed to bring her the most enormous satisfaction and gratitude that she had been so privileged as to have lived her life amid such majestic splendour. Earlier this summer, when it had seemed that she was doomed to marry and be whisked away to the mind numbing dullness of a Zurich suburb, she had faced the unthinkable prospect of losing her beloved valley. She had fought a desperate rear-guard action to cling onto it under increasing pressure from her parents. Her efforts had seemed futile however and she had begun to resign herself to suburban life with a man she was not at all sure she cared for enough.

Fate had decreed otherwise however. The Toggenburg had had a new and glamorous resident in the shape of Daniela Devin, Switzerland's rising new star and, from the moment Sarah had met Daniela, their destinies had become intertwined. Daniela had fallen in love almost immediately with the lovely and unpretentious Sarah and Sarah for her part had been instantly entranced by her new friend even while struggling to come to terms with the significance of her attraction to her. It had been a hard battle for Sarah but, in the end, a victorious one. Through Daniela she had found the love she had desired and, as importantly, she had secured her life in the Toggenburg among the mountains and people she loved. The Zurich suburb was now just the echo of a partially remembered nightmare and Sarah had found happiness after all. But it had cost her.

Chapter Three

The cost of Sarah's victory could be measured partly by a meeting that was taking place, many kilometres to the west, at about the same time as Sarah was returning home from her day out in the Rhine Delta. In the beautiful city of Luzern, on the northern edge of the great lake of four cantons, the Vierwaldstattersee, Jessica had just left the railway station and was walking across the bridge, that spanned the river flowing out of the lake, on her way to meet her father. She was irritated by the fact. She had had plans for the afternoon that had had to be curtailed by her father's insistence upon meeting her. She wondered what the devil her father was doing in Luzern anyway.

Her parents lived near Ascona in the south of Switzerland on the far side of the Alps and it was rare for him to venture into these northern climes. Also there was a certain coolness between Jessica and her parents for the moment. It wasn't a major rift by any means. Jessica had already in her life experienced a massive fissure in her relationship with her parents when she had married a man without their approval. Fortunately that old wound was mostly healed by now, although Jessica was inclined to remind her parents of it whenever she felt that they were encroaching on her independence. While it had lasted, however, the division had been profound and bitter, although not, as Jessica was prepared to concede ruefully, as dramatic as her younger sister's own sudden bid for liberty this past summer.

Jessica was Sarah's elder sister, the eldest of the three children and had, until recently, held the title of the most rebellious and independent of the family. Sarah, by decisively rejecting her parents' choice of husband for her, thumbing her nose at her fiancées powerful and

33

influential family, causing a monumental rift with her father's business partner as a result, subjecting both families to public humiliation and ridicule and then finally declaring that she was gay and running off to shack up with some mysterious girlfriend somewhere or other had rather stolen Jessica's thunder as the rebel of the family and Jessica, secretly, almost envied her for it. Jessica had rather enjoyed the ensuing scandal. She hadn't thought that her younger sister had it in her.

Sarah had always seemed to be the meekest and most dutifully obedient of the three Fuchs children and, as the baby of the family, had always been rather pampered and indulged and something of her father's favourite. She hadn't been a spoilt child however and she'd always been deferential to her parents' wishes, rarely giving them cause to berate her for her conduct. She had never dated boys very much or stayed out late at night to her parents' consternation. She'd been a model student at school and university and, when her parents had hopefully pushed Alan in her direction as a future spouse to cement the alliance between them and the Bergers, their business allies, Sarah had voiced no protest and had quietly and meekly acquiesced in the arrangement. In short she had been the perfect daughter. You had always known that she would go on to achieve high academic results in her studies, would marry well with her parents' approval, live a sensible and respectful life and produce a gaggle of well-adjusted and well brought up grandchildren for her doting parents. It had seemed almost too good to be true. It *had* been too good to be true.

Even now, months later, Jessica still couldn't shake off the unreality that it had been Sarah that had been the one to drop such a momentous bombshell and liberate such a frightful skeleton from the family closet. Jessica herself was strong willed and certainly capable of throwing a spanner into the works. Even her younger brother John, in his quieter way, had a mind of his own and had further irritated his parents by his stubborn resistance to their plans for him. But Sarah? No! It was unthinkable. Jessica and John defying their parents' wishes was one thing but for Sarah to do so had shaken the very bedrock of the family stability. It was as if somebody had announced in a scientific journal that Galileo was wrong; the sun did revolve around the earth after all.

Jessica had been as shocked as anybody to discover that her younger sister was gay. It wasn't that she disapproved or was in any way homophobic for she had several gay friends. It was just that she had never suspected it or seen it coming. Sarah had never previously shown any interest in girls. Then again, her one long, if somewhat orchestrated relationship with Alan aside, she hadn't shown much interest in boys either, Jessica realised belatedly. In fact, Jessica had sometimes wondered if her younger sister had been a little emotionally retarded when it came to matters of sexuality. She'd always wanted Sarah to bring home some dreadfully unsuitable boyfriend sometime if only to demonstrate that she was suffering normal adolescent love pangs appropriate to her age but it had never happened.

Jessica remembered one conversation she'd had with Sarah when Sarah had been just sixteen; the age when most girls would have been living on hormones and mooning over one overly dramatic or tragic teenage love affair or another. She'd asked Sarah if she had any boyfriend yet. Sarah had just looked puzzled and said she had too much homework and no time for boys. "God! I should have seen it coming then." thought Jessica to herself. It was always the quiet ones wasn't it? She'd probably been gay all along and just nobody had seen it. Knowing Sarah she probably hadn't even realised it herself. Twenty two seemed a rather mature age to suddenly come to a realisation of your own sexuality but it was by no means unprecedented as Jessica well knew. Many people emerged as gay well into their lives and a few, a tragic few, lived with their secret hidden all their days.

Since Sarah's startling announcement, Jessica had been following events with interest. Sarah's mother was distraught and angry and could barely bear to mention Sarah's name. Her father had been torn, ever since, between agreeing with his wife concerning Sarah's conduct and frantic worries for his beloved estranged daughter. In the early days of the estrangement, they'd bombarded Sarah with messages and telephone calls beseeching her to come to her senses but Sarah's adamancy had been resolute and unyielding. She'd refused whatsoever to discuss the matter any further until such time as her parents accepted her orientation and decision. With such stubborn refusal on the part of both camps to compromise, all communications had ceased and the silence between them was thunderous. To her amusement, Jessica had found herself pressed into service as a sort of diplomatic go between to convey messages between the two factions that were no longer on speaking terms with each other.

It was the source of some irritation to Jessica and ultimately the cause of her own cooling of relations with her parents. Both sides had drawn up battle lines and there was undoubtedly some pressure on the neutral parties to decide on which side of the lines they stood. If she was frank with herself, Jessica had to admit that her sympathies lay mostly with Sarah. She had been deeply unhappy with Sarah's presumed engagement to Alan from the beginning; perceiving it to be little less than Sarah being sold off to the highest bidder for the gratification of her father's business interests. It had been, to all intents and purposes, an arranged marriage and Sarah's concerns about it had been merely brushed aside as irrelevant. Jessica had applauded Sarah's decision to terminate the relationship and had been deeply disgusted by her family's attempts to publicly bully Sarah into marriage.

On the other hand, she had at least sympathised with her parents' shock over Sarah's announcement that she was gay. She didn't share their sentiments that it was unnatural or shameful and neither did she agree with their expressed view that Sarah must have been corrupted by some outside influence. Nevertheless, she could at least understand what a profound shock it must have been to them and how difficult it must be for them to come to terms with it. They'd demonstrated the classic parental wringing of hands; the "where did we go wrong?" lamentations and the blinkered denial of facts that Jessica supposed nearly every parent experienced upon discovering that a child of theirs was gay. Jessica herself was trying for the moment to have a baby, although so far without success, and it brought it home to you what parents must have to go through when you were trying to be one yourself. Would you lament the loss of the grandchildren you thought you would never have or rue the big day when you proudly saw the fruit of your loins in her wedding dress that you thought would never happen now? It would be hard to readjust.

Despite this sympathy with her parents' dilemma, however, Jessica was starting to lose patience with them. It was all very well to go through a period of shock and readjustment but, in Jessica's opinion, things were starting to get out of hand. The rift had widened to an alarming extent and, as yet, there was no sign of her parents coming to accept Sarah's homosexuality. It was beginning to get unpleasantly personal and Jessica wished that her parents would start to be a little more mature and understanding about Sarah's life. They were still talking as if Sarah's being gay was some sort of aberration; still in denial and they talked about Sarah "coming to her senses" as if Sarah was suddenly going to come running home and tell them it had all been a terrible mistake and she wasn't gay after all. Jessica sometimes felt like shaking some sense into them. Why couldn't they just say "Ok our daughter is gay. It's not her fault and it's not our fault. It's just the way things are." and then everybody could move on and get back to the business of living. But no. They were still intractably enclosed in a dreamland of denial and blame, although they seemed unable to decide whether to lay that blame on Sarah for her "condition" or squarely at the feet of this mysterious girl she was apparently living with.

That was the one unknown factor in the whole sorry equation that *really* intrigued Jessica. In the months since her announcement, Sarah had steadfastly refused to reveal the identity of her girlfriend or to volunteer any information whatsoever about her. There had been good reason for this at the start for her father had threatened, at the beginning, to come to the Toggenburg and confront this woman that had apparently been such an insidious influence on his impressionable daughter and, furthermore, Alan and his family had made thinly veiled threats against her. So Sarah had defended her girlfriend behind an obdurate stone wall of anonymity. Jessica was beginning to shrewdly suspect however that this was not the whole story. The threat of her father to confront the girl had receded considerably. In fact, by now, it was unlikely that he would deign to meet the girl under any circumstances or even condescend to admitting her existence at all. Jessica guessed that Sarah had ulterior and more complex motives for concealing her girlfriend's identity.

That identity was a delicious mystery to Jessica. She was not an abnormally nosy person and she certainly had enough sensitivity not to pry, uninvited, into another person's private life but she couldn't help but speculate interestedly on this shadowy figure that had seemingly taken over her kid sister's life. She guessed that it was no ordinary young lesbian girl (if there was such a thing) that Sarah had fallen so comprehensively for. She was pretty sure that Sarah's amour wasn't just a farmer's daughter from the Toggenburg she'd run into.

For one thing she was rich. Jessica was certain about that. When Sarah had come to the Ticino for her ill-fated engagement party she'd been sporting expensive designer clothes and valuable jewellery that she'd been reticent about the source of. Certainly this woman had had a great deal of influence over Sarah for Jessica had never seen Sarah so elegantly or, come to that, so femininely dressed and Jessica was sure that Sarah's own finances would not stretch to the sort of expensive adornments she'd been wearing. It made Sarah's motivations for concealing her identity even more intriguing.

Perhaps she came of a rich family; a wealthy heiress or something. In that case perhaps the girl's family did not know of her relationship with Sarah and that was why Sarah was so reluctant for the information to become public knowledge. God in heaven she might even be a married woman, married to a wealthy man and Sarah was having a clandestine relationship with her. This house, Sarah was purportedly sharing with this woman, might even just be a little private love nest; this woman's holiday villa in the Toggenburg to which she flew whenever hubby was away on business.

These sort of things happened, Jessica knew. Just after the afore mentioned engagement party Sarah and her lover had mysteriously vanished away on holiday for two weeks together leaving no forwarding address or word to anybody as to their whereabouts. Sarah had told her later that they'd spent the two weeks alone on some little deserted island in the North Sea. It didn't exactly sound like the sort of destination that would have been chosen by a couple not concerned about their

39

relationship becoming known. Jessica suspected that Sarah might be playing a dangerous game.

Jessica paused on the main road bridge over the River Reuss and leaned on the balustrade to admire the sight of the Kapellbrucke and the old Water Tower just downstream. The Kapellbrucke was a long wooden, covered footbridge spanning the river and the oldest covered wooden bridge in Europe, dating from 1333. It was the city's most notable landmark and it had been a massive blow to civic pride when much of it had been destroyed in a catastrophic fire in 1993. It had been largely rebuilt after that but you could still see some of the charred timbers remaining. The greatest loss had been the old seventeenth century paintings depicting civic life that had decorated the interior walkway of the bridge. The Wasserturm, the old water tower at one end of the bridge, had escaped pretty much unscathed by the fire. That would have pleased Sarah, thought Jessica with a grin. Apparently there was a colony of Alpine Swifts that nested in the water tower according to Sarah. Despite her degree in history from Bern university, Sarah would have been far more concerned about her bloody birds than an ancient historical monument.

Jessica had a great fondness for Luzern. Her husband, Damien came from the city and she had met him here. They'd lived in the city in their first difficult years of marriage in a tiny bedsitter in the old quarter. Since then they had become more affluent and moved to a lovely old house near the small nearby town of Hergiswil on the banks of Lake Lucerne a little south of the city. She still liked to come into town though and still retained a great affection for the city.

She glanced at her watch. She was late. Doubtless her father would be tapping irritably on the. table in the restaurant they were meeting in by now. "Well let him!" thought Jessica. Perhaps it would teach him that his children were all grown adults by now and had other things to do with their lives, other than drop everything at the drop of a hat and come running at his parental order. Nevertheless she pushed away from the balustrade and walked on into the old town.

To give him his due, her father had picked out a very pleasant old establishment for their meeting. It was a large but cosy pub/restaurant popular with tourists and the smarter young locals in the heart of the old town. Jessica saw her father immediately, at a corner table rummaging through some papers from his briefcase and glancing at his watch. She walked over and kissed him quickly. "You're a bit late Jessica." He noted with a frown.

"Oh gee dad! I'm sorry. Does this mean I'll lose my executive bonus this year?"

"Don't be flippant Jessica. I was merely making an observation."

"Well in case you hadn't noticed dad, I do have a life and your call could have come at a more convenient time."

"In that case I'm sorry to have inconvenienced you. Can I offer you something to drink?"

"Yes. I'll take a large gin and tonic if you're offering."

Mr Fuchs raised an eyebrow. "Are you sure Jessica? I mean don't you have to drive back?"

"Thank you for your concern for my well-being father but I think I'm old enough to know not to drink and drive by now. As it happens I'm *not* driving. Damien's car is in for servicing and he's had to go through to Lausanne for the opening of his new exhibition this weekend so he's borrowed my car. Hence, I've been obliged to catch the train into town to come and see you so I hope you've got something worthwhile to say."

Mr Fuchs lowered his head apologetically. "Oh I'm sorry Jessica. I had no idea."

"No and you didn't think to ask either."

Mr Fuchs took a deep breath and regarded his hands on the table for a few seconds. When he spoke again his voice sounded sad and defeated. "I'm sorry Jessica. Am I really such a self-important tyrannical father?"

Jessica laughed lightly. "Sure you are. I don't know how you and mum have managed to live together for twenty six years without murdering each other. You're both a pair of unrepentant control freaks." Jessica saw her father wince at the remark and she became concerned. "Hey come on dad. Lighten up. I'm only kidding."

Her father nodded distractedly. "Yes. Well the least I can do by way of apology for putting you to so much trouble is to get you that drink and offer to drive you home later. I'm going past Hergiswil on my way home and it's not far out of my way."

Jessica blinked. "You're driving back over the Gotthard tonight?"

Her father nodded and raised a hand to catch a waitress's attention. "Yes. I've been in Zurich on business and since I was driving back this way today I decided to stop off to see you. If I'd known you were stuck without a car though I'd have come down to Hergiswil."

"You're working away on a weekend dad? Isn't mum pissed off with you?"

"Well yes she is but not for that reason Jess. To be honest I think she's glad to see me out of the house for a few days."

Jessica stared at her father in shock. "Dad is there something the matter between you and mum?"

Her father nodded once more. "I'm afraid so Jessica. In fact a week ago your mother mentioned the subject of divorce."

Jessica felt the blood drain out of her face. "Oh dad! No! Surely not!"

Mr Fuchs raised his hand. "Don't panic Jess. I think I've talked her out of it for the time being. At least we've agreed to table the matter until after your brother's wedding in the spring. It wouldn't do we've agreed to ruin your brother's wedding with possibly acrimonious discussions of divorce."

"Dad what the hell's happened?"

"Sarah, Jessica. That's what's happened."

"Oh for heaven's sake dad. You can't blame Sarah if your marriage is going through a rough patch. What the hell's *she* got to do with it?"

"I'd best get you that drink and then I'll tell you all about it."

Jessica had ordered a large gin and tonic somewhat rebelliously to make a point to her father but now, nursing her drink, she decided she needed it. "So what the hell's going on dad?"

Her father folded his hands together on the table and mustered his thoughts. "I'm afraid these last few weeks have been very difficult for your mother Jessica. Losing Sarah's marriage like that was bad enough to begin with. To compound the problem, as a result of the events of that horrible party, the story that the whole proposed marriage was a sham and arranged only for business convenience has spread pretty much through all our friends and acquaintances in the Ticino and caused a good deal of malicious gossip. Your mother has found herself somewhat marginalised by her former circle of friends."

"Oh Christ!" Jessica realised immediately how much that would hurt her mother. Mrs Fuchs was a dedicated socialite. Ostracism from the echelons of fashionable Ticino society would be devastating to her.

"Fortunately," Mr Fuchs continued, "The real reasons for Sarah's refusal to marry Alan have not become public so far. Your mother is terrified that Sarah's condition becomes known."

"Condition! For God's sake dad! She's only gay. It's not a life threatening, incurable disease."

"For God's sake don't say that Jess. I read recently that the incidence of AIDs is much higher among the homosexual community than among heterosexuals in Switzerland."

Jessica rolled her eyes to heaven. "I think you'll find dad that those statistics refer to homosexual *men*. The HIV infection rate among non drug using lesbians is one of the lowest of any societal sexual grouping. Sarah would have had more chance of catching AIDs if she'd been straight. In fact one of the commonest causes of HIV among gay women is when one of them decides to have a heterosexual fling. If you're frightened about Sarah catching AIDs you ought to be delighted that she's shacked up with another woman."

"You seem to know a lot about it Jess."

"Well I've done my research dad. When Sarah dropped her bombshell I was as taken aback by it as you are. It occurred to me then that, here I was, and I have a kid sister who's gay and I know absolutely damn all about it. Oh I know gay people to be sure but I didn't really know much about the subject in general and about gay women in particular. So I set about to inform myself about it. I wish that you and mum would do the same. You might not be so terrified about it if you learned more about the subject."

"Well anyway Jess, as far as all our friends are concerned, Sarah has nothing other than a perfectly normal healthy heterosexual appetite."

"Oh God! Listen to yourself dad. The very fact that you use words like that shows your ignorance. Do you honestly believe that Sarah is abnormal and unhealthy? There are millions of perfectly *normal* gay people. It's not an illness. There aren't hospital wings dedicated to caring for the incurably gay."

"Well you might have a hard time convincing your

44

mother of that Jessica. She believes that Sarah being gay reflects badly on herself as a mother. She's taken this very hard indeed Jess. Moreover she thinks that, if it were to become known that her daughter was gay, she would lose whatever is left of her own social standing and become an object of ridicule. As a result, she refuses to have anything to do with Sarah for the moment. In fact she even refuses to mention her name most of the time."

"I can't believe I'm hearing this dad. Sarah is her *daughter*! Surely her own daughter is more important to her than the bloody opinions of a bunch of trite, superficial, self-serving, socialite fucking gossips. I refuse to believe that my mother is as shallow as that."

"Jessica I think it goes deeper than that. I think your mother was truly heart broken by Sarah saying she was gay. She was equally heartbroken that the wedding she had so wanted for Sarah was dashed from her hands in such a way. I know what the gossips say and I know you think it too but it was never about marrying Sarah just to cement a business alliance with the Bergers Jess. We genuinely both believed that it was the best move for Sarah and that she would be happy and well cared for in the marriage."

"But you never asked Sarah if she thought so too dad." Jessica pointed out.

"I know that now Jessica but how could I have known it then? Sarah had never seemed to have any problem before concerning her marriage. Until that damn weekend of the party she'd not once raised any fundamental objection to marrying Alan. I thought her only concerns were that her mother was imposing too much on the wedding plans. I tried to persuade Alisha to involve Sarah more in the wedding arrangements and not to keep bulldozing Sarah's opinions with her own ideas but she said, and with justification, that Sarah didn't seem interested in the wedding plans. Not in our worst

45

nightmares could we have foreseen what was coming though. It was absolutely crushing. Your mother hasn't got over it. I don't know that she ever will."

"But what's all this got to do with you and mum and your marriage dad?"

"Well Jess when people are hurt to that extent they often look around for something to lash out at. I was the nearest whipping boy. Your mother was looking around to apportion blame for Sarah's... Sarah's... damn I don't want to say condition again."

"Let's just say Sarah's being gay then dad."

"Very well. Sarah's being gay. Naturally she pointed the accusing finger at me."

"Why the hell does she think it's *your* fault?"

"Oh she thinks I encouraged Sarah to be too much of a tomboy when she was younger, taking her hiking in the mountains and all that."

"Damn it dad! You took me hiking in the mountains when I was a kid. I used to love it. It didn't make me fucking gay though."

"I didn't say her reasons were necessarily rational Jessica. In spite of your earlier aspersions, I have taken the trouble to read a little bit about homosexuality since learning that my daughter identifies herself as such. I am well aware that contemporary psychological thinking argues that the reasons for a person's tendency to homosexuality are far more complex than that and that it is a common reaction among parents confronted with their children's homosexuality to look for faults in their own raising of the child. I am not entirely insensitive to the issues you know."

"I'm sorry dad. I underestimated you. Forgive me."

Her father waved his hand dismissively. "Oh don't concern yourself Jessica. I am not blameless in all this. I've handled the whole situation very badly from beginning to end. I know I should have done better but I honestly never saw it coming and when it did I was floundering in the dark, not knowing what to do. I let my worries get the better of me. I even went along to the Bergers and tried to persuade them that Sarah was just going through a phase and would come around in the end. Then Sarah phoned me on her graduation day and I was very abrupt with her and near as damn it ordered her to stop her foolishness and discuss the matter with Alan. She hung up the phone on me."

"Yes she told me dad."

"I didn't know what to do Jess. I couldn't admit to myself that Sarah was gay and I couldn't bring myself to accept it."

"And now dad? Are you beginning to accept it now?" asked Jessica quietly and compassionately.

"I don't know Jess. On the one hand the rational side of me says that yes you're right, homosexuality is a common and normal manifestation of the human condition and that I should take it on the chin and accept that my daughter is in no way diminished by her sexual orientation and that she is just the same person that I have always known and loved. On the other hand there is another side of me that just refuses to believe it."

"Presumably your researches into parental reactions have taught you that all that's pretty much par for the course as well dad I suppose."

"I know Jess. I suppose it's because I feel so helpless in the situation. I know what a cruel world it is and I can't bear the thought of my daughter being subjected to the sort of prejudice and ostracism that comes from being different. I want to protect her but I don't know how. Whatever she is and whatever she's done I still love my daughter dearly. I love all of you of course but you and John always struck me as much more robust; more able to take care of yourselves in the rough and tumble of life. Sarah always seemed more vulnerable.

"That's an illusion dad because she was the baby of

the family. I think Sarah's far more capable of looking after herself than you give her credit for."

"Perhaps you're right Jessica. I suppose, like many a foolish man before me, my daughter was growing to womanhood under my nose and I just failed to see it. I was still stuck thinking of her as a little girl."

"I think that's pretty normal for fathers as well dad."

"Well anyway Jess the upshot of all this is that I am now caught on the horns of a dilemma. The whole issue of Sarah has driven a wedge between your mother and I of sufficient seriousness that the word divorce has arisen."

"You can't get divorced dad. You and mum have been devoted to each other for over twenty six years."

"Trust me Jess. There is nothing I want less. For all her faults and foibles, and I am fully aware of them, I love your mother dearly and I simply could not imagine life without her. Somehow or other I have to fight to save my marriage now Jessica. And to save that marriage I have to come to a solution regarding Sarah. This is where I need your help."

"Dad you can't ask me to tell Sarah that you and mum are breaking up because she's gay. That's tantamount to emotional blackmail. I won't do it."

"I'm asking you to do nothing of the sort Jessica. In fact I'd prefer it if you kept this entire conversation to yourself. All I need you to do is reassure Sarah that I'm thinking about her and to keep an eye on her for me. I'm worried sick about her Jess."

"I'm not about to start butting into her private life dad."

"I'm not asking you to. All I want is for you to keep the communication lines open and to try and stop the breach becoming any wider than it is at present. I'm pulled between two forces Jess. On the one hand I have a wife I love, and who I'm desperately trying to hold onto,

48

and, on the other hand, a daughter I love dearly, that I'm worried to death about. Right now those are two conflicting interests. My daughter presumably despises me for the moment and my wife won't entertain the thought of having her anywhere near her. Your mother would be furious to know that I'd even discussed the matter with you Jess. Right now I daren't even call Sarah, let alone visit her or invite her to our home. The last time I tried to arrange a meeting with Sarah and ourselves, she insisted that her girlfriend be present and your mother flatly rejected the notion out of hand. She has a hard enough time even talking at all about Sarah never mind this mysterious girlfriend of hers! But I don't want Sarah to be completely convinced that I am ignoring her. I hope in time that your mother will come around and accept that what has happened has happened and that it's nobody's fault and we can put it behind us. Right now though I have to treat her with kid gloves or risk losing her Jess. I need you to understand that. I need you to keep the door ajar and hope that someday we can kick it open again."

"Just one thing dad."

"What's that Jess?"

"Sarah doesn't despise you. She loves you and always has. Never forget that."

Mr Fuchs choked. Jessica had never seen her father so close to tears. "Thank you Jessica. Your words mean a lot to me."

"But dad this is all crazy. You can't allow this to jeopardise your marriage. You've got to make mum see sense."

"How am I supposed to do that Jess?"

"Put your bloody foot down and tell her to stop being a bigoted blunder head and a social coward. Tell her that it's her daughter too and that she should be proud of her and bugger what the twittering imbeciles of Ticino society think about it. Knock a bit of bloody

49

sense into her. Since when has the flower of Swiss manhood let its womenfolk walk all over them? What kind of man are you?"

Mr Fuchs rubbed his chin wryly. "One that's been married to your mother for twenty six years I suppose."

Jessica laughed, disarmed by her father's unusually, uncharacteristic, self-depreciating irony. Her father could be often pompous and overly serious but there was a saving grace of humour about his character too. "Seriously though dad you're going to have to talk to her. We can't let this continue."

"I'll try my best Jessica."

Jessica reached into her handbag. "Look dad there's something I've been meaning to give you for some time. Maybe it might help."

Jessica handed over a pamphlet from an organisation with the acronym FELS on it. "What the devil is this?"

"It's a pamphlet from the Swiss chapter of PFLAG dad."

"What the blazes is PFLAG?"

"Parents, Families and Friends of Lesbians and Gays dad. It's a socio-political group for family members and friends of gay people. It gives such people a forum to stand up in support of their gay family members and friends."

"And how is this supposed to help?"

"Well one of its missions is to offer support to families when a family member has come out as gay and to offer counselling when a family is having a hard time coming to terms with it. The Swiss chapter is called Freundinnen, Freunde und Eltern von Lesben und Schwulen. They have meetings where family members of gay people can go along and share experiences and find support from other people that are experiencing the same difficulties. Maybe you could drag mum along."

"I doubt very much if she'd agree Jess. As for

counselling, well that's a sore subject. She's already tried to get me to convince Sarah to go for counselling in the hope that someone can, I suppose, cure her of her homosexuality."

"Oh God! Don't dare dad. Sarah would never forgive you."

"I know but what can I do? Your mother's even heard of some bloody Christian organisation that purports to wean people off the homosexual life style and convert them to ex-gays. God only knows where she dug that up from."

"For crying out loud dad, get her to desist from this line of reasoning. She'll be talking about shipping Sarah off to a nunnery at this rate."

Mr Fuchs raised an eyebrow. "Er possibly not such a good idea that I think."

Jessica laughed. "Yeah I see what you mean. That might be a bit like trying to cure an alcoholic by locking him up in a brewery." Jessica leaned back in her chair. "I'm glad we've had this talk dad. To be honest I thought that you were being a bit of a prick about Sarah being gay. I've misjudged you dad. Ok then I'll act as your go between and reassure Sarah as much as I can. If you need to set up a clandestine meeting with Sarah I'll set it up too."

"Thank you very much Jessica."

"There's one thing I think you might be missing though dad."

"And that is?"

"Sarah's girlfriend. I think you might have to ask Sarah if you could meet her."

"Why Jessica?"

"I don't know dad. I couldn't tell you myself. Call it intuition or a gut feeling but somehow I have the feeling that Sarah's girlfriend is going to be decisive in all this. Don't ask me why I think so though. I mean, I'm as much in the dark about her as you are."

Mr Fuchs ruffled his hair worriedly. "Well if Sarah's relationship with this woman lasts we may not be able to avoid meeting her. There's one last spanner in the works I haven't mentioned to you. I haven't dared tell your mother yet but, on the way up here on Thursday, I had to see some people in St Gallen so I came up over the San Bernadino pass, through Chur and down the Rhine valley. Since I was close by, I popped in to see John and Maria in Appenzell. They've more or less decided on a date for their wedding in early April and of course they have every intention of inviting Sarah to the wedding. What's more, they see absolutely no reason why they shouldn't invite Sarah's girlfriend as well."

Chapter Four

Mr Fuchs might have been even more concerned about his volatile wife had he known that, whilst he was talking to Jessica in the pub in Luzern, she was about to take independent action of her own. It had possibly been a mistake for Mr Fuchs to go away and leave his wife to brood on her own for, left to her own devices without some sort of steadying influence, she was all too likely to go off the rails and do something unbelievably foolish. She had decided to do just such a thing now. In a rash, impetuous decision, she had decided to phone Sarah.

Sarah was busy in the kitchen, humming contentedly to herself. Showered, changed and coiffed she was expecting Nicole shortly and so she was busily making her initial preparations for dinner. The kitchen was a scene of domestic harmony for the moment for Daniela's four cats were blissfully consuming their own evening meals from bowls scattered about the floor. Sarah had fed them just before beginning her own preparations to dine. The cats had taken very well to Sarah's permanent presence in the house considering that they quite clearly believed that the property belonged to them. Sarah liked cats and she had taken to the scruffy bunch immediately. When she had first heard that Daniela had four cats she had assumed that they would all be pampered pedigree Persians or Siamese or something appropriate to such a glamorous mistress. Instead they had turned out to be a rather battered gang of strays that had fostered themselves on Daniela's gullible kindness with ruthless exploitation. The incongruity amused Sarah and she found Daniela's fond affection for the motley crew endearing.

Busy with her domestic chores, Sarah was caught

by surprise by the chime of her mobile telephone. As a result she omitted to glance at the display screen to ascertain the caller before wiping her hands and keying the reply button. "Hello, is that you Sarah?"

Sarah started in surprise. Her mother hadn't called her in over a month. "Yes it's me mum. This is a surprise."

"Why should it be a surprise?"

"Well you haven't exactly shown any enthusiasm for talking to me recently you know mum."

"Well I wouldn't have thought that *that* should come as any surprise Sarah. You have after all gone out of your way to exclude your father and I from your life these past weeks. You can hardly be surprised therefore if we're reluctant to communicate with you."

Sarah blushed and felt her hackles rising. "That is unfair mother. The reason you are excluded from my life is because you so clearly want to have nothing to do with it. You never turned up for my graduation even though I told you weeks in advance when it was and you refused to come through to the Toggenburg to see me just because it would mean you having to meet my girlfriend. If you feel excluded from my life, I suggest that you take more interest in it."

"I am not about to go all the way to the Toggenburg just to have this woman you're seeing thrust under my nose Sarah."

"Well then that's your loss mother and I can hardly be blamed if you think that excludes you. I'm not about to hide my girlfriend in the cupboard just to pander to your sensibilities."

"Where are you now anyway?"

"I'm at home mother."

"Which home is that?"

Sarah rolled her eyes and prayed for patience. "The only one I have mother, the one I share with my girlfriend."

"Is she there?"

"My girlfriend?"

"I wish you'd stop calling her that Sarah. I mean the woman you've been seeing."

"Oddly enough I call her my girlfriend mother because she's my girlfriend. I find it strangely offensive that you keep referring to her as "this woman you've been seeing".

"I can't see what else I'm supposed to refer to her as. You haven't even told us the damn woman's name."

"You've never asked. Anyway if it makes you feel better she's called Danny."

Mrs Fuchs snorted loudly. "*Danny*! She's even got a man's name. I knew she'd be some awful butch. Where is she now anyway?"

Sarah's impatience was getting the better of her. "Oh let's see... it's Saturday isn't it? Wrestling practice is on Wednesdays so she must be out for rugby training today."

Mrs Fuchs ignored Sarah's heavy sarcasm. "What I mean is can you speak freely now?"

"Why on earth would you believe that my girlfriend's presence would prevent me from speaking freely mother? The only restrictions I'm placing on my speech for the moment is a desperate effort to keep my temper and refrain from using unfortunate vocabulary whilst listening to my girlfriend being insulted."

"I have something important to say to you Sarah and I need you to listen sensibly."

"I think that will rather depend on whether or not what you have to say is sensible mother. At the moment, I'm afraid I have my doubts."

"Sarah there is no need for you to make this choice."

"Choice? What choice mother?"

"The choice you seem to be making regarding your life for the moment. I've tried to be patient with you so far in the hope that you'd come to your senses without being told but now it has gone too far Sarah. Now I think you have to make some greater conscious effort to reverse the poor decisions you have made of late."

Sarah leaned against the kitchen top with her head swimming. "I'm sorry mother but you have me fuddled. I haven't the faintest idea what you're talking about."

"I know that it's difficult Sarah but there are people that can help you."

"Help me do what?"

"Why change your lifestyle of course."

"What sodding lifestyle?"

"Why your homosexual lifestyle of course."

"Oh my sainted aunt! What the devil are you blathering about mother?"

"What I'm trying to say Sarah is that it's not too late to alter your choice. There is still hope. I've been talking to some people who have offered to help you; help you escape from this lifestyle and revert back to the girl you were before you made such a poor choice to become homosexual."

"WHAT? Are you saying that I *chose* to become gay mother? Are you honestly sitting there and telling me that it's some terrible decision I made like getting involved in drugs or something and are you in all seriousness suggesting that there are people who will rescue me and lead me back on the road to salvation?"

"Exactly Sarah."

"Have you completely come adrift of your sodding marbles mother?"

"There is no need for you to lose your temper Sarah. All I want you to do is talk to these people."

"Who the hell are they?"

"It's a charitable organisation funded by some Christian group. They assure me that they have a very good record in helping people escape from the homosexual lifestyle. They've agreed to send a couple of people around to visit you and talk to you."

"If these people come anywhere near my front door I'll set the bloody dogs on them."

"I didn't think you had any dogs."

"I'll *buy* some!"

"I'm only asking you to listen to what they have to say Sarah. It's the least you can do."

"It's the *last* thing I'll do. Thank God I had the sense not to give you my new address."

"Well of course I shall need that Sarah. I shouldn't imagine that it would be too hard to obtain."

"Mother if you dare, if you even dare to infringe upon my privacy like this or in any way harass me through your blasted narrow minded bigotry I swear I shall not only never speak to you again but I shall furthermore take legal action to protect my privacy and, if necessary, I'll take out a restraining order from the courts to defend myself. You have completely stepped beyond the line mother. I will not tolerate this unwarranted invasion of my life in this way."

"Well I can see that you're in no mood to discuss this thing rationally Sarah."

"There's nothing *rational* in this entire crack brained idea of yours mother. I've never heard such a dollop of verbal garbage in my life."

"Sarah listen to me..."

"No *you* listen mother! I am gay mother. I didn't have a choice about that. It's not something I can reverse just because my mother doesn't approve of it. I am what I am and talking to a pair of earnest Christian fanatics eager to lead me back onto the path of righteousness isn't going to change that. I'm not ashamed or distressed about being gay mother. On the contrary I am perfectly happy and proud to be who I am. I am not living in some sordid and shameful sort of underground lifestyle. I am living a perfectly ordinary happy and fulfilled life with a woman I love dearly and if you cannot accept that life then please do me the common courtesy of staying out of it."

"There's no need to get angry Sarah."

"On the contrary I think there's every need to do so. Has my father put you up to this lunacy?"

"Oh I can get no sense out of your father these days."

"Mother I think the person most lacking the commodity of sense at the moment is yourself. Now you'll have to excuse me but I'm expecting a guest shortly and I have dinner to prepare."

"Sarah listen..."

"I'm through listening mother. Please call back when you've come to your right mind again."

Angrily Sarah snapped off the connection and leaned against the kitchen top breathing heavily. She swore under her breath and straightened up, determined not to let her mother's foolishness spoil her evening. As she did so, she heard Nicole's car pulling into the driveway. She glanced at the clock on the kitchen wall. It read half past six. Nicole was early. Sarah walked through into the living room just in time to greet Nicole who had walked straight into the house without the formality of knocking on the front door as befitting the status of an old friend. Sarah smiled in welcome. "Hi Nicky."

"Hi Foxy. Sorry I'm so early but I was just hanging around at home at a loose end so I thought I'd come over."

"Don't mention it. I'm glad to see you. You won't believe the conversation I've just had with my mother over the phone."

"Your mum phoned? Hell that's a turnaround isn't it? I mean she's barely spoken to you since you told that retarded boyfriend of yours to take his engagement ring and shove it up his arse."

"Well believe me it wasn't a phone call of

58

reconciliation. There have been no hatchets buried or peace pipes smoked. In fact hostilities are as intense as ever."

"Oh God! What happened?"

"Look Nicky I've only just started dinner. Come in the kitchen and I'll open a bottle of wine. I can tell you about it while I'm cooking."

Nicole was appalled by Sarah's rendition of the conversation between her mother and herself. She sat at the kitchen table whilst Sarah busied herself with the food and listened in disbelief. "Your mum's really lost the plot this time Foxy."

"I know. I don't think she'll ever get her head around my being gay. I suppose her background doesn't help."

"What do you mean?"

"Well she was a fashion model when she was younger Nicky. I suppose she was in the business of looking attractive to men and homosexuality is just so alien to her."

"That doesn't hold water Sarah. Fashion models dress up to look gorgeous for women not men. When was the last time you saw a man drooling over the pages of Cosmopolitan? It's women that read those sort of magazines, ogle the models and want to be just like them. Anyway I'd have thought that your mother would be cool on gays. I mean there's a hell of a lot of gay people in the fashion industry. It's practically dominated by them. You'd have thought that she would have been exposed to dozens of them in her career. So why's she giving you such a hard time about it?"

"Maybe it's just because I'm her daughter Nicky."

Nicole ran a hand through her blond hair. She was looking pretty today. She'd even put quite a modest dress on to come around for dinner which was an improvement on her usual line of outrageously short mini-skirts and tiny tops. "Are you sure your mum's not a couple of cans short of a six pack at the moment Sarah? This is some way beyond parental disapproval now. I mean it's starting to sound like a clinically definable obsession."

"I don't know Nicky. If I wasn't so furious with her, I'd be worried."

"Yeah..." Nicole started in surprise as her eye strayed to the big glass veranda doors leading out onto the back garden. "Er Sarah... did you know that you've got somebody's chicken scrabbling about on your back porch?"

Sarah pulled a face. "No it's one of ours I'm afraid; or one of ours by default anyway."

"You and Danny keep chickens?"

"Not through any fault of ours. We have an old guy that looks after the garden and does repairs around the place. Well while we were away on Helgoland his chicken coop collapsed for reasons as yet undetermined. Well, as it happened, there was an old chicken hut in the back garden near the barn and so Hans-Ruedi shifted all his chickens into our chicken coop on a purely temporary basis whilst he effected repairs and we've been lumbered with them ever since; devil the sign of their old quarters being put back into repair so far."

Nicole laughed. "God! How many have you got?"

"Nearly two dozen of the damn things. Danny was a bit put out when we came home to find the place infested with chickens but we've sort of got used to them by now. At least we get nice fresh eggs out of them. If you want to take some eggs home with you just help yourself. We've got more than we know what to do with."

"Don't the cats have them?"

"Nah! The cats are far too well fed and lazy to bother about trying to take on something as big as a chicken. Roddy, that's the tabby one over there, does a bit of mousing in the barn in a desultory sort of way but the others can't even be bothered to do that much generally."

"So you've got two dozen and stuck with them."

"Well for the moment we have. I should imagine we'll have a certain attrition of numbers as time goes on. We're a little bit too close to the woodland here. The local Goshawks regard chicken runs as handy convenience stores. We've already lost one to a hawk."

"What about foxes?"

"Not a problem usually, as long as you lock the coop up securely by night. Foxes are pretty much nocturnal." Sarah peered into her saucepan. "Dinner will be ready in a few minutes. Do you mind eating in the kitchen?"

Nicole shrugged. "Suits me. We always used to eat together in the kitchen back at the cottage. This kitchen's a bit posher than that though."

"Well ok. Do you want to be setting the table while I finish tossing the salad?"

"Sure if you tell me where everything is. I've never been in your kitchen before."

"Cutlery in that drawer over there, plates and so in the cupboard above and you'll find paper napkins in the cabinet next to the table."

They sat down to eat. Nicole wolfed her food ravenously enough to make Sarah worry about whether she was eating properly. "God I've missed your cooking." She told Sarah.

Sarah regarded her concernedly. "I'm sorry Nicky. Does the house feel empty without me there anymore?"

Nicole shrugged. "Well I might not be in it much longer."

"Oh?"

"No. I just got a notice from the landlady. She's sold the property. I know she's been threatening to do so for years but she's really gone and done it this time. I don't suppose the new owners are going to want to keep me on as a tenant so it looks like I'm on my bike. I had a word with Heike Muller yesterday. She says there might be a room going at her place I could have."

Sarah frowned. "I thought you couldn't stand Heike Muller."

"She's not that bad. Anyway it's a matter of needs must. Even if the new owners didn't throw me out I can't afford to stay there. I can't expect you to keep paying half the rent when you don't live there anymore and now there might not be much work going until the winter season at the hotel."

Sarah laid her cutlery to one side and passed a basket over to Nicole. "Here have the last piece of garlic bread." Nicole took the offering thankfully. She'd been too polite to take it without being offered. Sarah thought for a moment. "If the new owner let you stay and you could afford it, would you?"

"Yes. I love the old place although it's not the same without you around anymore.

"I could come over and stay when Danny's away sometimes Nicky. She's going to be away on tour a lot this winter and it gets pretty lonely in this big place on my own."

"Well I don't think it's likely to happen Sarah. I'm pretty sure the new owner isn't going to want a sitting tenant and you can't keep on paying the rent."

"I'm not going to keep paying rent Nicky. I cancelled the standing order last week. It seemed a pretty stupid idea to be paying rent to myself."

Nicole sat up and looked at her in surprise. "What the hell do you mean?"

"*I'm* your new landlady Nicky; or, to be more precise, Danny and I are. We signed the deeds for the property before she went away. She owns that house now and you can take it from me that you *will* be able to afford the rent!"

Nicole reeled in shock. "You are kidding me!"

"Not at all. It's something we talked about weeks

ago. We didn't want to tell you before the deal was signed though."

Nicole ran a hand through her hair. "Is that legal Sarah? I mean aren't there laws about foreign nationals owning more than one property in Switzerland?"

"Danny's *not* a foreign national Nicky. She's got dual nationality. She has a Swiss passport. Her father is Swiss."

"Oh I see. Oh Christ! This is a turn up. Why the hell did she want to want to buy the house?"

"I think she considers it a sound investment Nicky and it means you won't have to find somewhere new to live."

"She can't just buy a bloody house to stop me being put out on the street Sarah!"

"Don't bank on it Nicky. It's not the only investment she's making locally either."

"Is she buying up half the bloody valley?"

Sarah laughed. "No not quite. She is however investing some money in Peter and Simon's new pub."

"Oh wow!" This was exciting news. Peter and Simon had lately acquired the little rustic pub at the feet of the chairlift up to Oberdorf where Sarah and Daniela lived. They had great ideas for the new location but the patronage of the Toggenburg's very own pop superstar would be a potential goldmine.

Sarah leaned across and tapped on the table. "Yes and I think that you and I can take the chairlift down tomorrow and see them. I think that it's time you had a talk with them."

"What about?"

"About the new staff they're going to be needing once the place is up and running."

"You think they'd take me on?"

"Er the best friend of their business partner's girlfriend? I think we can take that as a no-brainer Nicky."

Nicole looked shell-shocked. "My God! That'd be a hell of a lot more fun than waiting on tables in the Hirschen."

Sarah grinned. "I'd say the job's yours. In fact I already spoke to Pete and Simon about it. They'd love to have you aboard."

"Why are you doing all this Sarah?"

"I can't imagine Nicky. Maybe it's because I care about you. *We* care about you. Danny was adamant that we make sure that you're all right Nicky. She's been worried about you and so have I."

Nicole squirmed uncomfortably. "You... you want to make sure I'm all right?"

"Danny would consider she had abrogated her duty by not doing so.

"I...I'm not sure I feel entirely comfortable about this Sarah."

"Why not?"

"Well is it... I mean is it because Danny feels well... guilty?"

"Why should she feel guilty Nicky?"

"You know why Sarah. She thinks she took you away from me."

Sarah shook her head slowly. "You're way off base Nicky. Oh I know that Danny did feel bad because she believed that she'd taken away the woman you loved but this isn't about guilt Nicky. Danny genuinely cares for you and she knows as well how much you mean to me. You've got to understand how Danny's mind works Nicky. There's not a single bone in her body that can even contemplate the alien concept of hating somebody. Love rules Danny. It rules her completely. It's where she's at."

Sarah shook her head wistfully, "You know Nicky, when I first met Danny, I was impressed by the way she was able to talk to people and make them feel special as if they were the best thing that had happened to her all

64

day. I thought it must be some kind of trick that you learned when you became famous like some kind of charm and charisma. I mean, she knows so many people that it didn't seem possible that she could be that interested in all of them. As I got to know her better though, I realised that it wasn't just some kind of trick. She's really like that. She's absolutely fascinated by people. She observes them avidly; can't get enough of them. She doesn't just see a person in front of her she sees a story; a journey through life and she wants to know about it; share it. To her, life is this incredible adventure populated by all these amazing people that she wants to reach out and touch the lives of. I've seen her sit for hours at her computer answering her fan mail just thrilled that she and her music have become a little part of somebody's life. It's not the adoration she craves. She feels almost embarrassed by that. It's just the thought; the idea of sharing something together. She might do a concert in front of two thousand people but, to her, it's not her performing to those people it's her and two thousand people all having fun together. She likes to pick people out in the audience when she's performing and watch them throughout the concert and try to make a personal contact with them; a shared smile or maybe she'll say something on the microphone to make them feel included. She genuinely loves people; loves them in spite of all their failings and idiocies. That's her magic. It's what makes her irresistible.

"And if she loves people in general then those people close to her she becomes devoted to. I sometimes worry that a really ruthless person could terribly exploit her but somehow it doesn't seem to happen. I think her love is so genuine that even really bad apples find themselves wanting to be better people as a result of meeting her. When it comes to the people within her life, money just becomes an irrelevancy to Danny. I'm always protesting that she shouldn't spend so much money on me but she just looks puzzled. What else would she spend her money on, she'd wonder, if not those things dearest to her? It's not that she tries to buy affection. She's just genuinely happy that she's fortunate enough to have enough money so that she can take care of the people that mean a lot to her and her loved ones. Take Elrika, our house keeper."

"Is she the woman that answers the phone sometimes?"

"That's her. Well when Danny first came to live in the Toggenburg Elrika was the first person that came around to welcome her. Elrika didn't even know who Danny was. She just wanted to make a new neighbour feel at home. She'd even baked her an apple tart. Danny was incredibly touched by that. Elrika was an old widow with very little income so Danny took her on as a housekeeper to look after the house and her cats and so on while she was away and paid her well. Now, of course, I live here. Now I'm a pretty tidy housekeeper myself..."

Nicole snorted. "Anally retentive, is how I would have put it."

Sarah ignored the interruption. "Anyway, since I've been here, there is actually no good reason whatsoever for keeping Elrika on. So now we have to keep inventing ruses just to keep Elrika on the payroll because there's no way that Danny is going to see her go short. We've got her making new curtains for the guest bedrooms even though we simply don't need them. She even still comes in to do the laundry. I have to sit on my hands. I mean I'm perfectly capable of putting my own dirty drawers in the washing machine. I mean I suppose Danny could just pay her a pension and have done but it goes further than money. Elrika is a proud old lady and she wants to feel useful so Danny will go to any lengths to convince her that this household would collapse in ruin without her continual support. Of course, in a very real sense, she *is* useful to Danny. She's a part of her life now and she loves her. Loving people is the bread and butter of daily existence to Danny. Elrika is performing a vital function in Danny's life just by always being there."

Nicole raised an eyebrow. "And me?"

"Of course Nicky. Danny adores you and even more so because you are important to me. Do you remember that night at Gamplut when you and Pete threw that going away party for me when we thought I was leaving to go to the Ticino and get married?"

"More than you do. You were bladdered."

"Well then you'll recall that you were pissed off because I turned up with Danny after we'd been hiking up on the Alpstein for three days."

"I've already said sorry for that Sarah. I was jealous. I'm not proud of myself."

"Well you were being a bitch to Danny and I was furious with you. I caught up with her in the ladies after you'd had word with her and I was spitting blood. I said something stupid like I was never going to speak to you again and she turned on me. She said something like "Don't *ever* say that again! Nicole is the first love in your life! Don't *ever* lose her because of me!" It's the only time I've ever seen her angry. The thought that she would be responsible for two people that loved each other falling out was unbearable to her. That's the way she thinks.

"This thing about the house is similar Nicky. As far as Danny is concerned she hasn't thrown her money away. On the contrary, she's invested wisely in a property that will only increase in value as time goes by and, at the same time, she has secured the place where you live and is important to me as well. Everybody wins. It's a no-brainer as far as she's concerned. It's the same thing with Pete and Simon. They are important to us too so, naturally, she wants to put the money up front to get their new business up and running. Now with Danny's name and support behind it, that pub it can't lose. They're even going to theme it on Danny's music. Tourists will want to flock there just because of her name attached to it and it'll be the new place to go in the valley for all the younger generation. Pete and Simon make money hand over fist, Danny gets a good return on her investment and we're all in an exciting new venture together. Everybody wins again."

Nicole swilled her wine in her glass thoughtfully. "She's quite some lady your girlfriend Sarah."

"She's the most remarkable person I have ever known Nicky. You know I wake up every morning and ask myself why; why has this extraordinary woman fallen in love with me? I don't know the answer to that one."

Nicole pulled a face. "I do."

"You know what the real problem is Nicky?"

"I think I can guess Sarah. It's your mum and dad right."

Sarah nodded. "Yes. That's really tearing Danny up. She's a sight more sympathetic towards my parents than I am at the moment. She's really upset that I'm estranged from them. She's always trying to make me more understanding of their concerns. She feels terrible at having been the cause of such a break with them. I don't think she'll be truly happy; I don't think *we'll* be truly happy, until we've resolved that one. I think Danny believes that I've taken too radical a stance on this and taken a position from which I'm refusing to move without compromise."

"Well you have been pretty stubborn about it Foxy."

"Possibly Nicky. But there are principles involved here too. I let my parents control my life for too long. If I bend on this issue, I'm handing control back to them. I'm not asking much; just the right to be who I am and with the person I want to be with. I don't think that that is an unreasonable demand. I know any sort of conflict breaks Danny's heart but I can't yield on this one Nicky. It's fundamental to me. It's a basic right to my own life and my parents have to accept it."

"So why won't you tell them who your girlfriend is?"

"Because it should be *irrelevant* Nicky. I've offered them the chance to meet my girlfriend and they don't want to. Right now they think that she's just some ordinary girl and they're not interested in her. Well they should be. It shouldn't matter if my girlfriend is just the butcher's daughter or something. Of course they'll go absolutely crazy when they finally find out that my girlfriend is a famous celebrity. Right now they're scared shit less that all their friends will find out that their daughter is gay and living with another woman. Can you imagine what they're going to think when they find out that the siren that's stolen their darling little Sarah from them is one of the most high profile gay people in Switzerland and liable to be linked with her on prime time television?"

"Well I know we keep saying it Foxy but it's not a secret you're going to be able to keep forever. Don't you think it would be better to tell them before the paparazzi do?"

"No I don't. I mean I don't want them to learn it from the newspapers but, on the other hand, I want them to accept that I have a girlfriend whoever she is. Who I have fallen in love with should have nothing to do with that person's fame. The day that they are able to say, "Yes we accept that you're gay and have a girlfriend and we'd like to meet her.", then that is soon enough for them to learn who she is. Right now though they're not prepared to go that distance and, until they do, then my life is no concern of theirs."

"I don't mean to criticise you Foxy but I think you might be making a mistake. You're risking this thing becoming public knowledge before they're ready to do that and if it does then you risk making the fracture even bigger than it is now."

"Well what the hell would *you* do?"

"Easy! I'd just put Danny into the car, drive down to your mum and dad's house in Ticino, bang on the bloody door and say, "Mum, dad, ready or not, I want you to meet my girlfriend." Sure they'll probably fall over in a dead faint but all you'd have to do then is sit back and let Danny take care of it. You've said it yourself. Danny's irresistible. Let her loose on your mum and dad for five minutes and they'll be taking her into the bosom of the family like a long lost daughter. What's more, you know it."

Sarah sighed. "There are principles involved here Nicky."

"I wonder how many fucking wars started because people were too fond of their bloody principles and unwilling to bend on them Foxy."

"I think you might be underestimating my parents capacity for obdurate resistance Nicky."

"I think there's a bit of obdurate resistance in both camps Sarah. One of you is going to have to pick up an olive branch. You've said yourself that Danny likes everybody to win. Well who's winning here? Nobody as far as I can see."

Sarah held her hands up. "Let's just table this subject for the moment Nicky. I don't really want to talk about it."

Nicole shrugged. "If you want Foxy. I stand by what I said though. Danny's your ace in the pack. You can't hide her up your sleeve until the game's over. Use her. Unleash her on your parents. Your Danny's the kind of person that changes lives."

Sarah smiled. "Yes she does and there's another person whose life is about to change as a result."

Nicole inclined her head interestedly. "Oh yes?

Who's that?"

"Well when will you be seeing Charlie again?"

Nicole's face took on an instant mask like expression of feigned casualness and non-commitment. "Oh er...dunno. I sometimes bump into her when I'm through in Winterthur. Why do you ask?"

"Well when you see her you can officially inform her that she's got a new job for the winter. Danny needs her as a bass guitarist."

Nicole's jaw dropped open. "Oh wow! You're kidding!"

"Not at all. I got a phone call from Danny this afternoon and heard it straight from the horse's mouth and if you dare tell Danny I called her a horse I'll put some of the more startling examples of invertebrate pond life I collected from the Schwendisee the other day in your bedclothes one night."

Nicole ignored the threat in her enthusiasm. "Are you serious Sarah? Charlie's going on the road with Danny's band?"

"Well I think they need to do some rehearsing and so forth first but, yes, those are the facts."

"This is brilliant. I know Charlie had an audition with Danny some weeks ago in the studio in Zurich but she didn't know if she'd been good enough."

"Well you may reassure her that Danny thinks she's a very talented bassist and just the person she wants to fill in on the winter tours."

"This is just fantastic. I have to phone her. Damn I've hardly any credit on my phone. Can I use yours Sarah?"

Sarah sat back with her tongue in her cheek. "You want to phone her *now*? Can't it wait until you er... bump into her in Winterthur one day?"

"Come on Sarah. This is big news."

Sarah grinned at her. "Go on then. Use the phone in the living room; my mobile's on charge. You can be

71

telling her the news while I put the dirty plates in the dishwasher and go lock up the bloody chickens for the night."

Chapter Five

When Sarah returned from her chores, she found Nicole sat on the big sofa in the living room, interestedly examining some DVDs on the coffee table. "Er do you want coffee Nicky?"

"I'll stick with wine thanks Sarah."

"Ok I'll go grab another bottle. Did you get through to Charlie?"

"Yeah."

"And? What did she say?"

"I don't know really. She was babbling incoherently. As far as I could tell, the gist of it was that she was ecstatically happy. This is huge for her Sarah. It's not just that it's her first big break to play with a big band on tour. Danny's her idol. She worships her. This is her every dream come true. I don't think the shock has set in yet. She'll be staggering around in a daze right now."

"She does know that it's just to fill in while Danny's regular bassist takes a time out for his wife's baby doesn't she?"

"Oh yeah. That was made clear from the start Sarah but she's still over the moon. I mean it's a hell of a chance for her. Just the fact that she's backed Daniela Devin will open doors for her all over the place. She's not had much work since her last band split up."

"I'm pleased for her. I like Charlie a lot."

"She thinks the world of you Sarah." Nicole bit her lip. "Look Danny's not back until Monday right?"

"Yes. Why?"

"Well do you fancy driving through to Winterthur tomorrow? Charlie wants to buy us dinner to celebrate and she'd like you to come so she can thank you for introducing her to Danny."

"I think that's a good idea. Why don't we ask Pete and Simon along too and make an evening out of it. Simon's an old friend of Charlie's."

"Yes that's an idea." Nicole frowned. "Wait a minute though. Won't we have to take two cars in that case?"

"Er what's wrong with my car? It's plenty big enough for four people, five if we have to drive Charlie around as well."

"Well I thought Pete and Sime could travel in Simon's Porsche and, since she's not using it, you and I could do the thing in style and go in Danny's car."

"Dream on! I know you Nicky. You just want to get your mitts on Danny's Ferrari. Forget it. I'm not letting you loose with four hundred and ninety horse power under your arse. You're a big enough menace in your little Renault. We'll take *my* car thank you. That way we can designate one of the boys as driver on the way home and we can let our hair down and have a drink."

Nicole grinned sheepishly. "Ok then. You have a point. I suppose Simon will be designated driver as usual. Poor Simon. He always ends up having to be the sober one."

"That's because he's the best driver of any of us. Do you think you ought to call Charlie back and make sure it's ok if Pete and Simon tag along? Obviously we won't expect her to pay for dinner if there're five of us."

"I'm sure she'll be cool about it. Simon's one of her best friends after all and she loves Peter. I'll call her in the morning after we've seen Peter and Simon. Anyway you'll not get much sense out of her right now. She'll probably be dancing through the streets of Winterthur naked at the moment."

"Where are we meeting up; the Planet?"

"I don't know Sarah. I said I'd call tomorrow to confirm."

"I should imagine it will be. The Planet's Charlie's

favourite place." Sarah smiled. "Do you know how it got its name Nicky?"

"No idea."

"That DVD you're holding; it's named after a coffee shop stroke bar in that."

"This one; "The L Word"? What's it about?"

"It was a cult TV series on American television Nicky about a group of lesbian women in Los Angeles. I've got the first full four series on DVD. There's this lesbian coffee house where they all meet in it called the Planet. The bar in Winterthur took the name."

"I was going to ask you about these DVDs Sarah. It's not your usual sort of thing is it? I mean what's this..."Nina's heavenly Delights"... what the hell's that?"

"Oh it's a lesbian romance between a Scottish girl and an Indian girl whose family have a curry house in Glasgow. It's a lovely film."

"And this?"

"The Truth about Jane" That's a film about a young high school girl coming out as gay and her parents problems with that."

"So it struck a chord huh?"

"You might say that."

"And this one... "The Incredibly True Adventure of Two Girls in Love"? Am I right in assuming that this is another lesbian film?"

"Yes it is and that one there... "Gray Matters" is a romantic lesbian comedy. It's sweet."

"And this... "If These Walls Could Talk"... another lesbian film?"

"Well it's actually "If These Walls Could Talk 2"... it's a sequel. They were made for television films. This one is cut into three segments and explores three separate lesbian relationships in the same house at different times from the early nineteen sixties to the year two thousand. The third part is my favourite. It's got Sharon Stone and Ellen Degeneres in it."

"I've heard of Sharon Stone but who the hell is Ellen Degeneres?"

"If you were a lesbian you wouldn't need to ask that. She's just about one of the world's most iconic lesbian celebrities. She's an American comedienne, actress and talk show host. Back in the nineties she had this sitcom on American TV. It was very funny but it was dead straight, the girl next door, family stuff. But Degeneres was gay and very closeted; afraid to come out and lose her career. Then, in 1997, she decided she couldn't lie about her sexuality any more so she decided to publicly announce that she was gay. She was just about the first mainstream television actress to do so. She actually kept hinting at it and, in the sitcom, her character comes out at the same time, mirroring her real life journey. It was huge and it caused a sensation. The show had the biggest audience it had ever had for the episode when the character reveals that she's gay. Millions tuned in. In one state they even banned it on air so the public hired cinemas and showed it on cable to rapturous audiences. The whole of Hollywood held its collective breath apparently to see if she would get away with it. There were an awful lot of closeted gays in the movie and television business and, if Ellen could do it and get away with it, then it could open the floodgates. It was an incredibly brave thing to do and ground breaking. It nearly did cost Ellen her career, in fact, because Disney, who owned the television company, got uncomfortable as the show explored more and more gay themes in its last series. They were under pressure from all sorts of fanatical religious right wing groups denouncing them for promoting homosexuality and eroding American family values, and the rest, so eventually they pulled the plug. She didn't work again for nearly three years. Now however she has her own talk show and it's massive in America. She's married to a drop dead gorgeous Australian actress called Portia Di

76

Rossi. I couldn't find any DVDs of her sitcom but I've got the full fourth and fifth series of the show downloaded on the computer, from You Tube and places, as well as loads of stuff from her talk show and even the film of her wedding to Portia." Sarah blushed and looked sheepish. "I'm a bit of a fan of hers I'm afraid."

"And I've never heard of her. Does that make me straight?"

"Ok I could have phrased that better. I hadn't heard of her either until a few weeks ago. Actually, if I lived in America, I would have heard of her because she's very famous there and popular with both straight and gay people."

Nicole picked up one of the DVDs and shook her head in bewilderment. "What the hell's all this about Sarah? Two months ago you would never have watched stuff like this and now you don't watch anything else seemingly. What is it? You suddenly find out you're gay and now you're bloody well obsessed with it."

Sarah sat down on the sofa alongside Nicole and gave a little smile of embarrassment. "Well of course I do watch other things but you're right to some extent. I suppose I have spent an awful lot of time watching things about lesbians and reading all sorts of stuff about it and what have you. You have to remember this is all very new to me Nicky and before this summer I had no idea about the gay culture or anything about gay women. I remember the first time I met Charlie in Winterthur, she started telling me stuff about gay issues and I felt incredibly ignorant. I mean how could I call myself gay and know so little about the whole thing?"

"So, of course, in true Sarah style, you decided that if a thing's worth doing it's worth overdoing."

"Well it was even worse for me than just any girl coming to terms with her sexuality Nicky. I mean I'm not just gay but I also happen to be the girlfriend of just about the most publicly prominent gay woman in

Switzerland if not Europe. I mean Danny's not just a musician who happens to be gay, she's a figurehead for gay women all over the world. She's a leader in many respects for gay women; an icon and spokeswoman. She was the star billing at last year's Gay Pride festival in Zurich. That was the Euro Pride festival last year and it was just about the biggest gay event on the continent. I never realised just how big the thing was. Here's Danny standing up for all the world to see and declaring herself gay and her timid little girlfriend is cowering in the background scared to death of anybody finding out about her and totally ignorant of gay matters. So, at the very least, I had to try and inform myself more about the subject. So I've been researching it; looking at gay literature, films, television and culture in general. If I'm going to live with the country's most high profile lesbian the least I can do is become expert on it."

"God! You're really taking this seriously aren't you?"

"Yes I am but it's been a revelation to me as well. I feel connected, in a way, to all the other gay people in the world in a way I didn't before. I mean all the problems I've had in coming out are just the same as everybody goes through. You could rewrite my story a million times over for millions of different people. I think one of the worst things about coming to terms with being gay is this terrible feeling of loneliness; of being different from everybody else and thinking nobody will want to know you. Ok I was lucky because I had good friends around me to support me but, even so, there was this awful feeling of isolation. Then you start looking and you suddenly realise that you're *not* alone. There're millions of people just like you and all going through exactly the same thing as you are. There's nothing unique or odd or, dare I say it, queer about you at all. It's as normal as any other growing up pang. Some people just grow up one way and others another way. It's nothing to get excited or worried or threatened by. It's about as worrying as being born blond."

"What's wrong with being blond?" demanded Nicole indignantly.

Sarah patted her on the knee. "Nothing at all sweetheart. Your secret is safe with me. I think you're lovely blond. Of course you're going to have to come out and tell your parents one day you know. Your mother will be devastated. She'll blame herself for letting you watch Olivia Newton John films when you were a little girl."

"Ha ha!"

"Anyway it's better than that bloody awful pink dye you had your hair in at the beginning of summer."

"Ok so that wasn't one of my better fashion statements."

"You looked like you'd been in an industrial accident involving a candy floss machine."

"There's no need to get personal Sarah. Until you met Danny you weren't exactly known for your own ground breaking reputation in haut couture and fashion yourself. I don't think scuffed hiking boots and grubby jeans quite caught on at this year's Paris shows you know."

Sarah gave her a playful push. "Come on let's just chill out and have a nice girly night in. I'll go get another bottle of wine and we can curl up on the sofa and watch a movie." Sarah pointed to the television. "We've got a bit better TV here than we had back in the Alpli." That was putting it mildly. The huge plasma, high definition TV screen in the living room was the biggest Nicole had ever seen.

"Er are you sure that it's all right for me to stay here tonight Sarah?"

"Of course it is darling. We can even share a bed if you want."

"Christ! I don't know about that."

"We've shared a bed before Nicky."

"Yes but... well that was before."

"Before I met Danny or before you met Charlie Nicky?" asked Sarah innocently.

"What the hell are you talking about?"

"Nothing. Just kidding you. Come on what film shall we watch?"

"Well you know what you've got in your collection."

"How about watching a lesbo film then?"

"Oh Christ! Does it involve embarrassing sex scenes?"

"You might pick up a few tips." Sarah picked up a DVD. "How about this one you were looking at earlier... "Gray Matters"... it's just a silly bit of nonsense really but it's funny and light entertainment. A brother and his sister fall in love with the same girl with predictably hilarious results. It's got an appearance by the English actress Rachel Shelley who plays Helen Peabody in the L Word in it and she's gorgeous."

"God! Once a geek always a geek. Three months ago you didn't even know who Daniela Devin was now you can reel off the names and characters of every actress who ever played a lesbian in Hollywood."

"After that we can put "Nina's Heavenly Delights" on. That's one of my favourites. One of the lead characters is played by a Scottish actress called Laura Fraser who has played another role as a lesbian in Glasgow in a BBC series called "Lip Service" that came out recently."

"Are you trying to recruit me or something by showing me all these lesbian films?"

"Well we need a new toaster oven."

"What?"

"Never mind. It's an old joke from an Ellen Degeneres show."

"Look just go and get the bloody wine will you and

I'll see if I can operate your DVD player and set about corrupting myself."

Chapter Six

It was nearly noon by the time that Nicole and Sarah left the house next morning to walk down the incline to the chair lift station at Oberdorf. Summer seemed reluctant to leave that autumn for it was another glorious day, with the sun glittering in a cloudless sky and the air so clear that they could pick out people strolling about on the valley floor below as easily as if they'd been insects crawling around their shoes. Hardly a breath of wind stirred the among the forest canopies and there was the ringing call of a big Black Woodpecker sounding from the depths of the woods. The air was scented with fresh cut hay as the farmers of the valley harvested the last of the meadow grass for winter fodder and a few late butterflies still wavered between the last of the meadow flowers. It was a wonderful day to be abroad on and a shame that the two girls had slept so late to so little take advantage of it.

In fact, their tardiness this morning was due to the fact that they had sat up into the early hours of the morning working their way steadily through Sarah's collection of lesbian films and TV shows. To Sarah's amusement, Nicole had started to enjoy the fare on offer in spite of herself. They'd watched "Gray Matters", then "Nina's Heavenly Delights" and after that "The Truth about Jane" and Nicole had enjoyed them all. Whilst they were on a roll Sarah had decided to expose Nicole to "The L Word" and they'd managed to watch the first three episodes before they'd fallen asleep on the couch. Nicole had already got involved in the story and they'd been discussing it all morning over breakfast and on their way to the chair lift. "So who's your favourite character so far?" Sarah was asking Nicole.

Nicole pondered for a moment. "I like Shane." She

decided. "She's so mad she's cool."

Sarah raised an eyebrow. "Oh really? Don't you think she looks a little like Charlie?"

"Nicole's face assumed the mask of indifference she habitually adopted when Charmaine's name was mentioned. "Can't say I'd noticed. By the way I didn't see that actress, what's her name, you know the one that was in "Gray Matters" in the show."

"Oh she doesn't join until the second series. Actually there's another actor from that film in the series. You remember the Scottish taxi driver?"

"Oh yeah. He was cute."

"Yes well he plays a gay man in the third series."

"How many of those actors and actresses are really gay... I mean in real life... do you think?"

"Not as many as you might imagine actually. I looked them up. Katherine Moennig who plays Shane is supposed to be gay but she's never come out and admitted it even though she's played quite a few gay roles. Leisha Hailey who plays Alice is openly gay but not many of the others. The woman that plays Bette is married and has kids although apparently she's acted as a Grand Marshall at the San Francisco Gay Pride Parade. I don't know what that says about her. Laurel Holloman who plays Tina is a divorcee with a child although she plays a butch lesbian in "The Incredibly True Adventure of Two Girls in Love" as well as the L Word. The woman that plays Dana isn't gay and neither is Mia Kirshner who plays Jenny as far as I know but I might be wrong there. I mean she's thirty five and not married as far as I can tell."

"I wonder if Jenny's going to get off with that Marina chick."

"Well you'll have to watch the next episodes."

"Is she straight or what?"

"Wait and see."

Nicole grinned. "Charlie told me this joke. What's

the difference between a straight girl and a lesbian?"

"I've no idea."

"About three Jack Daniel's and cokes."

"I see and what was her next line... what are you drinking?"

"Give me a break Foxy. Just because I've spent a night with you watching bloody lesbian films doesn't make me gay you know."

"Of course not Nicky."

Charlie's just a friend right."

"Of course she is."

"We just meet up sometimes when I'm in Winterthur."

"As you do..."

"Anyway I was driving."

"Yes Nicky. I understand."

"Then why are you smirking?"

"I'm not smirking. I was just admiring you. You look really pretty in that dress."

Nicole smoothed the borrowed dress over her limbs self-consciously. "Are you sure Danny won't mind me borrowing one of her dresses?"

"Cheeky bitch! It's one of *my* dresses."

"Seriously?"

"Of course it is. You don't think I'm going to start handing out the contents of Danny's wardrobe do you?"

"Ok I'm sorry. It's an understandable error though. Until this summer I could probably have counted the number of times I'd seen you in a dress on the fingers of one hand. Now every time I see you you've got some fabulous new addition to your wardrobe."

"Hey, I've got a rock and roll singer as a girlfriend. I've got appearances to keep up."

"Oh yeah! Right!"

Sarah sighed. "I don't know why it is Nicky. I just found out that I like dressing up nicely. It never used to bother me really before but I've changed." Sarah grinned, "I wasn't being entirely facetious though. You can't walk around looking like a tramp when the most gorgeous woman in Switzerland is holding on to your hand."

"That's a point. What am I going to wear tonight? I'll have to pop home some time today to find something."

"You don't need to. Those shoes you're wearing go with most things and I'm sure I can find you something pretty for Charmaine."

"Don't start on me again Sarah. I told you. She's..."

"Just a friend. Of course she is. I'm sorry Nicky. It slipped my mind."

"Bitch!"

Sarah laughed and slapped Nicole's bottom affectionately. "I'm not being a bitch Nicky. I really like Charlie. I think she'd be good for you."

"You're crazy!"

"Why for heaven's sake Nicky? God knows she'd be a sight of an improvement on some of the bloody awful men you've dated the last couple of years."

"Look Sarah just because I once told you that I had a crush on you..."

"Had a crush on me for years..."

"Ok had a crush on you for years. It doesn't mean..."

"Kept saucy pictures of me on your computer..."

"So I had a few pictures of you..."

"Told me that you'd always wanted me..."

"Well ok but..."

"And kissed me if I recall."

"Doesn't mean that..."

"What Nicole? Doesn't mean that you're gay? Hmm. Methinks the lady doth protest too much."

"Listen Sarah..."

They were approaching the chairlift now and the little restaurant at the top of the lift. Sarah suddenly grabbed Nicole's hand and dragged her to one side, seating her on a wooden bench by the children's playground. "No *you* listen a minute Nicole. I'm not trying to make fun of you or tease you... well a little bit maybe... but there's something you ought to know. Do you remember that scene in "The L Word" where Dana can't figure out whether the cute red headed sous-chef is gay or not and she has to drag all her friends down to the club to try and suss her out?"

"God yes. That was funny."

"Do you remember the word they used? They said that Dana didn't have any "gaydar"."

"Vaguely. What's "gaydar" anyway?"

"Like gay radar Nicky. It's a sort of sixth sense by which gay people detect other people that are gay. Now I don't know what that is particularly myself very much. I think it's something that comes with experience. Nevertheless other gay people do have it and it might or might not interest you to know that you show up as a big blip on the gaydar screen."

"*What*?" yelped Nicole, appalled.

"Danny thought you were gay pretty much from the moment she saw you. Elke and Angelica both reckon you're gay and I'm as sure as death and taxes that Charmaine thinks so too."

"This is ridiculous."

"Well I don't know exactly *what* you've been talking about with Charmaine but I know for a fact that you haven't been discussing the Grasshoppers' chances in the football league this year. Answer me truthfully. Have you slept with her?"

"Don't be ridiculous Sarah."

"I'm not being ridiculous Nicky. I know for a fact that if you haven't slept with her it's not for want of trying on Charlie's side. She fancies the hell out of you."

"I don't sleep with girls Sarah."

"Don't sleep or haven't slept with them?"

86

"Amounts to the same thing doesn't it?"

"Not at all. Just because you've never slept with a woman doesn't assume the certainty that you never will. Tell me have you ever been attracted to a woman?"

"You know I have. I was attracted to you... still am."

"And Charlie? Are you attracted to her?"

"None of your damn business."

"We'll take that as a yes shall we?"

"You can take nothing of the sort. Look Sarah just because I like Charlie and she's a good friend and because she's gay it doesn't mean that I'm sleeping with her. Sure she's flirted with me sometimes but that's the way she is."

"I know Nicky. She tried to seduce me into bed the first time I met her."

"I know. She told me."

"She bought a bottle of wine and tried to get me drunk. I only wanted a small beer."

"That was before she knew you were dating the most beautiful lesbian woman in Switzerland Sarah."

"Mind you it was nothing compared to the bloody effort Rozella went to, to try and drag me into the bushes."

"Oh! Rozella..." Nicole went quiet for a moment. Rozella was a sensitive subject. She was Daniela's photographer for her album covers and Sarah had met her quite by chance in the Ticino. She was also just about the most predatory gay girl that Sarah had so far met, with smoky "come to bed eyes" and ruthlessly single-minded in her pursuit of attractive girls. In the summer she had been photographing a collection of young women with an eye to making a magazine spread of the young womanhood of Switzerland. Daniela had mischievously suggested Nicole as a model and, in late August, Nicole had spent a day modelling for her. Nicole had insisted that the photo shoot had been entirely professional and that Rozella had paid competitive industry prices for the shoot. Other than that Sarah had been able to extract very little information from Nicole who seemed rather embarrassed about the whole thing. There had been no further word about the affair and Nicole tended to avoid the subject when it came up. Sarah rather suspected that Nicole was saying rather less than the truth about the whole thing.

"Yes whatever is happening about those photos Rozella took of you Nicky?"

"I dunno. Nothing I suppose. I've not heard anything since."

"I thought she was dead keen to do something with them."

"Maybe she decided they weren't good enough."

"Did you sign a release form giving her permission to use them?"

"Yeah and she said she might be able to get me some more modelling work but I haven't had a peep out of her for a month. Anyway look are we going to get on this bloody chairlift or not."

"Yes I suppose so. The boys will be wondering where we are." Sarah had phoned that morning to say they were coming to visit.

They climbed on to the chairlift platform and jumped onto a passing chair, pulling the bar down over their waists and were whisked off down the cable, their feet dangling high above the pastures and the forest floor as they rode down through the gap in the lower woods. Sarah realised that she had got no further towards understanding exactly what was going on between Nicole and Charmaine but she decided to table the subject for the moment. It would be interesting to see Nicole and Charmaine together that evening.

The little pub was only a few yards away from the bottom of the cable car and it was in a charming location on the valley floor and very secluded. The nearest concentration of houses was at Wildhaus perched on the hillside opposite the chairlift and separated by a wide swathe of marshy meadows which were dotted with thistles in late summer and a wonderful place to find little parties of Goldfinches and the occasional Whinchat. Sarah recognised Simon's old Porsche parked outside the pub and the battered, ancient Land Rover pick up that the two men were using to ferry materials for the renovations on their new pub. The outside beer garden of the pub was littered with planks of wood, a couple of old settles, several wooden tables, a large roll of carpet and several large paint pots. There was the sound of a power drill from the interior. Sarah and Nicole stepped up onto the beer garden terrace. "Yoohoo! Anyone there?" Sarah called out.

Simon stepped out from the interior with a grin, dressed in a seriously degraded pair of old dungarees liberally smeared with paint. He was an almost ridiculously fine looking man, tall with dark hair and dark soulful eyes, lithe and athletic and, together with his partner Peter formed, one half of probably the best looking pair of young men in the valley to the despair of the local girls who considered it little other than a criminal waste that two such hunks had only eyes for each other. "Hi girls!" boomed Simon, "Welcome to the asylum."

Sarah smiled hugely. Once upon a day she had been jealous of Simon. She had been hurt and shocked to discover that her lifelong friend Peter was gay and in a relationship with this man. Since then however she had come to know Simon and was dearly fond of him. She would never forget that, while Peter had been rather upset with her and judgemental in the early days of her relationship with Daniela, Simon had been surprisingly supportive. He had treated Sarah like a younger sister ever since and he adored her. He turned to yell through the open door of the pub. "Pete! Get your arse out here!

Sarah and Nicky are here." He turned to the girls. "We were just doing something embarrassing with a set of shelving." he explained. Peter emerged brushing dust off his old overalls and passing a hand through his habitually ill-kempt blond hair. He was another fine looking man and Sarah had once fancied herself in love with him in the days before Daniela had so decisively captured her heart. He was a modest man to the point of shyness and his endearing timidity with the opposite sex had long been the last unclimbed peak in the Toggenburg to challenge the seductive wiles of the local lasses. Peter had resisted all advances, however, although, even then, very few had guessed the truth until Simon had appeared in his life. Looking at him now, Sarah decided that he had never looked happier. His grey eyes seemed more animated than she could ever remember. Previously she had always had the curious feeling that his eyes were focussed elsewhere; on some distant horizon only he could see and searching for something. It seemed he had found what he was looking for. Simon was clearing debris away from the benches at one of the beer garden terrace tables. "Come on girls. Sit yourselves down. Pete fetch us some beers out of the fridge."

"This place looks like a bomb site." Nicole commented.

"Appearances are deceptive." Simon told her. "Actually we're making brilliant progress. We're far further forward than I dared hope."

"So when's the big opening going to be?" asked Sarah.

"Unless there are any unforeseeable difficulties, in December, in time for the winter season. I think we should easy make it. The actual pub should be ready to go long before that. It's the big barn at the back that's going to take the most work."

"What are you going to use that for?" asked Nicole in interest.

"We're converting it into a dance hall and live music venue Nicky. It's a perfect location because our nearest neighbours are miles away so we've no problem with noise. We've got big plans for it."

Peter, arriving with the beer, overheard the conversation. "We're hoping to get Danny to put in a guest appearance on our opening night. I don't know if she'll go for it though."

Sarah shrugged. "I don't see why not. After all she's a business partner in the venture so it would be in her interest to give the place a kick start."

Simon flipped open the top of his beer bottle. "We wouldn't expect her with her full band or anything. We thought maybe she could do a short acoustic set or something."

"Sounds fine. Danny isn't fazed by small locations. She once did an impromptu little set on an old upright piano for the guests in the Santis hut when we were hiking up there."

"I think it's a brilliant idea." enthused Nicole. "You'd pack the whole bloody valley in."

"Well it would certainly give us a big boost at the beginning." Simon agreed. "We could probably get the local newspapers in. You can't ask for better publicity on your opening than that."

"You'll have to consult Danny about her touring schedule." Sarah warned. "She's got a lot on this winter."

"Sure, sure." said Simon with a nod. "In fact we'd be wise to time our opening to coincide with Danny's free time. We don't expect her to put on a full concert of course but even a couple of numbers would be a massive boost."

"Why don't you get that band you booked for Sarah's going away party at Gamplut?" Nicole suggested. "Danny got up and sang a couple of songs with them and it was great."

"Now there's an idea." mused Peter. "We could ask them if they're available. They weren't too expensive as far as I recall."

Simon grinned. "They'd probably do the gig for nothing if we tell them that Danny will be putting in a guest appearance. Hell I don't suppose they get much chance to work with a big star like that."

"I think you all have to talk with Danny before you go off the rails and start planning something." Sarah cautioned. "I'm sure she'll be sympathetic but she's got her own agenda to keep to as well."

"You're right Sarah." Simon agreed. "We won't do anything without her agreement. We wouldn't be opening this place at all without Danny's support and she who pays the piper calls the tune."

"Sarah said something about a job that you might have going for me Simon." Nicole intervened.

Simon took a swig of his beer and nodded. "That's right Nicky. When we're up and running, we're going to be needing some staff if you're up for it. I don't know how much we're going to be able to pay you yet though." Sarah hid a smile and held her peace. She was fairly sure that Danny would ensure that Nicole had a decent working wage.

"I'd be interested in any case." Nicole assured Simon. "I wouldn't mind too much about the money to begin with. I just think it would be exciting to be part of the whole thing."

"What about your job at the Hirschen Nicky?" asked Peter.

"Well it's pretty much fading out on me right now Pete. They'll be running on skeleton staff for the off season and they haven't talked to me yet about the winter season."

"I don't know that we can offer you anything until December Nicky." Simon told her.

"Well maybe you could use some help in renovating

Simon. I wouldn't want paying. I'll do it for tea and biscuits. I'm a dab hand with a paint brush."

"We might take you up on that offer."

Peter looked around. "Have you girls walked down? I don't see your car anywhere."

"We took the chairlift Pete." Sarah informed him. Nicky stayed over at our place last night."

"How long does that cable car run anyway?" asked Simon, who was a newcomer in the Toggenburg.

Peter answered him. "Oh they'll just be running on weekends for the moment Sime. They'll probably close down altogether around mid-month and open again come the winter season."

"Listen boys." interrupted Sarah. "When are you going to be finished working today?"

"We haven't really thought about it yet Sarah." Simon said interestedly. "Why? Did you have something planned?"

"Well yes as it happens. We have good news. Danny's taking on Charlie as a bassist for her winter tours."

Simon slapped a hand on the table delightedly. "Wow! That's fantastic. She must be thrilled."

"Yes Nicky told her last night. Anyway she's invited Nicky and I out for dinner tonight in Winterthur to celebrate. We wondered if you two fancied coming along."

Simon leaned back with a grin. "That sounds like a great idea. How about it Pete?"

"Suits me. We could do with a night off."

"Well it would be better for me." Sarah pointed out. "Otherwise I'm just going to be a wallflower while Nicky and Charlie are carousing together."

Nicole glared at her. "Tell Danny to pick up some flowers and grapes on her way back on Monday. She'll need them when she visits you in hospital after I brain you with that piece of two by four over there."

"How were you thinking of getting there Sarah?" asked Simon.

"I thought we could take my car. It's got the most room."

"Sounds logical. Are you going to pick us up then?"

"Well actually Simon I was wondering if you wouldn't mind driving up to the house before we set off. I need your help on something."

"Oh yes?"

"Yes. How are you with a DVR?"

"A Digital Video Recorder? Fine. They're straight forward enough. Why?"

"Well I need to record a television show tonight but I'm a bit of an idiot with things like that. I wondered if you'd be able to set it up on timer to record while we're in Winterthur."

"It's not another bloody lesbian drama is it Sarah?" Nicole asked. "Sarah's been trying to brainwash me by bombarding me with lesbian films and television." she explained to Simon and Peter.

"Well you could call it that." confessed Sarah sheepishly. "Actually it's Danny. She's appearing on a chat show on German television tonight. I wanted to record it."

"Oh brilliant!" Nicole declared enthusiastically. "Danny on telly. We can watch it when we get back."

Simon nodded. "Well it shouldn't be a problem Sarah, as long as you know the channel and time. I'm assuming that your DVR is more or less the same sort of thing as mine."

"I'd like to see Danny on television myself." Peter remarked. "Where is this interview Sarah?"

"In Berlin. Danny did a big concert there last night. She has another interview this afternoon but I think that's on a local station."

"Well then when are we supposed to be meeting Charlie in Winterthur then?"

"I phoned her this morning Simon." Nicole answered. "We said around seven or seven thirty."

"Sounds fine. Shall we come around to your place at about half past five then Sarah?"

Sarah frowned. It surely won't take us two hours to drive to Winterthur Simon."

"I thought we'd better give ourselves enough time Sarah especially if you want me to wrestle with your DVR."

"Yes and we might hit rush hour traffic." remarked Nicole."

Sarah looked at her pityingly. "On a *Sunday* Nicky?"

"Oh of course! Stupid of me."

"Are we meeting Charlie at the Planet?" asked Simon.

Nicole nodded. "Yes. That's what we've agreed."

Peter rubbed his chin thoughtfully with a mischievous twinkle in his eye. "I guess we'd better chaperone Sarah then Simon. Danny will have our guts for garters if we let some ambitious dyke get her claws into her!"

"Hey what about me?" demanded Nicole indignantly.

"Oh you've got Charlie to look after you." Nicole glared at him in speechless outrage as Simon and Sarah dissolved into laughter.

"Anyway," said Sarah at last. "Aren't you going to show us around?" Simon and Peter had been busy. The two girls were impressed with the progress on the pub although there was still a long way to go. Not least of their problems was the living accommodation over the pub. At the moment the two men were occupying a pair of rooms and a small bathroom whilst they endeavoured to make the rest of their living quarters fit for habitation. They didn't seem to mind the inconvenience. They were embarked on an adventure together and, being men, would probably have been perfectly content living in a tent in the back garden. They were sharing a small bedroom whilst the master bedroom was being decorated but Sarah noted that they were still trying to personalise it. She was touched to see a photograph of herself among the pictures on a small table by the window. Peter had kept a photo of his oldest and dearest friend in his bedroom for years.

Finally the two girls took their leave and walked back across to the chairlift for the ride back up to Oberdorf. "Do you want to eat anything before Pete and Simon come around for us Nicky?" Sarah asked as they mounted the chairlift.

"I'm fine Sarah. We had a really late breakfast and if we're going out for a big dinner we'd better save our appetites."

"Where was Charlie thinking of going for dinner anyway?"

"Oh she knows this Chinese place in Winterthur she rates."

Sarah brightened. "Oh lovely! I was just thinking yesterday that I'd like to eat Chinese. I passed that old restaurant on the barge in the river in the Rhine Delta and, if I hadn't been coming home to cook dinner for you, I'd have been sorely tempted to go in and stuff myself."

"What do you think of the pub then?"

Sarah nodded in satisfaction. "I think it's going to be great. They seem to have some really good ideas for it and it'll be the best thing to happen to the valley in years. I mean there's hardly any sort of night life in the valley for the moment apart from the bar and disco at the Hirschen and the disco at the Sternen in Unterwasser. I think they'll make a bomb."

"I think so too." Nicole agreed. "This could be a winter to remember."

Chapter Seven

It was a little after seven when Sarah found a place to park in Winterthur. Sarah had an odd fondness for Winterthur. It was a small provincial city of about 100,000 inhabitants on the main E60 highway north east of Zurich. It wasn't exactly a city that registered much on the tourist radar for it was virtually unknown outside of Switzerland. It was an industrial city founded largely on engineering. If this conjures up images of grim factories, smoking chimney stacks and steel mills then the imagination in question isn't familiar with Switzerland; a nation so wholeheartedly devoted to orderliness and appearance that it even managed to make its industrial quarters look picturesque.

In fact, any visitor to the town centre would have been struck by just how attractive it was with its extensive parks and broad, café lined streets and pedestrian precincts. Even the worst of the traffic was diverted out of the city centre and the public transport system consisted of electric trolley buses that whispered almost silently around the streets. It was a laid back kind of city, inviting to stroll around in and for perusing its fine shopping centres and generally much cheaper than the neighbouring giant of Zurich. For such a small city it was surprisingly lively as well. It was a young sort of place, full of students, studying at the technical colleges or the Zurich university branch of applied sciences, and there was an active social life as a result. It also had a small, but active and vibrant, gay community.

The Planet was one of the epicentres of this gay community although it was by no means exclusively gay. Switzerland, some of its antiquated legislation notwithstanding, is generally a tolerant sort of country and it was by no means unusual to find heterosexual and gay people mixing together in the same bars. During the day time, therefore, the Planet was a fairly mixed sort of place although it tended to become rather more emphatically gay during the evenings. It was patronised by gays of both sexes but it was far more lesbian than most gay bars tend to be and it was the central focus of the city's lesbian community. It was not particularly a place for picking people up although of course that did happen. It was more a meeting point and, as an aside, a forum for activist groups in the gay community of Winterthur. The city's representation at the Zurich Gay Pride festival was organised at the Planet. There were regular meetings of the Pink Cross, FELS, a local group called the Rainbow Warriors (an organisation of environmentally conscious gays) and other gay groups. It was an important hub of gay life in the city and it celebrated the fact. It even had a rainbow flag, the international gay banner over the door.

Charmaine was waiting for them when they arrived in the Planet. She had grown her hair somewhat since the first time Sarah had met her but she still retained the slightly boyish look. It wasn't that she was masculine by any means. Charmaine didn't regard herself as butch although she rarely dressed in a particularly feminine sort of way. She habitually wore jeans or trousers often with a shirt or blouse and a jacket. Tonight her ensemble was typical. She wore stylish jeans and a short sleeved shirt. She carried a leather jacket over her shoulder and a leather choker about her slender neck. If the impression was slightly butch it was belied by her face which was impishly pretty with generous lips and eyes that danced with amusement and passion. Her dark hair was feathered, just reaching the nape of her neck and she wore a single earring in her left ear. Sarah was slightly confused about that because she thought that gay people were supposed to wear the earring on the right but she supposed that that idea was out of vogue somewhat nowadays. Certainly Charmaine's choice of earring left no room for ambiguity, however, for it was an old lesbian emblem; two intertwined Venus symbols. Charmaine was also wearing a simple gold chain around her neck that was vaguely familiar.

Charmaine was also quite clearly excited for, as soon as she saw the party, she leapt from her seat and flew across the bar to greet them. Simon, Sarah and Peter all glanced at each other in amusement as Charmaine flung herself at Nicole in a warm embrace, kissing her ardently. Nicole stiffened visibly under the assault and blushed furiously trying desperately to untangle herself. Sarah bit back a smile as she saw Nicole whispering furiously to Charmaine and flashing warnings with her eyes. Charmaine cooled noticeably as a result and turned to embrace Sarah instead. Sarah accepted the hug of greeting warmly. She liked Charmaine a lot. Peter and Simon exchanged hugs and kisses with her as well and Simon held her at arm's length for a moment to look at her the better. "Well congratulations Charlie." he told her. "Nicky and Sarah told us the good news today."

Charmaine laughed. "I still can't believe it myself. Nicky phoned me up yesterday to tell me and then this morning Danny called me from Germany to make it official. I've been on a high all day."

Peter patted her on the shoulder. "It couldn't have happened to a better person Charlie. Come on then. What's everybody drinking?"

Sarah hesitated. "Er I don't know if I should drink Pete."

Simon pushed her playfully. "Go ahead and have a drink Sarah. I've already figured that I'm the designated driver home tonight."

Sarah grinned gratefully. "Why thank you kind sir. I'll have a white wine in that case."

"Why don't we just get a bottle?" suggested Nicole.

Charmaine looked smug. "I'm ahead of you all. I've already got two bottles on ice. You guys grab a table. Simon you can help me carry them over. You can be getting yourself a coke or what have you while we're at it."

The bar was only half full and they had little trouble finding a table surrounded by comfortable settles. Nicole eased alongside Sarah still looking flustered by Charmaine's effusive greeting. "I wish Charlie wouldn't do that." She grumbled.

"Do what?" asked Sarah in amusement.

"Well... you know... jump all over you and slobber all over your face like that."

Sarah held a hand to her mouth. "Oh gosh yes. How *embarrassing* it must be for you."

"It's not funny Sarah. What are people going to think?"

"Blimey yes! They might think she's *gay* or something." Sarah slapped herself on the head. "Oh just a minute... silly me... she *is* gay." Sarah leaned forward to whisper conspiratorially. "Never mind Nicky. I don't think anybody will *mind* in here."

"You're asking for a fucking slap Miss Fuchs."

Sarah giggled happily. She was enjoying teasing Nicole. "I wonder when we're going on to this restaurant. I'm hungry."

"Well I shouldn't imagine we'll be too long in here." Peter remarked. "I don't suppose the restaurants are going to be open that late on Sundays."

"We're in town now Pete." Nicole told him exasperatedly. "Not the back of beyond in the Toggenburg."

Charmaine and Simon returned with the wine. Simon was clutching a bottle of alcohol free beer resignedly. Charmaine distributed glasses animatedly. "Hey everybody. Thanks for coming through. This is a big day for me." She shook her head disbelievingly.

100

"God! I still can't believe it. To think this would happen just because I tried to chat up the best looking girl in town one day."

Simon guffawed. "You can be thankful that Danny's an understanding sort of person Charlie. Not many people would offer you a job after you've tried to pinch their girlfriend."

"Hmmph fat chance! I was on a hiding to nothing there."

For the next few minutes they listened to Charmaine excitedly talk about her new career opportunity. Nicole seemed a little subdued however. Eventually she wrinkled her nose. "Can't we do something about the music? They're always playing bloody Madonna in here."

"What's wrong with Madonna?" demanded Charmaine indignantly. "She's a massive gay icon Nicky. She's been a supporter and friend of the gay movement from the beginning. Saying you think Madonna is pants in a gay bar is about as socially acceptable as smearing creosote on the Mona Lisa."

Nicole looked a bit miffed at this rebuke so Sarah intervened smoothly. "When are we going to the restaurant Charlie?"

Charlie bit her lip uncertainly. "Er I've put the booking back an hour Sarah. We're not due until nine."

"Oh? Why?"

"Well because there's another gay icon to pay homage to first. Danny told me that she's in a live interview on German television at eight o'clock this evening so they're putting it up on the TV screens here."

Sarah's eyes opened wide. "Seriously?"

Charmaine looked at her in puzzlement. "You didn't know she was on the telly today?"

"Yes of course! But why would they show it in here?"

Charmaine laughed. "Oh God Sarah! You're

101

kidding aren't you? Danny's *our* gay superstar. Switzerland's very own. They always have her on when she's on the telly. God they'd stop everything to watch if she was appearing in a cornflakes advert. Don't you know what she means to gay people in this country?"

"Well I knew she was admired sure but..."

"She's fucking *worshipped* Sarah. And now of course everybody in the bar knows that I'm going to be playing with her. God! Everybody's going to be glued to that television set when she comes on."

Simon burst into laughter. "And to think we spent twenty bloody minutes programming your DVR Sarah."

Sarah looked hunted. "But... but does that mean that everybody... I mean that everyone knows..."

Charmaine shook her head. "Relax Sarah. Nobody knows a thing about you and Danny. Fuck knows why you want to keep it a secret though. Any other dyke in the country would be shouting it from the rooftops."

"I'd prefer not to have the paparazzi camped out on my doorstep Charlie."

"Take it easy Sarah. I'm not telling anyone about you. You're just a good friend of Simon and Nicky if anyone asks."

Nicole sat bolt upright. "Wait a minute. Are you saying that everyone here knows *me*?"

Charmaine looked at her in puzzlement. "Well sure. I mean you have been in here quite a bit recently. People notice a new face turning up regularly."

Sarah raised an ironic eyebrow. "Oh? Become quite a regular here recently have you Nicky?"

"Er... I haven't been in that much. Charlie's exaggerating."

Simon's tongue seemed to be welded to the inside of his cheek. "I'd er... be careful if I was you Nicky. Some of the girls in here might get the wrong impression and think you're available."

Nicole spluttered but before she could say anything

sensible Charmaine responded. "Nah! They wouldn't dare. Not while she's with me."

Nicole seemed to have turned a delicate shade of green. Simon leaned back on his couch and placed the tips of his fingers together. "Now that would be the supreme irony wouldn't it? Sarah here might be remaining undercover but not the girl associated with Daniela Devin's new bass guitar player. You might have the paparazzi camped out on *your* front lawn Nicky."

Nicole rose in confusion. "Er I need the ladies." She swept out quickly.

Charmaine held her hands up in bewilderment. "What's up with *her*?"

Sarah rose to her feet. "I'd better go see she's ok." Sarah found Nicole in the ladies looking set faced. "Nicole are you ok?"

"Of course I am."

"So why did you dash off like that?"

"I'm just fed up of people jumping to conclusions."

"Such as the conclusion that you've been seeing Charmaine?"

"I haven't Sarah. Well only as a friend."

"It doesn't look as if Charlie's interpreted it that way Nicky."

"I haven't done anything with her Sarah."

"Nothing? Nothing at all?"

"Well all right so I kissed her once."

"You *kissed* her?"

"It was nothing Sarah. We'd had a bit to drink and we were just playing around."

"And just where did this infamous intimacy take place? Back at her place perhaps?"

"No! Not at all. I've never been to her place. It was in here. In the bar I mean."

"In the bar? In public? In front of half the lesbians in Winterthur? And now you're complaining that people are jumping to conclusions?"

"I'm telling you it was nothing."

"And you seriously expect me to believe it?"

"Yes I do. Why wouldn't you?"

"Nicky I lived with you for close on four years in between university."

"Don't be pulling the "I know you too well" card Sarah. I thought I knew you too but you surprised me anyway by being gay. Don't think that now you're out as gay that you can see gay in everybody else."

"I wasn't going to say I know you too well Nicky. What I was about to say is that, while there are many things about you that are a mystery, the contents of your wardrobe is not one of them."

"What are you trying to say?"

"I know every item of clothing you possess Nicky and every item of..." Sarah paused for dramatic effect. "Every item of jewellery."

Nicole paled. "What do you mean?"

"I mean Nicky, why is Charmaine wearing your gold chain around her neck?"

"Oh! Oh that."

"Yes that!"

"Oh she just took a fancy to it one day so I... I er gave it to her." Nicole was shaking.

"Just like that huh? Oh sure Charlie take my 22 carat gold chain if you feel like. I never wear the damn thing anyway."

"It's nothing Sarah." Nicole seemed on the brink of tears.

Sarah took hold of Nicole by the shoulders. "You keep saying that Nicky but..."

Sarah would have elaborated but at that moment a girl walked into the ladies. She took a long appraising look and smirked. "Sorry girls. Am I interrupting something?"

Nicole leaned against the washbasin and groaned comically. Sarah grinned and took her by the elbow. "No

104

we were just leaving thank you." Hastily she steered Nicole back out into the bar. "Let's go and sit at the bar for a couple of minutes Nicky. I think you could do with a shot of something and we need to talk."

"What about the others."

"Don't worry about them I'll shoot them some bullshit or other." She steered Nicole to the bar. "Stay there and order us two brandies. I'll go tell the others we'll only be two minutes."

The party was concerned. "What's the matter with Nicky Sarah?" asked Charmaine in agitation.

Sarah smiled at her reassuringly. "Oh nothing Charlie. She just came over a bit funny so I've sat her down for a quick stiff drink. I just have to talk to her quickly. We'll only be a few minutes."

"Is she feeling poorly or something?" asked Peter.

"Extraction pains I think Pete. She might have had a small accident."

"Accident? What kind of accident?" demanded Charmaine worriedly. "I'd better go see her."

Sarah put her hand on Charmaine's shoulder. "Let me deal with it Charlie. It's not serious."

"But you said an accident."

"Not a life threatening one. I think she may have bumped her head on the closet door. Don't worry about it. I'll sort her."

When Sarah returned to Nicole she found her distracted. Two young girls were sat on a settle in a corner near the small dance floor apparently trying to set new standards for indecent public behaviour. Their mouths were locked together with the tenacity of limpets and they were pawing at each other hungrily. Nicole couldn't tear her eyes away. Sarah slapped her sharply on the leg. "Stop staring Nicky. It's rude."

Nicole swallowed and blushed. "Sarah can I ask you something?"

"Go ahead."

"When you and Danny... I mean when you and Danny are well... alone..." Nicole tailed off helplessly.

"Spit it out Nicky."

"I mean like... when you're... well in bed...well what do you.... well *do*?"

"Are you actually trying to garner details about our sex life Nicky?"

"Well I suppose so. I mean what is it that two girls actually do together?"

Sarah sighed. "Is that what your problem is Nicky? Are you just scared because you don't know what to do with a girl?"

"I just wondered Sarah."

"Look Nicky darling. I am not about to go into the details of my sex life whilst sat at the bar in a gay pub. If you require more specific instruction in lesbian sex then wait until we're somewhere more private and I'll try and give you the benefit of my limited experience. Better yet if you don't know how it works then get Charlie to teach you. I'm sure she'll be all too willing."

"But there's nothing going on Sarah..."

"Look just shut up and listen for a moment Nicky. Now it may be possible that there really is nothing going on. Maybe you really just think that you're just good friends. Possibly you never intended to give Charlie any other impression. If that is so then you'd better tell her that right sharpish because you can take it from me that that isn't how she sees it at all. I've seen the way she looks at you and I've seen the way talks about you. Right now, I'd say she was pretty damn well smitten with you. If you really wanted nothing more than a platonic relationship then kissing her in full public view and giving her a gold necklace wasn't the way to demonstrate that. Now, right now, she's looking a bit hurt. This is her big day and you've barely said a civil word to her since we said hello.

"Now it might be just speculation on my half but it

occurs to me that you were uncomfortable with her showing such overt affection to you on arrival in front of me, Simon and Pete. Now maybe you're trying to put some distance between the pair of you just in case you think we're all going to think something terrible about you. God knows what that could be. It surely can't be fear that we might think that you're gay as if we'd all give a flying fuck if you are or not. Or are you just frightened of showing something to yourself? I don't know Nicky. What I do know is that I like Charlie a lot. Now if you have no feelings for her then you'd better apologise for giving her the wrong impression and ask humbly if she'll forgive you and if you can still be friends anyway. If, on the other hand, you *do* have some feelings for her then I suggest that instead of planting your arse about as far away from her on the table as you can get that you go and sit next to her, apologise for being such a prick and start treating her as a person as wonderful as she is deserves to be treated. Don't worry about what Pete and Simon and I think. There isn't one of us that's going to think the worse of you because you fell for a girl as nice as Charlie, for heaven's sake."

"Sarah... I... I can't. I'm not ready for something like this."

"There was an awful lot of tension on that word "this" there Nicky. I'm presuming that "this" is something rather more than you've been admitting to."

Nicole looked miserable. "I know Charlie really likes me Sarah. She's said so. I know she wants to sleep with me too but..."

"But what Nicky?"

"That would mean that..."

"That you'd have to be gay?"

Nicole nodded unhappily. "I don't know if I can do that."

"What? Be gay? That's not something you have much choice about Nicky. If you are then you are. You had feelings for me for a long time that went beyond the bounds of platonic relations Nicky. Now I think you're starting to realise that you can have these feelings for other women too and it's frightening you. You're attracted to Charlie aren't you?" Nicole nodded dumbly. "Well then what are you going to do? Keep pretending that it's not really happening? You should talk to my parents. They could teach you a lot about the delusional power of denial."

"It's easy for you Sarah."

"Oh right! Come on Nicky. You know as well as I do the agonies I went through when I first realised I was gay. I'm still going through them. It's not easy. It *never* is. Elke was unhappily married to a man for fifteen years before she finally accepted that she's gay. Have you ever talked to Charlie about what it was like for her coming out as gay?"

"No. We've not really talked about it."

"Well do so. She had a hard time. Her parents more or less threw her out on the street. None of her old friends wanted to talk to her anymore. You've got it easy by comparison. Your best friends are all gay for heaven's sake. You couldn't get much more support than that. As for your parents, they'd be a damn sight more understanding than mine are. Your mum would probably be delighted. She thinks you're too boring as it is. She can't understand why a daughter of hers has never been arrested for assaulting a police officer in a human rights demonstration or something. I mean we're talking about a woman whose husband proposed to her the day he had to bail her out of prison for public disorder. She'll be hanging up the rainbow flag in the back garden and running the local branch of PFLAG in a twinkling."

"Oh God! Don't mention my mum." Nicole sighed. "What the hell do I do Sarah?"

"Just go with your heart Nicky. You don't have to rush into bed or anything but just stop fighting against who you are. If we go back to the table and Charmaine takes your hand, don't treat it like it's carrying some infectious disease or something. She thinks a lot about you Nicky. This is a big day for her. Don't spoil it by being a pussy."

"I'll try Sarah. But this isn't going to be easy for me."

Sarah took her hand and kissed her. "Now then you've just kissed another girl in a gay bar. You'll be starting to get a reputation."

"Stop making fun of me."

"I'm sorry Nicky. I just want you to be happy. You know what? Last night when I told you that Charlie was going to be Danny's new bassist you looked so happy and couldn't wait to tell her. That's how I want you to look now."

Nicole took a deep breath. "Ok let's go back to the others then."

"That's my girl."

They arrived back at the table at a critical moment. Just as Charmaine was about to ask what was going on, the music in the bar stopped and the sound from the television came over the speakers. "Hey, shut up everyone!" said Simon excitedly. "They've got Danny's interview on."

Sarah was astonished to see the whole bar fall silent. Everyone was riveted to the television screen. A beautifully coiffed, cool looking hostess was sat on a couch smiling at the camera. "My next guest tonight is one of Europe's biggest musical talents, with millions of album sales, numerous musical industry awards and a worldwide fan base. Please welcome the lovely and talented Miss Daniela Devin."

Sarah felt her heart miss a beat as Daniela walked on to the set to a burst of one of her own songs and the rapturous applause of the studio audience. "God! She looks stunning." yipped Nicole, caught up in the

109

excitement. She did too. Daniela always had the knack of capturing an audience with an entrance and it had not deserted her now. She was dressed quite simply in a pretty floral dress and high heels but her wavy blond locks shone under the studio lights like burnished gold and her smile was captivatingly lovely. She looked radiant and heartbreakingly beautiful. Sarah glanced around her at the other people in the bar and shook her head in wonder. Her own pride in Daniela was mirrored on every face present. Daniela belonged to everybody here. The hostess rose and embraced her warmly before ushering her to a facing couch as the applause died away. "Well hello there and thanks for coming on the show Danny. You don't mind if I call you Danny do you?"

"Not at all and thank you for having me Sabrina."

The voice was the lovely modulated rich warmth that had torn a hole in Sarah's heart the first time Daniela had ever spoken to her. Sarah could hear Charmaine whispering to Nicole. "Sabrina Handelmeyer's a well-known gay on German television."

"I must say you look absolutely terrific tonight Danny." The hostess was telling her warmly.

"Why thank you. That's kind of you to say."

"Well these are big days for you at the moment aren't they? You have the new CD coming out shortly and a big schedule of tours for this winter. You must be very busy."

"Oh yes it's been a bit hectic over the last couple of weeks and it's going to get worse this winter I think. Still we managed to get most of the recording for the album done before the beginning of summer and I've had a nice break."

"You also performed here in Berlin last night Danny. I couldn't get to the show personally but I've talked to people who did and I listened to the reviews on the radio this morning. It sounds like it was a hell of a concert."

110

"Yes we had a terrific concert and the audience were just wonderful. We were really made to feel welcome, as always in Berlin. We always like playing here."

"There wasn't quite a universal welcome though was there Danny. I understand that there were some anti-gay demonstrators outside the concert hall." Sarah blinked in surprise and worry. Daniela hadn't mentioned any demonstration when she's phoned that morning. There were a few boos and angry mutterings around the bar.

Daniela smiled. "Yes there were some; just a handful; half a dozen or so misguided people. Presumably they couldn't get tickets."

After the laughter died down the hostess continued. "Is it true that one of the demonstrators threw a Bible at you?"

Daniela laughed easily. "Oh I wouldn't put it as dramatically as that. This lady tossed a Bible at me for me to catch. I think she thought that if I read it I might change my sinful ways."

"Did you catch it?"

"Yes I did. I thought it was no way to treat a book which so many people consider sacred but then I suppose the lady had all the best intentions in trying to save me."

"Do you think she'll succeed?"

Daniela laughed again. "Didn't Jesus say, "Let he who is without sin cast the first stone."?"

"Or the first Bible for that!"

"Or the first Bible."

"Does it worry you that some Christians condemn you for being gay?"

"Well Sabrina you know people will read into the Bible what they want to hear many times. It's common knowledge that I was married at a young age to a man. It didn't work out obviously because I was gay but one

111

thing stuck in my mind from my wedding ceremony. It was something the preacher read from the Bible to solemnise the vows we were to make. He read "Do not press me to leave you or to turn back from following you! Where you go, I will go; where you lodge I will lodge; your people shall be my people, and your God my God. Where you die, I will die — there will I be buried. May the Lord do thus and so to me, and more as well, if even death parts me from you!" That always struck me as a beautiful pledge of love and it turns out that it is a common quote in Christian marriage ceremonies. It was only years later that I discovered that it was what Ruth said to Naomi in the book of Ruth. It was actually the pledge of love from one woman to another. I find it hard to reconcile that with a belief that a Christian God could frown upon the love between two people whatever gender they might happen to be."

The applause was thunderous in the studio and it was repeated among the clientele in the Planet. "She's just fucking awesome!" enthused Charmaine who quite clearly hero worshipped Daniela. The camera zoomed in for a close up on Daniela and Sarah caught her breath. Glinting in the lights in her bosom was a little pendant in white gold in the form of an Edelweiss with cluster of tiny diamonds. Sarah recognised it immediately. She had bought it as a present for Daniela the very day she had first met Charmaine in this pub. It had cost her nearly a thousand francs which had been a substantial amount of money for her. Of course it was a trifling expense for a multi millionairess such as Daniela but here she was, wearing it on prime time television. Sarah knew in an instant that Daniela had worn it for her; had wanted her to see it and know that she was thinking about her. It was a little private message beamed across the continent just for her. Sarah felt such an up-welling of emotion in her throat she thought she would choke.

"But seriously," the hostess was continuing. "How

do you react to demonstrations like that?"

"I try not to Sabrina. The way I see it is that there were two thousand people in that concert hall last night all projecting love and there were half a dozen sad people outside in the rain with a message of hate. Now the press might want to fasten on to those half a dozen people and their message and I suppose that's their privilege and what they think will sell newspapers but it sort of misses the point don't you think? I don't know why it should be newsworthy that some people hate some people and want to hurt them and completely uninteresting that most people just want to love other people. I suppose it's because the latter is so usual isn't it? I mean when did you last see a headline that blared "Joe Bloggs fell in love yesterday and everything is wonderful for him? So what? Happens all the time. Where's the news in that?"

The hostess nodded. "Yes I suppose we can all identify with that. Bad news sells papers. Nevertheless, as a prominent gay artist, you frequently attract media attention because of your sexual orientation. Does that ever bother you? I mean don't you ever wish that people would judge you just by your music and not because you're gay?"

"Not at all Sabrina. For one thing people don't only buy my records or come to my concerts because I'm gay. My music is not exclusive. I write songs for people regardless of their sexuality. I'm also a woman but that doesn't mean that I only write songs for women or that only women buy my music. Michael Jackson was an Afro American but it doesn't follow that only Afro Americans loved his music or that it is judged by that criteria. If I was a terrible musician people wouldn't buy my music regardless of whether I was gay or not. Having said that, being gay is an important part of who I am and I am certainly not going to evade that issue. I see it as a moral responsibility to declare that I'm gay in fact. I

113

think that as prominent artists we have a responsibility to stand up and tell the world that we're gay. I know you feel the same way too Sabrina. There are an awful lot of frightened lonely people out there trying to come to terms with who they are. They fear ridicule, bullying, social ostracism, even losing their jobs, friends and family because they are gay. Every time somebody, such as you and I, who are privileged to be in the public eye, stands up and says "Yes I'm gay" we send a message to those people; a message of hope. We're saying you're not alone. If we're brave enough to stand up and be who we are then so can you. I think that's very important." This time the applause was long and heartfelt.

"So you see yourself as a gay role model then?"

"I think anybody in the public eye, whatever they do or whoever they are, is a role model to somebody. I think we have to be very conscious of that. We have to have a sense of duty to our public and realise that what we do and say will be scrutinised and possibly imitated by the people who follow us. As to being specifically a gay role model I couldn't tell you. Certainly I am very aware of the enormous debt I owe to the gay communities around the world who are among my most loyal fans. I believe that as long as I am in the public eye I have the duty to speak up for the gay minority and try never to let them down. They've never let me down after all. I wouldn't be where I am now without them."

The hostess waited until the inevitable applause had died down. "Well thanks for that Danny. I'm sure that few people have contributed a more positive image of the gay community than yourself. But let's move on for the moment and talk about your new CD. I have an advance copy here." She held up the CD for the camera. "It's called "Endearments and Estrangements". Why did you pick that as a title?"

"Well because it occurred to me that so often love can come at the cost of other people dear to you. I found

114

that sad and it was one of the themes that I explored on the album."

"It sounds a bit gay dare I say."

Daniela tossed her hair back and laughed. "I dare say it does. I suppose it's a common theme for a gay person to risk losing the people close to them because they declare their for love for somebody of the same sex."

"Well I've listened to the album and I've got to say that it's terrific; your best yet."

"Why thank you. I'm pleased you like it."

"Oh I do. So when is it going to hit the stores?"

"We're due to launch it at the beginning of December."

"Well I'd advise everybody to go out and buy it. It really is that good. Do you have promotional tours to launch the album?"

"Yes. We have one tour in December then a break for Christmas and another tour starting in January."

"And will you be back here in Germany on those tours?"

"Of course. I have a big following of fans here in Germany and I wouldn't want to let them down. We'll be in Stuttgart, Köln and Frankfurt in December. Then we're back here in Berlin in January, as well as Hamburg and Dortmund."

"Of course you have an affection for Germany apart from your fans as well don't you? I understand you even take your holidays in Germany. You mentioned before the show that you spent two weeks on Helgoland back in August."

"Yes that's right. I've been to Helgoland several times. I love the place and I'd like to say hello to all my friends there especially Rudi who is the wonderful man who helped make our stay in August so special."

The hostess lifted an eyebrow. "Oh so you weren't alone then?" Sarah was holding her breath.

"No. I was with a friend."

"Oh Really? A special friend perhaps?"

"Stop fishing for gossip Sabrina."

The hostess laughed easily. "Well it was you who said we should tell more good news Danny. Anyway let's move on. I understand that there's been a bit of reshuffling with the band for your next tour Danny. Is that a breakup or something? What's it all about?"

"Oh nothing so dramatic Sabrina. Leo, my bass player, is taking a time out for the winter. His wife is expecting a baby around the beginning of December and so naturally he wants to spend some time at home with her. So it means we have to have another bass player for the winter tours to fill in."

"And have you picked a replacement?"

"Oh yes and an exciting one I think. She's a young woman from Switzerland called Charmaine Voller and she's an exciting new talent." The bar erupted in cheers as Charmaine buried her face in her hands in a comical mix of ecstasy and embarrassment. "We tried her out in audition a few weeks ago and she was just fabulous. I think there's a great future in store for her."

"You have a bit of a reputation for blooding new unknown talent don't you Danny?"

"Yes I suppose that comes from my own experiences when I was touring out of the back of an old van looking for a break myself. I never lost sight of my roots. There's an awful lot of untapped talent out there that just needs the chance if somebody would only take the trouble to look for it."

"So you met this girl in Switzerland where you live?"

"Yes... through a mutual friend."

"And would you mind me asking if she's gay?"

Daniela laughed. "You never give up do you Sabrina? As it happens, yes, she is gay."

Charmaine buried her face once more and groaned. "Oh God! Now everybody's going to think *I'm* Danny's damn girlfriend."

Nicole smirked and glanced at the furiously blushing Sarah. "Well it wouldn't be a problem if the future Mrs Devin stood up to be counted."

Simon grinned. "I think she's brilliant. What a lovely red herring to toss to the media." Sarah was apparently trying to sink into the floorboards.

The talk show hostess was relentless. "Come on Danny. Give your fans something to cheer about. It's been absolutely ages since you were last seen dating anybody. Isn't there anybody special in your life at the moment?"

"I'd rather not talk about my personal life at the moment Sabrina. It's a little private."

"And your new bass player has nothing to do with it?"

"You'll have to wait and see."

"Well on that hint we'll have to end off there because we're right out of time. I've been talking to Daniela Devin whose new album, "Endearments and Estrangements" will be in the stores at the beginning of December. Thank you Danny and we hope to see you again soon."

"Thank *you* Sabrina."

There was a thunderous applause once more from the studio audience and the hostess was saying "We'll take a short break there. Right after this we'll be..." The barman cut off the television and restarted the music. The bar came alive with a buzz of excited discussion.

Nicole wiped a hand across her brow. "Whew! That was quite an interview. For a minute I thought she was going to out you there for sure Sarah."

"Don't say that. My heart was in my mouth."

Any hope that Nicole could do anything to repair her earlier cooling of relations with Charmaine seemed to have vanished. Charmaine was being surrounded by well-wishers excited at hearing her confirmation as

Daniela's new bass player on the television. She was having a hard time of it. "Hey!" one girl demanded. "Are you really seeing Danny Devin?"

"Hell Claire. I'm just playing in her band ok."

"Well don't let her find out you've been going out with that Nicole chick." another girl remarked

"She won't mind at all. I'm just her bloody bass player."

"Hey does that mean that Nicole's free?" asked yet another of the crowd surrounding her hopefully.

"Isn't she with that drop dead gorgeous little piece with the long chestnut hair?" asked yet another. "They were being awfully cosy together on the bar earlier."

"That's just a good friend of Nicky's and Simon's guy Peter." said Charmaine hastily, feeling as if she was losing control of events.

"But she's gay right?" persisted the girl. "Are you saying she's not with Nicky?"

"No they're just friends."

"Hmm I wonder if she'd like a drink."

At this point Simon waded into the crowd to rescue her. "Charlie if we're going to catch that restaurant we'd better be making a move soon."

"Oh sure. Look girls I've got to go. Catch you all later right."

They extracted themselves with difficulty from the bar. Out on the street Charmaine ran a hand through her hair and took a deep breath. "Christ what a day!"

Chapter Eight

The day was by no means over. The Chinese restaurant was some way out of the city centre and so they had to drive in Sarah's car to get there. It was a good choice, in spite of that, for it was refreshingly modern without being sterile and the setting was pleasant, the service excellent and the food beyond reproach. They ordered spicy hot and sour soup and spring rolls for starters and, for the main courses, they all ordered a variety of different dishes so that everybody could try a little of everything. Simon set the mood by insisting that everybody had to eat with chopsticks. The results were variable. Sarah managed reasonable well as did Charmaine. Simon was smugly expert with the challenging eating utensils but Peter was quite frankly hopeless and Nicole disgraced herself by propelling a battered ball of pork half way across the restaurant onto somebody else's table where its progress was finally halted by a flask of hot rice wine.

Despite these amusing interludes, however, the atmosphere around the table was somewhat strained. There were complex undercurrents eroding the camaraderie over dinner and these involved the three women present. To begin with there was Charmaine. On the face of it there was absolutely no reason for Charmaine to be feeling anything but deliriously happy. It, after all, was tantamount to a dream come true for her. A chance to play the bass guitar with one of the continent's greatest current stars was not exactly the sort of thing that happened every day. It was a life changing career move; one that opened up galaxies of possibilities for an ambitious aspiring musician. Yet, since leaving the Planet, Charmaine had looked curiously troubled. The first of Charmaine's troubles involved Nicole.

She had been receiving oddly mixed signals from Nicole all evening and she was frankly baffled by them. She had expected Nicole to be ecstatically happy for her but Nicole had seemed nervous and reserved. Then there'd been the puzzling incident with Sarah in the Planet. Charmaine was acutely aware of the fact that there was something of an ambiguous relationship between Sarah and Nicole. Nicole, she was aware, had been, and probably still was, deeply in love with Sarah. Despite Nicole's assurances that there was no further worry on that score due to Sarah's total commitment to Daniela, Charmaine was still worried about it. For one thing, Nicole was still resisting taking the nascent relationship between them to any higher level.

Nicole's assertions that nothing had happened between them were by and large correct even if she'd been less than truthful regarding the developing affection drawing them together. Nicole had protested that she was not ready for a lesbian relationship and had begged for time to sort out the conflicting emotions tearing her apart. Charmaine suspected otherwise. It had not escaped her notice that Nicole had been considerably more reticent about displaying affection to her while Sarah was present. Furthermore, when Nicole had seemed upset, it had been Sarah that rushed off to attend to her and they'd had a private conversation together, the gist of which was still a mystery to Charmaine. Somebody had noted that they'd seemed very close in private with each other during their absence and Charmaine felt hurt and confused about it.

Sarah was an enigma to Charmaine. She was a truly beautiful girl and possessed of a warm and loving nature, it was true. Also, she was the girl who Daniela adored above all others. There was no doubt about Daniela's feelings for her. Charmaine had seen the two of them together and Daniela's love for her lovely country girl had been blindingly obvious. Furthermore, when

120

together with Daniela, Sarah showed every indication of reciprocating those feelings. And yet there were oddities. To Charmaine, Sarah's reluctance to publicly declare herself as Daniela's girlfriend was quite simply incomprehensible. If she'd been in Sarah's shoes, Charmaine would have wanted the whole world to know about it. She was sure that the clandestine nature of the relationship had nothing to do with Daniela. Daniela wouldn't have cared less who knew that she loved Sarah, Charmaine believed. So it was Sarah then that was the source of this baffling secrecy. Yet Sarah was quite prepared to appear in public in a gay bar and even kiss a friend in it. So it went deeper than Sarah merely hiding her sexuality. It almost felt as if Sarah was being unfaithful in some way to Daniela; as if she was playing some game that Daniela was not going to like. After all she knew that Nicole had stayed overnight with Sarah last night and in Daniela's own house at that. Charmaine worshipped Daniela and she had growing feelings for Nicole. Somehow Sarah seemed to be undermining her loyalties to both of them as if she was playing a love triangle with Nicole that threatened all of them.

To compound the situation were Daniela's rather obfuscating remarks in the television interview. To be sure, Charmaine had been thrilled to be named as Daniela's new bassist so publicly but her failure to deny outright that Charmaine was the mysterious new girlfriend that Sabrina Handelmeyer had so obviously sniffed out complicated matters immensely. Already she had seen that the clientele of the Planet were suspecting that there was some truth in the innuendo and there was no bigger witch's cauldron of gossip anywhere than a clique of lesbians. It was almost certain that her name would be publicly attached to Daniela's in no time. What was she supposed to do about it? If Daniela was genuinely trying to protect the identity of Sarah then Charmaine could hardly now come out and deny the rumour and point to Sarah. For one thing Charmaine's own career now rested on Daniela and she wasn't about to queer her pitch by offending her new boss. Then again however, if there was some sort of public perception of her as Daniela Devin's clandestine lover, then her own actions would come under intense scrutiny. How the devil was she to pursue a relationship with Nicole if everybody thought she was cheating on Daniela by doing so and she could only kill the rumour by the fatal course of pointing out that it was Sarah who was Daniela's love and not she?

It was a quandary and she tentatively raised the subject over dinner. "Why the hell did Danny leave that question unanswered?" Charmaine asked the company. "What am I going to do if everybody thinks I'm Danny's girlfriend now?" Sarah blushed deeply and seemed to be concentrating on her food fixedly.

Simon thought about it for a second. "I think Danny was just trying to lay a smoke screen Charlie. She never actually said that you were she just left the question open to interpretation. It's not your fault if people jump to the wrong conclusion. I'd just deny it if I was you and let people think what they will." Privately Simon was of the opinion that it was no bad thing if people's attention was redirected. It would take the heat away from Sarah and Simon thought that was probably why Daniela had left such an open question in the first place. Daniela was capable of considerable subtlety.

"I suppose you're right." conceded Charmaine, "It's no skin off *my* nose if the world thinks I'm going out with the most beautiful lesbian women in Switzerland!" She glanced pointedly at Sarah who blushed even deeper and avoided her eye.

Nicole swallowed and shuffled uncomfortably. Ever since her conversation with Sarah in the Planet she had been agonising over how to proceed. At least she was sitting next to Charmaine now and trying to be more friendly but she was aware that Charmaine seemed a little distracted now. Even more worrying was the change that had come over Sarah. Ever since that television interview Sarah had been subdued and unwilling to talk. Nicole knew her friend well enough to know that she was brooding over something. She looked genuinely upset.

It was true. Sarah felt terrible. That interview had been like a dagger in her heart threatening to destroy her new, hard won and fragile happiness. She had felt such an ache for Daniela while watching her on the television yet every nuance of the interview had made her feel worse. Daniela had worn the necklace she had given her, telling her even at that distance she was always in her thoughts. Her eyes had lit up when she'd talked about that fortnight on Helgoland and she'd had the radiant glow of a woman in love. Yet Sarah felt so very unworthy of that love now. Throughout the interview she had been terrified of Daniela identifying the love in her life. Yet Daniela had talked of the courage to be able to stand forth and be counted. She had even had to face demonstrators accosting her on the street because of her sexuality. She had dealt with the problem with characteristic serenity and diplomacy. This was a woman of courage and high principles; unafraid to stand up for what she believed in and prepared to let the world judge her for who she was. Yet her girlfriend was a timorous coward that hid behind her apron strings and didn't have the guts to stand up and say, "this is my woman!"

Sarah had seen how proud everybody in the bar had been over their adopted star. Daniela was like a queen to them while she, this extraordinary woman's so-called girlfriend, had been trembling in her boots at the thought of being exposed as such. Why was she so frightened? Was it because she feared that her old way of life; the old Sarah who could walk abroad on her mountains in comfortable obscurity, would be threatened by the glare of publicity upon her. Why had she been able to tell her family that she was gay and yet conceal the identity of the woman she loved? It was true that she had invited her parents to visit whenever they wanted and meet her girlfriend but, if she was honest with herself, she knew that she had been safe in such an invitation because they would never agree to such an invitation. So why was she so afraid of them knowing?

It was largely because she knew that having their daughter connected with such a public figure would horrify her parents. As long as they believed that her girlfriend was some unknown girl of perfectly obscure background they could maintain the pretence that she didn't exist. Sarah lived far enough away from the Ticino to preclude her parents' having to admit to their circle of friends and acquaintances that their daughter was gay. If they knew the truth they would realise that Sarah was all too likely to come to the public eye and be recognised throughout Switzerland as gay. It would be a fatal blow. They would probably disown her completely. Sarah was terrified of losing that last slender bridge to her family.

She knew too that there was a part of her that was even embarrassed by her relationship with a person like Daniela. She had thought of telling her sister the truth about her girlfriend but even then she had baulked at doing so. She had a complex relationship with her elder sister. She had always been the baby looking up to her more worldly and sophisticated sister. She had felt for a long time that her sister had been somewhat exasperated by her obedience to her parents' wishes; had felt her to be somewhat immature and without the strength of character to defy them. Jessica had been almost proud of her when she had finally broken the engagement with Alan and told her parents she was gay. But Sarah wondered how she would feel when she learned that the person she had broken the engagement off for was a pop star.

Somehow it seemed an awfully immature, girly thing to do. Teenage girls were supposed to fall in love with pop idols not grown women who were demanding of their parents the right to be taken seriously as adults. Even Nicole, at the beginning of her relationship with Daniela, had questioned whether or not she was just beglamoured by a famous singer. Her parents' expressed view that it was just a phase she was going through would seem all the more credible in the light of the fact that her lover was such a person and even Jessica would begin to have her doubts.

And yet, as her friends continually reminded her, she would not be able to hide forever. And why should she? She knew that Daniela was being extraordinarily patient with her. She was even now throwing a defensive wall around her to protect her from the public eye. Why should Daniela have to do that? Why couldn't she have a girlfriend as courageous as she; who was willing to state that she loved her and damn what anybody else thought about it? Here she was, a very public gay figure, and she couldn't even tell the world about her girlfriend. Sarah felt truly ashamed. Worse yet she felt hypocritical! Only an hour or so before she had been berating Nicole because she was unwilling to show her affection for Charmaine in public and yet Nicole's cowardice didn't begin to compare to hers. She was living in some cloud cuckoo land of denial; some bizarre fantasy that the world she inhabited with Daniela would remain hidden and private. Daniela would surely not tolerate that forever and nor would that world remain hidden for long.

When Daniela phoned her toward the end of dinner, Sarah took the call in the ladies of the restaurant but she was too ashamed of her fears to talk much about them and in any case Daniela sounded tired and just wanted to come home. Sarah didn't want to bother her with her concerns. She did tell Daniela that she was out with the others in Winterthur celebrating Charmaine's new job however. "Yes I have to get together and speak to her." Daniela remarked.

"You could see her tomorrow when you get back."

"I won't really fancy stopping off at Winterthur on my way home Sarah."

"Well Charlie could come back with us to the Toggenburg tonight and stay over Danny."

Daniela laughed. "You mean stay with Nicky?"

"I don't know Danny but it might work don't you think? I could invite them both to stay over and see what happens. I could use the fact that you'd like to see Charlie tomorrow as a pretext. Nicky could drive Charlie back after you've talked to her."

"It's an idea Sarah. Test them out and see if they'll go for it."

"We saw your interview on the telly in the Planet Danny."

"Oh God! Was it torrid? Bloody Sabrina was being a bloody nosy pain in the arse."

"You were wonderful Danny. I...I thought you handled it really well. Everybody in the bar was cheering you. I...I wish I had the courage that you have in public."

"I've had a few years of experience Sarah. You haven't."

Sarah swallowed. "I...I was frightened Danny... I don't know why. I was frightened that people would... well...find out about us."

"Don't worry Sarah. I'm not about to tell anybody about you on live television."

"Danny... I...I'm not proud of it. I think I've let you down today."

"You couldn't let me down Sarah. It's perfectly understandable that you're nervous about it. I'm nervous too Sarah although perhaps for different reasons. Don't beat yourself over the head about it. We'll talk when I get home. Until then, just stay cool."

"Oh Danny you were wearing my necklace."

"And I am so glad you saw it Sarah. I haven't taken it off all the time I've been gone. I've missed you so much."

"You never mentioned when you phoned up this morning that you'd had demonstrators accosting you at the concert."

"I didn't want to worry you sweetheart. It was nothing honestly. I've had to put up with these crackpots before. They're harmless."

"Danny I miss you. I didn't think it was going to be so bad with you gone but I've felt so lonely. What's it going to be like when you go away for longer tours this winter?"

"We'll talk about that too Sarah. I've missed you terribly as well. Maybe we have to rethink a few things. But listen I'm home tomorrow and it's weeks before I have to take another protracted leave so let's just enjoy the moment shall we."

"I'm sorry. I didn't want to bother you with my worries. You sound tired."

"I'm knackered darling. I'm back in my hotel room and I'm going to flake out in a minute. I just didn't want to go to bed without hearing your voice."

"I'd better get back to the others then and let you sleep."

"Send my love to everybody."

"Of course. Is it ok then if I invite Charlie over? I mean if you don't feel like seeing her tomorrow then I won't."

"Of course it's ok. I'd like to see her. Are you going to put Nicky and Charlie in the same room?"

"I'd better play that one by ear Danny. Nicky's wringing her hands and playing hard to get."

"Don't push her too hard Sarah. This won't be easy for her. Tell you what; put them in the two adjoining bedrooms with the shared bathroom. That way they can take it from there and you can pretend not to notice if they end up in the same bed together."

Sarah giggled. Talking to Daniela had restored her humour somewhat. "Yes that's an idea. Nicky will smell a rat but at least it'll give her a get out clause."

"Exactly. Listen honey I can barely keep my eyes open. I'm going to have to crash."

"Oh I'm sorry. Get some sleep then. I'll see you tomorrow. Love you!"

"I love you too Sarah. Until tomorrow."

"Sweet dreams."

"Of you always. Goodnight darling."

Sarah was putting her phone away as the door to the ladies opened and Charmaine walked in. Charmaine looked at her curiously. "Was that Danny on the phone?"

"Yes it was."

"Did she have anything to say?"

"Not a lot mostly Charlie. She's had a busy few days and she's tired. She did say that she wanted to talk to you tomorrow though."

"Yeah! I guess we're going to have to start putting a few things together." Charmaine looked distracted and uncomfortable.

"Is there something on your mind Charlie?"

Charmaine nodded and hesitated. "Well... yes there is Sarah."

"Do you want to tell me about it?"

"What's going on with Nicky?"

Sarah was taken aback by the sudden bluntness of Charmaine's question. "In what respect Charmaine?"

"Well is there something going on between you two?"

Sarah blinked in surprise. "Between me and Nicky? Well yes there is. We've been best friends ever since we were kids. Of course there's something going on. If you mean are we sleeping together, however, then the answer

128

is no."

"So why is she being so distant with me because you're here?"

Sarah smiled. "Oh Charlie you've got the wrong end of the stick. It's got nothing to do with me in particular."

"You were having a pretty cosy chat with her in the Planet and you kissed her."

"I often kiss Nicole Charlie. She's my best friend. As for the chat we were having it was about you."

"About me?"

"Yes I was telling her to stop being an arse hole and to start treating you properly because she'd hardly had a word to say to you since we came in."

Charmaine blinked and bit her lip. "Oh!"

"Yes and I furthermore told her that I thought you were just the person for her and that she ought to stop pussy footing around and realise it."

Charmaine shuffled guiltily. "I'm sorry Sarah. I've made a prick of myself. I... I didn't understand."

"Don't mention it. Are you fond of Nicole?"

"Yes I am but I don't know how much she likes me."

"She likes you a lot Charlie. She just can't bring herself to admit it to you or herself."

"But why?"

"Charlie you must remember what it was like when you were first coming out."

"Yeah! Rough!"

"Well it's just as hard for Nicky if not more so. She's never confessed to feeling anything for another woman before Charlie. It's completely foreign ground to her. She's always had a bit of a reputation for the boys."

"You mean she's bi?"

"I don't think it's as simple as that Charlie. She used to go through boyfriends like water but none of them ever lasted. I can see now it was because none of

129

them ever had what she was looking for. What she was looking for, and never dared to say, was a girl. Now she's having to face up to that and you have to be patient with her. She's never slept with a girl Charlie. She's way out of her league here. She comes up against a girl like you who's openly gay and proud of it and she doesn't know what to do. Right now she's an emotional mess and you're going to have to be very gentle with her. She's out of her comfort zone so you're going to have to take it as it comes."

"I don't have much choice either way Sarah. I only get to see her when she comes through to Winterthur and then only for a couple of hours at a time. It's hardly a whirlwind romance."

"Well I was coming to that Charlie. I said that Danny wants to see you tomorrow. Well she's had a busy few days and she wants to get home so she doesn't really want to come to Winterthur if she doesn't have to. So I suggested that maybe you'd like to come back with us to our place in the Toggenburg tonight. You could see Danny when she gets back tomorrow. She's taking an early flight out of Tempelhof in the morning and expects to be back in the early afternoon. I don't know if you've got anything on tomorrow of course."

"Good God no! I've nothing *that* important."

"Well then Nicky is staying overnight as well..." Sarah left the rest of the statement unsaid.

Charmaine looked at her eagerly. "Where would we sleep?"

"Well I'm going to put you diplomatically in separate bedrooms, Charlie, otherwise Nicky will feel like she's being coerced into bed with you. But the rooms are adjoining each other and they share the same bathroom so maybe after a couple of nightcaps you might just have a chance of enticing her into your room."

Charmaine nodded with a grin. "Oh God! Do you think she'll go for it?"

"I don't know Charlie. We might be pushing her too hard and too soon. I'm just asking you to treat her with kid gloves and don't try to push her into something she's not ready for. She's a bit mixed up for the moment and we don't want to spook her."

"I've got it Sarah. I'll be as gentle as a lamb."

"Thank you Charlie. I appreciate it. Look we'd better get back to the others."

Nicole looked at the two of them suspiciously when they returned. "You two have been a hell of a long time." she remarked sourly.

Sarah put on a breezy face. "Oh we just had Danny on the phone. She needs to have a long talk with Charlie about the winter tour programme tomorrow so she's invited Charlie over to the house tonight so she can see her when she gets back. Charlie's got nothing on tomorrow so she's agreed."

Nicole closed her mouth hastily, aware that she was beginning to look like a paralysed goldfish. "Charlie's staying tonight?" she asked in a hoarse squeak.

"Yes that's right. I thought that Simon and Pete might want to stop for a nightcap as well when we get back."

"How's Charlie supposed to get back after she's seen Danny?" asked Peter.

"Well I thought Nicky might be able to run her home if it's not too much trouble. You're not working tomorrow are you Nicky?"

"Hey, I can always take the train if it's too much hassle." volunteered Charmaine.

Nicole looked haunted. "No, no. It won't be any trouble Charlie."

"Well then that's settled." declared Sarah in satisfaction.

Simon looked at his watch. "Well if it's nightcaps round at Sarah's then we'd better pay our bill and get going."

Charmaine held up a hand. "No you don't. This was my idea and my treat. I'll pick up the bill."

Sarah looked askance. "We can't let you pay the whole bill Charmaine. It'll come to a bloody fortune."

"I insist Sarah. This was my party and I insist on paying."

"Well if you're sure you can afford it."

"Sure I can. I'm the bass guitarist with one of the biggest bands in Europe remember." Charmaine laughed merrily. "You guys get our coats and I'll go sort it out."

As soon as Charmaine was out of earshot, Nicole grabbed Sarah's arm. "What the hell are you playing at inviting Charlie over?" she demanded in a furious whisper.

"Why nothing Nicky. Danny needs to talk to her and I can't ask her to drive over to Winterthur as soon as she gets home. It seemed the perfect solution. Charlie's got nothing on tomorrow."

"I couldn't give a shit what she hasn't got on tomorrow. It's what she might not have on tonight I'm worried about. Where the hell's she supposed to sleep?"

"You'll have separate rooms if that's what's worrying you."

"Separate rooms?"

"Yes...unless of course you'd prefer to share."

"Have you lost your marbles?"

"Well then in due reverence of your chastity you can have a room on your own."

"What if she comes into my room?"

"Well you could say "I'm sorry but I find you repulsive and your presence is offensive to me.""

"Don't be stupid Sarah."

"Or alternatively you could move over in bed and make room. Entirely your choice of course."

"Oh thanks Sarah!"

Peter came up behind. "Er your coat Sarah." Gallantly he held it out for her.

"Why thank you sir. Ah here comes Charmaine. Shall we leave then ladies and gentlemen?"

Chapter Nine

Sarah loved the scent of fresh brewed coffee first thing in the morning. To her the aroma was evocative of domestic tranquillity and home comfort; your own home, another day to look forward to and peace and security within the walls you inhabited. Sarah had not dressed since her morning shower. She had merely pulled a silk robe around herself and donned a pair of slippers. She was enjoying the luxury of walking about the house and attending to her early duties while barely dressed.

The big house was warm despite the fact that the weather outside had taken a turn for the worse overnight. Sarah was aware that Daniela had installed a sophisticated central heating system that provided not only constant air temperature from the radiators but also a deliciously warm floor from the under floor heating. It was also well insulated and draught free. Sarah knew that Daniela was not afraid to rough it when circumstances dictated but, in the privacy of her own home, she was hedonistic and considered that clothes were for decoration only. If she couldn't walk about comfortably naked then she considered the house too cold.

It was quite new to Sarah. She loved the old cottage she had shared with Nicole for so many years but she was well aware that, on a cold winter's morning, parts of it could be quite chilly. They'd had to switch an electric heater on in the morning to warm the kitchen over breakfast for example and, although the living room was cosy enough with a log fire in the grate in the evenings, they'd rarely used it in the daytime in winter. This overall fuggy warmth wherever you were in the house felt almost decadent. There was cold rain with a hint of sleet beating against the double glazed French windows in the kitchen but the kitchen itself was cosy, bright with light and music was playing over the radio.

Sarah felt happy. The dark misgivings she had experienced yesterday evening had left her and she hummed contentedly as she poured herself a mug of coffee. She had left the kitchen door open so that the sound of music and the aroma of coffee could circulate around the house and suggest to her guests that it was time to be up and about. Hans-Ruedi, the gardener and handyman, was pottering about in the old barn that was part of the property, on some mysterious mission of his own. He had been in early to deliver fresh bread, rolls and croissants and he'd left a basket of fresh, big brown eggs from the chicken coop by the kitchen door.

Although Sarah and Daniela had grumbled somewhat about suddenly finding themselves hosting a whole flock of unwanted poultry to begin with, they had, nevertheless, been seduced into acceptance by the bounteous harvest of eggs the industrious hens produced. Daniela had declared them to be the best eggs she had ever tasted; huge wholesome things with the sort of glorious enormous orange yolks that only chickens that spent their days scrabbling around in the dirt outside seemed able to produce.

Hans-Ruedi was a welcome source of additions to their diet in many respects in fact. On his own property he maintained a well-managed vegetable garden and he was continually pressing fresh vegetables on them. He also kept his hand in helping out with the local dairy farmers and supplied them with as much fresh milk, cream, homemade butter and cheese as they could have wished for. He also kept a little livestock of his own; rabbits, the odd pig or two and his beloved goats. A fortnight ago he had slaughtered a pig and Sarah and Daniela had a freezer full of prime cuts of pork, lots of belly slices, some delicious homemade sausages and a side of home cured bacon. For a man of his age Hans-Ruedi kept himself inordinately busy. They had a fine store of apples from his little orchard and jars of honey from the hives he kept up on the alp. Their housekeeper Elrika added to this largesse with her own contributions for she was a fine cook and baker of some renown in the Toggenburg. Scarcely a week would go by without her delivering the fruits of her labour to the household. They had shelves filled with her jams, preserves and pickles and an enormous blackberry tart nestling alongside an equally daunting apple pie awaiting their attention in the fridge. It appeared, as Daniela had once amusedly observed, as if the domestic help were under the misapprehension that the two young ladies of the house would starve to death without constant vigilance.

Well there was certainly no shortage of sustenance for the morning repast for Sarah's two guests, once they deigned to bless the breakfast table with their presence, she thought with satisfaction. The fridge and cupboards were bulging with food. Sarah took a seat at the kitchen table. It was one of her favourite seats in the house for there was a fine view out over the garden to the woods beyond and the tips of the mountains could be seen beyond on days when the sky was clear. Today the distant view was choked by low lying cloud however and Sarah had to be content to watch the bedraggled looking chickens making tentative forays out into the weather.

She decided to ask Hans-Ruedi to build them a bird table in the garden within view of the kitchen. It would be heavenly to sit here in the winter with snow on the ground and watch the birds at the table in the morning. Perhaps they'd have to put some chicken wire around it to keep the cats at bay. Sarah snorted at the thought. The cats in question had already dined on fresh chopped kidneys and were now reclining somnolently around the kitchen giving every appearance of intending to sleep until the next meal was available. They were quite frankly the laziest gang of felines Sarah had ever come across. She had held the door open for them that morning in case they had felt intrepid enough to venture abroad. The cats had taken one look at the prevailing weather conditions and declined the offer aloofly. The garden birds would have little to fear from this collection of idle layabouts.

Happily Sarah opened the cook book she had taken down from the shelf. She had a mind to cook something special for Daniela on her return that evening. She was still experimenting with Chinese food and she had managed to get hold of some black bean sauce at an outlet selling oriental spices and condiments in Buchs. She had half a kilo of chicken breast that needed using, a bunch of green onions, a couple of green peppers, onions and garlic cloves. She frowned in thought. She knew that they had sesame oil and soy sauce in the pantry but she couldn't remember if there was any cornflower left to thicken the sauce. Worriedly she stood to take a look in the cupboard. To her satisfaction there was about half a cupful left in the tin. She didn't need that much. Her perusal revealed another problem however. They'd run out of stock cubes and the recipe called for chicken stock. It was a blow. It seemed like an awful lot of hassle to drive over to Wildhaus just to buy a packet of stock cubes! Then another thought relieved her concern. At some point during the day she had to go over to Schwendi to return a couple of DVDs she had borrowed from Angelica at the Hotel Toggenburg. They were bound to have some chicken stock in the hotel kitchen.

Contentedly she returned to her coffee and reading. She felt foolishly excited she knew. Daniela was coming home. She glanced at the kitchen clock wondering whether to phone her. She decided not to. Daniela would probably already be at the airport in Berlin by now and she'd doubtless call if there were any delays. Sarah wondered if Daniela would bring her a present from Germany. It was likely she knew. Daniela normally didn't even manage to have a day in Zurich without remembering to bring something home for her. Sarah didn't really care if she did or didn't. As long as she returned home safely that would be present enough.

There would be no question of entertaining guests tonight. She wanted Daniela all for herself. She'd cook them both a nice meal, light a big log fire in the living room, burn some candles and they'd eat by the light of the flickering flames. She had a good bottle of Chablis to go with the dinner and, as a pièce de resistance, she had a bottle of Japanese saké that she had bought in town and had been saving for a special occasion. She had even bought a set of little ceramic sake cups which she had learned were called choko and an accompanying flask called a tokkuri. They would finish their meal with hot saké by the fireplace.

Then they would make love. Sarah tingled at the thought. Before she had met Daniela Sarah had thought herself to be somewhat inadequate sexually. Sex had seemingly never particularly interested her. Sex with her boyfriend had been unsatisfying and anticlimactic. She had masturbated and fantasised of course but the reality of sex had never lived up to her expectations. It had all felt rather awkward and short with none of the lingering sensuality she had imagined in her fantasies. She had begun to fear that she might be rather backward in that regard; frigid even. But then Daniela had exploded into her life.

With Daniela Sarah had discovered a whole realm of sexual intensity she had scarcely imagined even in her wildest fantasies. It had been both the greatest joy and surprise of her life. In the days when she had first known Daniela, Sarah had resisted becoming her lover although she had teetered dangerously on the edge of succumbing to her growing feelings. They had finally become lovers just two days before Sarah was due to travel to her parents' home in the Ticino to become officially engaged. It had been a revelation. Sarah had never known such an excitement and satisfaction. She had imagined that it would be she that would surrender to Daniela's patient seduction but in fact Daniela had cleverly manoeuvred her into a dominant role and had made her take the lead. Sarah had been delighted to discover that she could so excite Daniela as to make her lose all reason, leave her senseless with passion and reduce her to whimpering jelly cradled in her arms. When Sarah had surrendered her dominance and allowed Daniela to take the lead she had thought for a moment she was going to faint. In three years with her boyfriend Sarah could remember just one orgasm. In that first wild night with Daniela she had counted at least six. From that moment on it had been a foregone conclusion. She had gone to the Ticino with only one real intention in her mind; to rid herself as quickly as possible of her boyfriend and arranged marriage and then fly straight back to the arms of her impossible lover.

They had become greedy for each other staying up until late in the night to explore their new found pleasure. They had spent two weeks on Helgoland where they had become almost careless in their passion; making love among the sand dunes or rutting among the seals on the beach as the sun set over the sea. Back in the Toggenburg that passion had not diminished an iota. They had made love in every room in the house including the barn. Daniela had teased Sarah one day by preparing breakfast clad only in a silly flowery apron. When Sarah had pawed at her hungrily she had slapped her hand and pushed her away so Sarah had chased her around the kitchen, wrestled with her and dragged her over her knee to spank her amidst mock protests of indignation and much giggling. Breakfast had been ruined long before they had slaked their lust on the kitchen floor.

At night they had often gone for walks among the meadows and woods and made love by starlight or beneath the rays of the sun. Even in broad daylight one or the other would drag the other aside on one of their walks and pull them into the grass or against a tree; their excitement enhanced by the danger of it. They had very nearly been caught red handed several times and they pushed the boundaries of their luck perilously; daring each other to more and more outrageous escapades. On one occasion they had picked flowers in the meadows and decorated themselves with them and dared each other to walk across a meadow clad only in flowers. They had taken photographs and the startling results were locked away in a file on Daniela's computer for fond reminiscence. On another occasion Sarah had fulfilled a promise to allow Daniela to paint her naked among the wild flowers in a little sunny corner up at Gamsalp. They had nearly come unstuck for they had heard voices and Sarah had managed to cover herself in the nick of time before a whole party of hikers had rounded a corner. The hikers had recognised Daniela and politely asked for her autograph. Daniela had obliged them whilst Sarah had blushed furiously in the background aware that the half-finished nude portrait of her lay in plain view for all to see. When the hikers had taken their leave Daniela had ordered Sarah to undress once more and had refused to allow her cover herself again until the portrait was complete. The result was beautiful and touching and, much to Sarah's continual embarrassment whilst entertaining visitors, Daniela had insisted on hanging it proudly in the living room. The previous evening Charmaine had admired it openly. Sarah had blushed with chagrin but at the same time she was secretly pleased and touched by Daniela's obvious and overt pride in her.

So, yes, tonight they would make love. That was

inevitable. Having been separated for the past days they would be feverish for each other. Sarah's eyes glazed at the thought and her fingers stroked the pages of her cookbook sensually as she dreamed of the velvet softness of Daniela's skin, the heavy luxury of her golden hair and the deep invitation of her enormous blue eyes. Sarah loved everything about Daniela's body. She could never tire of touching it and caressing it. She had discovered that the feel of Daniela's skin altered perceptibly when Daniela became aroused. It just seemed to feel different; almost as if there was some kind of electric charge running through it. Sarah had puzzled over this phenomenon. Perhaps the flood of blood to the outer layers of the skin warmed it and gave it a different feel or was it the tiny almost invisible hairs on the skin erecting and giving that odd feeling. Whatever it was it was so noticeable that Sarah could reach over in the night in their bedroom and detect it even in the dark. Daniela knew that she could too, for, one night, Sarah had leaned forward to murmur, "Don't try pretending to be asleep Miss Devin. I know damn well you're awake." and Daniela had given that little chuckle of deep happiness that Sarah loved so well and turned to clasp her lips to hers.

It wasn't just the feel of Daniela's body that Sarah loved either. She was a feast for the eye and Sarah could rarely tear her gaze away. Neatly coiffed, cosmetically adorned and stylishly clad, Daniela was a stunningly beautiful woman; admired warmly even by a public who knew of her sexual orientation. She had made the pages of glamour magazines regularly with no hint of airbrushing or other photographic skulduggery required. She had the sort of body that came so close to perfection that it reeked of injustice; as if it was simply unfair that somebody who was so talented, so charming and so serenely gentle in character should also be blessed with such breath taking beauty.

Daniela was not shy about her appearance. She had appeared naked on her own album covers and she was uninhibited about displaying herself to the point of exhibitionism. Their mutual friend Rozella had taken the photos for the albums and had enthused profusely about her favourite model. Rozella's dearest wish was to photograph Daniela and Sarah naked together. So far Sarah had resisted the temptation but privately she was excited by the thought. But the vision of Daniela that Sarah loved the most was not the one that made it onto the front cover of the glossy magazines but rather the morning sight of Daniela awakening in bed without her make-up on, her hair a tangled ruin and her eyes still misty with sleep. Sarah could never get enough of that sight nor ever resist the urge to bring her lover to full awakening with urgent caresses.

Touch and sight were not the only senses that Daniela excited in Sarah. She loved the scent of Daniela; even the taste of her and she could listen for hours to her voice. Of course Daniela's voice had enraptured millions with her singing but even a request to pass the sugar bowl sounded like music to Sarah. She had never heard such an entrancing timbre to anybody's voice before. It was thrilling in its richness and irresistible in its promise. Daniela knew exactly how to manipulate Sarah with her voice and she utilised it ruthlessly. If Sarah was annoyed with her about something she could turn on a kittenish submissive little tone instantly and Sarah was so much putty in her hands.

She was an incorrigible tease as well and she knew how to lower her tone into a seductive deep contralto that would drive Sarah's libido off the scale. She delighted in playing this game; sometimes stopping in the middle of a crowded supermarket to lean forward and murmur something outrageous punctuated by a tiny caress of her finger and then giggle triumphantly as Sarah blushed crimson and glared at her in frustrated exasperation. She had turned mundane shopping trips into private erotic adventures and she played it so well that they could barely get the shopping bags through the front door before Sarah was tearing her clothes off.

She had even exploited Sarah's finicky house-keeping to tease her. Sarah knew that Daniela deliberately left items of her underwear lying carelessly about to irritate her sense of tidiness and titillate her imagination. The most extreme case of this had occurred one day when she had come home from working at the hotel. Parking her car at the side of the house, she had entered by the kitchen door, as was her habit, and found, to her annoyance, Daniela's shoes lying carelessly on the back step. Clicking her tongue irritably, she had picked them up and walked into the kitchen. There she had found Daniela's blouse draped haphazardly over the back of the chair. Berating her partner's untidiness, she had picked that up too and marched through into the living room to take issue on the matter. There had been no sign of Daniela but one of her skirts had been lying on the floor. Adding this item to her burden, Sarah had taken the stairs to return the clothes to the bedroom. Then she had burst into laughter. Daniela had draped her bra over the stairs. Sarah had found Daniela's knickers adorning the bedroom door handle and she had marched in to find Daniela lying naked on the bed, looking triumphant and with a rose clamped between her teeth. Life with Daniela was always exciting.

"Is there any more coffee in that pot?"

Sarah jumped at the sudden voice. She had been so lost in daydreams that she hadn't noticed Nicole entering the kitchen. "Nicky! You startled me." She looked at her friend fondly. Nicole was wearing a bathrobe and her hair was damp. "Sure there's coffee. Help yourself. But do I get a morning kiss first?" Bashfully Nicole stepped forward to peck Sarah on the cheek. Sarah's revelry had put her in a languidly sensual mood however and

Nicole's token kiss was inadequate. She pulled Nicole to her firmly and kissed her full on the mouth letting the embrace linger. Nicole squirmed for the briefest moment but then she melted with the tiniest of sobs. Her bathrobe was dangerously loose over her breasts and Sarah could feel the heat of her body through her silk dressing gown. Abruptly Sarah broke the embrace with a laugh and ruffled Nicole's hair. "Why have you come downstairs with your hair still wet?"

"I...I didn't have a hair dryer."

"There was one on the dressing table in your room you muppet."

Nicole looked haunted. "Oh! I...I never saw it."

Sarah turned away to hide her smile. Of course Nicole would have overlooked the convenience provided. "Well grab yourself a cup of coffee Nicky and then you'd better go dry your hair before breakfast."

Nicole was staring at her in confusion. "Why did you do that?"

"Do what?"

"You know bloody well what! Why did you kiss me like that? I thought you were going to drag me down on the kitchen floor."

Sarah grinned and slipped a hand around her waist. "Well Charlie already suspects that I have evil designs on her girlfriend so I might as well be hung for a sheep as a lamb."

"You're teasing me."

"Maybe." Sarah winked at her. "Maybe I'm thinking that you and I will get pretty lonely during the long winter months whilst our girlfriends are away on tour."

Nicole swallowed. "What makes you think that Charlie's my girlfriend all of a sudden?"

Sarah grinned mischievously. "Well I don't really know Nicky. Perhaps it's something to do with the fact that you've come down to breakfast undressed and with your hair wet after I left not only a hair dryer in full view on your dressing table but also a change of clothes for you on the end of your bed. I left a nightgown out for you as well. I don't suppose you saw that either."

"All right I shared a room with Charlie. That doesn't say anything happened."

"No? Did one of the cats give you that love bite on the side of your neck then?"

Hastily Nicole pulled the collar of her bathrobe up. "Oh shit!"

"Relax Nicky. Just loving friends here. Where is Charlie anyway?"

"Under the shower."

"Well grab some coffee and then go and put a rocket under her arse. It's nearly ten o'clock and I'm waiting to get breakfast on. I'm famished. I don't know why. After all I ate in that restaurant last night, I thought I wouldn't need to eat for the rest of the week!"

"That's Chinese food for you." Nicole poured herself coffee and nodded at the cookbook on the kitchen table. "Is that a Chinese cook book?"

"Yes. I'm going to try to cook chicken in black bean sauce for Danny this evening. I've been running through an inventory of the ingredients."

"When's Danny due home?"

Sarah glanced at the clock. "She should be just about boarding the plane by now. I think the flight from Berlin takes about an hour and a quarter, then call it maybe two hours, two and a half hours to pick up her baggage and drive home. She should be back early this afternoon."

Nicole cradled her coffee and took a seat at the kitchen table. "Is she chartering a private jet then?"

"Yes. The charter company does her a special rate as a regular customer. I should think the plane will be a bit bigger than the one we took to Helgoland though. The rest of the band is flying with her." Sarah and

Daniela had flown on a tiny business jet accommodating a maximum of four passengers when they had taken off on holiday.

"What about all the gear?"

"Oh that'll be travelling by road in the wagons with the road crew Nicky. It's a long haul. Danny says that it's a twelve to fourteen hour trip in the wagons from Berlin."

"Poor bastards. The road crew I mean. The band flies home in style but the poor bloody roadies have to spend all bloody day humping gear and driving home."

"They're well paid Nicky. Danny looks after her road crew like family. She says that good roadies are worth their weight in gold and, however big a star you think you are, you're buggered without a good road crew behind you, so she pampers them something rotten."

Nicole nodded. "What's for breakfast anyway?"

"Eggs. We have over production problems. We can't consume the sodding things as fast as the chickens lay them."

"Suits me."

"How do you want them; fried, scrambled, boiled, poached?"

"Soft boiled sounds fine to me."

Sarah looked up as Charmaine entered the kitchen. "Hi everybody. Hmm I can smell coffee."

"Fresh brewed Charlie." Sarah told her, "Grab a mug from the cupboard by the sink."

"Thanks." Charmaine paused to bend and kiss Nicole. Nicole blushed but, to Sarah's satisfaction, accepted the kiss.

"I see you managed to get dressed Charlie." Sarah observed. "Which is more than Nicky and I have managed!"

"Where are my clothes anyway Sarah?" asked Nicole, "I mean the clothes I came in on Saturday."

"I put them in the wash Nicky. I put you out a clean

146

dress and knickers last night. You'll have to skip the bra I'm afraid though. I don't have one in your size."

Nicole frowned and looked out of the window. "Doesn't look like the kind of weather for a dress Sarah."

"What's the problem? You won't be going anywhere until this afternoon will you and, in any case, you only have to drive home. Anyway it looks like it's clearing up a little."

How did Simon and Peter get home last night anyway?" asked Charmaine.

Sarah raised an eyebrow, surprised at the question. "Well I suppose they drove home."

Charmaine shook her head. "Can't have done. I took a look out front when I came down. Simon's Porsche is still in the front drive."

"They must have walked down the hill." Nicole remarked. "Simon did tuck away a fair bit of the contents of your brandy bottle last night Sarah."

"They wouldn't be likely to get stopped at that time of night on a back road in the Toggenburg Nicky." Sarah pointed out.

"No but that little road down to Eggenwaldi is no place to be driving in the dark in a powerful car when you've half a bottle of brandy under your belt."

Sarah shrugged. "Well he's got a long walk up the hill to pick his car up today then. The chairlift is only running on the weekends for the moment."

"Maybe Pete will run him up in his clapped out old Land Rover." Nicole suggested.

"Yes possibly." Sarah stood up decisively. "Anyway I'm hungry. Let's get some breakfast on. Are boiled eggs ok for you Charlie?"

"Anything. I could eat a horse this morning."

Before Sarah could begin preparations for breakfast however a burst of music announced an incoming call on her mobile. Sarah frowned in puzzlement. "Oh that might be Danny. Strange. I thought she'd be on the plane by now." She picked up the phone but it wasn't Daniela's number. She didn't recognise the number on the screen. Curious, she pressed the answer button. "Hello?"

"Hello is that Sarah?"

"Yes, speaking."

"Hi Sarah! Maria here."

Sarah was pleasantly surprised. Maria was her brother John's girlfriend; no, more than that now, she corrected herself, his *fiancée*. Maria was a lovely girl. Sarah liked her a lot. "Maria! How lovely to hear from you. How are you?"

"I'm fine Sarah. And you?"

"Oh I'm fine too Maria. Hey, I haven't congratulated you personally yet. Have you set a date yet?"

"Yes Sarah. We're getting married the first week of April."

"Wow! That's fantastic. Hey, we're going to be sisters in law."

Maria laughed. "That's right. Don't think of it as losing a brother but as gaining a sister."

"I'm really pleased for you Maria. It's about time that somebody took a firm hand on that big oaf of a brother of mine."

"I'll soon kick him into shape Sarah. Listen I don't have much time right now Sarah but I wanted to ask if you were doing anything special this week."

Sarah frowned. "Well I hadn't planned anything particularly Maria. Why?"

"Well John's going to be away on a job in Austria for the next couple of days and I was wondering if you'd like to come through to Appenzell and meet up. I wanted to speak to you."

Sarah's brow furrowed thoughtfully. "About anything in particular Maria?"

"Well yes Sarah. John and I have had a bit of a talk. John's a bit upset about what's happened between you and your family and how it affects our wedding and all that. We're both a bit upset actually and I wanted to talk to you about it. I thought with John being away it would be an ideal opportunity for you and I to get together and have a talk. After all we're going to be sisters in law and I don't want whatever's happened between you and your parents to cast a cloud over that. I thought we could meet up in Appenzell and maybe drive up and have lunch in that little restaurant at Wasserauen."

It sounded like a pleasant idea to Sarah. Wasserauen was a beautiful spot up a valley from Appenzell on the side of a small stream where the little local railway line ended. Beyond Wasserauen was nothing other than the bulk of the great Säntis massif that separated the tiny isolated Canton of Appenzell from the Toggenburg. "Er what day were you thinking of Maria?"

"I thought perhaps Wednesday if that was convenient Sarah."

"Well it sounds fine Maria but could I get back to you to confirm."

"Oh might there be a problem with Wednesday?"

Sarah swallowed. "Er not as such Maria. It's just that my... my girlfriend has been away on business these last few days and she's coming home today. I don't know if she has any plans or not."

"That's ok Sarah. I understand. You can call me back if it's inconvenient. Or, if you like, you're very welcome to bring your girlfriend along as well. I'd love to meet her."

Sarah bit her lip. "I don't know. I...I'd have to ask her. She might not be able to. She's very busy at the moment."

"Well if she's busy then she can spare you for the day. I'd love to meet up with you in any case."

"Well I'll try Maria. I'd like to see you."

"In that case give me a call on this number as soon as you know more. I have to dash now. Hopefully we'll see each other on Wednesday."

"Yes. Hopefully."

"Ok. Until then, Bye bye."

"Goodbye Maria." Sarah signed off and committed the number to the memory on her phone.

"Who was that Sarah?" asked Nicole.

"Maria, my brother's fiancée. She wants to meet me this week." Sarah ran a hand through her hair agitatedly. "Now what the hell's all that about?"

Chapter Ten

Daniela finally came home at a little before two o'clock in the afternoon. Before her car had even fully stopped in the driveway, Sarah was flying out of the front door to greet her. Daniela leapt from the hired limousine and rushed to meet her. The chauffeur shuffled his feet uncomfortably in the background as the two girls embraced, nearly dancing each other around the front drive in their joy at being reunited. Sarah dashed tears from her eyes as she smothered Daniela's face in kisses. "Look at me!" she laughed in exasperation, "It's only been a few days and here I am crying like a baby. It's pathetic isn't it?"

Daniela gripped her fiercely. "God Sarah! I've missed you. These last few days have been torment."

Sarah held her at arm's length to look at her. As always, the beauty of Daniela made her catch her breath. Sarah had always felt that if there was a God then he must have been feeling in a particularly benevolent mood the day he created Daniela. From the luxurious mane of golden hair, through her exquisitely fined boned face with its enormous and captivating deep blue eyes; her long elegant neck and beautifully proportioned figure Daniela was almost perfection to Sarah's love struck eyes. To her it seemed as if no detail had been overlooked in the creation of this masterpiece. The skin was clear, smooth and unblemished, the breasts firm and perfect, the legs long and slender; even the hands were elegant and expressive. The smile that lit up that maddeningly lovely face glowed with happiness and almost child-like wonder. It always amazed Sarah to see that expression in Daniela's face. She knew that her own face must be a picture of wonder; wonder that such a beautiful and extraordinary woman belonged to her. To see that wonder reciprocated in Daniela's eyes was astonishing. To love was one thing. To know that that heart rending love was returned in equal measure made you feel giddy with delirium.

At last Daniela kissed her again and grinned. "Come on darling. The driver will think he's going to be here all day. Give me a hand with my luggage." On the face of it, Daniela's luggage would appear to have been somewhat extravagant considering that she had only been away a little over a week. Sarah knew however that Daniela needed a large wardrobe on tour. She'd sometimes change costumes as many as three times during a concert and there'd be assorted other public appearances; photo shoots, television interviews; even turning up at a concert hall she'd need something other than the outfits she would be performing in. On tour Daniela was always under pressure to appear her best before her public. She'd easily have to change her dress as many as six times in a single day and be constantly aware of her coiffure and cosmetics. If you exposed yourself to the public eye you had a duty almost to please that eye. It was something that never left Daniela; this awareness of her public appearance. Even hiking in the mountains with Sarah she contrived to look stunning at all times. It had become second nature to her and if the pressure of public expectation occasionally wearied her then you would scarcely have noticed for she carried it off with easy grace and charm. It did, however, mean a lot of luggage.

Sarah had been astonished when she had first encountered Daniela's wardrobe. Most girls would have managed to find room for their clothes in the bedroom closets. Daniela's wardrobe took up two entire rooms in the house. Daniela had been sheepishly apologetic over her extensive collection almost as if she imagined that Sarah would find her hopelessly vain and conceited to require so many clothes. Sarah herself could have comfortably fitted her own wardrobe into that space allocated to Daniela's collection of shoes. But, in a very real sense, Daniela's clothes were her working clothes. She had a public image to maintain. It required hard work and dedication to uphold and Daniela was conscientious about it, perfecting her appearance with the same attention to detail as she lavished on her song writing and music. She was a consummate performer and she was acutely aware that her appearance was a part of her performance. Early in their relationship Sarah had been astounded to learn that Daniela's physical appearance was insured for millions. Daniela had considered that to be simple prudence. It wasn't vanity as such; just a responsible protection of her assets.

They manhandled Daniela's luggage up the drive. In addition to her cases of clothes she had several shopping bags and a couple of guitars. It seemed as if Daniela was bringing her work home. Daniela regarded the collection of cars in the driveway in amusement. Her Ferrari was taking up the available garage space whilst Sarah's BMW was nestled alongside Nicole's little Renault and Simon's Porsche. "Blimey!" she remarked. "While the cat's away.... Have you been throwing wild parties while I've been in Germany?"

"There's only Nicky and Charlie here. Simon and Pete stopped for a nightcap last night and it looks like Simon decided he'd drunk too much because he's left his car here."

"Nicky's still here then. Good. I need to talk to her."

"Oh? What about? Is there a problem?"

"Well there could be. Let's go say hello." Daniela hugged Nicole and Charmaine fondly before collapsing heavily on a sofa in the living room. "I am knackered!" she declared feelingly. "Thank God I'm home. Sarah sweetheart do we have any beer in the house?"

"Of course we do."

"Then be a darling and grab me a bottle honey."

153

"Sure. Anyone else want a beer?" There was universal assent and Sarah went to the fridge to fetch them. Returning, she handed out the beers and then nestled down next to Daniela on the sofa. Daniela cuddled close and took her hand.

"So how were the concerts Danny?" asked Charmaine in interest.

"Brilliant; especially Berlin. We got three encores. I thought they were never going to let us go."

"We saw your television interview."

Daniela pulled a face. "Oh I owe you an apology there Charlie. I didn't really want to announce that you were joining the band so publicly like that but the media had got hold of the story that Leo was leaving the band and they had me over a barrel a bit. God knows there's been enough drama with the band members and the last thing I needed was a load of speculation about personal rifts, and what have you, so I decided the best thing was to come out openly and say what was happening."

Charmaine grinned. "Hey! I didn't mind. I was made up in fact. Even my mum and dad phoned up to congratulate me. That's a big deal."

Sarah frowned. "Why Charlie? I mean why wouldn't they be pleased for you?"

Charmaine shrugged. "Well you know how it is with my folks Sarah. We went through a tough time when I came out as being gay and they've never really come to terms with it. I thought that when Danny said that I was gay on television they'd freak out but all they wanted to talk about was that I was Danny's new bassist. My mum was thrilled and dad was trying to sell me a new bank account." Charmaine's father was a bank manager. He had long lamented his daughter's financial insolvency and he considered her musical career to be completely at odds with what he envisaged as a stable respectable income. Doubtless he was most pleasantly surprised that she now had a possible source of wealth.

Daniela smiled. "I'm pleased Charlie. Look we're going to have to have a long talk. We need to be doing a good deal of work over the next few weeks. We've got a lot of important engagements coming up and we've quite a bit of new material as well so the whole band has to get together and practice. Our practice studio is in Zurich. Is that going to be a problem?"

"Hell no. It's only a few minutes on the train."

"Well some of our practice sessions can go on well into the night but I'll probably be able to drop you off on the way home."

"Does this mean you're going to be away a lot?" asked Sarah with a frown.

Daniela gripped her hand. "It'll be only during the day for the most part honey. I'll be home every night and we won't be practising every day. You can come up to Zurich with us if you want. Maybe we can press you into service as a backing vocalist."

Sarah raised an eyebrow. "I hardly think so."

Daniela laughed. "I don't see why not. You've got a lovely voice." She paused to nod at her luggage still residing in a large pile in the corner. "Oh yes Charlie I have something for you. Nicky could you pass over that guitar case; the black one?" Nicole picked up the case, surprised at the heaviness of it. "Could you pass it to Charlie please?"

Charmaine took the case in puzzlement. "What's this then Danny?"

"I thought you needed a new instrument Charlie. I think you'll find it matches your style of playing but if you can't get on with it we can always change."

With her mouth open Charmaine opened the guitar case. "*Oh my God*!" Disbelievingly she pulled the guitar from the case and stared at it looking stunned. The guitar had an elegantly shaped body of maple wood in black with a long maple neck and rosewood fret board. It looked stylish and professional; even a little sexy.

155

Charmaine was having trouble speaking. "I don't believe it!" she croaked at last.

"I hope you like it Charlie." Daniela told her. "You'll get a lot more punch up on your treble notes and a nice beefy sustain on the bass range. You've got a through neck design and struss rods in the neck which help to give you that attack and sustain. There're a couple of things you'll have to get used to. For one thing the volume and tone controls are in the reverse position to most guitars so you've got the tone knobs at the top and volume below. That's a bit awkward to begin with if you're used to the standard layout. Also the fret board is lacquered as opposed to the matt finish most guitars have. It makes it a bit slippier than maybe you're used to although I don't think it's as big an issue on a bass guitar as it would be on a normal guitar. Your other difficulty might be the resonating bar over your bridge pick-up. That can get in the way if you want to play slap on it. Of course you can remove the bar but you might lose a bit of your sustain if you do that."

Charmaine was stroking the guitar like a lover and crooning softly. "It's.... it's wonderful!" she breathed.

Nicole was watching Charmaine's new infatuation with amusement. "Is it a good guitar then Charlie?" she asked.

"Good!" she choked. She seemed lost for words. "It's... it's a fucking Jetglo Rickenbacker 4003! This is like the fucking guitar I've waited all my life to own."

Daniela laughed. "Well she's all yours now Charlie. With all due respect I think you'll get more out of her than you can with your old beat up Yamaha."

"Can I plug her in Danny? I want to try her out."

Daniela grinned. "Later Charlie. We'll go out back and you can play with her to your heart's content." Daniela had the hayloft in the old barn converted into a little studio.

Whilst Charlie caressed her new love fondly Sarah

leaned across to whisper in Daniela's ear. "Have you brought *me* a present back from Germany then?"

Daniela grinned and kissed her. "Oh yes! I've brought you a couple. You might want to wait until we don't have guests around before I show you them however." Sarah giggled happily.

Daniela sat upright and became more serious. "Oh yes Nicky I have something to show you."

"What me?" Nicole looked surprised.

"Yes and I'm afraid it's maybe not something good. I feel bad about this Nicky because I'm at least partially responsible."

"What the hell is it?"

In response Daniela reached into a plastic shopping bag. "You'd better take a look at this Nicky." She tossed a magazine over the coffee table to Nicole.

Nicole picked up the magazine in puzzlement. "What's this?"

"It's called L-Mag. It's a glossy publication for lesbians published in Berlin and distributed in Germany, Austria and Switzerland Nicky. You might want to check out page twenty four."

Nicole opened the magazine and gasped in horror. The magazine had run an article on the photographic work of Rozella Fangio; a talented gay photographer from Switzerland. The article included a brief biography and included the information that Rozella was the official photographer for the publicity stills and album covers of the well-known gay performing artist Daniela Devin and, in case anyone had missed the point, there was a reproduction of Daniela's last album cover to prove the point. Accompanying the article was a several page spread of Rozella's latest work. It was a collection of nude portraits of beautiful girls set in Switzerland entitled "Sapphic Switzerland; the gay girls of the Helvetian Republic".

The portraits were artistically stunning; clearly the

work of a truly talented photographer; erotic without being pornographic and set against a magnificent backdrop of clearly recognisable Swiss landscapes. Some of them had evidently been taken early in the morning when the locations had been relatively free of the general public such as the eye catching photo of the dark haired beauty dabbling in Lake Geneva with the famous landmark of Geneva's great water spout in the background or the red haired little vixen posing alongside the statue of Wilhelm Tell in Altdorf. There was a gorgeous picture of a naked brunette with a Swiss flag draped across her shoulders resting on a rock with the iconic bulk of the Matterhorn behind her and another of a smiling girl with flowers in her hair carrying a milk urn surrounded by Swiss Brown cows. The pride of the collection however was a picture of a truly lovely little blond girl, wearing a chain of daisies around her neck and a smile, posing among the meadow flowers with the Toggenburg's Churfirsten mountains receding into the distance behind her. It was Nicole!

Nicole dropped the magazine back on the coffee table in shock. "Oh my God!" she yipped in alarm.

Daniela held up her hands. "I'm sorry Nicky. I had no idea that Rosy was going to do something like this with the photos she took of you."

"The fucking bitch!" Nicole fumed. "The sodding, fucking bitch!"

Charmaine picked up the magazine in interest. "Hey! You look *gorgeous* Nicky. Can I have this?"

"I'll sue the bitch! I fucking swear I will!"

Daniela grimaced. "I'm not sure you can Nicky. After all you did sign a release form for the photos."

"I didn't sign a fucking form for her to tell the whole of fucking Europe that I was *gay.*" Nicole declared feelingly.

Daniela wrung her hands together. "I'm sorry Nicky. I can see that you're upset but let's calm down for a minute. She hasn't revealed your name on the photo."

"A fat lot of fucking good that is. The whole world can see that it's me on that photo."

"Relax Nicky." said Daniela soothingly. "That magazine is only likely to be seen by gay women. It has a pretty limited distribution. It's not the kind of publication you're going to find on the shelves down your local newsagents."

"I think it's brilliant." declared Charmaine enthusiastically. "I think you look great Nicky."

"Can I see it?" asked Sarah eagerly. Charmaine passed the magazine over. Sarah examined it closely. "You look lovely Nicky."

"Oh for fuck's sake!"

"No you do." Sarah insisted. "It's the best photo I've ever seen of you." Sarah meant it too. She knew that Rozella was a talented photographer but the picture of Nicole was quite frankly astonishing in its virtuosity. It wasn't just the beautiful setting or technical perfection but there was a real artist's eye to it. Rozella had captured the impish mischievousness combined with just the right amount of self-consciousness remarkably. Nicole looked utterly priceless in the picture; a girl teased into being just a little bit naughty and yet so natural among the splendour of the beauty around her. Rozella had displayed not only the loveliness of Nicole's naked body but somehow she had caught the essence of her spirit too. It was a photograph to fall in love with. Sarah swore to herself that she would possess a copy of this picture.

Daniela was inclined to agree. "I must say Nicky you do look stunning in that photo."

"You're all barking mad!" raged Nicole. "What happens when my mum and dad see that picture?"

Daniela waved her hands palm downwards in a gesture of calming. "I don't think your parents are *going* to see it Nicky unless they subscribe to lesbian magazines. I think it will be pretty limited in its audience. If anybody does see it then they're obviously the sort of person who reads that kind of magazine and hardly in a position to cast stones. Did Rozella pay you for the shoot Nicky?"

"Well yes... I mean she paid me for the day's modelling and I signed a contract giving me a percentage if the pictures were published."

"Well then you probably have some money coming to you. I don't suppose it will be that much given the limited market and I think Rozella should have consulted you before selling the pictures to L-Mag. I picked up the magazine in Berlin and I phoned Rozella straight away to ask what the devil she thought she was playing at. In her defence, she was horrified when I told her that you would not be the kind of person that would wish to be publicly announced as gay. For all Rozella's faults she is generally a very discreet person. She was mortified and very apologetic. She had assumed that you were outwardly gay and would have no problem with it. She was devastated when I disabused her of the notion. She thought you were out."

Nicole was striding the carpet with her head in her hands. "But I'm not."

Charmaine grabbed her suddenly and dragged her down onto the armchair beside her with a grin. "Well you are *now* Schatz. I think it's brilliant. What a way to come out. I'm proud of you."

"Oh God!" groaned Nicole comically.

Daniela sucked air in between her teeth. "It gets worse Nicky." she told her.

"Oh God! Please no."

"I'm sorry Nicky. I really am but there's another reason why Rozella was so upset when I called her."

"Don't tell me. The bitch wants to make me the new face of lesbian Switzerland."

Daniela winced. "Well actually you might not be far

160

off. Apparently her agents have seen the photos and they're impressed. She says that they're falling over backwards and flashing money in her face to sign you up for more work. She reckons there could be some real money in this for the pair of you Nicky. When I told her that you were probably going to tell her to shove it up her arse she was destroyed. Rozella likes money almost as much as she likes pretty girls."

"She's taking the piss."

Daniela sighed. "Well I can imagine your feelings Nicky. I'll tell her that that's a no shall I?"

Charmaine grasped Nicole around the waist. "But why Nicky? You're just gorgeous on camera. Think about it. How many gay girls are there that are photo models? You could be cutting edge; a whole new look. You could be the glamorous, sexy lesbian of modelling. In one swoop you can strike a blow for the gay woman; show the world that a woman can be gay, out, beautiful and sexy. Think what that will mean to all those poor young girls out there terrified that their best friend is going to find out that they're in love with them."

Nicole looked desperate with Charmaine's arm around her. "I'm not bloody glamorous."

Charmaine nuzzled her fondly. Nicole looked as if she wanted the ground to open up and swallow her. "*I* think you're glamorous." Charmaine assured her.

Daniela smiled. "Actually Nicky I think I agree with Charlie here. I've always thought you were a pretty girl but having seen these photos I have to say that you are quite stunning on film. You're a natural in front of the camera. I'm not at all surprised that Rozella's agents are champing at the bit wanting to sign you up. I see many lovely young women in my line of business with aspirations to be models but I've rarely seen a girl that projects such a natural, girl next door charm as you. Rozella was positively drooling over you. There's only one other girl apart from myself she would love to have

161

as a regular model as much as you."

Nicole frowned. "Who's that then?"

Daniela grinned and squeezed Sarah. "She's sat next to me."

Sarah started violently. "Hey! Leave me out of this."

Charmaine slapped her leg gleefully. "Wow! Now there's a portfolio. The three best looking lesbians in Switzerland."

Nicole squirmed uncomfortably. "But..." she hesitated. "I mean I'm... I... I'm not..." she tailed off helplessly.

Daniela raised an eyebrow. "Not what Nicky....*gay*?" Nicole blushed and lowered her head.

Sarah looked equally uncomfortable. She rose hurriedly. "Well this is getting out of hand. Nicky being a photo model is one thing but Rozella thinking she can lure me in front of a camera lens is another. Listen Danny are you hungry? I was going to cook for us this evening but if you like I can fix you something quick right now."

Daniela shook her head. "I ate on the plane honey. I'll wait for this evening. What about you and Charlie though Nicky? Have you eaten?"

Charlie answered. "I'm fine Danny. We had a late breakfast. Nicky's going to drive me home this evening. I was going to rustle up a couple of steaks for us when we got back to my place."

Daniela smiled warmly. "That sounds nice. I do hope that you're in no rush to get home after you've dropped Charlie off Nicky." Nicole blushed but kept her peace. "Well if it's all right with you Charlie," Daniela continued, "I need to have a talk with you about our practice schedules and the new tours before you go." She turned to Sarah. "Is it all right if I have a chat with Charlie sweetheart? I don't want to seem to be neglecting you as soon as I'm home but we do have a lot of business to cover."

Sarah shook her head. "Of course it's ok Danny. I have to pop over to the Toggenburg to see Elke in any case." Sarah turned to address Nicole. "Fancy coming out as well Nicky...er I'll rephrase that... do you want to come along as well? If Danny and Charlie are going to be talking shop we might as well leave them to it for an hour or so."

Nicole swallowed. "Ok. Suits me. Maybe I can go drown myself in the Schwendisee on the way over."

"Good. The weather's cleared a bit so we can walk over. I could do with some fresh air."

Chapter Eleven

Nicole was still grumbling as they walked down the road towards Schwendi where their mutual friend Elke ran the Hotel Toggenburg. "I just don't bloody believe this." she remarked sourly although by now her protestations of disbelief were beginning to sound repetitive. "How the fuck have I ended up being more out than *you* are?"

Sarah squeezed Nicole's hand. She'd taken her hand as they had left the house and she held on to it as they walked. Nicole had been surprised and a little uncomfortable to begin with. Sarah had never held her hand before. But Sarah's habits had changed since Daniela had come into her life. Daniela loved to hold Sarah's hand when they strolled about out of doors. Even in the days before they had become lovers, from their first ever meeting in fact, Daniela had naturally taken Sarah's hand as they walked. From being a little embarrassed about it to begin with, Sarah had come to love the small intimacy. It wasn't a sensual pleasure but more a physical connection of togetherness; a sort of sisterly solidarity and gently private communication. She had got so used to the contact of Daniela's hand on the quiet back roads of the Toggenburg that it now seemed the most natural thing in the world to take hold of Nicole's hand. Nicole had started with surprise but she had relaxed after a while and was even beginning to enjoy it.

"Well Charlie seemed pleased by your...er public exposure Nicky." Sarah observed, a tad impishly.

Nicole grimaced. "Oh God Sarah! I suppose you're waiting for an explanation of what happened last night."

"Nicky sweetheart. You don't owe me any explanations about what happened between you and

164

Charlie." Sarah gave her hand another squeeze. "On the other hand you *do* owe me an explanation regarding your little photo shoot with Rozella Fangio. I think you've been a little less than candid about the details of that particular episode. I thought that you'd just taken a few perfectly respectable fully dressed portraits and what have you. You didn't mention that you'd been flaunting up the back of Thurwis in front of Rozella's camera without a stitch of clothing on. Personally I thought Charlie took it rather well. If you'd been *my* girlfriend I'd have been asking some pointed questions about what the hell you were playing at, cavorting around in your birthday suit, on a quiet alpine meadow, with one of the most notorious skirt chasers in Switzerland."

"Leave it off Sarah. Don't even go there all right."

"Ok... your problem I suppose."

"Then stop giving me disapproving sniffs."

"I'm not Nicky. Really I'm not. I wasn't being judgemental actually. I just wanted to know why you couldn't confide in me. We've been best friends ever since we were kids. We've always told each other everything."

"Er not always Sarah. You were pretty cagey with me when you first started seeing Danny."

"I didn't tell you any lies."

"You didn't tell me the whole truth either."

"To be honest I didn't really *know* the whole truth Nicky. I was as confused about it as you were."

"Well then you should be able to sympathise with how I feel. I'm not exactly crystal clear about what's going on with me as well at the moment Sarah."

Sarah paused to brush Nicole's face with her lips. "I know Nicky. I'm not trying to push you or anything. I just want you to know that if there's anybody you can talk to about it it's me."

"So why did you sound so pissed off because I was posing nude for Rozella?"

"Hell Nicky! I couldn't give a damn about what happened with you and Rosy. If your photo shoot went beyond the call of purely professional requirements I can understand that. Rosy's an act of God. She's a very sexy girl and very difficult to say no to. Damn it Nicky she's seen me without any clothes on as well and if I hadn't happened to be the girlfriend of her most important client I wouldn't have stood a chance. I don't think I'd have wanted one anyway. If I'd have been as single and free as you I wouldn't have put up more than token resistance."

"How the hell as she seen *you* without your clothes on?"

"I first met her on the beach by the river at Intragna when I was down in Ticino for my ill-fated engagement party. I wasn't wearing anything more than you were in those photos." For all her protestations of veracity Sarah was being a little economical with the truth. In fact she'd been wearing her bikini at the time but she had played a dangerous stalking game around the secluded beach with Rozella. Eventually she'd teased her quarry by leaving her bikini on a rock and changing into a flimsy sarong. Rozella had stolen her bikini and refused to give it back until Sarah shed her wrap to re-don her bikini. It had been delicious fun although it had ended innocently enough. Daniela had laughed richly when Sarah had contritely confessed to her misdemeanour and then pulled her over her knee to spank her; a deeply gratifying consequence culminating in mutual satisfaction.

Nicole looked thoughtful for a second. "So nothing happened then?"

Sarah shook her head. "No, nothing."

"You can tell me you know. I won't tell Danny."

"Nicky seriously, nothing happened. If anything had have done, Danny would know, believe me. I'm not the best liar at the best of times but to Danny I can't lie worth a damn. She'd know I was telling a porky as soon as I opened my mouth."

A small smile crossed Nicole's face. "Well you missed a treat then."

Sarah stopped in the middle of the road and stared at Nicole. "*What*?"

Nicole shuffled her feet guiltily. "I said you missed a treat because you can take it from me that Rosy's forgotten more about the art of sex than most people ever knew in their life."

"Nicole Richardson! So you *did* get up to hanky panky with Rozella."

"Hell Sarah I wanted to know what it was like. I mooned over you all those years sure but it never really hit home to me that the consequence of that was actually having sex with a girl. It wasn't until you got together with Danny that I started really thinking about it. Then I couldn't think of anything else. Shit I started walking down the street looking at other girls and wondering what it would be like to.... well you know... with them."

Sarah laughed. "Oh God yes! I know *that* feeling."

"Well I didn't know what it would be like. I mean I must have slept with half the boys in the bloody valley but all of a sudden I felt like a virgin again. I started going to bed and dreaming about it. It was more than just curiosity. I was obsessed by it."

Sarah laughed shortly. "Oh Christ! Rosy would have picked that up in a second. You were a sitting duck."

"I'm not complaining Sarah. It was by far and away the best sex I've ever had in my life. I was like a limp dish rag by the time Rosy had finished with me. I told her to just leave me there in that meadow for the crows to pick over and let my family know so they could come along and put up a little cross to remember me by."

Sarah frowned. "Just a minute Nicky. Last night in the bar you were asking me what it was that two girls do together. It sounds as if you weren't quite as inexperienced as you were making out to be."

Nicole shook her head vigorously. "No Sarah. I wanted to know. I mean I didn't exactly take much of a participant role with Rozella. She just hit me like a force of nature. One minute I'm sat there with no clothes on feeling a bit randy and exhibitionist if you know what I mean and the next minute I'm on my back in the grass vaguely wondering how much the aftershocks are registering on the Richter scale. I don't know how much Rosy got out of it though. I mean I must have been pretty crap. It was the first time I ever went with a girl. I hadn't a clue about what to do."

Sarah leaned against a fence post whilst she controlled her laughter. "Oh God! This is priceless. What did Rosy say?"

"She just picks up her camera again and says, "Now you are ready." and starts photographing me again."

Sarah's eyes grew wide in astonishment. "Oh God! Don't tell me that that photo in the magazine was after..."

Nicole nodded wryly. "Oh yes. Rosy's got some interesting theories about the best way to prepare her models for a photo shoot Sarah."

"Christ! What about all those other girls in that spread?"

"Take a look at them Sarah. Take a *good* look. They're all glowing and flushed with dumb ass grins on their faces. You've only had to be on the end of one of Rosy's preparatory inductions personally to be able to recognise that look in an instance."

"Oh my God! Then that photo spread was to all intents and purposes a photographic record of Rozella's conquests."

"More or less. I suppose it's slightly more artistic than carving a notch in the bed post."

"Oh hell! No wonder you nearly passed out when

Danny handed you that magazine."

"Yes and you'll also understand why I jumped like a gaffed salmon when Danny mentioned that Rosy was keen for me to participate in some future modelling work."

"Oh God!"

"Quite. And while we're on the subject I wouldn't enquire too deeply into Danny's professional relationship with Signorina Fangio if you don't want to hear any uncomfortable truths."

"Oh God!" Sarah looked shocked at the thought. Then she shook her head. "No! I don't believe it. Their relationship is purely business only. Rozella told me so herself."

"Well she'd be bound to say that wouldn't she Sarah?"

Sarah paused in concentration. "Yes... yes I suppose she would. Certainly Danny's under no illusions about what Rozella's like."

"Well there you go. You're not jealous are you?"

Sarah ran a hand through her hair distractedly. "I don't know. I suppose I shouldn't be because Rozella took the photos for her new album last spring before I even knew Danny. In any case I'm hardly in a position to berate Danny for her behaviour when I spent an afternoon flirting with Rosy myself. Bloody hell! Rosy's a sodding menace isn't she?"

"She's a phenomena Sarah. If she ever decides to publish her memoirs there'll be carnage."

"And you Nicky? I mean what are you going to say if she wafts a modelling contract under your nose?"

"Hell I don't know. To be honest I really got off on that photo shoot. I suppose there's a bit of an exhibitionist streak in me. Of course I didn't know the bitch was going to publish it in a fucking gay magazine. Still I might have thought about it but..."

"But what?"

"Well it's a bit more complicated now isn't it?"

"You mean Charlie?"

"Yeah...I suppose I do."

"You told me yesterday that there was nothing happening between you."

"That was yesterday."

"Ah so I assume that relations have moved on to a more intimate footing since then."

"Oh like and you didn't know they would? You must think I'm simple, Sarah Fuchs, if you think I don't know why you put us in adjoining bedrooms. You knew bloody well we'd end up in the same bed."

Sarah giggled. "I didn't force you Nicky. I left you a perfectly acceptable escape clause."

"My arse! You engineered the whole bloody thing."

"So are you complaining?"

Nicole shook her head. "No I suppose not. I like Charlie and it was fun."

"More fun than Rozella?"

"Whole different ball game Sarah. Rosy's not somebody you have a lot of control over. You just lie there and whisper, "Help rape!" and hope that nobody hears you. Charlie's different. She's more sweet; more loving. You get assaulted in the nicest possible way by Rosy but Charlie... well Charlie's the sort of girl you could fall in love with."

"And are you...I mean in love with her?"

"I don't know Sarah. It's all too new for me. I'm just learning what it's like with a girl. I don't know if I'm ready for a serious relationship with one."

"I fell into a relationship with the first girl I ever slept with Nicky."

"Yes but that's you Sarah. You're not exactly the kind of girl known for sleeping around. If you were going to sleep with any girl it was going to be serious. I'm different. I've got a bit of previous when it comes to playing around."

"That was with boys Nicky." Sarah pointed out. "Yes you never had a relationship worth a damn with any of them but this is different isn't it? You never found the right boy because maybe there wasn't such a thing. But could you find the right girl?"

"I thought I'd already found her Sarah. I was in love with you. Damn it I still am."

"Oh Nicky..."

Nicole held her hands up. "Don't panic Sarah. I'm not so dumb that I think I'm going to steal you away from Danny. I'm just mentioning it. I tell you what though it was a very bad idea to kiss me this morning before breakfast. I'd spent the night finding out that I really like making love with girls and then you go and kiss me while my libido rating's off the scale. You've no idea how close your dressing gown came to being a crumpled heap on the floor. I'd cool the sisterly affection if you don't want to make life even more complicated than it is if I were you."

Sarah snorted. "And this is the girl who has been protesting that she's not gay. I must say Nicky that, for somebody ostensibly agonising over her sexuality, you're doing a damn poor job of ambiguity. First of all you go frolicking with a notorious gay predator like Rozella, then you start having a relationship with a bass guitar player, who has been publicly declared gay on television, before threatening to seduce the girlfriend of the lead singer, who is one of the continent's most famous lesbians, and, just in case there's anybody left who hasn't got the message, you contrive to get your naked portrait blazoned across one of the biggest lesbian magazines in the German language. And to think you accused *me* of not doing things by half. You're not so much as coming out of the closet as chopping up the bloody thing for firewood. I'd slow down if I was you."

"I suppose it does look bad." Nicole conceded.

"Don't make the same mistakes as you did with

men Nicky. Charlie's a nice girl. I wouldn't like to see you hurt her."

"I don't want to hurt her Sarah. I like Charlie a lot. Maybe you're right. Maybe I ought to try a relationship for a change. There's just one trouble."

"What's that?"

"Well with blokes it was a different thing Sarah. I kept moving around because they never seemed to have what I was looking for. All right Sarah...don't say it. I know what you're going to say. Well ok now maybe I have found what I'm looking for. It's true. Girls are much more exciting. And Jesus but they're beautiful. I never realised how many gorgeous girls there are in the world. I'm finding myself looking at them all the time now. God did you see those two girls snogging on that couch in the Planet last night? I couldn't take my eyes off them."

"I *had* noticed." remarked Sarah aloofly.

"Well it's just that as soon as I'm starting to discover how much I like girls it seems downright unfair to be in a relationship and find all those gorgeous creatures are off limits. They're just too exciting."

"Oh God Nicky! You're hopeless."

"I'm sorry Sarah. I mean I really like Charlie but I just don't know if I'm ready for a serious relationship. I mean this is like a whole new world to explore and I've barely started. I want to try with Charlie but I know damn well I'm going to have a hard time keeping my knickers on when she's not around."

"Look Nicky please don't mess Charlie around. She's a nice girl and I think she's fond of you."

"Ok Sarah I've got the message. I've got enough to worry about without a lecture on morality from you. What the hell am I going to do about those bloody photos?"

"I don't see what you can do. They're pretty much in the public domain now. You can't put the cat back in the bag."

"What if somebody around here gets to see them?"

"Then they'll be the kind of person that buys lesbian magazines Nicky and hardly in a position to throw stones. The worst that can happen is that some woman might come up to you in the Hirschen and ask you if you're doing anything tomorrow night. Who knows, we might flush some surprises out into the open. There's a gorgeous girl who works in the Migros in Wildhaus who's always a bit friendlier than customer service conventions require that I've wondered about. If she starts spending more time in the Hirschen on your shift then we can definitely put her down as a possible."

"Shut up Sarah! I'm serious. What if that bloody magazine comes to the notice of my parents?"

"Same scenario Nicky. I don't suppose your dad is going to be on the L-Mag subscription list although I wouldn't put it past your mum. Anyway if they do see it, by some fluke, then so be it. Your dad has had thirty years of being married to your mum so I doubt if anything can shock him anymore. He might ask you that, since you are gay, does this mean you'll start coming out to play golf with him. As for your mum she'll be chuffed to bits. You've never really done anything in your life against the conventions of society and shocked the neighbours before. You've been a terrible disappointment to her. If she finds out that you've been parading around nude in a lesbian magazine she'll clasp you to her bosom like the prodigal daughter returning to the fold. I wish *my* parents were half as tolerant as yours are likely to be."

"Oh God! I can't imagine it... telling my mum and dad that I'm gay I mean."

"You know what I've found is the hardest thing Nicky? It's not just the confessing that you're gay to other people it's the confessing of it to yourself. We still carry the stigma about it inside us. However much we know intellectually that being gay is nothing to be ashamed of, there's still that social conditioning inside us that tells us that it's wrong and some sort of dirty secret. I suppose that's why they have gay pride events because, however much we would wish it otherwise, there's still a lot of shame attached to being gay. I think that's what your problem is Nicky. I know it's my problem Nicky. I mean look at my awful behaviour last night."

"What awful behaviour? Your conduct was impeccable as far as I could see."

"Nicky honey…. I was sat in a gay bar and listening to everybody there extolling Danny's virtues as a spokeswoman and role model for the gay community and I didn't even have the guts to stand up and say that this amazing woman is my girlfriend. I'm not exactly proud of that Nicky."

"Sarah you're under no obligation to publicly declare your private life you know. That's why it's called *private.* Just because your girlfriend is a publicly visible gay woman, it doesn't follow that you have to be. If Danny had been a man you wouldn't have felt it incumbent on you to jump up and say, "Ok I'm heterosexual and that guy on the telly is my boyfriend." It would have sounded like boasting. Why should you feel bad about it just because you're gay? I mean I don't know much about it but, in an ideal world, wouldn't it be your business and nobody else's who you were sleeping with, be they man or woman. There's no moral obligation for you to shout your private life from the rooftops. Ok so maybe you shouldn't be ashamed of being gay but why should you be proud either? I mean shouldn't you be proud of things that you've done or achieved, not of things you really had no control over. So I was born blond. What of it? I'm not going to walk down the centre of Zurich on this year's blond pride parade."

"Well you have been keeping your hair shade in the

closet you know."

"If you mention my pink dye job one more time Sarah I won't speak to you again for the rest of the day."

"Ok we'll table the subject as taboo. Seriously though Nicky I think we've both got a lot to learn about being gay."

Nicole nodded seriously. "Yeah I guess so." Then she grinned impishly. "You know what though Sarah?"

"What?"

"It's going to be a fun education."

Sarah laughed. "I think you may be right. I know that my life has been ten times more exciting since Daniela came into it. I can't believe how boring and mundane it was before."

"Well you are a rock and roll singer's girlfriend."

"So are you now... well technically... Charlie's the bass player."

Nicole snorted with amusement. "God yes! This is ridiculous isn't it? How did we both end up on the official groupies list of the same rock and roll band?"

Sarah smiled at the thought. "Yes. Maybe we could go to one of their concerts together Nicky. I've never seen Danny play at a full concert... only impromptu guest appearances. You've at least been to one of her shows."

"Well we couldn't be better placed for getting free tickets could we? Maybe we could go on the road with the band. That would be fun."

"We'd be sitting ducks for the paparazzi."

"That's true. Mind you Rosy would be pleased. If she's getting interest in me now as an obscure country Swiss girl think of the mileage she could get out of me as part of the Daniela Devin's road show."

"Oh hell yes! Lesbian's on tour...the official calendar."

"We could form our own little group Sarah... the Bandwagon Dykes."

"Leave me out of this."

"Anyway we're nearly at the Hotel. What do you want to see Elke about anyway?"

"I'm returning a couple of DVDs I borrowed and I want to cadge a couple of stock cubes from the kitchen. Apart from that I want to see what Elke thinks of your photo shoot."

"You haven't brought that foul magazine with you have you?"

"Of course! Elke and Angelica will be thrilled to see it if they haven't already got their own copy that is."

"Oh my God!"

"Yes they might want to put a copy in the hotel foyer."

"I'll burn the bloody place to the ground if they do."

Chapter Twelve

It was bliss having Daniela home again. The wretched weather that had greeted her homecoming on the Monday had broken by Tuesday morning and the day had dawned into a glorious fresh early autumn day and the new snow that had fallen at high altitude during the night had crowned the tops of the mountains with a sugar frosting that glittered in the clear air and sparkling sunlight. Sarah and Daniela rose late after a night in which they had seemed to want to make up for the lost days apart. They'd made love well into the night and fallen asleep happily in each other's arms just content to be together cocooned for the moment from the world outside. They had no plans for the day other than to simply enjoy each other but the morning was so lovely and inviting that it seemed a shame to spend it indoors. They donned hiking boots, packed some warmer clothes in a rucksack, hung binoculars around their necks and stepped forth out of the house with no real notion of where they were heading. They discovered that the chair lift up to Gamsalp was still running so, impulsively, they decided to take it up and find some route to walk from there.

Gamsalp was an old favourite of Sarah's and it was one of the first places she had ever introduced Daniela to in the Toggenburg. The old Gasthaus at the top of the cable car was at an altitude of a shade under 1800 metres and it was bordered by a bewitching zone, on the edge of the upper tree line, of alpine shrub land set among limestone rocks. In the high summer it was a truly beautiful place with little patches of short grass liberally sprinkled with alpine flowers between the alpenrose bushes, reclining pines and dwarf mountain willows. Most of the flowers were finished for the season now but there was still a little touch of magic lingering in this corner of paradise. They took a drink at the Gasthaus and pondered their options. "I know." said Sarah, "Let's walk over to Voralpsee." Voralpsee was a beautiful alpine lake nestled beneath the Alvier mountain massif a couple of hours leisurely hiking over to the east. It was an easy hike as well for the lake was only 1123 metres above sea level making the walk from Gamsalp a steady descent. Overlooking the lake was a lovely little rustic hotel and restaurant for a drink at the end of the hike and there was an easy lower level hike back through the forests to Oberdorf. In the glorious sunshine it was a perfect afternoon's walk.

Daniela had even brought a small basket with her. Ever eager to tap into Sarah's encyclopaedic knowledge of natural history, she had discovered that Sarah, among her vast range of skills, was an expert mycologist. For once this skill went beyond mere appreciation of the living world for its own sake. Daniela loved to eat mushrooms and she could be greedy for them. To have a girlfriend who not only shared her passion for the culinary delights of mushrooms but could also confidently identify most species of wild mushrooms in the pastures and woodlands was a delightful bonus. Early autumn was just about the best time of the year to collect mushrooms and Daniela considered that the pleasure of any walk in the outdoors was hugely enhanced by the prospect of bringing home something delicious for tea. Daniela would never have dared to collect mushrooms on her own. She had been brought up mostly in England where people were scared to death of picking mushrooms, being under the erroneous impression that any mushroom not bought at a supermarket must be poisonous. People in Switzerland were more enlightened and mushroom collecting was a popular seasonal occupation in rural areas. Sarah had assured Daniela that the number of really dangerous mushrooms that you were likely to come across could be counted on the fingers of one hand and they were generally fairly easy to identify. They were hoping to find some Agaricus mushrooms in the pastures or woodlands and possibly even some boletes in the forest. Daniela had developed a taste for the big boletes called ceps. The smaller ones they fried, stir fried or added to omelettes and the bigger ones they turned into a delicious soup.

Best of all would be if they could find a troop of Chanterelles in the woods. These were Daniela's favourites. They could be cooked of course but Daniela just loved them raw in a salad with a little oil and lemon juice. Her eyes would light up at the sight of a group of Chanterelles under the trees. Sarah had been bemused by Daniela's new found passion for mushroom collecting. Ever since the end of August she had rarely gone out with Sarah on a walk without her little wicker basket in case they found some mushrooms and she had become adventurous, trying several different edible species.

Of course wild mushrooms were collected on a commercial scale in Switzerland and Daniela could just as easily have gone to a delicatessen to buy her mushrooms and she was certainly rich enough to afford the rather high prices the most sought after species commanded. But the act of finding and gathering her own food amidst the abundance of nature appealed to her on a very fundamental level. Sarah told her that she was reverting to her hunter-gatherer past but she empathised with this connection to nature. There was just something enormously satisfying about eating something that you had harvested with your own hands. On their holiday on Helgoland in August they had even eaten codling and flatfish they had caught themselves from the sea and declared them the best fish they had ever tasted.

So having decided on their itinerary for the afternoon, they set off to hike toward the east. Despite the lateness of the season nature was still busy. There were fewer butterflies than the abundance of the summer months but there was still the odd Small Tortoiseshell or migrant Painted Lady on the wing and they even saw a late Clouded Yellow dart rapidly past. Among the scrub in the Gamsalp there were still a few wrens, Dunnocks and late Lesser Whitethroats and Sarah pointed out a handsome little cock Redpoll in the reclining pines. Sarah was keeping an eye open for larger birds low on the ground among the scrub zone too. Earlier that summer, the first day in fact that she had ever met Daniela face to face, she had flushed a superb Blackcock from the scrub here. Black Grouse were scarce and elusive in the Toggenburg but this was one of the places to find one. She had no luck today though and neither did they see a Chamois; the mountain goat-antelopes called Gams in German and the origin of the name Gamsalp. This wasn't a surprise to Sarah. It was hunting season and the Chamois were wary.

There were other pleasures to compensate however. Their walk took them along the edge of the tree line at the Gamsalp and this was an interesting area ornithologically. Sarah always loved to walk with Daniela outdoors for Daniela was an enthusiastic student for Sarah's fount of knowledge. Sarah had spent most of her life walking the mountains, woods and lower pastures of the Toggenburg and she was a dedicated and expert naturalist. Her depth of knowledge in spite of her tender years was well respected in the valley and even grizzled veterans bowed to her expertise. Daniela was in awe of Sarah's seemingly endless store of information and her ability to instantly identify virtually every growing plant or living creature she came upon. She could listen to Sarah talk about the wildlife in the valley for hours and never tire of it. This deep connection with the natural world about her made Sarah irresistible. Daniela loved nature too but she was a rank novice

180

alongside Sarah. She was hungry for knowledge though and having an expert guide in Sarah alongside was a continual delight to her. Under Sarah's tuition she was slowly starting to gain experience and she was eager to learn. Sarah delighted in her girlfriend's enthusiastic endorsement of her passion and she coached her assiduously. She was surprised to see how quickly Daniela learned. She was forced to admit that Daniela was better at learning natural history from her than Sarah was at picking up the guitar from her lessons with Daniela.

Sarah scoured the trees for birds with her binoculars as the trail approached the forest edge. Almost immediately she saw a little brown bird scurrying furtively up the bole of a large pine. She grinned in pleasure. "OK Danny here's one for you. Check out the side of that pine tree there."

Daniela raised her binoculars to her eyes. They were the same mark as Sarah's, Zeiss Ikon, and another legacy from their holiday on Helgoland where she had bought them. "I can't see anything...Oh! Wait a minute... do you mean that little mousy thing clinging to the trunk?"

"That's the one! What do you make of that?"

Daniela frowned. "Is it a Treecreeper?"

"Very good. Which sort though?"

"Oh God! I don't know. There're two types aren't there?"

"Yes there's the Common Treecreeper and the Short Toed Treecreeper. Which one do you reckon that is?"

"God only knows Sarah. Well God and you at any rate. I presume there are other ways of telling them apart other than by measuring their bloody toenails."

Sarah laughed. "Well yes there are but it was a bit unfair of me to throw that one at you. They can be quite difficult to separate. Actually that's a Common Treecreeper. You can tell by the differences on their faces and the overall plumage on their mantles. The best diagnostic feature however is the contrast between the brown plumage of their upper parts and the white underparts. Do you see how there's a very clear dividing line between them? On a Short Toed it's much less noticeable because Short Toed's have a brownish flush on their flanks which blurs the distinction between the upper and under parts. It's easy to spot once you know what you're looking for."

"God it's a bit subtle for me."

"Well there's an easier way to tell them apart."

"What's that?"

"Habitat Danny. This is an example of two very similar birds occupying very different niches in the habitat. The German names give you the clue. In German a Treecreeper is called a Waldbaumlaufer or Forest Tree Runner while a Short Toed Treecreeper is called a Gartenbaumlaufer or Garden Tree Runner. Nearly every tree creeper you'll see in parks or gardens in towns or open country in the lowlands will be a Short Toed whereas here, in the forest, ninety nine times out of a hundred it'll be a Common Treecreeper. It's not an absolute rule but you'll be right most of the time if you follow it."

"It's cute whatever it's called. I thought it was a little mouse scuttling up the tree when I first saw it."

"They are endearing little things. I always like seeing them."

"Sarah! What's that thing in the second tree along from it?" Daniela sounded excited. "I'm sure I've seen one near the house before."

Sarah followed Daniela's pointed directions. It was a largish dark brown bird covered in whitish freckles. Even as Sarah looked at it, it emitted a harsh croak. Sarah smiled. "I thought we'd see at least one of those Danny. It's a Nutcracker; a kind of small crow of the mountain forests."

"Is this a good place to see them then?"

"Look at the tree it's in Danny."

"What about it? It's some sort of fir tree isn't it?"

"Tut tut tut! Nothing of the sort. It's a pine tree. To be more precise, it's an Arollo Pine. Nutcrackers *love* Arollo Pines. In fact, wherever you find Arollo Pines, you can be sure that Nutcrackers are not far away. The Gamsalp area has one of the only stands of Arollo Pines anywhere in the Toggenburg and it's a magnetic attraction to Nutcrackers."

"Do we have Arollo Pines near the house then because I'm sure I've seen one of those birds near us?"

"Oh no. You don't find Nutcrackers *only* in Arollo Pines. They're common enough in spruce forests as well and even in mixed woodland. But wherever you get Arollo Pines there'll be Nutcrackers as well." Sarah scanned the forest edges. "What about those little green birds further along Danny? Fancy trying your hand at those?"

"Shit you're putting me through it today. My first reaction is to say Greenfinches but I'll bet I'm wrong."

"Close but no cigar Danny. Actually they're Citril Finches. They're another bird of montane forests and the region along the tree line. In fact they're more closely related to canaries than they are to Greenfinches."

"Yes they're smaller than Greenfinches. I can see that now."

"We might get them near the house later in the season Danny. They tend to move to lower altitude a bit when winter sets in."

"We have to get that bird table up before winter Sarah. It'll be fun to watch the birds from the kitchen on winter mornings."

"Oh yes. It's amazing what you can get coming to your bird table in the winter. At the cottage in Alpli Nicole and I even had things like Alpine Accentors and Snowfinches visit our table from time to time. The only problem is the choughs. Gangs of Alpine Choughs invade the lower valley in the winter and they can mop up a bird table in no time. Still they tend to stay nearer the villages so we should be all right."

"I don't mind if they do gang up in our garden Sarah. I love the things." Daniela had been an enthusiastic fan of the little black crows with bright red legs and yellow bills ever since she'd first encountered them on the Chaserugg mountain. Their consummate mastery of the air and their piratical habits had endeared them to her for life. She could never tire of watching the roguish little bandits soaring on the thermals or swooping to rob food from the plates of diners on the terraces of mountain restaurants.

"Well let's push on." said Sarah. "We'll see if we can find some tits in the forest."

"That's my Sarah. Always on the lookout for some nice tits."

"I meant tits as in birds you shameless strumpet."

Daniela rolled her eyes innocently. "So did I darling. What did you think I meant?"

As the trail descended slowly they passed in and out of bands of coniferous woodland interspersed with marshy meadows. In the high summer these areas of damp ground were happy hunting places for orchids but most of the flowers were past their blooming season by now. A few flowers still lingered on however and Sarah found Marsh Felwort; a lovely dark purple bloom characteristic of these marshy places. It was in the woods however that they had the most luck this day. In the glorious weather the birds were active and vocal and the old mature spruce forests down towards Voralpsee held a wide selection of birds of the mountain forests. The trees seemed alive with the ubiquitous chaffinches. Nuthatches called loudly and there were even a few late Chiff Chaffs among the mix. One brightly coloured dumpy bird flitted ahead of them along an open ride in the forest and Daniela regarded it with satisfaction. "That one I do know." she declared firmly. "It's a bullfinch isn't it?"

Sarah nodded. "Go to the top of the class. Yes it's a male bullfinch. Those damn things were the bane of my life a couple of years ago."

"What's wrong with them? They're pretty birds and completely harmless I would have thought."

"Well you might not say that if you were an orchard grower. They're supposed to be a pest on cherry trees. That's not why they got on my wick though. Two years ago I set out on a quest to prove the existence of Pygmy Owls as a breeding bird in the Toggenburg forests. The trouble is that Pygmy Owls are tiny little birds and unbelievably elusive. You could hide regiments of the damn things in these forests. Anyway I hit on a plan. I had this tape recording of owl calls and songs and I thought if I learned to imitate a Pygmy Owl's song I might be able to get them to call back or even come to investigate." Sarah pulled a wry face. "It didn't work out. The trouble is that a Pygmy Owl's song sounds almost exactly like a bloody Bullfinch. I must have spent hours whistling away until I was blue in the face and my cheeks hurt and all I ever got were flaming bullfinches piping back at me and flitting around. I never did see a sodding Pygmy Owl."

"Poor Sarah. What a frustrating unfulfilled life you must lead."

"Stop taking the piss. It's important work to make a comprehensive survey of all the local breeding birds."

"Well where are these tits you've been promising me?"

Ignoring Daniela's teasing Sarah cocked her head on one side and listened for a moment. "I can hear some calling now Danny. Let's see if we can find them. There's one bird I really want you to see." In fact they found some small parties of tits quite easily. The commonest ones in the mixed flocks were the little Coal Tits and the larger Willow Tits which were both characteristic birds of coniferous woodland. There was also the odd Great Tit but, to begin with, Sarah couldn't find the bird she was looking for. Then a soft trilling sound alerted her and excitedly she scoured the trees for her target. "Got one!" she yipped at last. "In fact there's three or four. Look Danny." She pointed animatedly at a tree ahead of them.

Daniela raised her binoculars to her eyes and gazed at the small birds in the spruce's foliage. "Oh they're so *sweet.*" she gushed. Daniela had a tendency to anthropomorphise the creatures she saw but, in truth, the tiny birds were entrancing little things with comical looking speckled crests on the back of their heads. "What are they?"

Sarah grinned in pleasure. "I thought you'd like them." she declared in satisfaction. "They're Crested Tits. You often see them in mixed flocks with Willow and Coal Tits. They're real birds of the coniferous forests Danny. That's another one to see if we can get on our bird table in the winter. They're nice aren't they?"

"They're adorable. Are they rare?"

"Oh no they're common enough. They're a bit shyer than most tits though and quite timid so it's always nice to see them."

The Crested Tits were not the real highlight of their walk though. They heard the loud yelping call of a Black Woodpecker from some distance away and Daniela kept her eyes peeled for she had only ever seen one Black Woodpecker before. She liked woodpeckers and she'd seen quite a few of the common Great Spotted Woodpeckers by now which were among her favourites. Thus it was that Daniela first spotted the real star of their day out. Sarah was examining some moss on a tree stump interestedly when Daniela saw the black and white bird cross the open ride on a bouncing flight and come to alight on a dead spruce tree. "Sarah." she called. "There's a woodpecker on that dead tree. Is it a Great Spotted?"

Sarah tore her attention away from the moss to look without any great interest. Great Spotted Woodpeckers were so common as to hardly elicit much in the way of interest from her. When she looked however she drew her breath in sharply. "Is it hell!" she whispered excitedly. "It's a Three Toed Woodpecker. God it's a male as well."

"Is that good?"

"Good? It's bloody brilliant. That's the first one I've seen all year. We've got four species of woodpeckers resident in the Toggenburg and that one is by far and away the scarcest and most elusive of the lot. If I see two in a year it's been a good year." They stared at the bird in fascination. It was a handsome creature; very pied in black and white with bold black stripes on its face and a yellow crown to its head. When it finally finished its examination of the dead tree and flitted away into the dense canopy of the forest Sarah lowered her field glasses in profound satisfaction. "Well that was just great. Well done for spotting that Danny."

Daniela smiled in pleasure and placed an arm around Sarah's waist. "God what a place this is to live Sarah. I can't believe how lucky we are to live in a place as beautiful as this surrounded by so much wildlife. Every day feels like a new joy."

Sarah nodded soberly. "Yes and to think I once considered giving all this up for a life as a suburban housewife in Zurich. Thank God I met you when I did Danny. You saved my life."

"I think both our lives were saved that day I stopped to give you a lift to Schwendi Sarah. I always thought that I was good with words of love but every time I try to express how much I love you I find no words adequate."

Sarah blushed sheepishly. "I think you say things

pretty well Danny."

Daniela kissed her fondly. "Nothing like good enough Sarah but I try. I try a little bit better than you sometimes. You've had something on your mind ever since I came home. I'm still waiting for you to tell me what it is."

Sarah blinked, astonished as always by Daniela's deep perception. She lowered her eyes and gazed at the rough ground of the forest floor. "Why me Danny?" she asked huskily.

"What?"

"I said why me Danny. I mean of all the beautiful gay women in the world that would throw themselves at your feet in an instance why did you pick me?"

"Oh God Sarah! What kind of question is that? There isn't a woman alive that can match my Sarah."

"Rubbish Danny! There must be millions of them. I'm not exactly an exemplary girlfriend for you."

Daniela looked at her concernedly. "What the hell's all this about Sarah? We're committed to each other aren't we?"

Sarah nodded. "Yes Danny. At least I know I am. But somehow I don't feel worthy to be your girlfriend. I feel that I've let you down. I'm ashamed of myself."

Daniela raised an eyebrow. "Have you been getting up to mischief while my back's been turned Sarah?"

"No! No nothing like that. It... well it's just that you're such a role model for gay women and... well I don't think I live up to your standards."

"Sarah darling nobody's asking you to be some sort of role model. You're not a public figure. Why on earth should you be one?"

"Because I happen to be the girlfriend of the most famous gay woman in Switzerland Danny. Whether I like it or not, that comes with certain obligations attached. Every gay girl in this country looks up to you to carry the flag and I just hide in the background."

"Sarah sweetheart. Whatever has brought this on? I mean why are you suddenly worried about it?"

"We watched your television interview in the Planet Danny. They stopped the music and showed the whole interview in the bar."

"Yes Sarah you told me that. So what's that got to do with it?"

"Because ever gay person in that bar was riveted to that television screen. I never realised just how much you mean to gay people in this country. Everybody was so proud of you... like you were the gay queen of Switzerland or something. Everyone but me that is. I mean I was proud of you, of course, but I was that frightened of anybody figuring out that I was your girlfriend that I was hunkering down and trying to melt into the floorboards. Some of the girls there even thought that Charlie was your girlfriend. She denied it of course but if it had been true she would have been proud to let everybody know. Not me though. I felt like a complete coward. Even Nicky thought I was being a pussy. God how did it happen that Nicky is now more out in the public eye than your girlfriend? Here you are... a hero to every gay girl in this country and your girlfriend is too pusillanimous to even admit that she's together with you. What's the matter with me? Why can't I just come out and say that I'm with the most wonderful woman in the world and I'm proud of it? What the hell am I ashamed of?"

Daniela looked thoughtful for a moment. "Sarah I don't expect you to shout it out from the rooftops. You're not being a coward. What you've already done to tell your family and friends that you're gay wasn't the action of a coward sweetheart. It took courage and conviction honey. Wanting to keep our personal life private from the attentions of the media isn't a failure of courage Sarah. I've been exposed to the public eye for some years now. You haven't. It can be tough Sarah and

189

I don't think you're ready for that. In fact it's no bad thing, keeping our relationship to yourself. If you blurted it out in public, the media would start to suggest that you were exploiting our relationship to boost your own fame and public image. It doesn't matter that nothing of the sort would ever occur to you. The media can be pretty cruel like that. If they find out in their own time then it's a different matter. They can't make that accusation about somebody who keeps such a low profile. You'd garner a lot more respect that way. In any case we don't want intrusive media attention on our private life. I learned long ago to keep my private affairs apart from my public appearances. I don't crave publicity for its own sake and I don't want you to have to face it either. You're a quiet, home loving, country girl Sarah not a media icon. I love you just the way you are. I don't want to turn you into a celebrity just because you're my girlfriend. If you become famous I want it to be because of what you yourself achieve not through my reflected glory. So don't feel bad about hiding the fact that you're my girlfriend in a Winterthur gay bar for heaven's sake. So what if those girls there don't know? It's none of their damn business. The lesbian community can be the worst gossip mill in the world. Let 'em prattle."

Sarah frowned. "Did you deliberately throw Charlie as a red herring to that woman who interviewed you Danny?"

"No honey I didn't. She asked me who the replacement bass guitarist in the band was and I told her... nothing more nothing less. She asked me if Charlie was gay and I said yes. Charlie is quite open and out. The media would have found that out soon enough. If I'd denied it then the lie would soon have been exposed. But all I said was that Charlie was my new bassist and that she's gay. If the media wants to put two and two together and make six then that's their problem. I'm not in the business of trying to deceive anybody."

"What are we going to do when the media finds out who your real girlfriend is?"

Daniela sighed. "I don't know darling. We'll deal with that problem when it arises. I think you might find that the attention might be rather less than you think though."

"Why do you think that?"

"Well I tend to attract the most attention when I'm touring with the band. The only times my private life ever really under scrutiny was with my ex-husband and the singer in my band. Otherwise my private life is pretty boring from a scandal rag's point of view. Doubtless there'll be some speculation about any woman in my life but the paparazzi will soon get bored when they find out that the most interesting things we ever do are to go bird watching or mushroom collecting or something. We don't exactly make good gossip column material. After the initial story fades down we might have to endure the odd article in the ornithological press or something but, unless we lose the plot one day and decide to punch a photographer's lights out for him, they'll soon get fed up of staking us out. We've got other problems than that."

"Such as?"

"Dealing with your family Sarah. We can't hide from them indefinitely."

Sarah pulled a face. "I know Danny. In one way I suppose that this is what all this is about. My only real fear is what my parents' reaction is going to be."

"Do you really think they'll flip out just because your girlfriend is famous?"

"Yes I do Danny. My parents are pretty public persons themselves... especially my mother. I know for a fact that they haven't told anybody else among their circles that their daughter is gay." Sarah grimaced. "Hardly likely that is it? I mean they haven't even admitted it to themselves yet let alone anybody else. If it suddenly comes out in the papers that you're my

191

girlfriend they'll have a coronary. They're already having to deal with the fall-out from my refusing to marry Alan. If it becomes public that the reason I didn't marry him was because I'd run off with a female rock and roll singer there'll be a bloodbath."

"Isn't that all the more reason to talk to your parents before they read it in a paper somewhere?"

"I'm not exactly on talking terms at all with them at the moment Danny. I never told you this but my mum phoned me on Saturday."

Daniela raised her eyebrows. "Well that's progress isn't it? I mean she hasn't called you for over a month."

"It hardly counts as progress Danny. You haven't heard what she had to say." Briefly Sarah recounted the conversation she had endured with her mother over the telephone. "Can you believe it?" she concluded. "My mother actually thinks she can reverse my "choice" as she puts it. She thinks I decided to be gay just on a whim or something."

Daniela pondered as they ambled slowly through the woods. "It sounds as if your mother has been seeking help Sarah. Sadly she's gone to the wrong place. I mean it's understandable for someone who has discovered that their child is gay and is having a hard time accepting it to seek help from supportive groups. In a sense it's commendable that they do so. Unfortunately there are groups that will exploit that for the purposes of their own agendas. I've come across these groups purporting to convert people from homosexuality before. They're nearly always religious groups; usually conservative Christian movements. As you can understand they're more prevalent in the States than over here because you've got a powerful, fundamentalist, right wing Christian faction over there. The biggest group was called Exodus International formed of people who call themselves "ex-gays". There was an offshoot of them called Exodus Europe. They might be the sort of people getting their claws into your mother."

"They're loopy though surely Danny. They can't think that they can just persuade people not to be gay. It's barking."

"To you and I perhaps but to them it all makes perfect sense Sarah. If it's a religious tenet that homosexuality is basically wrong and a sin then you automatically have to assume that people have a choice as whether to be homosexual or not. If they don't have a choice; if it's something over which they have no control, then you lose the basic premise of sin because in order to sin you have to make a conscious choice to succumb to temptation and commit that sin. The question of choice is the most fundamental dividing line between those people arguing for gay rights and those opposing them. If being gay is truly something over which an individual has absolutely no choice about then you genuinely have to accord them equal rights alongside everybody else. You can't call it a sin to be born the way you are any more than you can call it a sin to be born black, Asian or Swiss for that matter. To deny equal rights for homosexuals you therefore have to argue that a person is gay by their own decision and, inherent in that assumption, that they can reverse that decision. You'll hear a lot of fundamentalist Christians argue that God loves the sinner but hates the sin. That's all very well but if the two things are synonymous you have a problem. If homosexuality is not an act of sin but a fundamental part of the sinner then God either loves the sin or hates the sinner and that doesn't sit well with fundamental Christian beliefs."

"But surely no gay people actually do convert because of these groups Danny."

"Oh they do Sarah; or at least they purport to. These groups run courses of something they call "conversion therapy" and they claim it can reverse a person's sexual orientation. In America there are even special camps run for teenagers that have been sent there by their parents to "cure" them of being gay. You can imagine the controversy that causes. The Mental Health authorities are understandably down on it. You know yourself the problems a person has to face in coming to terms with their sexuality. Imagine the damage you could do to a vulnerable teenager struggling with guilt and the shame heaped upon them in that sort of social background."

"So these teenagers are not given a choice about having a choice?"

"It's a good way of putting it Sarah. Of course not all ex-gays are coerced into conversion. In many cases they voluntarily join such groups. Some people just never get to grips with their own sexuality and genuinely believe the Christian burden of guilt and that it must somehow be all their own fault. There's still a lot of stigma and shame attached to being gay. Imagine how much more so that is for a person who has been brought up in a very religious background that becomes aware that they are gay. Their own sexual feelings are completely at odds with everything they've been brought up to believe in. In a sense groups such as Exodus provide a support group for people so tortured by that dichotomy. It's an opt out clause. Sadly there aren't that many groups for Christian gays. The long hostility of many Christian denominations towards homosexuality has tended to polarise the argument and draw up battle lines so most gay people are suspicious of or directly hostile to the church. There's little outlet therefore for people who are both gay and very religious to reconcile the two aspects."

"So they do "convert" then?"

"After a fashion Sarah. The problem with this so-called conversion therapy is that it simply doesn't work. I mean by that, that a person doesn't just stop being gay and suddenly become heterosexual. Even many people who call themselves ex-gays are the first to admit that they haven't stopped having sexual feelings towards their own sex. In fact there have been a lot of high profile cases of prominent members of ex-gay groups being caught having gay sex with the very people they are treating in therapy. What the therapy does do is simply to suppress the person's homosexuality and create an illusion of living a straight lifestyle. Even some large ex-gay groups have conceded that it's not possible to change a person's sexual orientation. They focus now on simply changing their lifestyle so that the person is no longer actively homosexual."

"Can they do that?"

"According to Christian belief, of course they can. Christianity has a long history of sexual suppression. Roman Catholic priests are supposedly celibate after all and monks and nuns are also supposed to eschew all sexual activity whatever their orientation. It makes perfectly logical sense for a Christian to argue that a person might be gay but is obliged not to have relations with the same sex. What they're targeting then is not sexual orientation but sexual orientation *identity* and that's a very different thing."

"Erm... what's the distinction?"

"Oh it's a crucial distinction Sarah. Sexual orientation is how you feel sexually for other people but sexual identity is how you identify those feelings. When you draw up battle lines and assign labels you define group identities. Now everybody likes to put people in boxes. People like to put *themselves* in boxes. To a person feeling that their sexual orientation is different to those of other people around them it's a frighteningly lonely experience. Their first feeling that they're not alone comes with discovering that there are other people just like them. There's a group to which they belong; a society or sub-culture in which they can find a place and are not ostracised. That's very comforting and hence they identify with a specific lifestyle based around that sub-culture. Everything becomes black or white. You're gay or you're not gay. You were born straight or you were born gay; end of story. It's us and them.

The trouble is that it's not that easy. It never is. People are so infinitely variable that you're always going to have trouble putting them into boxes. Look at me. I have a child from a heterosexual relationship. I was married to a straight man. Yet here I am, considered to be a gay role model for heaven's sake. What about you Sarah? You were in a completely heterosexual relationship for years before you met me. Then there's Elke. She was married to a man for fifteen years. Or Nicole for that matter; the scourge of every straight man in the Toggenburg and now she has a girlfriend. Which box are you going to put her in?"

Sarah frowned thoughtfully. "Are you saying that we have a choice after all?"

"Not at all. I don't think we can choose our sexual orientation. As to whether we're born with that orientation or whether it's a combination of genetic inheritance and childhood experience I don't know although I suspect it's more complicated than we give credit for. I also don't think that sexual orientation itself is so straightforward. I believe that our sexual feelings are a lot more complex than the categories we try to put them into. I suspect that nearly everybody has had feelings for another person that falls outside of their identity. I simply don't believe that hetero sexual people never have feelings towards people of their own sex and neither do I believe that gay people never have feelings for the opposite sex. Even most gay people have trouble with bisexuality. You often hear gays grumbling about bisexuals as if bisexuals ought to make up their minds whether they're one thing or another which is pretty ironic don't you think for a group that insists they have no choice over their own sexual orientation.

"Yet bisexuality is troubling. It doesn't fit neatly

into any box because it's an intermediate stage. It's actually quite rare to find a bisexual that is equally attracted to both sexes. Usually they are more inclined to one or the other. So where do you put them on the line? Do you assign sub groupings to describe a person who is bisexual but more gay than straight or a person who is mostly straight but sleeps with their own sex too? The problem is, therefore, not their sexual orientation but their sexual identity. To what grouping do they belong? In terms of sexual orientation is there in fact any grouping possible at all? Doesn't everybody fit somewhere on a line between completely heterosexual and exclusively homosexual? How the hell do you categorise something as variable and subtle as human sexuality?"

Sarah thought hard for a moment. "What you're saying then is that people don't change their sexuality but they can change which sexual group they identify with."

"Yes, essentially. I don't think that sexuality is necessarily fixed either though. The world is full of people who spent a large proportion of their life being of one sexual orientation and then suddenly changing that. I'm not saying that they have a *choice* about it. It just happens. People change. It may be that there has been a suppressed side to their sexuality all along and due to circumstances or changes in their later life these suppressed feelings come to the fore and change their lives. There's been a lot of talk in recent years for example of the number of women approaching or passing menopause that suddenly abandon their former heterosexual orientation to find intimacy with other women. Some argue that it's a result of the hormonal changes that come about with that passage of life. Others say that it's a backlash against years of not finding fulfilment in their married lives and finding the tenderness and loving they've always yearned for with another woman. I don't know the truth but, again, I suspect that it's a lot more complicated than simply a single factor. Whatever the reason however, it is a recognisably more common trait. It's not only straight people that can change either. I have a friend, a gay man, who fell in love with a woman in his late thirties. He was terrified about any of his gay friends finding out about it. He feared social ostracism from his own sexual identity group. Life's given you a bum deal when you have to come out twice in your life."

"So you're saying that these... these ex-gay groups just try to alter a person's lifestyle... who they identify with. They're saying that it's ok to be gay just don't act like it. Isn't that just trying to put everything back into the closet?"

"Hell yes! Society always wants people to come with identifiable labels Sarah. Just tick the box that describes you. I suppose we impose that sort of labelling on ourselves. Everybody has a deep yearning to belong to some grouping within society. We just go along and find out which box best fits us and then retreat into it. We're even prepared to make compromises concerning who we really are just so we fit into our box. All societies are like that Sarah. The gay society can be just as intolerant of those who don't fit into its own criteria as any other grouping sometimes. In an ideal world it shouldn't matter a damn what your sexual orientations are. You shouldn't have to say I'm gay or I'm straight or any other thing any more than you should have to declare that you have blue eyes or ginger hair. But what can you do? We still haven't evolved enough for it not to matter what race we are born into let alone what sexuality we have. Being different is always a problem for any society looking for uniformity. There are six point nine billion people in the world Sarah and every single one of them is unique. The day we can acknowledge that as a basic truth we might be getting somewhere. Until then I suppose we'll just keep trying to squeeze round pegs into square holes and drive ourselves mad in the process. Don't be too mad at your mum Sarah. She's just trying to get you back into the box she always thought you belonged in. Funnily enough you should forgive her for that. It shows that she cares in her own misguided way. She's worried about you. What you have to do is show her that you're able to live a perfectly happy, healthy life whatever your sexual orientation might be. Once she sees that her daughter is happy and fulfilled in her life then she'll soon come around."

Sarah laughed shortly. "God don't we make an awful fuss about sex?"

"Oh God yes! But then that's what makes us human. Human beings are the most sexual animal on the planet. Our sexuality is fundamental to us. Life would be a lot easier for us if we just had occasional regular breeding seasons like other animals. We could just do our shagging, raise our young and then forget about it until next season. But we're not like that. We're the sexual animal and we sure as hell love to make things complicated."

Sarah grinned. "Well if there are six point nine billion of us and counting then maybe being gay isn't such a bad thing after all."

Daniela laughed, "I actually read an article once by some guy who argued that the increasing visibility of gay people was not merely a product of greater tolerance but also because the percentage of gay people was actually increasing in reaction to population pressure. He theorised that over populating societies become far more receptive to homosexuality as a sort of inbuilt population control. I don't know if there's a word of truth in it. It strikes me that there's more holes in that argument than the average piece of Emmental cheese."

Sarah laughed with Daniela. She loved to listen to

Daniela when she spoke of things close to her heart. There was a sort of gentle wisdom to Daniela that belied her youthful years as if she was much older than she really was. She invited you to smile at all the absurdities of people and forgive them and love them for them. She even understood and sympathised with the very people who were against everything she stood for. Even for those people that hated her she would feel only sadness and not animosity. Sarah loved her for it and blessed her for the rosy tints through which she viewed the world with such empathy and understanding.

They were deep into the forest now and approaching the Voralpsee. At the end of their trail they emerged from the dense coniferous woods onto a track overlooking meadows surrounded by trees to their right that swept down to the beautiful Voralpsee; the little alpine lake nestling at the feet of the Alvier mountain massif. A tiny country road penetrated this far up into the alp from the Rhine valley far below and terminated at a charming country guest house. This was their destination and they dropped their rucksacks in the beer garden and eased onto a wooden bench to enjoy the sunshine. From the edge of the beer garden the adjoining meadow fell steeply away and the lake glimmered tantalisingly in the alp below back dropped by towering mountains. It was a richly satisfying view and well worth the hike to find it.

"Why have you never brought me here before?" demanded Daniela. "This is just gorgeous."

"Danny there's thousands of places in the Toggenburg that are gorgeous that I haven't had time to show you yet. Be patient."

"I want to see them all. What are those mountains over there?"

"That's the Alviergruppe or Alvier group. Basically we have three major mountain groups around us. There's the Alpstein which is the group we've hiked over when we went up the Santis and that's split into three

200

subgroups; the northern, central and southern groups. Then we have the Churfirsten which as you know is the ridge of mountains from the Chaserugg in the east to Selun in the west and then there's this group called the Alvier group."

"Is Alvier the highest mountain of the group then?"

"No that's the Gamsberg at 2,395 metres. The Alvier is 2,345 metres. It's a nice mountain. There's a lovely, very simple mountain hut right on the summit that I've stayed at several times. It's run by the same people that have the mountain gasthaus at Palfries on the way up to the summit. The summit hut is pretty basic I'm afraid if you ever want to go up there in the summer. Don't expect en suite rooms and hot baths. It just has a simple dormitory and no electricity. Everything's gas lit and the house menu runs to things like sausages and cheese macaroni or goulash soup and brown bread."

"It sounds heavenly."

"It is. I like to go up there sometimes." Sarah glanced around. The beer garden was empty and there was no sign of any serving staff. "God this place is quiet."

"Are you sure it's open Sarah? I mean it's late in the season for them isn't it?"

"Oh no they're still open. They don't close for the winter until the beginning of November. They probably just haven't noticed us arrive. I'll go inside and grab someone. What would you like?"

"A bottle of beer will do me just fine Sarah."

When Sarah returned from the interior of the gasthaus she found Daniela looking preoccupied. Sarah had two bottles of beer and two glasses on a tray. The waitress in the gasthaus had been reading a magazine, clearly bored on a quiet day. She'd been apologetic however and had offered to carry the drinks out but Sarah had thanked her and told her she'd take them herself. Sarah didn't know the girl who was serving, who seemed to have an Eastern European accent. She was pretty Sarah thought and had the mischievous twinkle to her eye that Sarah often found attractive. Sarah wondered idly if the girl was gay or at least not averse to a little hanky panky with her own sex for she was quite flirtatious with her. Sarah had to smile at herself. Ever since coming to an acceptance of her own sexuality she was starting to ponder the same thing about any girl with a pretty face. She even found herself flirting just a little with them on occasion. She was surprised how often strange girls seemed to show signs of attraction for her. Either there were a lot more gay girls in the world than she had given credit for or they had an uncanny ability to spot their own. If this girl was gay then Sarah had one sure fire way of finding out. She'd make the girl serve them at their table for the next drink. If she *was* gay she'd probably fall down in a dead faint at having to serve Daniela Devin.

Daniela took her beer and poured a glass for herself. "There was a lovely little black and white bird on that little tree just there while you were inside Sarah. He's gone now. I wish you'd been here. I'd love to know what it was."

"Not a woodpecker then?"

"Oh no. I know what a woodpecker looks like. It was too small anyway; about the size of a Robin or something."

"Very black and white was it?"

"Oh yes. Strikingly so. Mostly black on top but white underneath."

"It sounds like a Pied Flycatcher Danny. I'll have to show you a picture of one when we get home and see if you recognise it."

"Do we get many of them around here?"

"Not really Danny. Oh we get a few along the valley bottom in the Toggenburg during summer but they're not really a mountain species. This is migration time however and birds turn up in all sorts of places. I even saw a couple of Yellow Wagtails on the meadows down there as we were coming up to the restaurant."

Daniela nodded distractedly and let her eyes wander mistily across the view. She seemed to have something on her mind. Finally she spoke. "I've been meaning to talk to you about something Sarah."

"Oh yes?"

"Yes and our conversation when we were walking here made me think that it was about time I did."

"You're being very mysterious Danny."

Daniela laughed gently. "Not really Sarah. It's just something a little bit personal that I need to consult you about. You know that we have the new album coming out at the beginning of December?"

"Yes of course."

"Well I've already started working on the next album Sarah. I've got a lot of new material I'm working on and I'm excited about it."

"Well great Danny! It's not much of a surprise though. I knew you were busy composing new material."

"Yes I have. I was stuck for some time last spring thinking of a new concept for the next album but then in the summer I found new inspiration and the stuff just seems to be flowing out of me now. I'm feeling really creative and I don't think I've been as excited as this about a new project since my first album."

"That's brilliant Danny! What was the inspiration for this project?"

"Don't you know?"

"Well you don't really talk to me about your song writing Danny."

"The album will be about *you* Sarah."

Sarah choked on a mouthful of beer. "*What*?"

"Well to be more precise it will be about you, the Toggenburg and love Sarah; the three most important things in my life right now in fact."

203

Sarah took a deep breath. "Oh God! I... I don't know what to say."

Daniela leaned forward. "Do you remember when we first met and I said I was writing a song for you?"

Sarah blinked in shock. "Yes but I never heard anything more about it."

"Well the song really came into focus the first day you took me up to Gamsalp. I remember sitting on a rock and just watching you while you examined the wild flowers. You just looked so precious and so at ease within your own natural environment. It was a beautiful vision of you and somehow you just seemed so in harmony with the beauty around you. I felt such an up-swelling of love at that moment I thought my heart would stop. I swore then that somehow I would try and capture you within your home; your garden. I called the song "Sarah's Garden" and I wanted it to show how the woman I loved was a part of this beautiful valley; how you belonged here as much as the flowers in the alpine meadows. I wanted to convey the Toggenburg as your garden like some mystical garden of Eden with you as some sort of spirit or Goddess at the heart of it."

"I'm not a goddess Danny."

"In a sense you are because you embody this land in the spirit of your heart. You're the lady of the meadows, woods and mountains; the nymph of the springs and streams. You're the friend of every little fly on every little flower. You soar with the eagles on the thermals on the mountainsides or play with the marmots on the high pastures. This is your world; your playground; your garden. If you'd left this land to marry Alan this would have been a sadder place for it. You are indivisible from these mountains now Sarah. That which I have most come to love is right here; my Sarah and her garden." Daniela paused sadly. "But I'm worried Sarah."

"About what?"

"I want to write music about you and your garden

204

Sarah. I want to express this love in me in the best way I know by writing songs that will touch the heart of those that understand. You are my inspiration and the joy in me that demands such an expression. But what if by writing about it I destroy the magic. I said earlier today that our private life is just that; private. But on the other hand I want to share my love through music. That's a dichotomy Sarah. This garden is fragile. If I turn the spotlight of outside examination on it do I risk losing something so personal and precious to me? Right now this feels like a secret place; a little private paradise of our own; a place where we can walk hand in hand in the garden of our love. That is so precious to me that I'm frightened to take down the garden walls and let the world peer in. Am I making sense to you?"

"You mean that you're hesitating about writing about something that is private to us because you would open up our relationship to public scrutiny."

"Something like that yes."

Sarah thought for a few moments. "I don't know how to advise you Danny. All I can say is that if you feel deeply about it you'll probably end up writing about it. I'm no artist myself Danny but I think most artists run the same risk of letting the public peer into their most private thoughts don't they. I mean isn't that what great art is really all about; the artist laying their own soul bare and letting the world see things through their own eyes. In the end will you have any choice about the matter? Isn't there an old saying that talent does what it can but genius does what it must? If those songs are telling you to write them then you'll write them."

"Writing them is one thing Sarah; putting them on an album and selling them is another."

Sarah pondered deeply. "I don't know Danny. I mean nobody ever wrote a love song about me before. I feel.... well I feel incredibly touched and honoured."

"I could always change the names to protect you I

suppose Sarah."

"Would you feel comfortable about that?"

Daniela ran a hand through her hair ruefully. "I don't know. It'll feel odd. I'm not sure I could belt out the stuff with as much passion if I called the song Lucy's garden or something!"

Sarah grinned. "You could always call it Andy's garden."

Daniela laughed. "Hell no!" Andy was a private nickname Daniela had for Sarah in the bedroom. It was short for Andromeda and Sarah had retaliated by calling Daniela Percy after Perseus. "That name stays secret." she declared firmly." Daniela took a sip of her beer thoughtfully. "Anyway Sarah it's not an imminent crisis. I can't see the material being ready for the public domain in anything like the near future. I just wanted to know what you thought about it. We've got all the time in the world to pull the plug on it if we're uncomfortable with it."

"Will you be practising any of this new material with the band?"

"Oh no. Not yet anyway. We've got enough to do perfecting all the stuff off the new album with Charlie without me introducing an entirely new body of material. It'll be going on the back burner for the moment. In any case it needs more work from me before I unleash it on the band."

"Well shall we just leave it at that for the moment? We can discuss it more when it's closer to a finished product and I've had the chance to hear what you're singing about me." Sarah laughed. "Anyway it's not unprecedented. At that party at Gamplut you sang a song with my name in it in public and deliberately dedicated it to me. I was proud."

Daniela lifted Sarah's hand from the table and kissed it gently. "You're just adorable Sarah." She glanced at her empty glass. "God did I drink all that so quickly? I must have worked up a thirst on the trail. Shall we have another one before we head off back?"

"Suits me. We can do whatever you want as long as it's just the two of us. You're off again to rehearse in Zurich tomorrow so today I'm going to be really greedy and selfish. I want you all to myself."

Daniela smiled at her. "We haven't tried those toys I brought back from Germany yet. We can give them a test run tonight."

"God! Do they include instruction manuals? What the hell's that thing like a harness with a dildo on?"

"It's a strap-on Sarah dearest; fucking one's girlfriend for the purpose of."

"Bloody hell! Which one of us is supposed to wear it?"

"We'll see who feels like topping who tonight or I suppose we could just toss a coin. Then again we could take turns."

"Oh my! Don't wear yourself out if you have be up early to go to Zurich tomorrow."

"Oh yes talking of which I have some things to take with me to Zurich in the morning and I'm picking up Charlie in Winterthur. Can I take your car?"

"Sure of course." Sarah slapped a hand on her forehead. "Oh damn! Wait a minute. I was going to go to Appenzell to see Maria tomorrow."

Daniela frowned. "Maria? Not another of your little bits of fluff on the side is it?"

"Stop it Danny. Maria's my brother's fiancée. I've told you that. She called me up yesterday and said she'd like to get together for lunch tomorrow and talk about her wedding. I think she's feeling bad about my estrangement from my parents and wanted to show some solidarity. It's her way of telling me that I'm welcome at her wedding whatever my parents think about it."

"Well you should go Sarah. Anything that rebuilds the bridges between you and your family is important."

"Well I thought I would since you're going to be rehearsing in Zurich all day and there's no point in me going to Zurich with you and just hanging about around the studio like a spare prick all day."

"Is it going to be inconvenient then if I take the BMW?"

"No you go ahead Danny. I suppose I can take the train."

"Is that easy?"

Sarah pulled a face. "Well no as it happens. It's a bitch of a trip. Appenzell's only on the other side of the Alpstein effectively but it's a sod of a place to get into with public transport. I'll have to walk down to Unterwasser and catch a bus to Nesslau. From Nesslau I have to take the train to Wattwil and change in Wattwil for another train to Gossau and then change again for the train to Appenzell. It's a lot of fanning around."

"Well take my car then!"

Sarah sat bolt upright. "What? Me take the Ferrari?"

"Sure. Why not? You probably drive the thing better than I do. You've had Simon to show you the ropes."

"Oh hell! I don't know Danny. I'm going to have a lot of explaining to do to Maria if I turn up in about two hundred grand's worth of Ferrari convertible."

"So park it out of sight and tell her you came on the train."

Sarah bit her lip in uncertainty. She quite fancied the idea of taking the Ferrari out for a spin on her own. "Are you sure you don't mind?"

"Hell no! Just be careful ok. I couldn't care less if you bend the car but just don't hurt yourself doing it all right?"

"Ok. I'll do it. I'll be careful I promise. Come on let's see if we can find the bone idle waitress that's supposed to be serving us and get some more beer."

Chapter Thirteen

Summer seemed reluctant to surrender the field to encroaching winter that autumn for the following day was, if anything, even more glorious than the preceding one. Daniela took her leave in Sarah's car, just after breakfast, leaving Sarah with little to do, other than some tidying up, until it was time to set off for her afternoon meeting with Maria in Appenzell. But the sun was shining brilliantly outdoors and, by ten o'clock, Sarah could endure it indoors no longer. She was chafing at the bit for the rare chance to take Daniela's powerful car out for a spin on her own. Excitedly, she wondered what she should wear for her meeting. It was the car that decided for her. Daniela's Ferrari was a somewhat hard to overlook, sleek beauty in traditional Ferrari red racing colours with white leather upholstery on the interior. She would look hopelessly incongruous, dressing modestly with such a flamboyant automobile around herself, Sarah decided. Very well then, if she was going to swan about the countryside posing it up in such a car she would dress the part. Happily she set out to raid Daniela's extensive wardrobes.

Daniela and Sarah took such a similar size in clothes that Sarah could usually rely on finding something to fit her among Daniela's collection. Daniela didn't mind these forays into her wardrobe. She had so many clothes that a sizeable percentage of them were redundant in any case. In fact Daniela was forever dipping into her own collection to dress Sarah up. She so delighted in dressing Sarah up that Sarah had once somewhat sourly asked her if she was supposed to be her girlfriend or her Barbie doll. But Daniela was incorrigible in this respect and Sarah was by now accustomed to deferring to Daniela's wishes in her choice of clothes whenever she appeared in public. Sarah was not the most fashion conscious of girls, it has to be said, but she had a true expert at her disposal when it came to matters of haut couture.

The trouble was that Daniela had so many clothes it was nearly impossible for Sarah to choose anything appropriate from her vast collection. One dress did jump out of the wardrobe and grasp her attention however. Under any other circumstances Sarah would have run a mile at the merest glance of this dress for, while it was stylishly classical and of simple but elegant lines, it was an eye dazzling scarlet in colour; almost exactly the same hue as the Ferrari in fact. Sarah laughed at herself for even contemplating the dress. She had never in her life dreamed that one day she might actually consider several hundred thousand francs worth of Ferrari convertible as a fashion accessory. She had never worn a red dress in all her days. Daniela would look fabulous in the dress, she knew, but that was hardly surprising. Daniela could have donned a nun's habit and still managed to look glamorous in it. Uncertainly Sarah lifted the dress down from the hanger. It certainly would match the car. She bit her lip in indecision. Part of her quite fancied the idea of dressing up to kill for an afternoon's run out in the Ferrari but the conservative voice of the old Sarah was horrified at the folly of turning up for a lunch date in a place as backwardly conservative as Appenzell in so striking an ensemble.

Sarah needed help on this one. She keyed Daniela's number on her mobile phone. To her surprise Daniela answered at once. Sarah had thought that she would still be driving. "Hi Danny. Where are you?"

"In Winterthur Sarah. We're a bit ahead of schedule as it happens so Charlie and I have stopped for a coffee. What's up?"

"I just wondered if I could borrow one of your dresses for today."

"Of course you can honey. Which one?"

"Well I thought that if I was going out in the Ferrari it might be an idea to colour match it and I've found a lovely red dress of yours that's exactly the right colour. I'm not sure about it though."

"I think I know the dress you mean. Put it on by all means. That'll shake the peasants in Appenzell up a bit."

"Don't you think it might be a bit over the top?"

"Not at all honey. You can carry that dress off. You'll knock 'em dead sweetheart. It'll be good for you to put on the old painted vixen look for a change."

"Well what should I wear with it? The interior of the car's white so I thought maybe white shoes and a handbag might suit."

"God no Sarah! Don't mix red and white for heaven's sake or you'll look like a street girl! Go for silver, black or red for accessories. There's a pair of red shoes that'll fit you in my shoe cabinets and I've got a red and black handbag or a silver one you can carry. Don't go over mad with jewellery either. If you're wearing red you have to avoid anything flamboyant in the way of jewellery or you risk looking hopelessly overdressed because red itself is such an in your face colour."

"What about my pearls?"

"Maybe but pearls are a bit old fashioned if you're going to whammy the public in red. Something simple in silver or white gold would be better. I know! If you look in the top right hand drawer of my dressing table there's a little box with a simple silver chain and a tear drop ruby pendant and matching earrings in it. That'll be perfect. They're quite conservative and tasteful so you won't come over as ostentatious."

"Should I paint my nails red?"

"Yes that'll probably be ok but don't go mad on the lipstick or you'll look like a slut. Oh yes and there's a couple of belts you can wear with that dress. There's a

211

silver one if you go with the silver handbag or a black one if you take the other one. If you tie your hair back use a black or a red ribbon."

Sarah giggled. "Oh God! I'm going to look like Gina Lollobrigida on an off day."

"You'll look fabulous honey. It's about time somebody brought a bit of colour to Appenzell."

Sarah laughed. "Ok the hell with it. I'll do it. My family already thinks I'm a scarlet woman anyway."

She heard Daniela's soft laugh on the other end of the phone. "Ok sweetheart. Have fun you hear and I'll see you this evening."

Sarah grimaced slightly when she regarded herself in the mirror in her choice of ensemble. For somebody who was protesting her reasons for keeping a low profile she certainly seemed to be going out of her way to get noticed. Nevertheless, from a purely aesthetic point of view, she had to admit that she looked stunning. It was so against her nature to wear such bold colours but having done so she had the appearance to bring them to life. Her hair with its hint of coppery sheen seemed to glow more fiery with the red dress and the tanned hues of her skin complemented the startling colour. The dress came just to her knees and flattered her shapely legs whilst its classical simplicity hugged her curves sensually. She was quite pleased with the result if somewhat nervous about it. Yet it was not a costume to be nervous about so she tossed her hair back with a flourish and tried to look confident. Red was no colour for timidity. If you wore red there was nowhere to hide. She had to walk into Appenzell like she owned it today. She had a statement to make.

Donning a pair of sunglasses she took the Ferrari out of the garage. The F 430 Spider convertible was a seriously wicked looking machine; sleek and predatory in appearance. Its 4.3 litre V8 engine developed four hundred and eighty three horse power and gave the car a top speed in excess of three hundred kilometres an hour. It was not a machine for the faint hearted. Sarah had been scared to death of it when Simon had first taught her how to drive it. But Simon knew his business when it came to fast sports cars and she had gained confidence under his patient tutelage. Once she had passed the hurdle of her early nervousness she had begun to enjoy the car and she found it exhilarating. It rode much more smoothly than she had at first anticipated; firm yet tractable and the traction controls tamed the beast within to tolerable handling conditions if you were too timid to allow it to run wild. She knew that in the hands of a true expert, such as Simon, the car, with its precise accurate handling, its grip in the corners and its enormous reserves of power, was nearly untouchable on the road. Sarah was well aware that she could not do the car justice but, in her chic red dress and her hair tied back at least she looked the part.

Of course it was no good looking the part if nobody could actually see you. The day was so lovely in any case it would have been a shame not to drive with the roof down. Sarah had only ever lowered the Ferrari's roof once under Daniela's instruction but it was not difficult. The process was automatic taking about twenty seconds of complex powered metal origami for the roof to fold away into a recess above the engine bay. Biting her lip in repressed excitement Sarah took her place behind the wheel and stroked it lovingly. She was feeling dangerously titillated, dressed in red with over four hundred and eighty horses champing at the bit under her bottom. Taking a deep breath she pressed the big red start button on the left hand side of the steering wheel and the machine snarled into life beneath her, frightening a pair of crows from the trees near the house.

Sarah had never really considered herself a connoisseur of automotive engine noise. Simon, she knew, could enter a state worryingly resembling sexual ecstasy at the roar of a powerful engine. Peter had once told her a funny story about that. Apparently they had been test driving some big fast super car one day and the road had gone through a tunnel. Simon had nearly had an orgasm at the growl of the engine in the tunnel, Peter had told her, and, no sooner had they emerged at the other end, than Simon had turned the car around, wound down the windows and gone straight back into the tunnel. Peter had had to endure driving through that tunnel half a dozen times before he could prevail upon Simon to stop playing and press on. Simon would have been quite happy driving backwards and forwards through that tunnel all day long.

Even Sarah, however, was prepared to concede that there was something thrilling about the thunderous symphony from the Ferrari's V8 engine. It always came as a little of a surprise to her. The car was so sleek and streamlined that it looked like something from a science fiction movie and you half expected it to produce some sort of whooshing zapping noise from a special effects sound machine or perhaps a sibilant hissing noise. When instead it produced a feral roar of rage, like some trapped savage animal in a cave, it was intimidating. Sarah would have known that noise anywhere. In the days when she had first been dating Daniela, and perhaps waiting for her to come and pick her up in the car, she had been aware of Daniela's imminent arrival well before seeing her for you could hear that engine from miles away. In Sarah's memory, therefore, the car's growl was forever associated in her mind with her excitement of seeing Daniela.

On the right hand side of the steering wheel was another control. This was a sophisticated traction control setting. It had four settings or five if you counted being able to switch it off altogether. One was for slow and difficult conditions. There was a second for normal road conditions and the two top settings; one for sport mode and the other for racing mode. Daringly Sarah turned the setting to sports mode. Her perilous over exuberance didn't quite stretch to racing mode. Tentatively she eased the car out onto the little road in front of the house.

The Ferrari wasn't a car that did tentative however. On the little back road leading from Oberdorf over to Schwendi Sarah felt as if she was sitting on an unexploded bomb. Even the merest dab of her foot on the accelerator pedal and the car threatened to leap out of control and career off down the hillside on a wild rampage. She passed a little stone trough and slowed the car to look at it fondly. It was the very trough she had been sitting on, trying to extract a stone from her boot, the day she had first met Daniela. Daniela had driven up in this same car and offered her a lift. Sarah giggled to herself. She had been wearing a very short tennis dress and had had her leg held high whilst she examined a blister on her heel. Daniela had told her that the picture of her so displaying herself had been like a red rag to a bull and Daniela had nearly thrown herself over the steering column, so hard had she stamped on the brakes.

Just before Schwendi, Sarah rounded the tight left hand turn and allowed a little power to make the engine sing as she took the short straight before the hamlet. There was another sharp right hand bend and then she was passing the Hotel Toggenburg; the establishment of her friend and mentor Elke and where Sarah worked in her spare time. The noise of her approach must have alerted the occupants for, as Sarah approached the hotel, she saw Angelica, Elke's girlfriend waving to her at the side of the road. Sarah lifted off the pedal and allowed the car to grumble to a halt. Angelica's eyes were dancing with amusement. "Hello. Who's this little sex siren out on the prowl then?" she asked. "I think you must have taken a wrong turn dear. You're miles away from Monte Carlo."

Sarah grinned. She adored Angelica, a warm

mischievous beauty with an infectious, heart melting smile of perpetual good humour. "Hi Angie!" she said. "What are you doing?"

"Oh I just popped out for a minute to the Schwendi. I was just coming back when I heard the car. What are *you* doing? Where's Danny?"

"She's in Zurich rehearsing for the day."

"While the cat's away huh...."

"Nothing of the sort Angie. Danny's taken my car for the day and I have to go to Appenzell to meet my brother's fiancée so I've borrowed *her* car."

"Well you look red hot darling. Literally red hot. Are you sure this is a wise move Sarah sweetie? Appenzell's hardly renowned for its tolerance of saucy bold young ladies, strutting their stuff along the Hauptgasse. They'll probably tar and feather you and ride you out of town on a rail."

Sarah frowned. "Oh do you think I've gone a bit OTT?"

Angelica laughed. "Not as far as I'm concerned honey. I think you look gorgeous. You'll probably scandalise every peasant in Appenzell though, which is no bad thing. If ever there was a town that needed scandalising it's Appenzell. It's high time that some woman dragged the place kicking and screaming into the twenty first century."

Sarah grimaced. "I just felt like dressing up a bit fancy for a drive in the Ferrari. I didn't want to draw attention to myself."

"Darling you'll be about as unnoticeable as an artillery strike on the market place."

"Maybe I should go home and change into something a little more modest."

"Don't you dare. You just walk into that town like you own the place. It's the last feeble bastion of male chauvinism, still twitching sister. So go in there, finish it off and then dance on the fucker's grave."

Sarah laughed. "I just dressed up a bit fancy Angie. I'm not out to make a feminist statement."

"Well you look fabulous. If I didn't have to look after the shop today I'd go put my sauciest frock on and join you. We could take the place by storm together. Lock up your daughters Appenzell."

"You're hopeless Angie. Where's Elke anyway?"

"Gone down into town on business so I'm stuck with the place for the afternoon. It's dead as well and I'm going out of my skin with boredom. You fancy a coffee before you set off?"

"I'd better not Angie. I've got plenty of time to get to my meeting but I'm a bit unused to driving this beast so I'd better allow myself enough time. I've still got to get petrol in Nesslau as well."

"Ok sweetheart. Pop in for a drink on your way home if it's not too late then and mind how you drive in that thing. That's a powerful motor you've got under your pretty little fanny so don't have an accident ok."

"I'll be careful Angie."

"Ok Sarah knock 'em dead and take care."

"Thanks Angie. I'll catch you later."

Sarah drove away in high good humour; stimulated as always by meeting Angelica. Angelica was always fun and an irrepressible flirt. She always managed to raise your spirits. The road down the hill from the hanging valley side from Schwendi to Unterwasser was steep and winding and Sarah negotiated it gingerly. Once on the relatively flat bottom of the valley, however, she dabbed more boldly on the pedal and felt the exhilarating surge of power from the car. The main road along the valley bottom towards Nesslau was quiet for the moment and, daringly, she let the car forge ahead. The sheer burst of acceleration was almost terrifying. The speed limit along this road was eighty kilometres an hour. The Ferrari took less than three seconds to violate this regulation. Ahead of Sarah was a tractor pulling a trailer; an almost inevitable hazard in the rural Toggenburg. Sarah pulled out and passed the lumbering vehicle with an authoritative snarl from the engine. There were two young lads sat on the trailer that Sarah recognised so she sounded the car's horn in greeting, receiving some lewd gestures and loud whistles in return. Grinning she allowed herself a moment of flamboyant exuberance and pressed on the pedal leaving the tractor vanishing behind in her wake. She passed the yellow and black post bus with equal flair with the wind whipping in her hair and began to enjoy herself. This car was fun.

There was a bottleneck in Nesslau. They were doing something mysterious to the road and a temporary set of traffic lights brought her to a halt with the car throbbing in frustration beneath her. A young man passing on the street regarded her with undisguised admiration as she tapped on the steering wheel impatiently. Sarah pulled a wry grin. "Forget it son." she thought to herself in amusement. "You're the wrong sex." A minute later she pulled into the service station. The Ferrari was a thirsty machine. Visits to the filling station were liable to be frequent. Sarah topped the tank up and paid with her bank card. She tried not to flinch at the cost. Sarah was normally a frugal girl but her bank account was robust and healthy and augmented by Daniela's insistence on providing her with a generous personal allowance. She could equally, of course, have charged the cost of filling the tank to Daniela's account but that seemed unduly mean considering that Daniela provided nearly everything for the household. There was a young pretty girl on serving duty at the filling station and she regarded the car with unfettered envy and also, Sarah rather thought, was unduly friendly to Sarah which was far more to the point than the attentions she had received from the local male population so far on her journey.

The road from Nesslau to Appenzell was a winding scenic route, following a small valley up to a watershed near Schwagalp before descending again via Urnasch and finally into the valley of the Sitter, in which reposed the town of Appenzell. In the high summer or on weekends this could be a busy road for the cable car to the summit of Mount Santis left from Schwagalp and was a popular tourist destination. It was quieter today although there was just enough traffic on the road to frustrate any ambitions Sarah might have had about giving the Ferrari its head. She became stuck behind a touring coach for some distance before a view of open road beyond allowed her to pull out and floor the accelerator to pass and there were a few seconds of intoxicating thrill as the blood red car liberated itself from the encumbrance. Finally she turned right at Urnasch and followed the side of the railway line down into the little land of Appenzell.

Emerging at a somewhat higher elevation from the town, Sarah had a panoramic view over this odd little enclave of Switzerland. It was one of her favourite views. The landscape around the town of Appenzell was quite characteristic and unique. The town was surrounded by odd, small, round topped hills grazed by cattle and often topped with little copses with the mountains forming a backdrop to this curiously verdant little hidden valley, dotted about with rustic farmhouses. Sarah often thought that the whole landscape looked contrived, like a miniature landscape you might see on a particularly ambitious model railway layout. It was almost comforting in its curious cosiness as if the inhabitants of the valley had fashioned the landscape into a homely little sanctuary hidden among the mountains. The landscape had been reproduced countless times in the naive art of the region and, seeing it, you could almost understand why the people here had such an introverted, insular outlook. It was somehow divorced from outside reality; a smug little, concealed and self-contained world that marched to its own pace and turned in upon itself. It was like stepping into a fairy story. This was the heart of the half canton of Appenzell Innerhoden; one of the most conservatively independent rural backwaters of Switzerland. Its population was infamous for its obstinate resistance to change and its mistrust of outside influence. Sarah had lived only some twenty kilometres away for most of her life, had visited it countless times and yet she could still never shake off the feeling of being an outsider here.

As Sarah drove down into the town, this feeling of not belonging was stronger than ever. It was the day in Appenzell when the farmers from the outlying districts came into town for the morning market and lingered into the afternoon to socialise with each other. There were small knots of men in the traditional brown trousers and green pullovers of the local farmers stood around on every street corner in earnest conversation. As Sarah passed in her extravagant automobile, they paused to remove their pipes from their mouths and blink in her direction, which was about as close as an expression of dumbfounded astonishment as you were likely to get in Appenzell. Sarah began to deeply regret her rashness in being so visible today. Her flamboyant entrance could hardly have been more noticeable if she'd been part of a travelling circus unexpectedly finding its way into town. Hastily she looked for somewhere quiet to park the car.

The town was busy today though and parking limited but, finally, she found a temporary spot close to the market place. She closed up the car and left it with some reluctance. Doubtless this was one of the safest places in the world to leave a car unattended but Sarah still felt nervous about abandoning it. It was no ordinary car, after all, and extremely difficult to overlook. She'd hate to have to go home on the train and tell Daniela that she'd just had her car stolen. Not that Daniela would mind all that much Sarah realised ruefully. Daniela had never been entirely comfortable with her car which had originally been a gift from her band. She'd harboured a surreptitious hope that somebody would nick it ever since it had come into her possession and it was insured after all.

Sarah was meeting Maria in a pub close to the town square. Sarah winced at the thought. The pub would almost certainly be crowded with farmers today who would be drinking steadily, playing jass and doubtless rendering the air unbreathable with tobacco fumes from their pipes. Switzerland was gradually implementing bans on smoking in public places at a cantonal level but, true to form, the good folk of Appenzell, to whom any form of outside interference was anathema, were stolidly resisting any infringement on their ancient rights to fill the interior of any drinking establishment with foul reeking vapours.

Crossing the square, Sarah paused to enact her own little personal ritual which she invariably performed whenever she visited Appenzell. She went to touch the tree. This tree was growing in the centre of the square and was surrounded by a wooden bench. It was a young, healthy and robust tree although not in any way particularly noteworthy in appearance or dimension. Nevertheless it was one of the most notable trees in Switzerland and, to a woman, one of the most significant. This tree had been planted when Sarah was a very young child and it had replaced a magnificent predecessor that had graced the square for hundreds of years. The old tree had stood as a symbol of unchanging continuity, dominating the square for as long as anyone could remember. This new tree, in the most basic of fashion, represented the dawning of a new age; the disturbing winds of change blowing into the valley and threatening the time honoured rural constancy of life in the canton. It was the ladies tree.

You would be hard pushed, thought Sarah, to find anywhere else in the world where the most visible

221

symbol of women's rights was a single tree but that was the case in Appenzell. Appenzell had been the last place in Switzerland, indeed just about the last place in Europe, to grant women the right of equal suffrage in local elections. The country as a whole had been somewhat tardy in this respect and women had not gained the right to vote in Federal elections until 1971. The right of suffrage for local elections had been left, somewhat negligently, to the decision of the assorted cantons in the Confederation but most cantons had fallen into line with the Federal policy fairly quickly. Not so Appenzell Innerhoden, however. Resentful of Federal interference in its local affairs the half canton had stubbornly held out for nearly another two decades.

Local elections in Appenzell were somewhat unusual. This was not a place that held much truck with the modern trappings of secret ballots and voting booths. Any issue up for vote was taken to the annual Landsgemeinde or general assembly on the main square where it was debated, spoken upon from a dais and finally decided by a show of hands from the electorate. From time immemorial, the men folk of the canton had filed importantly into the roped off centre of the square beneath the shadow of the venerable old tree to hear speakers argue for or against any item on the agenda before raising their hand in favour of whichever pro or contrary view. It was an age old affirmation of Appenzell's democratic inheritance and the local people had been richly proud of it and the magnificent tree that presided solemnly over the proceedings.

Naturally, of course, women had been excluded from this pompous ritual and were confined outside the rope although on hand to offer advice if their slow witted husbands were uncertain as to which way to vote. That was the way it had been for as long as living memory could recall but, by the end of the nineteen eighties, there had been an ominous change in the wind blowing around this solid institution. By now universal suffrage had been in place all over Switzerland and it was becoming a national embarrassment that Appenzell still refused to grant women the right to vote. On several occasions since 1971, the electorate, which of course was exclusively male, had turned down the right of female suffrage but when the issue once again emerged in the Landsgemeinde in 1990 most outsiders would have predicted that the canton could surely not once more deny this basic right. After all Appenzell was, by now, unique in being the last remaining enclave on the entire continent, more or less, to have not granted female suffrage. Giving women the vote was surely only a formality. Such an analysis, however, underestimated the stubborn, obstinate resistance of Appenzell's manhood.

There had been few local elections in living memory that had generated quite so much heated controversy as the Landsgemeinde of 1990 nor any other that so disrupted domestic harmony within the canton. The women of Appenzell were finally losing patience with their men folk and the men were retreating from the bitter disputes over the dinner table to circle the wagons with their comrades in the pub. For weeks the issue had polarised the community and the battle lines drawn between the sexes. It had been a richly comic scenario and if the men of Appenzell had been anxious that this piece of dirty laundry could be kept from the outside public eye, then they were soon to be disillusioned. The rancorous debate had finally come to the attention of the national media and from there to international interest. For the first time the little hidden canton had found itself at the centre of attention and under the merciless scrutiny of the outside world. It was an uncomfortable place to be.

After weeks of the most acrimonious dispute the day of the assembly had dawned in April 1990. The atmosphere in the canton had been tense to the point of being unbearable. The vultures of the outside world were gathering too. The Landsgemeinde often attracted curious tourists to witness the archaic machinations of Appenzell democracy but now, with the interest excited by the media over this divisive vote, there'd been thousands of them. Worse yet had been the hundreds of newspaper reporters and even television crews. Appenzellers hate to be the centre of attention and this intimidating spectator horde had added to the tension already at breaking point around the square. The men had shuffled nervously into the arena whilst their women folk stood on the outside in grim phalanxes glaring at them. It had felt like an explosion was about to occur.

Cocooned within the roped off centre of the square, however, the men had begun to recover their confidence and the banners of revolution had hardly been in evidence. Outside observers had listened to the ensuing debate within the square with growing disbelief. Speaker after speaker had stepped onto the dais to forward the sort of argument that most neutral spectators thought had vanished back in the 19th century. One man had thunderously proclaimed that his wife already had the God given right to bear his children so why on earth should she want the vote. Another had plaintively bleated that if his wife had the vote then the next thing she'd want would be to hold office in the local government and then how was she supposed to be home in time to have his dinner on in the table in the evening.

The disbelief among the spectators had given way to amusement and finally outright hilarity. Red faced men within the compound had heard the arguments they held sacred being greeted by hoots of derision and sallies of laughter. Finally a vote had been demanded and held. Proudly, in this last desperate stand, the men of Appenzell had gone down fighting. The right of women's suffrage had been voted down by a massive sixty five percent of the male electorate to the ironical cheers and irreverent laughter of the watching neutrals.

It had been the final straw. The men of Appenzell would have easily brushed off any serious concern about their decision. They would have pompously invoked their cantonal rights to self-determination in the face of outrage or outside condemnation. But when the results of the election had bubbled over into being the best joke in Switzerland it was another matter. There'd always been somewhat of an unfortunate tendency for outsiders to make fun of Appenzellers and not take them too seriously but now the ribbing became merciless. Even the serious national papers couldn't resist the joke and had lampooned the canton gleefully. Even in countries that had never even heard of Appenzell the canton had become a laughing stock. The obdurate resistance of Appenzell's proud manhood had crumbled under universal ridicule.

Tottering under this assault the male members of the canton could put up only feeble resistance when one Appenzell lady, fed up with the men and unwilling to expose the canton to any further derision, had taken the matter to the Federal Court in Bern. By this time the Federal authorities, under the scrutiny of international attention, had been seriously embarrassed by this evidence of retardation in a country eager to portray itself as cosmopolitan and sophisticated. Thus the Federal Court had overturned the Landsgemeinde's vote and insisted that Appenzell stop making a fool of the entire country and give women the vote. The women had won the right to vote after all.

The sequel to this was poignant. As if bowing before the new age that had dawned, the old tree that had stood so long and magnificently at the very heart of Appenzell's democracy, at centre stage of the square in the Landsgemeinde, had promptly given up the battle and died. This death of a much loved icon of the canton sent shock waves through the community and many a grizzled old veteran of the war of the sexes would be heard to grumble over his beer in the pub that it was only to be expected. You gave women the vote and now look what happens. The old tree had been reverently taken away and chopped up. In its place, a new sapling had been planted and solemnly, if a little bitterly, dedicated to the women of Appenzell. Now it held pride of place at the centre of each Landsgemeinde and the sisters of the canton stood beneath its boughs each year in affirmation of their victory in the long war for equality. Sarah loved it.

For all that it was a hard place to take seriously, Appenzell was a most attractive little town thought Sarah. The main streets were dominated by grand old timber houses, elaborately decorated with colourful designs and festooned with flower boxes. The floral and abstract designs painted on the gables, balconies and window shutters of the houses always reminded Sarah of the designs on old fashioned wooden gypsy caravans and it may not have been an accidental resemblance. She had once talked with a man at university who held the theory that the Appenzellers were originally quite distinct racially from the surrounding peoples of eastern Switzerland. He was of the theory that the population had been originally gypsies, possibly fleeing persecution, who had settled defensively in the hidden corner of this sparsely populated region. As evidence he had cited the resemblance of the traditional Appenzell art to gypsy art and the physical characteristics of the local people who were noted for being small and dark haired. Sarah didn't know how true the gentleman's theories were but it would explain a great deal about these folk, not least of which would be their insularity.

Certainly the Appenzell people were recognisably distinct in features and stature. Their small stature was a standing joke in Switzerland and the source of endless gags. Whether that had anything to do with a specific racial ancestry or whether it was more due to a reluctance to expand the local gene pool, Sarah was uncertain. Certainly the latter factor must have had some bearing on keeping the characteristics of the folk so distinct. Appenzellers tended to marry Appenzellers and, until very recent times, any young man finding his bride in distant parts was regarded a little askance. It was so marked a fact of local life indeed that even marrying someone from the outer canton of Appenzell Ausserhoden was regarded as somewhat of a scandal. Sarah's brother John, of course, was in no way related to anybody in Appenzell and, in settling in the canton and taking an Appenzell girl, he had set tongues wagging in no uncertain manner. Maria apparently had had to endure numerous occasions on which an older lady had enquired sadly of her if there hadn't been a nice Appenzell lad to wed. John was not only not an Appenzeller he wasn't even completely Swiss. He might as well have come from Alpha Centauri as far as the local populace was concerned.

The pub where Sarah was meeting Maria was as crowded as Sarah had feared. Sarah's entrance into the establishment was spectacular. Eyebrows were raised; card games temporarily halted; beer mugs paused between table top and mouth; pipes removed from mouths in surprise. It wasn't exactly a clamorous response but, by Appenzell's standards, it was as sensational as a porn star walking naked into a monastery. Sarah blushed with the eyes of the company upon her. To her great relief she saw Maria sat at a table almost immediately. She was looking pretty in a green dress and smiling at Sarah across the crowded pub. Sarah hastily joined her. Maria rose and kissed her on both cheeks her eyes sparkling. "Hoi Sarahli. My God you look stunning."

"Hoi Maria. Thank you. I could have done to look a little more inconspicuous though I'm afraid. I forgot it was the farmer's day in town. I feel like a bloody Jezebel."

Maria laughed warmly. "Ach take no notice of the peasants. Defenestration is illegal in Appenzell so you won't get chucked out of the window. Come on take a seat. What'll you have to drink? Beer? Wine?"

"I'll just have a coke thanks Maria. I'm driving."

Maria looked surprised. "Driving? I didn't know you had a car."

"Oh I've had a car since August Maria but I'm not in it today. I.... er I borrowed someone else's because my car is being used."

Maria looked at her shrewdly. "Ok. Coke it is." She glanced around contemptuously at the farmers who were trying not to stare. "If any of this lot gives you any grief, tell him to go play with himself."

As Maria walked to the bar to gain the waiter's attention Sarah took the time to regard her fondly. Maria was a warm beauty with wavy dark hair that fell over her shoulders, a slender figure and deep brown eyes. She was a small girl. Alongside John, who was a tall and muscular man, she looked diminutive which naturally afforded much amusement to other people given the Appenzellers' reputation for lack of stature. Tiny she might have been in comparison to her man but there was no doubt at all about who was the boss in that relationship. She dominated her giant of a man easily.

John was a rather shy and reserved sort of man and he'd found a perfect foil in the feisty extrovert of a girl he had fallen in love with. She was a determined sort of girl unlikely to accept not getting her own way and, while she was good natured, she nevertheless had a temper to her. John was outclassed in any argument with her and content mostly to defer to her wishes. It was a standing joke between Sarah and her sister Jessica that John probably didn't dare pull a pair of socks on in the morning without consulting Maria. Although she was an

228

Appenzeller herself Maria had always gone her own way and it was characteristic of her that she had taken an outsider as a man. She had little patience with the conservative morality of the elder generation and had long had a reputation for scandalising the most stuffy of local dignitaries; a class of people she waged unrelenting warfare against. It was a one sided battle. Few people dared to get on the wrong side of her on when her dander was up. Sarah adored her.

Whilst Maria was away at the bar a group of men at the next table regarded Sarah sourly. Sarah blushed deeply and diverted her attention to the table top. Maria, returning from the bar, noticed the attention her future sister in law was drawing immediately. She glared at the men defiantly. "What the hell are you lot staring at?" she demanded indignantly. "Haven't you ever seen a *real* woman before?" The men hastily busied themselves with their card game muttering under their breaths. Maria took her seat and turned to Sarah. "I tell you what Sarah let's have this drink and then get the hell out of here." She raised her voice slightly. "There's too many retards in here."

Sarah repressed a grin. "Sounds fine to me Maria. Are we still going up to Wasseraun?"

"Yeah I thought we could get something to eat at the Alpenrose there."

"Great. I like the Alpenrose. How are we going to get up there?"

"Well I thought we could drive. I've parked my car a bit out of the centre though so we've got a bit of a walk. What about your car though? I mean where have you parked it?"

"Just on the other side of the market square Maria. I'm parked in a restricted time zone though so I'll have to move the car sooner or later."

"Well we could take your car if you want. Mine's fine where it is."

Sarah swallowed. "Well ok... I suppose so."

Maria looked at Sarah in long appraisal. "Wow!" she said at last. "I thought John and Jess were pulling my leg."

Sarah frowned. "What do you mean?"

"They said you'd blossomed Sarah; turned into a real beauty. Of course you were always a pretty girl but they said that you'd changed; grown up over the last year and turned into a real lady. I mean every time I ever met you, you were just a tomboy in your old jeans and look at you now. You look absolutely radiant."

Sarah blushed. "Well life's changed a bit for me over this past year Maria."

Maria nodded. "I'll bet it has. John told me all about what happened at that party at your folk's place in Ticino. My God. I wish I'd been there."

Sarah squirmed uncomfortably. "It's not an episode I'm very proud of Maria."

"Well you should be. John certainly is. He said you were absolutely awesome that weekend. He said he hardly recognised his kid sister. According to him you blew everybody away. Even Jessica says you outclassed everyone at that party."

"Have you been talking to my sister about me?"

"Of course Sarah. I talk to Jessie often on the phone. She never shuts up about that weekend in Ticino. She was amazed by you. Says she was never so proud of you before."

"Oh God! All I did Maria was chuck my boyfriend and break my parents' hearts."

Maria snorted. "Hmmph! No offence, Sarah, but you were well rid. I was never that keen on Alan and John couldn't stand him. As for his bloody family; well the less said the better. That relationship was forced on you by your mum and dad Sarah and you were perfectly right to get shut of it. John was always afraid that you'd end up marrying Alan just because you couldn't say no

230

to your parents. Well you proved him wrong honey. There's nothing to be ashamed of by taking control of your own life." Maria paused to look at Sarah slyly. "Anyway there's somebody new in your life now isn't there?"

Sarah nodded sheepishly. "Yes... yes there is."

Maria took Sarah's hand suddenly. "There's no need to be shy Sarah. I'm absolutely fine with that. Honestly I am. Actually I'm pleased for you."

"Pleased?"

"Yes Sarah. I don't know who this girl is that you've met but I can tell in an instance that she's good for you. I've never seen you looking so well and so happy. I'll be honest with you. When I first heard that you were... well you know..."

"Just say gay Maria."

"Ok when I heard that you were gay I was shocked and couldn't believe it to begin with. Now I couldn't give a monkey's toss whether a person is gay or not but I just hadn't imagined that you were. But it seems as if that you've found what you were looking for Sarah. Tell me something. Do you well... you know... *love* this girl that you're seeing?"

"Yes I do Maria... very much indeed. In fact I'm not just "seeing" her Maria. We live together."

"Then I'm pleased for you Sarah." Maria paused to take a sip of her drink. "I was rather hoping you were going to bring her along today actually. I'd love to meet her. I have this feeling... call it an instinct if you will... that she's somebody pretty special."

"Oh she is Maria... very special."

"Well why are you hiding her from us then? We want to meet her."

Sarah hesitated. "Oh I'm sure that you'll get to meet her sooner or later Maria. She is very busy and she's away from home quite a lot though."

"Well I look forward to seeing her. Jessica thinks

231

she must be quite a lot older than you."

"Oh hell! Is everybody sitting around speculating wildly on my girlfriend?"

"Well you've hardly given us much to go on Sarah."

"Well why does Jess think she's a lot older?"

"I don't know really. I guess because you seem to have matured a lot since meeting her." Maria was being a little cagey. The real reason for Jessica's suspicions was that she suspected that Sarah's girlfriend was rich; richer in fact that you would expect a young woman to be.

"Well she is a bit older than me Maria but not remarkably so. She's twenty five so she's not exactly geriatric or anything."

"Is she... well you know... pretty?"

Sarah raised an eyebrow. "Well obviously I think so Maria. What are you getting at?"

"Oh God I don't know how to say this. I mean is she well... you know... girly or more..." Maria tailed off helplessly.

Sarah laughed. "Are you trying to ask me if she's butch or something?"

Maria had the grace to look embarrassed. "Well yes I suppose so. Jessica thought that because you've started to look and dress more feminine that maybe your girlfriend was a bit on the well... boyish side."

Sarah had to laugh. "Oh God no Maria! It's a bit of a worn out cliché that feminine lesbians only date butch ones you know."

"I'm sorry Sarah. I don't really know that much about it."

"Well you can take it from me that my girlfriend is the most feminine woman I have ever met. If anything I'm the more butch of the two of us. She's the sort of beauty that stops traffic on busy streets Maria. If she walked into this pub now you'd be able to hear a pin drop."

"Wow! Really?"

"Yes and that's not just my, admittedly, biased opinion Maria. Anybody who's ever met her will tell you the same thing. She is absolutely, stunningly, knock out, drop dead gorgeous. I look like something the dog found dead in a ditch stood next to her. She's not only beautiful Maria but she's also the kindest, sweetest, most generous and loving person it has ever been my privilege to know."

"You really do love her don't you?"

"I wake up every morning and bless God for the gift of her Maria. My life has changed unrecognisably since she came into it."

Maria looked at Sarah for a second or two. "And is this... well this feeling reciprocated Sarah?"

"She told me many times she loved me long before I had the courage to admit I loved her Maria."

Maria shook her head with a smile. "I've never heard you talk like this about anyone before Sarah."

"I've never heard myself talk like this before either!"

Maria laughed warmly. "Well I'm dying to meet her. Finish up your coke Sarah and let's get the hell out of here. I'm getting hungry!"

Chapter Fourteen

Out on the street Maria took Sarah's arm boldly. "So which car are we going to take Sarah?"

Sarah hesitated nervously. "Er I... I don't know."

"Well my car is near the house Sarah so it's a bit silly for us to go all the way back for it if yours is near to hand and you have to move it anyway. In any case, if you're driving, I can have a glass of wine."

Sarah nodded in acknowledgement. "Well ok it makes sense. I don't really like the idea of leaving it parked out of sight for too long anyway. Just don't make a fuss when you see it ok?"

"Why what's wrong with it?"

"There's nothing *wrong* with it. It's just a bit unusual for me that's all."

"You intrigue me. All right I won't embarrass you. Let's go find it."

In spite of her promise, Maria did embarrass Sarah. She stood staring at the Ferrari in astonishment as Sarah shuffled her feet and blushed crimson at her reaction. "You have got to be kidding me!" she exclaimed. "*This* is it?"

"You said you weren't going to make a fuss."

"You said you'd come in a car not a bloody guided missile with wheels on." She whistled appreciatively. "What an absolute stunner. God! Who does it belong to?"

"Er... just a friend."

"Your girlfriend's?"

Sarah blushed again. "Well yes, as it happens. She's taken my car to go to Zurich today because she had some things to carry with her. This isn't the most practical machine for transporting luggage."

"Jesus! Can you handle this machine Sarah?"

"Well I managed to get here in one piece. Don't worry I've been taking lessons in it. I'm no Michael Schumacher but I think I can get us to Wasseraun without killing us."

"Wow! It's a convertible isn't it?"

"Yes. Shall I take the roof down?"

"Hell yes! Let's do the thing in style."

Seated in the Ferrari with the roof open Maria grinned in pure pleasure. "This is brilliant Sarah. Bugger Wasseraun! Let's hit the road and drive off to Milan."

"Behave Maria. I'm sure my brother would be less than amused to find that his future wife had just eloped to Italy with his lesbian sister."

Maria giggled. "God you make it sound romantic. What a scandal that would be. It almost makes me wish that I was into girls."

"I'm enough of a disgrace to my family as it is Maria."

The colour combination of her green dress and Sarah's red dress against the white upholstery of the car tickled Maria. "We look like an Italian flag." she declared in amusement; her delight in the car almost childlike. "Come on Sarah fire her up and let's see what she can do." If Sarah had felt self-conscious about driving through Appenzell in the open topped Ferrari her future sister in law had no such inhibitions. She posed it up outrageously as they wound their way through the traffic and affected such a studied disdain for a small group of whistling boys that Sarah burst into laughter. Beyond the outskirts of the village the road to Wasseraun was relatively clear and, under Maria's enthusiastic urging, Sarah pressed on the pedal and gave the car its head. Maria whooped in glee as the powerful machine surged along the narrow road. It was only a few kilometres to Wasseraun, however, and soon they were pulling into the car park at the Alpenrose guest house.

It was surprisingly busy given that it was mid-week.

The lovely autumn sunshine had tempted a number of people out to dine in the open air for the garden abutting the car park was nearly full. The guest house was picturesque with the trees surrounding it glowing in autumnal colours alongside the lovely painted building and the rippling notes of the nearby brook harmonising with the rustle of the breeze in the leaves. Their arrival had not gone unnoticed. Most of the customers in the garden were staring at them and Maria dismounted from the car with the airs and graces of arriving royalty.

A waitress serving in the garden who was an old school friend of Maria's detached herself from her charges and rushed out onto the car park to greet them. "Christ Maria!" she yipped excitedly, gazing at the car, "Where the hell have you pinched this?"

Maria grinned at her. "Not bad huh? It's not mine though Ursie. Have you met Sarah, John's sister before?"

The young woman shook her head. "No I don't think we've had the pleasure Fräulein." She held out her hand. "I'm Ursula."

Sarah smiled and took her hand warmly. "I'm pleased to meet you Ursula."

"Is this car yours then?"

Before Sarah could respond Maria jumped in. "Sure Ursie. It's a gift from her girlfriend."

Ursula blinked and looked uncomfortable. "Oh! I... I er see."

Sarah glared at Maria. "Take no notice of Maria Ursula. It's a friend's car. We've just borrowed it for the day."

Maria grinned and fumbled in her handbag for her phone. "Hey Ursie how about taking a picture of Sarah and me with the car huh?"

"Er sure."

Maria grabbed Sarah's hand and dragged her to the front of the car. "Come on Sarah let's sit on the front

236

end."

Sarah endured having to pose in front of the car with Maria before she was finally able to pull her away and into the restaurant garden. She seated her firmly down at a table and faced her. "What the hell are you playing at Maria?"

"What's the matter?"

"Saying that to Ursula...telling her that the car was a gift from my girlfriend."

"Well technically it is isn't it? Ok it's only for the day but she did give you it."

"Do you think you might ask me before outing me to a complete stranger Maria?"

Maria stared at Sarah perplexed. "Outing you?"

"Yes. Announcing to someone I've never met before that I'm a lesbian with a girlfriend."

Maria shook her head in puzzlement. "But Sarah I didn't think you were making a secret out of it. I thought you were... well open and out about it."

"Yes to whom I choose to be Maria. I don't have to tell everyone I meet that I'm gay you know. If I want someone to know I'm gay then I'll tell them myself."

Maria looked chastised. "I'm sorry Sarah. I didn't think it was such a big deal. I didn't mean to embarrass you or anything. I thought you didn't mind who knew. I thought it didn't matter."

Sarah sighed. "Well I suppose it doesn't really Maria but people can feel awkward if they have to confront that you're gay. It's not something I want to push in their faces."

"I'm sorry Sarah. It's just that..."

"Just what?"

Maria grinned sheepishly. "Well I don't really know many gay people other than from television and so on. I think it's really exciting to be going to have a gay sister in law. It adds a bit of glamour to things."

Sarah drew a deep breath. "There's nothing

glamorous about being gay Maria."

"There is when you cruise around in a Ferrari convertible." Maria pointed out.

Sarah grimaced in exasperation. "It's only a car Maria."

"Only a car she says. Look Sarah, I know about as much about cars as I do about particle physics but even I can see that that is one hell of a classy automobile and damn expensive. This girlfriend of yours must be loaded."

"She has a successful business Maria."

"She must have Sarah if she's only twenty five and she can afford wheels like that."

"Enough about the stupid car Maria. Let's order."

Maria took a traditional veal and mushrooms in cream sauce with butter rosti and a side salad. Sarah hesitated over the special hunting season menu with chamois and venison on it but finally decided on fish. She'd never been a great fish eater although she'd quite liked it. Daniela on the other hand loved fish and during their holiday on Helgoland they'd eaten fresh fish nearly every day. Sarah had developed a taste for it as a result. Of course the selection of fish on most Swiss menus was limited for it was not a particularly fish eating country but it did have some fish specialities. Sarah ordered Egli; fillets of perch from Lake Constance grilled with chopped almonds and lemon and accompanied by salty, boiled new potatoes and green salad. Maria washed her food down with a white wine from the Valais but Sarah stuck prudently to mineral water.

At last Sarah dabbed the corner of her mouth with her napkin and pushed her plate aside. "Hmm that was nice." she declared firmly.

"Do you want a dessert?" Maria asked.

"Oh no thank you. I wouldn't mind a coffee though."

"Ok I'll have one too." Maria lifted a hand to catch

238

Ursula's attention.

With a coffee in front of her, Sarah leaned back in her chair and looked at Maria. "So Maria. Why exactly did you want to see me today?"

Maria stirred her coffee thoughtfully. "Well it's about this stupid rift between you and your parents actually Sarah."

"Well it's not really your problem Maria. That's between my parents and I."

"It *is* my problem Sarah. After all we're very nearly family now. Your mum and dad have been pretty good to me Sarah."

"Well they like you Maria. You should feel privileged. You're just about the only life partner of their offspring that they actually approve of."

"You're being a bit harsh Sarah. They get on well enough with Jessie's husband."

"They do *now*. When Jess first married Damien though they cut the pair of them off like a leper colony. My mother was barely on speaking terms with Jess for nearly three years."

"Well they came around in the end Sarah; once they got to know Damien and realised that he was good for Jessie. I'm sure that they'll reconcile themselves with you and your girlfriend too given time."

"It's a bit of a different scenario I'm afraid Maria. Jess only married a man they disapproved of. She didn't throw their choice of husband away in a public humiliation to run off with a woman. Jessie's misbehaviour wasn't in the same league as my conduct. I'll be lucky to get another civil word out of them as long as I live."

"I'm sure you're exaggerating Sarah. Your parents think the world of you. This rift must be as painful to them as it is to you."

Sarah looked vexed. "Maria if my parents are upset about any estrangement between us then they only have themselves to blame. I haven't any grounds for not wishing to communicate with my parents. The only problem between us is the fact that I felt unable to go through with a marriage they had arranged for me because I'm gay and in love with a woman. My sexuality and my love are non-negotiable and my parents refuse to accept that. They are the ones not talking to me Maria. I don't see what I'm supposed to do to change that."

Maria held up a hand. "Ok slow down Sarah. I'm not making any accusations or anything. I'm sure there were faults on both sides."

"What faults are those Maria? It isn't my *fault* that I'm gay and I'm certainly not going to accept any blame for falling in love with a wonderful woman."

"Please Sarah I'm not suggesting that either of those things were your fault. On the contrary I sympathise whole heartedly with you. I've already told you that I think you were well out of that marriage and I'm certainly not down on you for being gay. I just think that maybe things could have been handled a little better to avoid this... this breach between you."

Sarah shook her head in exasperation. "How could I have done things any better Maria? My parents painted me into a corner. You weren't at that bloody party in Ascona. My parents deliberately placed me in a position where I was given no choice in the matter Maria. It wasn't my intention to make a public scandal. I specifically made it plain to them that I did not want to be publicly engaged at that party but they went ahead and tried to bully me into it anyway. Bloody Alan jammed a ring on my finger in front of all the guests present without even the courtesy of asking for my consent. What the hell would *you* have done?"

"Probably worse than you did under the circumstances Sarah. Please, I know I wasn't at the party but John's told me the whole story and I agree you were forced into an impossible situation. He says you handled it magnificently. I'm not criticising you for that believe me. I'm mostly talking about what's happened since Sarah."

"And that is?"

"Well you know... this continuing separation. I know your parents are being difficult about it but don't you think that it's about time somebody started to heal the division."

"Maria my parents want nothing to do with me under my current circumstances. The only communication I've had with them over the last few weeks was from my mother over the telephone on Saturday. She'd been talking to some religious nut group that purported to be able to "cure" people of unnatural homosexual desires. She was keen for me to undergo a course of therapy with them it seems. I was so angry I hung up the phone on her."

"Well at least it shows she cares about you Sarah."

"If she truly cared about me Maria she would try to understand my sexuality and come to terms with it. not regard it as some shameful behaviour that's reversible through clean living and purity of mind. She seems to think that being gay was some sort of deliberate choice I've made. Right...being gay means having to face social ostracism, the loss of your friends and family, discrimination, ridicule, religious disapproval, marginalisation within society and all the emotional distress that comes with all that. Now who the fuck would want to *choose* that? I have no objection to talking with my mother and father Maria just as long as it makes any sense. I'm not going to sit there and be berated for my misbehaviour and listen to the woman I love being insulted and accused of corrupting their bloody daughter. Not once has it occurred to them to ask me if in fact I'm *happy* with my girlfriend. They're not interested in my life Maria. They didn't even turn up for my graduation. I phoned my dad on my graduation day

241

and all he had to say was a load of pompous bullshit about my misconduct and reprehensible behaviour. He even had the temerity to tell me that he'd been negotiating with Alan and that he'd persuaded Alan to take me back on the condition that I showed appropriate contrition and mended my wicked ways."

"Oh Christ! What did you say?"

"I told him to shove it up his arse essentially and I threatened to take legal action if Alan continued to harass me and my friends. I told him it was my graduation day which he'd forgotten and that I had expected him to show at least some paternal pride in my obtaining a first class degree instead of being ashamed of even being my father at all. It wasn't exactly what you would describe as a touching scene between a beloved and dutiful daughter and her proud devoted father. Apart from a terse communication confirming the repayment of some money I owed him that's the last communication I've had with him. Jess reports that the very mention of my name is taboo in my parents' house at the moment. I think we can take it that it goes a little way beyond some temporary misunderstanding don't you?"

But Sarah, things can't carry on like this."

"Well what can *I* do Maria? Am I supposed to go to my parents and tell them that I'm dropping my girlfriend, repenting of my homosexuality and intend to beg Alan's forgiveness and ask him to take me back?"

"Well of course not."

"Well that's all that would suit my parents it seems. There's not a lot of room for compromise in that negotiating stance is there?"

"There must be some sort of accommodation you can come to."

"To what end Maria?"

"To come to a situation where you're at least on talking terms with each other."

"I haven't closed the door to any communication Maria. I just want my parents to talk sense when they talk to me. I'm sure they've got plenty they want to say to me but not much that I want to hear for the moment."

Maria bit her lip thoughtfully. "Ok Sarah I can see that you're upset about your parents attitude to all this but you should perhaps try to understand their viewpoint as well."

"I *do* understand it Maria. I just think it's bigoted bullshit that's all."

"I don't mean it like that Sarah. What I mean is that you have to understand how difficult this must be for them. Parents are understandably going to be shocked when their daughter tells them that she's gay. They'll probably say a lot of things they don't mean before they can come to terms with it. It doesn't mean they don't love you or don't care about you."

Sarah sighed. "Maria I know I broke my parents' hearts. You don't have to tell me that. But what the hell else could I do? Perhaps it might have been kinder to tell a few white lies and hide the fact that I'm gay from them. I might perhaps have hidden the fact that I had a girlfriend from them. But they were trying to marry me off Maria. Lying wasn't an option. I had to act." Sarah shook her head. "Yes I know how difficult it must be for them to understand it but hell it's no picnic for me either. I've spent all my life trying to make my parents proud of me and now I'm a disgrace for something that isn't my fault. I love my parents Maria. How do you think I feel now that they consider me to be some sort of perverted deviant?" Sarah turned her head away to hide the tears that threatened her eyes.

Maria saw that Sarah was upset and she leaned over the table to take her hand compassionately. "Sarah don't cry. They don't think you're a deviant. They just don't understand that's all."

Sarah dabbed at her eyes with her napkin irritably.

"You know what's weird Maria? Actually I'm happier than I've ever been in my life. I've never known life to be so exciting and full of promise. I would have thought that my parents would have been pleased. But no. On the rare occasions when they've actually called me I can't even recall them actually asking how I am. There's been no "How are you doing Sarah?" or "How's life?" or even "What have you been doing lately?" It's like they're not interested in my life. They just assume that something's gone terribly wrong with me and it's their duty to admonish me for it. Not once have they actually asked me if I'm happy. They don't care about that."

"Of course they care Sarah. However misguided they are they always want what's best for you. If they really believe that being gay is something that a person can choose then it's understandable that they try to get you to change. It might be completely loopy but it shows that they're thinking about you. You've said yourself that being gay makes life a lot harder for a person. Of course they'd be concerned. Yes we know it's not something you can help but the trouble is that they don't *know* that. As far as they're concerned you've made a terrible decision which might prevent you from living a happy fulfilled life and they're upset about it. They just have to learn that that's what you are and there's nothing to be done about it."

"God you make it sound like an affliction Maria; as if I suffered from some congenital deformity."

"Stop it Sarah. I mean nothing of the sort and you know it. I'm just trying to see things from their viewpoint. I know for a fact that they always wanted to see you happy and comfortable. In their own blinkered way, even marrying you off to Alan seemed like a good idea. I know that John thinks it was just a cosy business deal between your parents and the Bergers but I know that your father particularly was concerned that you'd be happy. He was always pleased that you were going to marry somebody who would be rich enough to provide a comfortable life for his daughter. Material wealth means a lot to your dad. He'd be terrified at the thought of you without any means in life.

Sarah snorted in grim amusement. "Well I think he can rest assured on that point." She waved a hand in the direction of the Ferrari on the car park. "Does it look as though my gay lifestyle has left me in abject poverty?"

Maria laughed. "No I suppose not. Have you actually told your father that your girlfriend's rich?"

"It's none of his damn business. Why should it make any difference anyway? He's shown not the slightest interest in her in any other respect. He hasn't wanted to know if she's kind, or beautiful, or caring. He's obviously not interested in whether she's intelligent or talented. It seems a matter of indifference to him whether she loves me or makes me happy. Why, therefore, should it be of any concern to him whether she has money or not?"

"It'd put his mind at ease Sarah. He probably thinks you're living on dry bread and boiled dish rags at the moment."

"Well I'd rather he took an interest in my girlfriend from some regard other than crass materialism Maria. Don't you dare be telling him that I'm driving around in an expensive car if you talk to him. That's my business and I would prefer not to tell my parents that."

Maria shrugged. "Nothing to do with me Sarah. He might actually suspect it already however. I know Jessie does."

"Jess knows nothing about my girlfriend."

"Well no but she certainly figured out that she's got money behind her Sarah. She said you were dressing up in expensive designer clothes and carrying a small fortune around in jewellery."

"She was exaggerating Maria. I don't dress up that extravagantly. I'm not a kept woman you know. I have my own money and I work as well. Ok my girlfriend's generous with her things and she likes to see me dress up nicely but half of the stuff I wear is just borrowed. Even this dress is one of hers I borrowed for the day just so I could match with the car!"

Maria raised her eyebrows and glanced at the car. "God, that's a hell of fashion accessory. Not many people use a Ferrari convertible as costume jewellery."

"All right Maria. Maybe I was a bit over the top."

"Not at all. You look great." Maria thought for a second. "Tell me something Sarah. How did your friend Nicole take it when you told her you were gay? I mean you lived with her for years didn't you?"

"Oh she was a bit shocked to begin with but she's cool about it now."

"It must have been a bit weird for her Sarah. I mean she shared a house with you all that time and then you turn out to be gay. Isn't she worried about people jumping to the wrong conclusions about her?"

Sarah suppressed a smile. Maria had no idea. Sarah had no intention of outing Nicole and her currently complicated private life however. "I think Nicky's reputation with the boys probably dampened down any rumours Maria."

"You're still friends with her though?"

"Of course I am. She's my best friend. Why would anything like that come between us?"

"Oh I'm not suggesting it would necessarily but some people can be funny about it; your parents being a case in point."

"No Nicky's fine. She gets on well with my girlfriend too."

"Really? That's interesting."

Sarah regarded Maria carefully. "Maria you're taking one hell of a long time to come to the point."

"What do you mean?"

"You haven't dragged me all the way out here to

246

Appenzell just to discuss my private life with me Maria. I realise that you're concerned about my problems with my parents and you want to show support for me and I appreciate it. But you've got other things on your mind as well haven't you?"

Maria nodded shamefacedly. "Well yes... yes I do. I'm just a bit worried as to quite how to approach the subject."

"Well just try spitting it out and let's see what happens."

"Well there's a couple of problems actually Sarah. I want your advice and to see how you feel about things. For one thing there's my wedding."

"Oh?"

"Yes. Ever since John told your parents that we were getting married your mum's been on the phone every other day it seems like."

"Well I'm not surprised. Since I dashed her hoped for big wedding for me from her hands she'll have jumped at the chance to stick her oar into yours. John's just about the last chance she'll have to have a proper wedding for one of her children. Just don't let her try to start organising it for you."

"Oh God no. I don't think she would anyway. I'm sure she realises that it's the bride's family that does all that. Still she's excited about it."

Sarah heaved a sigh. "Poor mum. You know she and dad had a really hasty marriage. She was about six months gone with Jessica and it was a rushed affair by necessity. She's always regretted not having a big dream wedding of her own. Of course she wanted her daughters to have the big wedding she never had but it all went tits up on her. Jess eloped with a man she disapproved of and married in a registry office. Mum didn't even go to the wedding. She was damn determined that I'd have that big wedding and then look what happened. What a disappointment it must have been for her."

"Well at least she'll see her son married off with all the trimmings Sarah although it's not quite the same thing I realise."

"Well anyway... what about the wedding."

"Well of course I've consulted with your mum about the guest list because we have to know how many members of your family are going to be there. We've got a couple of your aunties and uncles, possibly your grandparents, your mam and dad of course and you and Jess. Now Jess will be coming with Damien naturally..."

"Oh, oh! I see where this is going."

"Well *there's* the problem. You see when John and I first started making up guest lists, before we'd even formally announced the date, we had you down to attend with Alan in just the same way that my sisters will be bringing their boyfriends. Of course that's a bit redundant now isn't it? Anyway John and I have decided to invite you and your girlfriend."

"Oh Christ! Have you told my mother this?"

"Well yes I did tell her over the phone."

"Oh my God! What did she say?"

"Damn all to me. She just went all quiet and thoughtful. Later however she phoned John up and went ballistic. She said it was bad enough for you to be there after bringing such a disgrace to your own engagement but it was quite unthinkable for you to be dragging along some woman you were sleeping with. I'm sorry Sarah but these are her words not mine. She said it would be a scandal and we couldn't possibly sully the occasion with you and your girlfriend."

Sarah lowered her head. "Well I suppose I should have expected it."

"John went mad with his mum Sarah. They had a flaming row on the phone and John said he was inviting you and your partner whatever she thought. If she didn't like it... tough! She didn't have to come. He said you were his kid sister and of course you would be there. He said that if everybody else was invited along with their partners it would be downright disrespectful to you to not invite yours. He was pretty adamant about it."

"Oh God Maria I don't want my family feud to spoil your big day."

Maria shook her head. "I agree with John Sarah. This was one of the reasons I wanted to see you today. I want you to know that both John and I fully support you in your relationship with your girlfriend and that we would like both of you to come to our wedding. We've talked this over quite a lot and we don't see why you should be singled out and treated as a pariah just because of your parents' bigotry. Everybody else is coming with their partners or spouses so we're not going to make an exception in your case just because your mum and dad are homophobic."

Sarah gripped her napkin agitatedly. "Maria I don't think this is a good idea."

"Why ever not?"

"Because you'll be bringing my family's dirty laundry to the wedding and it shouldn't be about that. This is supposed to be a happy family occasion. The last thing you want is family tension lurking in the background."

"Hmmph! There's always family tensions at weddings. At Petra Baurmann's wedding last year the bride's father had a brawl with his sister's husband at the reception. There's always some sort of family row brewing under the surface. My uncle's on the guest list and he and dad haven't spoken to each other for fifteen years!"

"It's not like this though Maria. I've just thrown my own wedding back in my mother's face. If I now turn up with my girlfriend it'll be like a deliberate affront. The whole wedding party will be looking at me and my girlfriend. That's not right. This is supposed to be *your* big day. You don't want to turn it into a confrontation.

Everybody's supposed to be looking at you not the scandalous pair of lesbians that have had the temerity to flounce in."

"Rubbish Sarah. If people have got a problem with you bringing your girlfriend then it's their problem. Anyway who will know? It's not as if we're going to announce on the invitation that you're being accompanied by your girlfriend. For all anyone will know she's just a friend of yours. I don't suppose you're going to be snogging her in public or anything and I don't suppose your mum and dad will want to broadcast her relationship to you. That's what I meant before about making some compromises. John and I have talked it over and we think that you and your parents can come to a mutual understanding. If you show appropriate discretion and not push your relationship in anybody's face then they will promise to be civil to both you and your girlfriend and not make a scene. Nobody will be any the wiser. She'll just be a friend of yours same as Nicole. In fact we thought we'd invite Nicole as well. John knows her from way back and they've always been friends. Nobody will think that Nicole's a lesbian so why will they think the same about your girlfriend as long as you keep it discreet?" Sarah winced inside. Just as long as Nicky didn't bring *her* girlfriend as well....or both of them, for that matter. Oh God! Rozella would create carnage.

"Is this why you wanted to know if my girlfriend was girly looking or butch? Did you want to know if she *looked* like a lesbian or something?"

"Well I suppose that was on my mind to some extent. I mean your mum and dad won't be the only homophobes there Sarah. My family's pretty conservative you know. They're Appenzellers after all. My dad hasn't got much time for what he calls fags and queers. But you said she's a very feminine looking girl so there's no reason why anyone would know."

Sarah rolled her eyes to heaven. They would soon bloody well know when Sarah came walking in with the most well-known gay pop singer in Switzerland. Daniela Devin was not somebody that was going to be easy to overlook. "Oh hell I don't know about this Maria."

"Why for heaven's sake?"

"Well I don't think that my girlfriend is quite the sort of person that will fade into the background Maria. She's a pretty spectacular girl and she will turn heads. Every male at the wedding party will want to dance with her and she'll attract attention however discreet we are."

"Oh are you worried about her dancing with people? I mean would she be affronted by men asking her to dance? Surely it's not too onerous. I mean everybody dances with everyone else at weddings. It doesn't mean anything. I had to dance with old Herr Grueber at Petra's wedding and he smelled like the back of his own cow shed."

"Oh I don't think she would mind Maria but she still isn't going to just drop out of sight. Everybody will want to know about her. She'll stand out like a whore in a nunnery at an Appenzell wedding... not that I'm calling my girlfriend a whore you understand. It's just that she's well.... the sort of person that could bring an earthquake to a grinding halt. You won't be able to hide her or her relationship to me for very long. Trust me on this."

Maria frowned. "Are you saying then that you'd be uncomfortable bringing her?"

"I'm uncomfortable about ruining your wedding day with an avoidable scandal Maria. I'm not ashamed of my girlfriend. On the contrary I'm proud of her but if I come with her then I'll be pushing my sexuality and hers in the face of everyone there. It doesn't matter how discreet we try to be. We might not even speak a word to each other for the entire duration of events but everybody there will know and right sharpish at that. My girlfriend moreover is completely honest and open and very affectionate. I can't ask her to hide her feelings for me. For one thing, she wouldn't know how. In some respects she's quite innocent like that. She can't understand why anybody could possibly be offended by her loving somebody else. When I first knew her she always used to take my hand whenever we walked somewhere. I was really shy about it but it's the most natural thing in the world to her. She wears her heart on her sleeve. There's no pretence at all about her. If somebody asks her about me she'll quite simply say that I'm her girlfriend. It wouldn't occur to her to fib about it. She's a very private sort of person but in private conversation she has nothing to hide." Sarah paused. "There's another thing about her too. She is very honest about being gay. She has strong feelings about not having to pander to society's prejudices and hide who she is. She might even feel quite offended to be asked to pretend that she's straight. To her that would be akin to agreeing with people that she has something to be ashamed about. I'm not sure that I don't agree with her as well. Why should we have to hide? I'm sure Jess won't hide the fact that she dearly loves her husband in public and I wouldn't expect you and John to do it either. Why should we behave differently?"

"I'm not sure I'm following this Sarah. You say it's a bad idea then if you bring your girlfriend but if you don't aren't you just hiding her anyway? That's even worse than just being discreet in public Sarah. Nobody's asking you to lie about anything; just not to make a big thing out of it. I mean even if you turn up alone people will want to ask questions. A lot of people at that wedding will know that you used to be in a long term relationship with Alan. What are you going to say to them when they ask where he is?"

"Just that we've broken up."

"And when they want to know what happened?"

"Well I'll tell them it's my business." Sarah

frowned. "I take your point though. At some point I'll be lying through my back teeth. Apart from that I'd have to try and explain to my girlfriend why I don't want her to come and I seriously don't want to do that. In fact Maria I wasn't actually suggesting coming without her. I think it's a bad idea if I come at all, with or without my girlfriend."

Maria looked shocked. "Sarah! You *can't* not come to your brother's wedding."

"Maria if I come to that wedding it'll be a disaster. My mother would never forgive me and neither would my father. My mother's right, it would ruin your big day. I've already said it but I'll say it again. This is your day. You want nothing to detract from that. I'm just the black sheep who'll bring scandal and ill repute to the affair. It's better if I stay away... really it is."

Maria rapped sharply on the table. "This is crap Sarah! I won't have it. John and I both really want you to come. You can't just be a wimp and run away and hide just because your mother disapproves. If you've got nothing to be ashamed of and you're not a coward then you'll be at our wedding... *with* your girlfriend."

"It's not that easy Maria."

"It is easy. We've already told your mother where we stand. Now for God's sake don't *you* let us down and bug out." Maria leaned forward in her chair and hesitated for a moment. "In any case there's another reason why it's important to me that you come with your girlfriend."

"What's that?"

Maria took a deep breath. "What I have to say has to be in the strictest confidence Sarah. Not a word of this to anyone apart from your girlfriend. Promise?"

"Of course I promise."

"Well your story sort of hit a chord with me you might say. You're not the only one with homophobic parents."

Sarah stared at her in shock. "What on earth do you mean?"

"I mean that my mum and dad don't take too kindly to the thought of one of their kids being gay either."

Sarah was speechless for a second. "Please don't tell me that you're gay Maria." she gasped at last.

Maria guffawed. "Not me you drip. I'm not gay. Oh I've wondered what it would be like to ... well you know... with a girl sometimes... I mean who hasn't? But no I'm too much into boys and I'm happy enough with the fellah I've got thank you. No it's my brother... my younger brother."

"What Albert?" Sarah was amazed.

"That's him. Well he told me this past summer that he was gay. I'm the only person he's ever told and I've never said a word to anyone else apart from John until now. He's only eighteen and he's scared to death Sarah. Mum keeps trying to fix him up with her friend's daughters and dad keeps asking him when he's going to get a girlfriend. He's terrified of them finding out about him. I'm the only person in the family he can really talk to and so he poured it all out over a couple of beers last June. He was absolutely in bits about it Sarah and I'm worried to death about him. He looks more and more desperate by the day. The trouble is I don't know how to help him. I know nothing about being gay or anything. I don't even really know any gay people apart from you and my hairdresser so I don't know where to send him for advice."

"Oh God! Albert! Does he have a boyfriend or anything?"

Maria shook her head. "Not as far as I know. I think there was some boy at school he was madly in love with but I don't think anything ever came of it. I don't think he'd know where to start to look for a boyfriend to be honest. There's not exactly a rocking gay scene in Appenzell you know. It wouldn't surprise me in the least if he was still a virgin. He does know however that he's attracted to men. He says he's always been attracted to them. He says he's been like that as long as he can remember. He's always been frightened to let anyone see it though. I think telling me was the hardest thing he'd ever done."

Sarah nodded grimly. "I can relate to that."

"Well if telling me, who's the closest family member he has, was hard enough can you imagine the agonies he'll have about telling mum and dad? He'd rather kill himself."

"Don't *say* that Maria! People do you know... gay people I mean. Teenage gay people have the highest rates of suicide of any peer group in society. Society doesn't make it easy for young people trying to come to terms with their sexuality."

"Oh God! You're scaring me Sarah."

"I'm serious Maria. You're right to be scared. I can tell you from first-hand experience how scary it is to have to confront this in yourself and I've had a relatively easy time of it. I've had a loving and understanding girlfriend to help me through it. Your Albert though is going through all this on his own and, in a background like Appenzell, that doesn't bear thinking about."

"Well exactly Sarah. You can see why it's important to me then that you and your girlfriend come to my wedding."

"I don't see why that would make a difference Maria."

"Of course it would. Listen I kept what Albert told me to myself after he confided in me but I didn't know what to do. He was looking more and more miserable every day. You really scare me when you talk about young gay kids committing suicide Sarah because Albert is just the kind of person who would think of things like that. He's always been a bit sensitive and fragile if you know what I mean. He used to get bullied at school quite a lot but dad just told him to stop being a wimp and stand up for himself. The trouble is that he's got no real friends he can confide in and no gay friends at all. He's got nobody to relate to. Like you said; he's on his own apart from me and I don't know what to do to help him."

Sarah nodded sadly. "That's the hardest part Maria; the loneliness, the feeling that you're different from everybody else in the world around you."

Maria nodded in agreement. "Yes and young people more than anybody have a need to belong somewhere. He must feel totally isolated and unwanted. If the rest of the family and people he knows find out about him being gay it will be a catastrophe for him. He swore me to secrecy Sarah. The worst thing in the world for him is for anybody else to find out."

"Oh God Maria he'll not keep it a secret forever or, if he does, it'll make his life a misery. Every gay person you'll talk to will tell you the same thing. Everybody goes through the same agony about the people in their life finding out that they're gay. For some it's harder than others but it's a process that everybody goes through. It's never easy. But, unless you want to spend the rest of your life living a lie and making yourself miserable, it's a process that you have to go through."

"Yes Sarah and, reading between the lines, it's not just a process that the person in question has to go through. It's also a process that the person's family and friends have to go through as well. They have to come to terms with it too. You only have to witness what you and your family are going through. Well my brother and my family are going to have to go through it as well Sarah. You're right that Albert's not going to keep it a secret for long. In fact, if I'm honest about it, he's doing a pretty poor job of it as it is. He's not exactly the most macho sort of boy and it hasn't escaped many people's notice that he's never had a girlfriend. He's not exactly a mincing queen but he is a bit limp wristed if you know what I mean." Maria pulled a wry face. "When we were kids he used to like dressing up in my clothes. I should have seen the writing on the wall then."

"Not all gay men are into cross dressing Maria and they're not all feminine either. He might be transgender for all you know."

"Transgender?"

"You know somebody born into the wrong sex body Maria; a person born a boy but who feels like a girl inside. It's a lot more common than you think. I've been reading some stuff about it. There're millions of people walking about convinced that they're the wrong sex; men and women."

"Do you Sarah? I mean do you think you're the wrong sex?"

"Hell no! I'm perfectly happy being a woman. Just because I'm gay doesn't mean I feel like a man. In fact. since accepting my sexuality, I've felt more like a woman than I've ever done in my life. Don't ask me about the psychology of that. Maybe during the years that I suppressed my sexuality I was trying to suppress my gender identity as well. Now I've found out I can be both gay and a real woman too. The two things aren't exclusive. My girlfriend likes me as a girl not a man and nobody could possibly accuse my girlfriend of confused gender identity. She is all woman believe me."

"Well we're getting off the point. What I'm trying to say is that Albert's efforts to hide the fact that he's gay are getting thinner by the day. I know for a fact that a number of people are already talking about him. Mum and dad are probably the last people around that aren't asking questions."

Sarah sighed. "Mums and dads usually are."

"Yes well sooner or later it's all going to come out in the open and then God knows what Albert will do. It's his worst case scenario."

"Do you think that he wants *you* to tell them for

257

him?"

"I think the very thought of *anybody* telling them scares him witless. But sooner or later somebody's going to have to. This is where you come in."

"Maria! I'm damned if I'm going to be talked into outing your brother to his mum and dad."

"No, no, no Sarah. I don't mean that. Let me explain. After Albert told me he was gay I was at my wits end. I thought of telling mum and dad but I couldn't bear the thought. I thought they'd go mental. Then in August all this thing about you and your parents blew up. I was staggered when you turned out to be gay. It had never even occurred to me. When John told me all about what happened in Ascona I was flabbergasted. John was really protective about you. He was disgusted by your parents' reaction. That's when I told him that Albert was gay too."

"Was he shocked?"

"Not in the slightest. In fact I think he pretty much had already figured it out. Albert helps out with the business on occasions and so John knows him pretty well. He certainly wasn't put out by it."

Sarah shook her head wonderingly. "You know Maria, I underestimated John. He's such a reserved kind of man and keeps his own counsel for the most part. I thought he would be as appalled as my parents when I came out but if anything he's been the most sympathetic and understanding of anybody."

Maria smiled. "A lot of people make the mistake of underestimating John Sarah. He's basically a shy sort of man and he hides his timidity behind a cloak of reserve and gruffness. A lot of people think he's a bit stuffy as a result but just because he doesn't say much doesn't mean he doesn't think and if he's not the best man for expressing his feelings it doesn't mean he doesn't have any. In any case he adores you Sarah. You could have come out and announced that you were living with three

Norwegian sailors and a transvestite nun, wanted for murder and he would have taken your side."

Sarah laughed. "Anyway we're going off subject again."

"Yes I know. Well as I said John wasn't at all shocked. Anyway a few days after John came back from that notorious weekend in Ascona we were having dinner round at my mum and dad's and they asked about you."

"Oh Christ! What did you say?"

"Well mum and dad have always liked you a lot Sarah and they always ask about you. In fact my mum suggested having you as one of my bridesmaids."

"Absolutely out of the bloody question!"

"Relax Sarah. All the bridesmaids roles are already promised. Actually it would have been a good idea though. Not many people have a lesbian bridesmaid. It would have made it a bit ground breaking don't you think."

"Don't even think about it. My mother would have a coronary."

"Well it was a thought. Anyway, as I said they asked about you and how the engagement party went off. So John told them."

Sarah turned pale. "What?" she whispered, "All of it?"

"Oh yes. Everything. Everything from you exposing the marriage as a sham to handing Alan his ring back and leaving and the letter you wrote to your parents telling them you were gay and living with a woman. John told them the whole story."

"Oh my God! What the hell did they say?"

"Well thank heavens Albert wasn't there. He'd have passed out on the spot. As it was I was holding my breath to see what reaction they'd have." Maria laughed shortly. "Well it wasn't what I expected. They shocked of course but not half as much as I thought they'd be. Dad was taken aback a bit but even he said you couldn't force a lass into a marriage she didn't want. When John told them that your parents were refusing to talk to you or even mention your name, mum clucked her tongue and said that wasn't right. Whatever you'd done you were still their daughter and they ought to stick by you. They were a bit shocked to learn that you were gay of course but it was hardly the biblical denunciation I'd expected. Mum even went as far as to concede that there was a lot of it about nowadays and it didn't carry the same stigma as it did in their younger days. Of course I could, at this point, have pointed that there was quite a bit of it about under their own roof, but I kept my peace. Dad huffed a bit but did say that he had nothing against poufs in general as long as they left him alone. Not that any gay guy is going to make a pass at my dad, of course, but you get the gist. In any case, they felt quite sorry that there'd been a rift between you and your family. John stated quite firmly that, whatever your differences were with your parents, you were still welcome in our house and that he had every intention of inviting you and whoever you were seeing to our wedding. They were completely cool about that. Mum said of course you should come to the wedding. You were John's sister and it was only right that you should be there. Even dad couldn't see any reason not to invite you."

"Well I'm amazed Maria but I have to point out that it's one thing accepting somebody else as gay but quite another when it's your own child."

"Well yes but at least it shows some sort of hope Sarah. They can hardly side with you on this question and be completely the opposite with Albert. Doubtless there'd be a major storm but it sounds like they might come around to it after a while. In any case it's a lot more hopeful than either Albert or myself thought. I told Albert about it and suggested that maybe it was time for him to be honest with them but he's still too afraid. Now imagine that you and your girlfriend attend my wedding. If your mum and dad agree not to make a scene and Albert sees that there is life after being exposed to your parents it might give him the bottle to open out. He'll see that in spite of your parents' antagonism you're completely happy with your girlfriend. It'll show him that he's not alone. Other people have to go through with this and they come out the other side perfectly ok. It's not the end of the world. Life goes on. You and your girlfriend will be an example to him; two gay people that have done the hard work and reaped the rewards. If we introduce your girlfriend to my parents and they're ok with her, which they will be or I'll never forgive them, then he'll see that his mum and dad are not the homophobic monsters he thinks they are. Do you see what I mean?"

Sarah nodded slowly. "Yes I see where you're coming from." Sarah bit her lip in concentration. "Maria I can't give you an answer on this one straight away. It's something I'll have to talk over with my girlfriend. Can you give me a few days to make a decision?"

"Of course. Take all the time you want."

"You say Albert doesn't know any gay people."

"Not that I know of. He tells me that he went up to St Gallen one day when he'd heard about this gay bar there but in the end he couldn't pluck up the courage to walk in. He can be a bit wet I'm afraid."

"Poor kid. I know a few gay people by now. If he likes I could introduce him to some of them. Maybe I could take him out in the Winterthur gay scene one day and chaperone him."

"He'd bite your hand off. He'd be terrified to go on his own. Would you do that?"

"Maybe, but only if both you and he promise that you don't tell your parents that I did. The last thing I want is to be accused of corrupting their innocent son.

261

I'm the scarlet woman in my own family as it is and I don't want to be the same in yours as well thank you very much!"

"We won't breathe a word I promise. I'll tell Albert. He'll be thrilled."

"It's the least I can do. Everybody needs someone to hold their hand at this time in their life Maria. Give me a few days and we'll see what we can do. Albert might see things in a different light after he's talked to a few other young people with the same experiences as himself. I know I did. You're not so alone when you feel part of the community."

"Sarah you're a darling. Thank you so much. You've no idea what this means to me. I love my brother and I'm scared to death about him."

"I'll make sure he doesn't come to any harm Maria." Sarah glanced at her watch. "It's getting on. Won't John be coming home soon?"

"Yes he's due back this afternoon. I suppose I ought to be getting back."

"Do you want me to drop you off at your house? You can pick your car up later."

"Sure but John can go fetch the car. He'd probably have apoplexy at the thought of me driving home after a few drinks anyway."

"Ok then let's get the bill."

A little time later Sarah pulled up outside Maria and John's house on the outskirts of Appenzell. Maria turned to her fondly. "Do you want to come in for a coffee before you set off home Sarah?"

Sarah laughed. "Does my brother know that you invite lesbians in for coffee while he's away?"

Maria grinned wickedly. "It might turn him on. Most men have fantasies about getting it on with a pair of lesbians!"

"I think John might draw the line at any fantasies involving his own sister Maria."

"That might make him unusual around here Sarah. Well?"

"Well what?"

"Do you fancy a coffee or not?"

Sarah shook her head. "I'd better not Maria. It's getting on and my girlfriend said she'd be home by late afternoon. I'm supposed to be cooking dinner for her."

"Regular little housewife aren't you?"

Sarah smiled ruefully. "Yes I suppose I am. Weird isn't it?"

"Well you'd better get off then. I'd hate your missus to come home and find her dinner's not on the table."

Sarah took Maria's hand. "Thank you for today Maria. I appreciate your support."

"Thank *you* Sarah. You've put my mind at ease about Albert. Will you think about the wedding and everything?"

"I'm not promising anything Maria. I'll have to talk to my girlfriend but yes I'll think about it."

"Fair enough. Well goodbye then and give my love to your girlfriend and to Nicole when you see her."

Sarah leaned over and kissed Maria on the cheek. "Goodbye Maria and thanks again. Give my love to John."

Maria stepped out of the car and waved as Sarah eased the machine down the road. She turned to the front door of her house and fumbled in her bag for the keys. Before she could find them though, the door opened. John was stood there with a frown on his face. "Who the hell was that?" he demanded.

"John! God you startled me. I didn't think you were home yet."

John looked contrite. "Sorry honey but I saw you from the window. Who the hell was that in the flash car?"

Maria turned to look down the road where the Ferrari was just visible as it turned the corner. She had a smug grin on her face. "That sir, believe it or not, was your kid sister!"

Chapter Fifteen

Bathrooms are interesting places. If there was a single room in the house where it could be said that the veneer of pretensions and self-deceit was stripped away, it would have to be the bathroom. There was no hiding from yourself in a bathroom. They were shrines of brutal honesty. The bathroom was the place where vanity confronted itself in front of the mirror. It was the room where a young girl saw the growing of her breasts or discovered her first menstrual bleeding. It was here that a young boy examined his chin for the beginning of stubble and worried whether his penis was normal. Conversely an adult woman looked at herself in the bathroom mirror and saw the paunches of growing age begin their devastation on her once pristine youthful figure. It was the place where a man saw his hair receding or turning grey. It was a place of appraisals; a place to stand naked and stare the passing of the years in the face. It was where you confronted time and the change in your own body. Your passage through life was punctuated by the evidence in the bathroom; evidence that your body had changed along the arrow of time and that there was no going back. Sometimes the changes were small and incremental. Other times they were profound, immediate and life altering. In her own bathroom, on the morning following Sarah's visit to Appenzell, Jessica was experiencing such a life changing moment.

Her first reaction was fear. She would always remember that with a smile. It seemed that life was not without its ironies. This was karma; her rebelliousness coming back to haunt her. It was payback time. Now she would know how it felt. God, apparently, had a wicked sense of humour. She leaned against the bathroom sink with her heart beating wildly. She looked at the little device for the tenth time, almost hoping it was wrong. The evidence stared back at her relentlessly. Deny this if you can. There was a tap on the bathroom door. "Are you going to be long in there honey?" her husband called from without.

"Won't be a minute darling." She replied hoarsely. She took a deep breath and pulled a brush through her hair. The action seemed strange as if somehow the act of vanity had suddenly lost its meaning in the light of the new evidence. Everything had changed now. Everything she would ever do again would be altered by this new reality. Jessica was not a religious person but she prayed at that moment for strength. She wasn't sure who she was praying to; perhaps it was to something inside her; some inner strength; some essence of womanhood. With a last long searching look in the mirror she left the device on the side of the sink and surrendered the bathroom to her impatient husband. She took mental bets with herself as to whether her husband would notice it at all.

In the kitchen downstairs she put the coffee on to brew and took eggs from the fridge. She was making scrambled eggs for their breakfast. She leaned against the kitchen top biting her lip; distracted from the morning routine. She could hear Damien singing to himself in the bathroom. She looked at her hand. It was trembling slightly. In sudden decision she snatched up the telephone and dialled a number. "Hello. Is that Doctor Hirsten's surgery? I'd like to make an appointment please."

In the Toggenburg Sarah was already out and about. She was humming gently to one of Daniela's songs on the car's CD player as she eased her BMW up the narrow road to the Alpli side valley. She'd left Daniela in bed. Daniela was not a lazy person by any means but without any pressing urgency to rise she loved to linger

on in bed on occasion. Sarah smiled happily to herself.
The poor girl probably needed the sleep. Sarah had come
home in a markedly amorous mood following her
adventures with the Ferrari the day before. Daniela had
barely had time to finish her dinner before Sarah's
insistence had shooed the cats off the sofa and pulled her
feebly protesting girlfriend down to divest her of her
clothing.

Sarah had worriedly read about something called
"lesbian bed death"; a condition it appeared that affected
many lesbian couples in long term relationships when
the ardour between them cooled to vanishing point to be
replaced by simple companionship. Well they weren't at
that juncture yet and Sarah could scarcely imagine it.
The more she enjoyed Daniela the hungrier she seemed
to become for her. Nor could she detect any reduction in
willingness on Daniela's part. Daniela's protests had
been little more than simple teasing after all. Sarah's
"insatiable sexual appetite" was a standing joke with
Daniela but, in truth, she was delighted by her lover's
continual passion for her even while she teased her about
it mercilessly. She had refused to move out of bed this
morning declaring herself to be a ruined woman. Sarah
had told her with mock severity that if she wasn't up for
breakfast by the time she returned she could expect a
spanking. Daniela had pulled the bedclothes over her
head with a moan of lament and called upon God to
witness how she was abused. Sarah had thrown a pillow
at her and skipped out of the house, thoroughly pleased
with herself.

She pulled up outside the little cottage in the Alpli
with pleasure. Set in a sunny south facing valley that was
a major watershed to the main Toggenburg valley and
with the mountains of the Schaffberg, Silberplatten and
Santis surrounding it, this was the house she had shared
with Nicole for many years and it still seemed like a
second home to her. In fact she still kept a number of

things in her old bedroom and Nicole hadn't changed it a bit. This reluctance to sever her ties with the old house was not through any lack of commitment to her new life at the house at Oberdorf by any means. It was just a way to maintain her connection to Nicole and the lovely little cottage where they had been happy together.

Daniela certainly didn't mind. Indeed it had been Daniela's idea that Sarah maintained a second home with Nicole. She had been concerned that Sarah would feel lonely during her absences from home on tour and that it would be good idea for her to keep her old room at the cottage so that she could stay over whenever she wanted. Nicole had no objections either. On the contrary she was delighted. The house had seemed a lonely place since Sarah's departure and the thought that Sarah would continue to share it with her, albeit on a temporary basis, was entirely agreeable to her. In any case she was hardly in a position to object. Sarah and Daniela's names were now jointly on the deeds for the house. They *owned* it.

Sarah picked up her carrier bag from the passenger seat and jumped out of the car. Nicole's battered old Renault was in the drive. Acerbically Sarah noted that there was a new scrape on the side of it. Doubtless Nicole's erratic driving had led her to yet another misadventure with some inanimate object. Sarah grinned. Some things never changed. She let herself in at the kitchen door which was habitually unlocked. The kitchen was empty and the house seemed very quiet. "Hello!" she called loudly. "Anybody there?" Sarah grinned at the muffled sounds from upstairs and the furious whispering and started the percolator to make coffee. A minute or two later a bleary eyed, tangle haired looking Nicole appeared in the kitchen dressed in a somewhat frayed dressing gown. Sarah kissed her tousled friend affectionately. "Hi Nicky. I just put the coffee on. You look a mess."

"Thanks Sarah. I love you too. What the fuck are

you doing here?"

"I was just down to the village to pick up some fresh rolls for breakfast so I thought I'd bring you some as well. I've brought you some eggs from the chickens too. Where's Charlie?"

Nicole looked hunted. "How the hell did you know Charlie was here?"

Sarah affected a look of deep cogitation. "I don't know really. It must be some sort of indefinable feminine intuition; that and the fact that her jacket's hung over the back of the kitchen chair and that Danny dropped her off here on the way home yesterday."

Nicole swallowed. "Well Danny said it would save her having to pick up Charlie in Winterthur. They're rehearsing again today."

"Ah yes. News on that Nicky. There's been a hitch with one of the band members apparently. They're not rehearsing until this afternoon. Danny's not setting off to Zurich until lunchtime so you can have a nice leisurely morning."

"Oh! I see. Actually I was going to drive Charlie through myself. I found out I don't have to work today."

"Well if you want to you can go both go with Danny."

"Or I could drive them."

"Out of the question. If Charlie wants to risk the perils of the intensive care unit then that's her business but I'm damned if I'm letting you put the love of my life in mortal peril through your lunatic excuse for driving. Danny can drive."

"Why are you so mean to me Foxy?"

"Just realistic Nicky darling." Sarah took the coffee pot from the percolator. "Hey I went through to Appenzell to see Maria yesterday."

"You told me on Monday you were going to. I was there when Maria phoned up remember?"

"Yes of course you were. Anyway I went through to

269

see her."

"How did you get there? Charlie says that Danny took your car for the day. Did you go on the train?"

Sarah grinned wickedly. "No actually. I took Danny's Ferrari."

"Oh *what*? Wicked! Why didn't you call round for me you mean bitch? I wasn't doing anything yesterday. We could have gone together."

"Nicky I was supposed to be seeing Maria privately to talk about her concerns about my problems with my family and how that was going to reflect on the wedding guest list. Anyway she doesn't know who my girlfriend is and it wouldn't have done to fuel speculation by turning up accompanied by the most notorious gay slut in the whole Toggenburg."

"Fuck you Sarah!"

Sarah giggled and poured out three mugs of coffee. "Does Charlie take milk and sugar Nicky?"

"How the fuck do *I* know? This is the first time she's stayed over in this house." Nicole took the steaming mug proffered to her. "Anyway what happened in Appenzell? Weren't the locals a bit taken aback when you cruised in behind the wheel of Danny's Ferrari?"

"Oh hell yes! I had the hood down as well and, just to complete the image of a scarlet woman out to corrupt the Appenzell morality, I wore a saucy red dress to match."

"Christ! How did you get away with it? I'm surprised the peasantry didn't tar and feather you."

"I was too quick for them. A four hundred and ninety horse power sports car takes a lot of catching in a tractor."

"Jesus I wish I'd been there. I still think you're mean not taking me. You and me flouncing into Appenzell in Danny's Ferrari like a pair of brazen hussies out on the prowl would have given the local priest months of good material for his sermons on the corruption of the flesh. Lock up your daughters Appenzell! The Bandwagon Dykes just hit town."

Sarah giggled. She glanced toward the stairs. "Charlie's taking a long time."

Nicole shrugged. "Probably jumped under the shower. She thought that she was up for an early start to go to Zurich."

"Well you've got time for a nice leisurely breakfast now. There's a dozen eggs in that bag so maybe you could rustle up an omelette for her. I noticed at my place on Monday she likes a hearty breakfast."

"That's a good idea. Why don't you make a start on it while I go and get a shower?"

Sarah picked up a tea towel and threw it at her. "You can make your girlfriend's breakfast yourself you lazy bitch. I've got to get home and make my *own* girlfriend's breakfast without having to cater for yours as well thank you very much."

"Oh God! I'll end up being domesticated at this rate."

"About time too. Where has Charlie left her new guitar; in the studio in Zurich?"

"You're taking the piss. Leave it in Zurich? No fucking way! She's not let the thing out of her sight ever since Danny gave it to her. She'd have taken the sodding thing to bed if I hadn't put my foot down." Nicole paused thoughtfully. "Listen Sarah what were you planning on doing today?"

"I don't know really. I didn't have any plans as such."

"Why don't you come through to Zurich with us? I said I'd drive Charlie to Zurich but it seems a bit silly if Danny's going in your car again. So why don't all four of us go in your car. I'd quite like to see the studio and everything but if the band are going to be practising all afternoon it'll be a bit arse paralysing on my own. If you were there though, we could slip down into town and do

271

a bit of shopping or something while they're working."

Sarah thought for a moment. "Yes I'd like that. It sounds more fun than sitting at home on my own. Zurich's bloody expensive though."

"For fuck's sake Sarah! You've got a millionairess as a girlfriend. Just make her a really specially nice breakfast and see if you can't wheedle her credit card out of her. We can hit the town running."

"You're a bad girl Nicky. I am not about to exploit Danny for her money."

Nicole sighed. "Jesus! What's the point of having a rich girlfriend if you can't exploit her? Oh well have it your own way. Listen though; Charlie told me about this bar in Zurich where a lot of lezzies hang out during the day. Maybe we can go check it out."

Sarah placed a hand on her hip in exasperation. "Oh great! So while our girlfriends are busy at work you want to take me out on the prowl stalking skirt in some sleazy Zurich gay bar. For a girl that only a couple of weeks ago was stringently denying that she was gay, you seem to have taken to your new found sexual identity like a duck to water."

"Come on Foxy. It'll be fun."

"Nicky you can't seriously want to go picking up girls while Charlie is working. Jesus have you got no morals at all?"

"Who said anything about picking up girls? I just want to go and look; nothing more than that." Nicole ran a hand through her hair ruefully. "The last thing I need is another bloody woman in my life. Things are complicated enough as it is."

A flash of colour and movement caught Sarah's eye out of the kitchen window. She leaned forward to take a better look and froze. A car had pulled up outside the house and a middle aged lady was emerging from it. "Oh shit!" Sarah breathed.

Nicole blinked. "What is it?"

"It's life about to get even more complicated Nicky. It's your mum!"

Nicole sprang to her feet. "Oh Hell!"

"Quick Nicky, go and warn Charlie. I'll hold your mum up down here."

Nicole was wringing her hair in anxiety. "Christ Sarah don't tell her you've moved out. She doesn't know."

"What the hell do you mean?"

"I haven't told her anything about what's happened Sarah... you know about you and Danny and you being gay and what have you."

"Oh for fuck's sake! Look just go and warn Charlie. I'll try and run interference for you."

Nicole dashed from the kitchen frantically and Sarah drew a deep breath. A second or two later, after a quick tap on the kitchen door, Nicole's mother stepped in. Actually hobbled in would have been a better description. Mrs Richardson was walking with the aid of a stick. In July, the madcap lunacy that seemed to come naturally to the female line of the Richardson clan, had led Nicole's mother to the misguided notion that paragliding off mountain sides was a suitable weekend occupation for middle aged housewives with too much time on their hands. Inevitably she had broken her ankle in a botched landing and the healing process was proving to be protracted. Not that a seriously injured limb was in any way going to slow Mrs Richardson down of course. Even with the impediment of a broken ankle Mrs Richardson could arrive on the scene with the energy of a small tornado. She was a small woman, barely reaching up to Sarah's shoulder, but she more than compensated for her diminutive stature with the zeal and enthusiasm with which she embraced life and her devil may care attitude to the conventions of the conservative culture of her adopted country; conventions which she outraged with monotonous regularity. This was the woman, Sarah had to remind herself, that only a year or two ago had bungee jumped in the nude to protest the exploitation of animals for fur. If you took Sarah's sister Jessica's inclination to crusade on behalf of worthy causes and mixed it up with Nicole's penchant for chaos and getting into trouble, then raised the whole thing a notch or two then you had Mrs Richardson in a nutshell. She was madcap and adorable but, if you liked a quiet life, she was best taken in small doses.

Mrs Richardson seemed delighted to see Sarah. In fact her greeting was well on the high side of effusive. She grasped Sarah to her bosom in a bear hug and kissed her on both cheeks ardently. Sarah was a little taken aback. She had always had the most cordial of relations with Nicole's mother but this sudden effusion of affection was somewhat beyond the protocols of polite esteem. "Sarah!" Mrs Richardson breathed at last, "You look wonderful. I haven't seen you since last winter. My word what a beauty you've turned out to be."

Sarah disentangled herself bashfully. "Er thank you Mrs Richardson. You look well too... I mean apart from your foot of course. I do hope that you're well on the mend."

Mrs Richardson dismissed her injury with a wave of the hand. "Call me Jacqueline Sarah or better yet Jacky." Mrs Richardson took Sarah's hand and lowered her voice. "I mean you and Nicole have been... friends... for years now. I suppose that makes us nearly family."

Sarah blinked in confusion. "I beg your pardon?"

Mrs Richardson winked conspiratorially. "There's no need to pretend to me Sarah. No need to... how do you girls put it... no need to hide in the closet. You can be completely honest with me. I wasn't born in the dark ages you know. I'm just happy that my daughter has somebody like you to share her life with."

Sarah closed her mouth which was beginning to hang open embarrassingly. "Er yes... yes of course er...

p..please take a seat er Jacqueline. C...can I get you a cup of coffee."

Mrs Richardson took a chair at the kitchen table. "Yes thank you Sarah. I will have a quick cup. I can't stop long though. I'm on my way to see friends in Sargans. I just popped by to say hello. Is Nicole around?"

Sarah swallowed. "Er yes. She's upstairs. She has... I mean we have a guest staying for the night and she's just...er showing her where everything is."

"Oh good. I'll wait till she comes down then. I just wanted a quick word with you and her."

Sarah handed over a cup of coffee to Mrs Richardson. "Perhaps I'd better go and see what's keeping her." It was in Sarah's mind to dash upstairs to warn Nicole that the goalposts had been moved; moved so far in fact that it sounded as if they were playing in the opposite direction. Something very odd was going on. Before she could move, however, a hastily dressed Nicole reappeared in the kitchen looking haunted and nervous.

"Er...Hi mum." Nicole's glance flitted anxiously to Sarah over her mother's shoulder who was trying to flash warnings with her eyes.

Nicole's mother embraced her daughter warmly. She seemed in fine good humour. "I can't stop long Nicky." She told her. "I'm meeting friends in Sargans. I just popped by to see if you and Sarah are doing anything tomorrow evening."

Nicole was floundering in confusion. Sarah looked downright agitated. Charmaine was keeping out of the way upstairs and Nicole was guiltily all too aware of the presence of her lover. The intelligence that her mother was not stopping long was extremely gratifying but Sarah's demeanour indicated that something was amiss and she was missing it badly. Nicole cleared her throat. "Er I didn't have anything planned mum but I don't know about Sarah. Why?"

"Well I just wanted to invite you and Sarah to dinner that's all. I'd love to have the chance for us to sit down together and talk properly."

"Talk?" Nicole looked perplexed.

"Yes I think it's about time we all had a good long talk. Don't you?"

"Er... what about mum?"

Mrs Richardson grinned roguishly. "I think you probably know as well as I do Nicky. I just wanted to clear the air between us; let you know that you can confide in me whatever other people might think."

Nicole was looking comically confused. "Er... what?"

Mrs Richardson turned to Sarah smoothly. "You'll be able to make it won't you Sarah?"

Sarah swallowed. "Er... I'm not sure Mrs Richardson. I'll have to... er look at my er... schedule for tomorrow. Can I get back to you on that?"

"Of course, of course. If we can't meet up tomorrow then maybe we can get together next week sometime. I really would like to have a long talk with you however."

Sarah took a deep breath. "Well... I'll try Mrs Richardson but..."

"Excellent. I'll phone tomorrow to confirm. I thought we could have dinner at that hotel you used to work in Sarah... the Toggenburg wasn't it?"

"The Toggenburg?" Sarah's voice sounded unnaturally high pitched to her own ears.

"Well yes it's a nice restaurant there and I thought it was a bit more discreet than the Sternen in Unterwasser. It probably wouldn't do for us to dine at the Hirschen in Wildhaus since Nicky's working there. Shall we say about seven o'clock provisionally?"

"Well... I... still have to consult my schedule Mrs Richardson."

"Yes naturally. I'll call you tomorrow and we can make it a firm date." Mrs Richardson glanced at her watch and stood up. "I really have to fly now though. Do try and make it tomorrow girls. We really do need to talk." She embraced both of them fondly and hurried toward the door. "You two girls take care of each other now you hear and I'll talk to you tomorrow." Then she was gone leaving devastation in her wake.

Nicole blinked in bafflement and sagged against the kitchen top. "What the fuck was all that about?"

Sarah groaned and slumped down into a chair. "We're rumbled Nicky. Your mum's found out that we're gay."

"*Impossible*!"

"It's the only explanation. You didn't hear what she had to say while you were upstairs." Briefly Sarah gave the gist of the exchanges she'd had whilst Nicole had been absent from the room.

Nicole stared at her appalled. "She...she can't have found out. I don't believe it."

"What other explanation is there? She was being damn conspiratorial; wink, wink, nudge, nudge...she damn as near came out and said she knew we were gay."

"But...but...how the hell can she know anything?" Nicole paled. "You don't think that she's heard anything from anybody here in the valley do you?"

Sarah shook her head. "It doesn't hold water Nicky. Sure there are people in the valley that know I'm gay by now but those same people must know that I'm in a relationship with Danny. It doesn't sound as if your mum is party to that particular snippet of information. In fact she near as damn it called us two an item. I felt like the fucking daughter in law!"

Nicole churned a hand through her hair in agitation. "Well your family then?"

"Give me a break Nicky. My mother's not been on speaking terms with your mum ever since she wrote those articles on the exploitation of animals and the poor role models for adolescent girls evident in the fashion industry three years ago. My mum thinks yours is batty in the head."

"Well she *is* batty in the head. It still doesn't preclude the possibility that your mum's been in contact with my parents. You've said yourself that your parents have been trying to find out who your girlfriend is. I'd be the first person they thought of."

"I've told my family that you're not my girlfriend Nicky."

"So they don't believe you. I mean you haven't exactly been open and above board about the identity of your girlfriend. It's natural that they'd think that you were telling fibs to conceal who she really was."

"That's crazy. They know I don't even live here anymore."

"Only from you Sarah and they might think that you're pulling an elaborate deception. Anyway it doesn't matter what they think. Even if they only suspected, they might call up my mum and ask her if she knew whether you were having a relationship with me or not. Mum would instantly put two and two together and come up with five!"

Sarah bit her lip concernedly. "Maybe." She conceded.

"It's got to be that Sarah. How else would she know?"

"I don't know. Hell what a mess."

Nicole sank into a chair opposite and rested her face in her hands. "God! What am I going to do now?"

Sarah took a deep breath and placed her hands firmly on the kitchen table. "Let's not panic Nicky. Obviously your mum hasn't the full story and she's labouring under a misconception. I'll just have to tell your mum the truth that I'm gay but that I'm not having a relationship with you. I'll tell her I've moved out.

278

That'll let you off the hook."

"So I'm supposed to scuttle back into the closet am I?"

"If you want to tell your mum you're gay Nicky then that's *your* problem."

"Oh Christ! I don't know."

At this point a furtive head appeared around the kitchen door. "Er... is it safe for me to come out now?"

Sarah and Nicole jumped. In their anxiety they had quite forgotten about Charmaine. Nicole rose to her feet apologetically. "Oh Charlie I'm sorry. Sure, sure... come in."

Charmaine walked into the kitchen to exchange a brief kiss with Nicole. She glanced at the two girls intently. "What the hell's going on?"

Nicole groaned. "You've just missed all the fun Charlie. Some fucker's outed me to my mum."

Charmaine blinked. "Oh shit! What happened?"

Nicole nodded to a spare chair. "Grab a seat Charlie and we'll tell you all about it. Do you want coffee?"

"Please."

Over coffee Charmaine listened to the account of Mrs Richardson's whirlwind visit thoughtfully. Finally Nicole paused. "Well what do you think?"

Charmaine cogitated for a moment before replying. "Well I don't see what the problem is."

Nicole stared at her in disbelief. "No problem? You don't see a problem? There's my mum thinking I'm gay and having a relationship with Sarah apparently and you don't see a problem?"

"Well no. I mean she sounds cool about it. It sounds like a hell of a lot more positive reaction than I got when I came out to my fucking parents or that Sarah got from hers for that matter. I can't see a problem there."

"But...but... she thinks that me and Sarah..." Nicole tailed off in confusion.

"So what if she thinks that you're having a

relationship with Sarah? You can just tell her that it's not true and that you have another girlfriend."

"*What?*" squeaked Nicole. "Me tell my mum that I've got a girlfriend?"

"Well why not if she's already figured out that you're gay?"

"But she's only assuming that I'm gay because she knows that Sarah is and she thinks we're still sharing a house together."

"Er we're only assuming that Nicky." Sarah pointed out. "We don't know for sure that that's where she's coming from."

Charmaine nodded. "Yeah for all you know she might have seen that photo spread of you in that magazine."

Nicole turned white. "Oh God! Don't even say that."

Sarah shook her head. "Look guys I'm going to have to get going. Danny will be wondering where breakfast is."

Nicole looked at her desperately. "Are you still coming to Zurich Sarah? We need to have a serious conference and come up with a plan if we're seeing my mum tomorrow night."

Charmaine looked surprised. "What's this all about?"

Nicole answered. "Sarah's going to drive us up to Zurich Charlie. We thought we could do a bit of shopping while you and Danny are in the studio."

Sarah kept her face impassive at Nicole's somewhat edited version of her plans for the afternoon. "Yes well Danny and I will pick the pair of you up around lunchtime then. Now I really must go."

Chapter Sixteen

Jessica drove into Luzern around lunchtime. Damien was away for the day and she thought she might as well take lunch in town. She had plenty of time. Her appointment with Dr Hirsten wasn't until the afternoon. She felt a curious mix of dread and excitement over the prospect. She took a light luncheon in a quiet little café and tried to read a newspaper but she couldn't concentrate on it. Distractedly she fumbled in her handbag for her cigarettes before remembering that she'd thrown them in the bin this morning in a reformist mood. It added to her edginess. If ever there was a time when she needed nicotine to sooth her nerves it was now; just the very moment when it was the *last* thing she needed. She took a deep breath and tried to compose herself. She took her compact from her handbag and looked at herself critically in the hand mirror. She had to laugh at herself. As if she was going to *look* any different. She put the mirror down. "You're having bloody vapours." she told herself. She glanced at her watch. She had at least an hour and a half before her appointment. She might as well have another drink. That raised another problem. She really wanted a coffee. Was that safe? She erred on the side of caution and settled for a fruit juice. She was regarding the drink in front of her somewhat sourly when her mobile phone chimed. It was Maria.

"Hi Maria how are you?" she asked, pleased with the distraction.

"Hi Jessie. I'm fine thanks. What about you?"

Well that was a good question at the moment with her current status still unconfirmed so Jessica hedged. "Oh fine Maria. How's John?"

"Same as ever. He's kind of busy at the moment

though. Have you talked to your sister lately?"

"No. Why? Should I have done?"

"She came through to Appenzell yesterday Jessie."

"Oh really? Er...alone?"

"Yes. Actually she came though on my invitation. I wanted to talk to her about our wedding so I asked her to come through and have a bite to eat somewhere."

"I see." Jessica was already well briefed on Maria's concerns regarding the inclusion of Sarah on the wedding guest list.

"Yes and I'm a bit worried about it Jessie."

"What's the problem?"

"I don't think she wants to come."

"Rubbish Maria. She won't want to miss her brother's wedding."

"Well she didn't sound terribly keen on the idea to me. Unfortunately I had to tell her that your mum was kicking off about us inviting her and her girlfriend and she got all defensive and self-sacrificing about it."

Jessica swore under her breath. "Well what does it matter if my parents are homophobic bigots Maria? It's not *their* bloody wedding."

"Sarah reckons that there might be a scene Jessie. She doesn't want my day to be spoiled by some sort of showdown with her mum and dad."

"That's a load of crap. My parents might be stuck in the dark ages when it comes to issues of tolerance and understanding but at least their sense of social propriety and diplomacy are not in question. They'd never start a family row at someone else's wedding. I can't see Sarah starting a fight either. I think the worst you could expect is somewhat cool and restrained relations. They might not talk to each other but I think we can rule out the possibility of vulgar abuse and a food fight with the wedding cake."

"I think Sarah feels uncomfortable with the idea of being put in the public spotlight Jessie. She thinks it would be a scandal if she were to turn up with her girlfriend in tow and that everyone would be talking about her and throw a pall of gloom over the day."

"Well, immediate family members apart, who the fuck would know Maria? I mean as long as they don't actually push it in everybody's face and start pawing at each other during the reception there's nothing to tell anybody that her girlfriend is anything more than just another guest. I'm sure Sarah's not going to publicly announce that she's gay and introduce everyone to her girlfriend."

"Well I sort of tried to say that to her Jessie. It was bloody awkward though. I felt terrible about it. I mean in effect you're saying that we'd love you and your girlfriend to come along but would you mind awfully keeping your hands to yourselves and hide the fact that you're a couple. It's a horrible thing to ask anybody. I mean you wouldn't ask any heterosexual couple to do the same. You can't ask somebody not to hold hands and kiss their husband. Why should a gay couple have to conform to that rule just because of the narrow minded views of some of the guests?"

"I take your point but if Sarah really wants to avoid attention so as not to distract from the real purpose of the day then she'd be willing to do it I'm sure."

"I'm not sure she would though Jessie. Oh I don't mean that Sarah would go out of her way to cause a scandal and I'm sure she'd be perfectly willing to conceal her relationship in public although I don't think she likes the idea of doing so. The trouble is that it's not just about Sarah. There's her girlfriend as well. Sarah says that she's not the kind of girl that hides who she is and Sarah thinks it would be disrespectful to ask her to be. Even if she was willing to be discreet however Sarah doesn't think she'd be able to pull it off. According to Sarah, her girlfriend is not the kind of person that can fade into the background. Sarah reckons she'll stand out

283

like a sore thumb and have everybody gossiping about her within two minutes of her arrival in church."

"Well let 'em gossip. You don't care do you? Once you come gliding down the aisle looking drop dead gorgeous in your wedding frock nobody's going to be looking at Sarah's girlfriend."

"Oh I couldn't give a fuck what people think. To be honest, I think it would be cool to have a pair of lesbians among the company. All good weddings need a dash of family scandal in the mix. I don't think I've been to a wedding yet that doesn't have a few black sheep and skeletons among the assembled company. It keeps life interesting. At least it gives the gossips something else to talk about other than the failures of the bridal gown and the hash you make of the ceremony. God what kind wedding would it be without a few embarrassing relations present and the best man getting drunk and disgracing himself? It would be bloody soporific. At least Sarah and her girlfriend are going to be a sight more interesting and stimulating than most of the family friends my mum and dad insist on inviting."

"So what's the problem?"

"The problem is that Sarah is kicking about the idea of being a public spectacle. She's being all noble about it as well because she thinks that it's supposed to be my big day and she thinks she'll detract from that."

"She's going to be a scandal whatever she does Maria. She either turns up and invites gossip or she's conspicuous by her absence and tongues will wag even harder."

"Well yes but I really want her to come Jessie. Ok she could come alone but I think it's awful not to invite her partner as well. Everybody else expects to be able to bring their partners and I'm damned if I'm going to make an exception just because she's gay. Anyway I *want* her to bring her girlfriend. I've told you about the problem I have with my brother. Right now he's liable to

284

be the only gay person at that wedding; well the only one apart from possibly the deacon who you do hear stories about. I want to try and make my brother feel less marginalised; show him that he's not alone and that there are other people like him. I want him to meet other gay people and see that they can be happy and in love just like anyone else. If Sarah and her girlfriend turn up with Sarah's family it might make him less terrified about his own family finding out about his own sexuality."

Jessica pulled a face. "Er I'm not sure that my family is going to set a good example in that respect Maria. If your brother sees the reaction my mum and dad have to their gay daughter it'll probably make him more terrified than ever."

"Not if we can find some way to maintain reasonably cordial relations Jessie. That's why I wanted Sarah and her girlfriend to be... well a little discreet. The trouble is that I've told Albert that they're coming to the wedding. If Sarah baulks and bugs out now because she's scared of being in the public eye and of her parents what kind of message is that going to send to Albert? It would be devastating."

"I don't get it. Why does Sarah think her girlfriend is going to stand out so much? Does she look like a Russian weightlifter or something?"

"Ah well I was coming to that. The other reason I want Sarah to bring her girlfriend is that I'm bloody curious to meet her as well. The more I learn about this mysterious woman the more intrigued I become."

"Has she told you anything about her then Maria?"

"Very little Jessie. She's pretty reluctant to furnish details. She did give me some hints about her appearance however. The same as you, I thought maybe she thought that everyone would know the woman was gay because she looked like a lesbian."

"What do lesbians look like?"

"Well you know... sort of masculine... butch."

"I think that's a bit of a hoary cliché Maria."

"Well I suppose so but if this girl did look a bit like that it would explain a lot. Sarah however was insistent that she's nothing of the sort. According to her this girl is very feminine and drop dead gorgeous. Sarah says the police have to ask her to move along at busy intersections to prevent traffic congestion. Sarah says that if anything she, Sarah that is, is the butch one in the relationship."

"Sarah's not butch. Oh she's always been a bit tomboyish I suppose but there's nothing masculine really about her. You can't even call her tomboyish anymore. In the Ticino she was dressed up to kill every day; every inch the lady. Even my mum was impressed by her turn out."

"Oh I know Jessie. I can vouch for that one myself. I hardly recognised her when we met yesterday."

"Oh yes? Do tell."

"Well we met up in the Drei Konig and Sarah's entrance was quite something. She was wearing this knock out red dress and..."

"*Red*! You're kidding me. Sarah never wears red."

"Oh hell yes and not any old red mind. This was in your face blood red. Sarah said that since her family seem to regard her as a scarlet woman she might as well dress the part. She had red shoes on and ruby earrings and necklace to match."

"Christ!"

"She looked stunning. The place was crowded but, after she flounced in, for about twenty seconds the only sound you could hear was the soft plop of eyeballs hitting the floor."

"Bloody hell!"

"Oh it gets better Jessie. If I thought that a few grand's worth of rubies was enough of a fashion accessory I'd seen nothing yet. There's one thing we can take as confirmed Jessie. Whatever else her girlfriend

286

might be I think we can take it as read that she's filthy rich. The bloody woman must be rolling in the stuff."

"Why Maria?"

"Did you know that Sarah has a new car?"

"You're joking. What the hell has she got?"

"I've no idea. I'll bet a king's salary against a bucket of cow shit that it's not something cheap she picked up second hand at a used car lot though. She wasn't driving it yesterday. Apparently the girlfriend borrowed it for the day so Sarah had to make do with the girlfriend's wheels."

"Oh hell! What was she driving?"

"Only about a quarter of a million francs worth of blood red, convertible Ferrari sports car."

"You're taking the piss!"

"Not a bit of it. I've even got a picture of me and Sarah sat on the bonnet on my mobile to prove it. The only reason Sarah dressed up in red was so she'd match her bloody car for the day. We drove up to eat at the Alpenrose at Wasseraun with the hood down and it was amazing. We were like a pair of Hollywood starlets out for an afternoon drive. We parked the car just by the garden in the Alpenrose and it was drawing a crowd all the time we were there."

"Well fuck me! Who the hell is this girlfriend of Sarah's?"

"I don't know Jessie but I'm dying to meet her."

"Where the hell does her money come from?"

"Sarah said she's a successful business woman."

"But she told me that she's only twenty five."

"Same here. She's got to be a millionairess though and, according to Sarah, bloody gorgeous to boot. Life's not fair is it?"

"Whew! Hey Maria you've got to send me that photo on your mobile. This I've got to see."

"I'll text it to you. This doesn't solve the immediate problem though. How the hell do we persuade Sarah to bring herself and her girlfriend along to my wedding?"

Jessica thought for a moment. "I don't think there's a panic just yet Maria. Sarah hasn't exactly turned down the invitation flat has she?"

"No. She said she'd talk it over with her girlfriend."

"Maybe it's really her girlfriend who's kicking."

"I don't know Jessie but it didn't sound like it though."

"Well as far as I can tell then it's largely a case of getting my parents to occupy the same space as Sarah and her girlfriend for a few hours and to persuade Sarah that we can pull the thing off without war breaking out. I don't think my dad will be a problem Maria. I talked to him last Saturday and he's already trying to repair bridges and offer the tentative olive branch. It's my mum that's the problem. She's being bloody hysterical."

"Yes Sarah said her mum phoned her up last weekend and tried to persuade her to see some sort of Christian counsellor that offered some sort of reparative therapy for homosexuals."

"Oh Christ! Seriously?"

"Yes. Sarah was spitting blood about it. She says she refuses to talk to her parents again until such time as they talk sense."

"That'll be mum's bloody barmy idea. Dad mentioned to me that she had some loopy idea like this brewing in her head. I hope to fuck she hasn't caught religion or something. It'll be hard enough effecting a reconciliation without mum getting all evangelical about it."

"Sarah was furious about it. She says she hung up on her."

"I'm not bloody surprised. I can't think of anything more guaranteed to ruffle her feathers."

"Well it sounds to me like we've got our work cut out trying to bring those two together."

Again Jessica took a moment to ponder. "Well dad's

appointed me as sort of unofficial diplomatic go-between so I suppose it's up to me to cast a little oil on the troubled waters. I think I can probably make Sarah see sense. My mum's the problem. She can be one stubborn cow when she makes her mind up about something."

"Damn it Jessie why's she such hard work? Sarah is her *daughter* and John is her son. A wedding is supposed to be all about family. Surely she'd want all her own family present at her son's wedding."

"You *are* talking about a woman that never even turned up at her eldest daughter's wedding Maria."

"You're surely not suggesting that she'd refuse to come to her son's wedding just because Sarah was going to be there."

"No I don't think so Maria. I think she's pretty much learned her lesson in that regard and in any case she isn't going to want to alienate her entire family. John would never forgive her and neither would I; let alone Sarah." Jessica paused for a moment and grinned to herself. "Family. You're right Maria. It's all about family. I think I might have a little leverage in that respect."

"What sort of leverage?"

"Let's just say that I'm not above a little emotional blackmail in a good cause."

"What are you thinking?"

Jessica leaned back in her seat and smiled to herself. "I'll tell you later Maria. My mum's as stubborn as a mule but you can move a mule with the efficacious use of the old fashioned stick and a carrot and, Maria darling, I'm the girl that's carrying both of them."

Chapter Seventeen

"Well all I can say is that it's going to be an interesting encounter with your mum tomorrow Nicky." declared Sarah feelingly as she steered her BMW along the west bound autobahn a little outside Zurich. Nicole pulled a face. They had been discussing the episode with Nicole's mother ever since Sarah and Daniela had picked Nicole and Charmaine up for the drive to Zurich at lunch time. Daniela was occupying the passenger seat next to Sarah and looking serious but Sarah knew her well enough to know that she was highly amused by the situation and having a hard time keeping a straight face. Nicole was sat in the back with Charmaine and looking seriously agitated.

Charmaine was holding her hand supportively but still somewhat at a loss to understand why Nicole was making such a fuss about it. She had more than once stated firmly that she wished to hell that her own mother was as tolerant and understanding as Nicole's appeared to be. "Maybe I should come with you when you see your mum Nicky." she suggested tentatively.

Nicole jumped as if someone had stuck a hat pin into her nether portions. "Out of the bloody question!" she declared heatedly.

Daniela rolled her tongue in her cheek. "Why not Nicky?" she asked. "You're going to have to introduce Charlie to your parents sooner or later; get her feet under the table and all that. Doubtless your dad will want to take Charlie to one side and ask her if her intentions upon his daughter are serious and honourable and whether or not she will be able to maintain her in the fashion to which she is accustomed."

Sarah glared at Daniela. "You're not helping here Danny."

Daniela conceded an apologetic smile. "I'm sorry Nicky. I shouldn't make fun. I know this must be a bit traumatic for you. Still I can't help but agree with Charlie here. It sounds a bit of a storm in a teacup from what I can gather. Ok so your mum's got a bit of the wrong end of the stick and all that but to be honest I think most gay people would kill to have a mother as open minded as yours seems to be."

Nicole groaned. "I can't just come out and tell my mum that I'm seeing another girl Danny."

Daniela shrugged. "It sounds as if she's figured it out already Nicky. Just got the wrong girl is all."

Nicole blushed. "But I'd have to tell her that... that... I'm... well...."

Daniela raised an eyebrow. "What... gay? Tut tut. What a terrible admission that would be."

Nicole glanced at Charmaine hauntedly. "I'm not sure I'm ready for that yet."

Charmaine regarded her shrewdly. "By the sound of things your mum is more ready for that than you are Nicky." Nicole had the grace to look sheepish. Sarah for her part bit her lip and kept her peace. Charmaine's astute observation had pretty much hit the nail on the head. Charmaine wrapped her arms around Nicole affectionately. "Come on Fluffy it won't be all that bad."

Sarah and Daniela exchanged delighted glances. Daniela grinned wickedly and mouthed "*Fluffy!*" silently and Sarah had to put a hand over her mouth to stifle a giggle. Fortunately she was distracted by the necessity of overtaking a large heavy goods vehicle. Daniela became business like. "Listen Sarah, Nicky we're on a bit of a tight schedule today so I wonder if you wouldn't mind postponing seeing the studio and meeting the band till another day. I thought maybe we could all get together next week sometime for dinner and I could introduce you both properly to the guys."

Sarah nodded. "Ok Danny but won't it be a bit rude

if I drive you to the studio and just drop you off without saying hello?"

"No I was going to suggest that we drop you two off in town and then I drive Charlie and me to the studio. It's way out of the city centre. Anyway if you drop us off and drive into town you'll have a bitch of a time finding somewhere to park. Zurich's a bloody nightmare. We can pick the pair of you up later. If you like, I'll drive us home Sarah so you and Nicky can have a drink together after you've finished shopping."

Sarah frowned uncertainly. "How long do you expect to be Danny?"

Daniela paused to think. "I don't really know honey but we've got a fair bit I want to get through today. I'm thinking it's going to be seven o'clock at the earliest before we're through."

"Aren't you going to be late at the studio if you drop us off in town?" Sarah asked.

"We could drop Nicky and Sarah off at the tram station and they could take a tram into town." Charmaine suggested. "It's only a few minutes or so to the bahnhof. We could pick them up later in town when we're not so pushed for time."

Daniela nodded. "That's a good idea. We'd avoid most of the traffic that way. Would you two girls mind taking a tram into town?"

"No of course not." Sarah reassured her. "I'll just have to try not to get lost. I hardly know Zurich."

"It's ok I've got a street map." Nicole mentioned nonchalantly. Sarah glanced over her shoulder at Nicole and raised an enquiring eyebrow. Nicole's eyes fluttered guiltily. "What?" she asked defensively.

"Oh nothing." Sarah nodded. "Ok that sounds like a plan. Are you going to call me on my mobile when you're through at the studio then Danny?"

"Yes honey. Make sure you've got the damn thing turned on for a change! You just find yourselves a nice little pub somewhere and we'll come and pick you up."

Sarah nodded grimly and cast an acerbic glance in Nicole's direction. "Oh I'm sure we'll have no problem there!"

It *was* a good plan. There was a perfectly good tram halt on the way into town and Zurich, in common with most Swiss cities, had an excellent tram service. Sarah surrendered control of the BMW to Daniela at the kerbside by the tram halt and kissed her. Daniela patted her bottom and reached into her handbag. "Here honey, take my card and you and Nicole buy yourselves something nice to bring home."

"I don't need your credit card Danny." Sarah protested.

"Be a good girl and do as you're told. Zurich's an expensive place."

"But Danny I've got enough money in my own account. I've hardly touched my allowance this month."

"Yes but you tanked up the Ferrari yesterday and this beast this morning out of your own money."

"That's hardly going to break the bank Danny. Anyway it's mostly your money in my account and in any case.... Urgh!" Sarah's protestations were cut short in a strangled gurgle. Nicole had just clamped a hand over her mouth.

"She'll take it Danny." Nicole affirmed. "Now shut up Sarah."

Daniela laughed. "Yes shut up darling. You girls go and have fun." Daniela turned to wag a finger under Nicole's nose. "And you Miss Richardson behave yourself. If you contrive to get my girlfriend into trouble in the big city, I'll get Charlie to practice her slap riffs on your rump."

Nicole was the picture of wounded innocence. "I don't know Zurich well enough to *find* any trouble."

"I'll believe that when I see it." noted Daniela with a sour grin. "Ok Charlie we'd better cut these two loose and push on. I'll call you later Sarah. You two have fun ok and don't get into any mischief." With a last kiss Daniela and Charmaine abandoned them at the tram stop.

"I don't bloody believe you Foxy." Nicole grumbled as they stood at the tram stop clutching their handbags. "Fancy trying to talk your girlfriend out of giving you her bloody credit card. You must be soft in the head."

Sarah sighed heavily. "Well like it or not it looks like we're lumbered with the damn thing. I suppose that means we're going to have to do some shopping." Sarah uncharacteristically for a young woman was an unenthusiastic shopper; a fact which was the source of considerable incredulous astonishment to Nicole who could have quite happily made a career out of the pastime.

Nicole rolled her eyes to heaven. "You can bet your last bloody rappen on it. The Devin millions at our disposal and the whole of Zurich to spend it in? Damn right we're going to do some bloody shopping."

"I am not about to bankrupt my girlfriend just to pander to your ruthless avarice Nicole Richardson."

"Pah! She'll hardly notice."

"Hmph! I notice you didn't mention the other little item on the day's itinerary you have planned young lady."

"I haven't planned anything."

"My arse! Come on let's see it."

"See what?"

"This infamous street map you're carrying. I'm betting my last chemise it's got the precise location of every sleazy gay bar in Zurich marked down on it."

"What a load of rubbish. I just thought we needed some way to find our way about."

"Don't try to pull the wool over my eyes. I know you too well... Fluffy!"

Nicole groaned. "I'll bloody kill Charlie for calling

me that in public. How bloody embarrassing is that?"

"Don't change the subject. Let's see this map."

"All right, so maybe I have just marked down a couple of places where we could maybe go for a drink after we've done some shopping. What's wrong with that?"

"A couple?"

"Well ok half a dozen or so."

"Half a dozen? Are you dragging me into a gay pub crawl?"

"It's just to give us a little choice."

"Did Charlie tell you all about these dives?"

"Well she recommended one of them."

"And the rest?"

"I looked them up on the internet."

"Oh my God! What the hell are you dragging me into?"

"Chill Sarah. We're only going for a quiet drink and a look see. We've only ever been in the one gay bar. I thought it would be interesting to see a couple of others. Give us a bit of perspective and all that."

"Oh so all this mad scheme is just in the name of academic research is it; mere sociological investigation? The fact that you're tarted up to the max with your best dress on has got bugger all to do with this impartial inquiry I suppose."

"Hey we're on a day out in the big city. I couldn't dress up like a tramp could I?" Nicole protested. "Anyway you're looking pretty sharp yourself."

"Well yes but that's because I thought we were going to be meeting Danny's band and I didn't want to let Danny down in front of them."

"Well why should you attach more sinister motives to my desire to look nice today then?"

"Because I know you. I know when you're in hunting mode. You used to do this sort of thing all the time when you were chasing men."

"Well I'm *not* chasing men." Nicole pointed out. "And as for attracting girls, well I don't even know how to dress to attract lesbian girls so your base suspicions of my intentions are groundless. Anyway it's a good job that we're both well dressed. With Danny's credit card at our mercy we'll be wanting to hit the sort of boutiques that would chuck us out of the door on sight if we looked like a pair of hicks from the Toggenburg."

Sarah groaned theatrically. "Oh God! Today is going to be an ordeal."

"Stop whingeing Sarah. Have you got some change handy? Here comes the tram."

They stepped out of the tram at the main railway station and paused for a conference. Zurich was a big place for two country girls from the Toggenburg and they needed some sort of plan. At the station and to the south of them was a huge shopping area centred on the Bahnhofstrasse but this was a centre of seriously wealthy luxury shops and international fashion full of haut couture designer outlets and breathtakingly expensive jewellery stores. Even with Daniela's credit card at their disposal, Sarah baulked at the sort of prices they would face there. It was a wealthy person's territory and, rich girlfriend or not, Sarah felt hopelessly out of place there. "What's the problem?" demanded Nicole. "We've got money to burn haven't we?"

"My *girlfriend's* money." Sarah pointed out "I don't intend to start a conflagration in my beloved's bank account. In any case I don't feel comfortable in the sort of shops they have down the Bahnhofstrasse. They stare down their nose at you unless you're a millionaire."

"You *are* a millionaire."

"No, my *girlfriend's* a millionaire. I'm just a waitress in a rural hotel."

"I think you're splitting some seriously dodgy hairs Foxy. You live in an eight bedroomed country villa; drove us here in a seventy grand BMW SUV; went swanning around Appenzell yesterday in about a quarter of a million's worth of Ferrari convertible; you're wearing a frock that didn't cost a rappen less than a thousand francs and sporting another three grand's worth of bling on you and now you tell me that you're too humble to go shopping down the Bahnhofstrasse. Is it me that's losing the plot or you?"

"Well I think we'd be better off crossing the river and spending the afternoon in Niederdorf."

Nicole paused to consider. She had to concede that Sarah's idea was a good one. Close by the station the road crossed the river Limmat and, to the south east of the bridge, was one of the oldest quarters of the city; Niederdorf, a warren of pedestrian precincts swarming with shops, restaurants, cafés, nightclubs, bars and food stalls. It was a busy, fun part of town, more bohemian in character and younger and more trendy in nature, full of chic young boutiques and music shops. It was a more appropriate place for two young girls out for fun with a much more youthful crowd augmented by students from the university. It also incidentally happened to be, according to Nicole's detailed researches, the epicentre of the city's gay community scene with several bars, cafés and dance clubs in the neighbourhood. This, as far as Nicole was concerned, was the decisive factor. "Ok you've got a point." she allowed. "Let's cross the river and shelter in the shade of the trees."

Sarah blinked in surprise. It was a remarkably witty and subtle reference coming from Nicole. She pulled a face. "I think the Stonewall Inn is in Greenwich village, New York Nicky; not in Niederdorf."

They negotiated the busy intersection at the station and walked across the bridge. On the edge of Niederdorf they passed a small hotel where a spectacularly dressed young lady was lounging about outside. She was pretty enough for Nicole to submit her to an appraising look and she received an inviting smile back as a result.

297

Excitedly she whispered to Sarah. "That girl gave me a come on Sarah. I'm sure she did."

Sarah sighed. For a girl that was forever berating the rural backwardness of the Toggenburg, Nicole was surprisingly unworldly when it came to the trappings of urban life. Sarah was no city girl herself but at least her years at university in Bern had taught her to be a little more streetwise. "Forget it Nicky. I'm not letting you spend Danny's money like that."

"What the hell are you talking about?"

"She's a *prostitute* you muppet!"

"You're kidding me."

"Not at all. That hotel is doubtless her workplace."

"Why would she try to invite a girl?"

"She's probably having a slack day and prepared to bat her eyelashes at anybody who seems interested, regardless of their gender. I suppose it makes no odds to her. It's not as if she's interested in her clients for their sexual attraction or anything. Who knows, a pretty young girl might make a pleasant change from the usual fat, balding middle-aged men she normally does business with and you *were* leering at her. Maybe she thought that two well-dressed young girls might have a bit of money about them."

Nicole pondered. "I didn't think this was the red light district Sarah."

"It isn't really. Oh there are a few brothels and strip clubs in Niederdorf but the main red light region is around Langstrasse over on the west side of the river. Alan took me for dinner in a Brazilian restaurant there one day, when we were in Zurich. It's a pretty dodgy neighbourhood but apparently it's pretty tame compared with the red light districts in most big European cities." Sarah giggled. "Danny told me a funny story about the street girls in Zurich."

"Oh yes?"

"Yes. Apparently the local city council was trying to

clean up the city a bit and they tried to pass a civic ordinance forbidding prostitutes to ply their trade on the streets during peak trading hours. The local prostitutes' guild was outraged. They stood to lose a lot of business. As a result they all went on strike in protest."

"Oh come on!"

"It's true. Every single last working girl in the city went on strike. They even staged a demonstration and a rally in the city centre all dressed up in their working clothes, waving placards. Apparently it was one of the funniest demonstrations ever seen in the city. After all you don't see many protest strikes from a group of workers demanding *longer* working hours."

"Oh God! Only in Switzerland. Can you imagine a picket line outside a brothel?"

"Priceless isn't it? I wonder if they bussed scabs in from other cities to cross the picket lines."

"What happened in the end? Did they stop the ordinance or what?"

"I don't really know what happened although that young lady we just saw would seem to suggest that the protest was successful. It's two o'clock in the afternoon and she was definitely on duty. I suppose perhaps that sober heads in the city council may have reconsidered. After all, a group as colourful as that must be worth its weight in gold as a tourist attraction. The Langstrasse holds a big carnival every year that is one of the city's most salacious and popular entertainments. There's another thing too. I suspect that it doesn't do for people with fragile public reputations to piss off the city's prostitutes. God knows how many prominent civic figures there are who wouldn't wish their leisure activities to become public knowledge."

They turned on to the Niederdorfstrasse; the long pedestrian street that arrowed through the heart of the Niederdorf district. It was a fine day for a stroll down this bustling centre of the old town for the autumn sun was shining kindly and had lured thousands of people out onto the streets. It was a perfect day for people watching or, more specifically in Nicole's case, for girl watching. Sarah could sympathise with Nicole's new found fascination with her own gender. When Sarah had been first coming to terms with her own sexuality she had done much the same thing; going through to Winterthur to observe girls. It had been an exciting journey of discovery. Pretty girls were an endless source of fascination. The city was a perfect place to watch girls and, despite being October, the weather was still warm enough to tempt those girls out onto the street in clothes more notable for their decorative function rather than as a barrier against the elements.

Nicole was clearly excited at the opportunity to overtly look at attractive young girls; something she wouldn't have dreamed of doing in the Toggenburg. In truth, she was not alone. Sarah was enjoying the experience too. In spite of the fact that she was in a serious relationship with one of the most stunningly beautiful lesbian women in the country, Sarah was, nevertheless, not averse to the charms of a pretty girl even if they were only to look at. She *liked* looking at them. Furthermore her enjoyment was increased this day by the opportunity afforded to share the experience. Daniela often pointed out nice looking girls but Sarah was usually inhibited about doing the same by the feeling that it was somehow disrespectful to your girlfriend to be ogling other girls whilst in her presence. Also it was true that Daniela was so captivatingly lovely that, when with her, Sarah usually only had eyes for her and all other girls paled in comparison. Today however she was not only at liberty to admire the girls but also able to discuss their merits with an equally enthusiastic observer.

Nicole nudged Sarah. "Check out the girl on that café terrace; the one in the blue top. She's hot."

Sarah laughed. "She's also straight Nicky. Can't you point out a girl without a bloody great hunk of a fellah in tow for a change?"

"Hell I only want to look at her not shag her."

"Well your gaydar needs some fine tuning. So far every girl you've pointed out to me has either had the boyfriend in tow or been a prostitute."

"Well how the hell do you tell the difference anyway?"

Sarah scratched her head. "To be honest I'm not sure. Oh sometimes it's obvious. I mean you could tell Charmaine was gay straight away but a lot of the times gay girls don't look as if they're gay. It's fairly easy with the boyish looking girls but a lot of lesbians are pretty girly too. I mean most gay girls take years refining their gaydar to spot each other. Danny can pick out a gay girl a hundred metres away with unerring accuracy. I don't know how she does it."

"Well it's easy for her isn't it Sarah?"

"How do you mean?"

"Well she's just about the most well-known gay female in Switzerland Sarah. Any gay girl that sets eyes on her is going to light up like a Christmas tree. They'd stand out a mile."

"I see where you're coming from. Yes that's a good point. I think a lot of the time when I spot a gay girl on the street it's because they spot me as well. You get that "Is she or isn't she moment" and then you realise you're both looking at each other and wondering the same. Bingo! Contact!"

Nicole paused to consider. "Maybe we're too straight looking Sarah. If we're going to spot the gay girls maybe we should look a bit more lesbian and attract their notice." Nicole laughed shortly. "It's ironic isn't it? Before you met Danny and came out as gay you looked more lesbian than you do now."

"Hmmph! Have you noticed that you seem to be

dressing more girly since you started going out with Charlie?"

"Well it's not really helping us now is it?"

"Well we could try to look more gay."

"I suppose so. What are we going to do? Buy some more masculine cut clothes or get your hair cut short?"

"No fucking way! Danny loves my hair. She'd wring my neck if I had it shorn off."

"Well what do you suggest?"

"Well let's try holding hands. Better still put your arm around my waist. That should send a good enough signal to our spiritual sisters."

"You're taking the piss."

"Why not? Come on we're in Zurich. Nobody knows us here."

"Are you sure it would work. I mean we'd look like a couple and turn everybody off."

"We'd still attract attention and, as you already said, we're only trying to spot them, not shag them."

"Ok we'll give it a bash; just as long as we don't pull in a bunch of fellahs with lesbian fantasies."

"That's always going to be a risk."

As chance would have it, their luck was in for they had gone no further than a hundred and fifty metres when two girls passed them in the opposite direction. One girl might have been a little ambiguous in a short skirt and white top but the other girl wore a pair of stylish black trousers with a masculine style shirt and a black waistcoat. With her boyish hairstyle she looked the part even if she hadn't smiled openly at Nicole and Sarah. The two girls smiled back and there was an instant understanding between the four girls before they separated. Nicole was exultant at the triumph. "They were gorgeous." she declared. "Do you think they're a couple?"

"I don't know Nicky. They're both lesbian for sure though."

"How can you tell? I mean the tall girl was straightforward enough."

"Possibly a bad choice of words there Nicky."

"You know what I mean. The other girl though... I mean if you saw her on her own would you have known she was gay?"

"Didn't you see her earring?"

"No. What about it?"

"She was wearing a black triangle as an earring."

"Well what the fuck does that mean?"

"It's a lesbian identification symbol Nicky. Gay men use a pink triangle as a gay symbol and lesbians a black one. They're taken from the triangles that were obliged to be worn by gay inmates of the Nazi concentration camps of World War Two."

"You mean lesbians had to wear a black triangle on their prison clothes?"

"Not exactly. Certainly gay men had to wear a pink triangle. It's a bit more complicated with lesbians. Black triangles were the badge given to anti-social women. To the Nazis, any woman was anti-social who didn't conform to the stereotype of submissive housewife taking care of the home and breeding a new generation of Aryan babies for the fatherland and the greater glory of the master race and the Third Reich. Lesbians certainly came under that heading and so the lesbian subculture has appropriated the black triangle as its symbol."

"God where do you learn all this stuff?"

"I do my research. I've got the country's most famous lesbian as a girlfriend. I need to know this stuff."

"So a black triangle tells other gay women that you're gay?"

"Yes among other things."

"What other things? Are you telling me that there're more symbols and stuff you can wear on you to advertise your sexuality."

303

"Hell yes. There's the labrys, or double headed battle-axe which is a symbol that dates back to the Minoan civilisation or there's the lambda from the Greek letter which is a general gay symbol. Or you can wear various forms of the gay rainbow flag or, for lesbians, the double Venus symbol. There're loads of them."

"And you can buy this stuff as jewellery?"

"Sure you can. All sorts of stuff; necklaces, pendants, bangles, commitment rings, earrings you name it."

Nicole clapped her hands together. "That's it then! We're on a mission Sarah. Let's find a trendy alternative jewellery store and see if they've got some lesbian chic bling in stock."

"You're kidding."

"Straight up. Er... I'll rephrase that. I mean sure. Come on Sarah. We haven't even started to put a dent in your girlfriend's credit card yet."

If there was one thing that Zurich possessed in abundance it was jewellery stores. Most of the big brand leaders in jewellery and watch making, Cartier, Bucherer, Tiffany's, Swatch and the like, were concentrated around the Bahnhofstrasse but there were plenty of smaller and less well known outlets scattered around the city. Niederdorf was the perfect location to look for the kind of shop Nicole wanted to find and within a few minutes they had located a likely prospect. It was a trendy little boutique with a wide range of costume jewellery, trendy watches, Goth adornments and outrageous accessories clearly marketing the young crowd. You wouldn't go there to order a tiara. You *would* go there to buy a nose stud. Inside the shop, the girl who came across to serve them was wearing a black see through blouse over a black bra, skin tight black leather trousers, high black boots with huge platform heels, assorted piercings, heavy black eye-shadow and a scarlet streak in her jet black hair. It was all very encouraging.

"Greuzi." She greeted them. "Can I help you girls?"

Nicole's earlier confidence seemed to evaporate when it came to the test. She swallowed and blushed. "Er we're er... looking for... well er for well you know... girl's jewellery."

The girl gave Nicole an amused look. "*Girl's* jewellery? Do you think you could be a little more specific?"

Nicole took a deep breath and tried again. "Well you know jewellery for well... like two girls."

"*Two* girls?" the girl still seemed perplexed.

Nicole was becoming desperate. "Well that two girls might er like want to er wear to... er together like."

"I'm sorry Miss, I'm not catching your drift."

Steeling herself for one last effort Nicole lowered her voice. "Well you know something a girl might er want to buy for... well er... another girl."

Comprehension dawned at last. "Ah!" said the girl in an unnecessarily loud voice, "You mean like *lesbian* jewellery?"

Nicole cringed. The girl's voice had a carry like a well hit golf ball. Several other clients in the shop turned to stare in interest. Blushing furiously Nicole murmured "Yes."

"Sure we've got a range of Lez gear. Were you looking for anything in particular?"

"Er we just wanted to browse for the moment if that's ok."

"Sure I'll go dig out some things for you."

Nicole leaned back against a counter with a groan. "Oh god this is torment. Stop fucking laughing Sarah."

Sarah covered her mouth with her hand. "I can't help it. This is priceless."

In amelioration of Nicole's embarrassment it seemed as if they had hit the jackpot on the first attempt for the shop seemed to have an inexhaustible supply of lesbian related jewellery. The shop girl laid out tray after

305

tray of products for their perusal. It was a bewildering collection. Many of the lesbian symbols that Sarah had already mentioned were on offer but there were dozens of others. There was even a range of jewellery from the hit television series "The L Word" on display and some startling items that caught them by surprise. One of these latter consisted of two rings each with a Venus symbol on them connected by a thin silver chain. "What's this?" inquired Nicole, picking the object up in puzzlement.

"Nipple rings." the girl informed her succinctly. Nicole dropped the object as if it had come fresh out of a furnace.

Sarah also found a surprising item that caught her eye. It was a beautifully crafted white gold pendant on a chain with two interlocking Ds with a single large sapphire set in the centre. "This is lovely," she told the girl, "but what has it to do with lesbianism?"

"Ah that's from our new Daniela Devin collection... you know the lesbian singer."

"Yes.. er yes I've heard of her."

"Well the two Ds are her initials and the sapphire is a reference to her single "Blue Stone Lady"."

"Oh! I see."

Nicole grinned. "Now that you've just *got* to buy Foxy."

The shop girl looked uncertain. "It's a little pricy." she pointed out.

"I'll take it." said Sarah in sudden decision.

The girl blinked. "Of course. Do you want it gift wrapping?"

"Yes please."

The girl left to wrap Sarah's purchase. Sarah took a deep breath. "I don't believe I did that. That cost over eight hundred francs."

"Well you've got Danny's card."

"I'm not going to pay for it out of Danny's money you idiot. I can't use my girlfriend's card to buy a gift for her."

"But most of your own money is from Danny isn't it?"

"Not all of it. I still have all my wages from the Hotel which I've hardly touched because Danny picks up all the bills and I've still got a nice chunk of money in my savings account. Danny does give me a generous allowance but I use that mostly for housekeeping and to be honest I never spend as much as she gives me. I'm forever telling her that I don't need that much."

Nicole frowned. "Do you think that range of jewellery is an official endorsement by Danny, Sarah, or somebody just using her name. If so Danny may want to sue."

"Oh God that's a point. I don't know if she's copyrighted the use of her initials or anything. She's never mentioned endorsing a line of jewellery with her name on it."

Nicole shrugged. "Well we seem to have got distracted. Let's find something for us two."

By the time the shop girl had returned with Sarah's purchase they had made a choice. It was a fairly conservative one for they picked out two matching eighteen carat gold chains with double Venus pendants in the same material. They were understated but stylish and reasonably priced at a little over four hundred francs apiece. The shop girl was getting more interested by the minute. These two girls had money it seemed and she was on commission. She smiled at them. "Do you want these wrapping as well?" she asked.

"No need. Just put them in their boxes." Nicole told her. "We're wearing them today."

The girl lifted an eyebrow. "I see. Are you two a couple then?"

Nicole started. "Er... no. We're just good friends."

"Are you two from Zurich then?"

Sarah answered. "No we're just here for the day. We

live in the country in Canton St Gallen. We're going back sometime this evening.

The girl's interest rose another notch. "Is that so? Hey we close at seven o'clock this evening. Maybe you two girls would like to meet up for a drink before you head off home. There's a little bar just on the corner that's kind of nice."

Nicole swallowed. "Oh yes I saw it when we came up the street."

"Well if you fancy it I'll be there with my colleague just after seven. Pop in if you've nothing better to do."

Nicole and Sarah exchanged glances. "Er we'll think about it." Nicole told her. "We'll be hanging around until at least then I think."

"Great I hope to see you. I'll just go put these in a box for you."

Once she had left once more Nicole pulled a face and ran a hand through her hair. "Jesus! I think we just pulled Sarah. That bar is one of the one's on my list."

Sarah placed a hand on her hip and regarded Nicole with exasperation. "Oh just great! So now when Danny and Charlie come looking for us this evening they'll find we've just picked up a couple of shop girls. I can't even go shopping with you without you managing to get me into trouble."

"Relax we don't have to turn up. Anyway are we done here?"

"Not quite. You ought to buy something for Charlie."

"Eh? You're kidding. I can't do that."

"Why the hell not?"

"Well for one thing I can't afford it. Since you've set the precedent for not using Danny's money to buy her a present I can hardly now use her money to buy *my* girlfriend one."

"You don't need to. You paid me the rent for the house this month but as of the beginning of the month you didn't have to. I was going to give you it back but now I think you could use it to buy Charlie a present. If you're a bit short I'll lend you the rest."

Nicole grimaced. "I could have done with that money Sarah. I've hardly got any work at the moment."

"You've got plenty Nicky. For one thing you don't have to pay rent anymore. There'll still be some weekend work in the Hirschen and Simon and Peter need help decorating their new pub."

"They haven't got the money to pay me yet Sarah."

"No but Danny has. We were talking about it last night. Danny's putting a good deal of money into that pub and she says she'll pay you something for your efforts."

Nicole brightened. "Oh God! That'll be a blessing."

Sarah grinned and pinched Nicole's cheek. "Don't worry honey. We're not going to let you go short. On top of that, we've still got Danny's card for the rest of the day and there's another thing you haven't thought about."

"What's that?"

"Well I'm not the only one with a rich girlfriend now am I? Charlie may not earn as much as the regular band members but Danny is certainly going to make sure that she's well paid and doubtless there are going to be all sorts of opportunities for her now. She'll be rolling in the stuff so, if I were you, I'd stay on her sweet side and buy her that present. Call it casting bread upon the waters."

"Well what should I buy her?"

"Well as it happens I've seen just the thing in that case over there. Since we're buying necklaces for you, me and Danny it would look awful if we didn't do the same for her. It's not lesbian related but I think she'll like it."

"So show me."

It was a chunky pendant in fourteen carat gold on a

chain, fashioned in the shape of an electric guitar. Nicole loved it as soon as she saw it. It was fairly expensive at three hundred and fifty francs but she decided on it without hesitation. The shop girl returned to find that they had another purchase. She grinned. "Every time I take my eyes off you two you've bought something else. Maybe I ought to slip out for a coffee and you'll end up buying half the shop."

Nicole fingered the pendant lovingly. "I ought to have it engraved."

The shop girl nodded. "No problem there. We do free engraving the same day. It doesn't take long. You could come back before seven and we'll have it done for you and then we could go for that drink."

Nicole hesitated. "Ok then. Could you just engrave the letter N on the back?"

Sarah raised an eyebrow sardonically. "N for Nicole? Sure you don't want F for Fluffy?"

Nicole glared at her. "Somebody's asking for a slap around here."

Sarah laughed and turned to the shop girl. "Ok we'll collect it later on. Can we pay you now?"

Once the complex financial transactions were completed the two girls found themselves back out on the street. Sarah was looking shell shocked at having just spent two thousand francs on trivial jewellery but Nicole was only just gearing up for some serious shopping with a predatory gleam in her eye. She dragged Sarah away and they began to hit the shops in earnest.

Chapter Eighteen

By five o'clock, Sarah had had enough and called a time out. Nicole's enthusiasm for spending Daniela's money had worn her out and, in any case, if it continued like this, Sarah grumbled, then Daniela would be reduced to busking on street corners to make ends meet. Besides, the day was still warm enough to make the prospect of a glass of beer on a sunny cafe terrace an inviting prospect. Wearily Sarah deposited her bags beside a free table and lowered herself gratefully into a seat. Nicole was still grumbling a little. "We haven't even got to the shoe shops yet." she protested.

"Don't you think we've spent enough bloody money for one day?"

"Well you need a pair of shoes to go with that outfit you got in that last shop."

"Right now I need a sodding beer."

"Well I suppose we've got time to take a break. The shops won't close till seven o'clock."

"What happened to your original plan of dragging me round this collection of gay bars you have on your list?"

"Hell we've got ages to do that in."

Nicole was right. Whilst Nicole had tried on some skirts in one boutique Sarah had received a phone call from Daniela. She'd been apologetic. Things were taking longer than they had expected. She anticipated not being able to get away from the practice studio until nine o'clock. She told Sarah not to wait for them to eat if they were hungry. They'd probably get some take-aways in so she and Nicole ought to grab something in town. She was sorry that it was taking so long. Sarah reassured her that it was fine. "Are you having fun?" Daniela had asked.

Sarah had cringed. "Oh Danny I'm sorry but we're spending too much money. Nicky's dragging me around the shops like a woman possessed."

Daniela had chuckled softly. "Oh let her have a bit of fun Sarah. If she goes too mad I'll take it out of Charlie's pay."

"Oh God what would Charlie say?"

"I'm kidding, you doughnut! Seriously Sarah let her spend herself silly if she wants. She's not going to bankrupt us in a couple of hours shopping."

"She'll have a bloody good try."

"Sarah darling our CD sales are going viral. I checked out our finances this morning while you were out getting breakfast. We're considerably richer than we were yesterday but not as rich as we're going to be tomorrow in spite of anything Nicole can do to prevent it. Relax. Spend money and enjoy yourselves. I'll see you later. Love you."

"Love you too."

Despite Daniela's reassurance, the frugal part of Sarah still blanched at the amount of money they were spending and, in any case, she was already mightily fed up of the growing legion of shopping bags she was having to carry around. "Well I'm just about shopped out for one day." She told Nicole. "Anyway we have to eat sooner or later because Danny and Charlie won't be joining us for dinner and I'm damned if I want to wait until we get back to the Toggenburg before grabbing some calories. Don't forget too that we have to go back to that Jewellery store to pick up your pendant."

Nicole took a seat in surrender and rummaged in one of her bags to gloat over a top she had just bought. "Ok Sarah we'll give it a break for the day. Honestly though you need to connect up more with your feminine side. Most women with virtually unlimited credit at their disposal would have to be dragged screaming and kicking away from a shopping mall."

312

"I'm just not that into shopping Nicky. You know that."

Nicole sighed theatrically. "And to think you're the one that pulled a millionairess as a girlfriend. What a tragic waste."

"Oh shut up Nicky and see if you can grab that waiter's attention and get us some drinks. I want a beer."

Nicole rolled her eyes in mock despair. "Oh gosh Sarah! Are you sure you want to go that far? You can't live the high life all the time you know. This isn't St Tropez."

"I'm *thirsty* Nicky and I want a bloody beer."

"Oh well... hold the Dom Perignon Oenotheque 1995. Sarah wants a fucking beer." Nicole turned to attract the waiter's attention.

As the waiter saw to their order, Sarah reached into one of her bags and withdrew the two little boxes containing their double Venus pendants on their chains. "I thought the idea of these was that we were going to wear them today."

"Oh hell yes. I forgot. Let's put them on now."

Sarah opened a box and took one of the chains. "Ok come here, turn around and let me hang this on you. Lift your hair out of the way." Nicole complied and Sarah fastened the chain about her neck in great solemnity. Before releasing her Sarah leaned forward and kissed her gently on the side of the neck.

Nicole started. "What the hell did you do that for?"

"Just telling you I love you. You're a complete fruit cake and you drive me round the bend sometimes but I love you to bits anyway." She grasped Nicole's shoulders and whispered in her ear. "It's always a sign of love when you hang something around somebody's neck Nicky. Don't you know that?"

Nicole breathed deeply. "If you do that again Sarah we'll have to get a room."

"Hmmph! I'm not going into competition with your

bloody harem. Anyway what would Charlie say? You've got enough explaining to do regarding the two shop girls you're supposed to be meeting later."

"God you wouldn't tell her would you?"

"Your secrets are safe with me. Come on then. Help me with this other chain." Sarah turned her back and lifted her hair. Nicole swallowed and hung the chain about her neck with trembling fingers. Finally she managed to close the clasp and cleared her throat. Sarah turned her head slightly. "Well?"

"Well what?"

"My kiss you dibble dabble."

"Oh er... right." Nicole leaned forward to kiss her on the cheek but Sarah turned her head to catch her lips. They held the kiss for a long second.

"Ahem! Your drinks Frauleinen." The waiter was stood over them austerely. The two girls broke hastily and a blushing Sarah fumbled in her bag to pay.

When he had left them they broke into giggles. Nicole picked up her drink. "Sante" She fingered the pendant at her throat with a laugh. "You know something Sarah. I never knew being gay was so much fun."

Sarah regarded her sourly. "Maybe you should have tried it years ago."

"Seriously Sarah. It really is. The hunt is so much more exciting. Being straight is boring." Sarah grinned affectionately at her irrepressible friend. Nicole seemed truly liberated today. The chance to be completely out and unafraid in an environment where nobody knew her, other than good friends who shared her sexuality, was exhilarating to her. She seemed to have come alive. Her eyes were sparkling and she looked, well there was no other word for it really, *gay*. Of course she was enjoying the novelty and, furthermore, Nicole had inherited a good deal of deal of her mother's penchant for outrageousness. Being able to walk the street openly displaying a sexuality that many still considered taboo

314

was deliciously exciting to her. Spotting other girls of like mind was a triumph as if it connected her to some secret sisterhood beyond the confines of convention. It made the world a thrilling adventure.

"It's not all fun and games you know Nicky." Sarah cautioned. "It's all very well to flaunt it here in Zurich where we don't know anyone but it's a whole different game back home where you're surrounded by friends and family and people you have to hide it from. That's where the real test is." Sarah paused. "Are you listening Nicky?"

Well the answer to that was not really. Nicole had caught the eye of a very pretty girl passing on the street who she was sure had paused in mid stride to admire her and Sarah. Nicole smiled at her and raised a hand to wiggle her fingers in greeting. The girl hesitated for a fraction of a second before continuing on her way but she tossed her hair back flirtatiously and her walk became noticeably more languid and alluring. Nicole punched the air in triumph. "*Yes*! I think we can put her down as a definite Foxy."

Sarah leaned back in her chair and laughed. "God you're hopeless Nicky. If you were *my* girlfriend I'd bloody chain you up at night. I swear I would."

"Aww come on Sarah. She was cute."

"And just what would you have done if she had come over and joined us Nicky? You've already got a date at seven o'clock not to mention the fact that your regular girlfriend is turning up some time after nine."

Nicole seemed unfazed. "I didn't catch the name of that girl in the shop Sarah. Did you notice she had a piercing through her tongue? I bet that's fun when she goes down to lick..."

"*Too much information!*"

"Well it would be." Nicole shivered delightedly. "Sex with girls is great isn't it Sarah? It's loads more fun than with men. Oh I'm sure there must be some men out

315

there who know what they're doing but the vast majority of them are just hopeless. Women just know instinctively what turns each other on and they're so soft and sensual. I can't believe I never tried it before Rosy violated me on the alp that day."

Sarah shook her head fondly. "I think I'll buy Charlie a collar and lead."

Nicole took another sip of her drink. Sarah didn't know what the drink was. Nicole had picked it out off the cocktail menu. Sarah knew only that it was expensive and probably contained more alcohol than was good for her. Nicole seemed lost in thought for a moment. "You know Sarah there's only one thing I miss."

"Oh God! Now what?"

"Well you know... I quite like.... well being penetrated too."

"Oh for fuck's sake!"

Nicole held up her hand. "Don't get me wrong. I don't mean I miss men like that. Charlie can do more with her hands and mouth than most men have never dreamed of. Then there's this other thing she calls scissoring which is where you..."

"I'm aware of that particular position thank you Nicky."

"Anyway I'm not complaining or anything. It's just that when she tops me I'd like her to be able to penetrate me and give me a right good..."

"Ok, ok! I've got the picture. I think we can skip the details."

"I'm not being heterosexual about this Sarah. I mean if all men have got going for them is a dick then they're pretty much a waste of space aren't they. Still if Charlie had an auxiliary penis she'd be just about perfect."

"Well use a sodding dildo then."

"I suppose so. I don't know if Charlie's got one."

316

"Well you've got a vibrator. I know you have because you're always leaving it out after you've been playing with it."

"Yes I guess so."

"And if you like scissoring get one of those double headed flexible dildos so you can penetrate each other at the same time."

Nicole's eyes widened enthusiastically. "God! That sounds like fun Have you and Danny got one?"

"None of your bloody business."

"Come on Sarah. You can tell me. I'm a newbie at this sort of thing. I need some tips."

"Well we do have one as it so happens but I'm damned if I'm going into all the sordid details."

"Could we borrow it?"

"No you bloody well could not. Buy your own bloody toys. I'm damned if I'm letting you rifle through the contents of our bedside cabinet. Buy one yourself. Better yet buy Charlie a strap on."

"What the hell's a strap on?"

Sarah blushed. "Well it's like a dildo you wear with a sort of harness so it's like an artificial penis so you can simulate straight penetrative sex."

"Oh wow! Do you have one of those as well?"

"Well as it happens Danny brought one back from Berlin with her."

"Yes? And?"

"And what?"

"Details, details Sarah. I want details. You can't end a story in the middle. Have you tried it out yet?"

"Well yes we have."

"And?"

"Well it was fun."

"Yes?"

"What more do you want to know for Christ's sake?"

"Bloody hell Sarah! You haven't even begun. For

one thing which one of you used it?"

"Well we..."

"Come on Foxy. Don't be shy."

"Well we both had a go."

Nicole's jaw dropped open in delighted astonishment. "Oh wow! Jesus! Talk about a game of two halves. I've just got to have one of those. Do you think Danny could fetch one for us?"

Sarah rapped on the table top imperiously. "Danny's got better things to do with her time than supply you and your girlfriend with bedtime accessories Nicole Richardson. If you want one, then go and buy one yourself."

"I wouldn't know where."

"There's a perfectly good sex shop I noticed on the corner of Muhlgasse and Limmatquai Nicky. I'm sure they have an extensive range of sex aids there."

Nicole swallowed. "What? Go in a sex shop? You're kidding. I couldn't."

"Why not?"

"I... I just couldn't. I'd die of embarrassment."

"Plenty of people do Nicky. Where did you buy your vibrator?"

"A girl from school bought it for me. I dared her."

Sarah sat back with a wicked grin; the germ of an evil plan formulating in her mind. "Well I dare *you*. Let's see just how far this new found gay liberation of yours extends. I dare you to go in that shop and buy a strap-on dildo."

Nicole looked at her desperately. "I...I can't."

Sarah leaned forward to home in on her prey. "I tell you what. I'll do a deal with you. You go in and buy that strap on and I'll let you use Danny's card to buy that handbag you were after."

Nicole hesitated. It was a telling bribe. The handbag in question had been a bone of contention. They'd seen it in a boutique a little earlier and Nicole had fallen in love

318

with it. But it was a designer make costing the best part of eight hundred francs and Sarah had refused point blank to allow Nicole to squander Daniela's money on such an expensive triviality. Since then however she had received permission from Daniela to allow Nicole to indulge herself and she had already decided to treat Nicole to the bag. Now, however, she had a mind to make Nicole earn it. Nicole was wavering. The handbag was a temptation of the devil. "You'd really buy that for me?"

"Oh yes but only if you agree to buy that strap-on."

"This is fucking blackmail!"

Sarah smiled sweetly. "Yes it is isn't it?"

"Bitch!"

"Come on Fluffy. What's it to be?"

"If I have to go in to this fucking sex shop will you come with me?"

"Damn right I will. I wouldn't miss this for a king's ransom. This is payback time; revenge for that day you made me model that sodding bikini in that sports shop in Lisighaus."

"You vindictive cow!"

"So are you going to do it?"

Nicole took a deep breath. "All right bitch! I'll do it then." She sighed in defeat and tapped the side of her glass. "But I'm going to need another of these first."

Sometime later they were stood outside the sex shop in question or, to be more precise, Sarah was stood outside the shop, leaning against a wall with her arms folded, looking smug. Nicole was pacing up and down on the pavement looking agitated and had been doing for several minutes. Sarah glanced casually at her watch with a wicked grin. "I don't wish to jiggle your elbow Nicky dearest but it is nearly six o'clock. Bearing in mind that we still have to go back for your bag, should you manage to earn it, and still have to get back to the jewellers before seven then, if it were done, then 'twere

319

best done quickly."

Nicole glared at her. "You're bloody loving this aren't you?"

"I've had less agreeable shopping experiences I must confess."

Nicole growled an unfortunate epithet and steeled herself to the task in hand. "Ok let's do it before you misquote any more bloody Macbeth at me."

Her throwing down of the gauntlet to Nicole notwithstanding, Sarah had never been in a sex shop in her life. She was surprised. In her mind she had envisioned a somewhat seedy, dark little interior populated by furtive old men guiltily thumbing their way through dirty magazines. Doubtless in the back streets of the red light districts of many European cities there were indeed shops that fitted that description. This however was a fashionable quarter of Zurich and even the sex shops tended to be on the up-market side. With its chic stylish interior, glossy displays and neon lighting this shop could have been any fashion outlet in the city as long as you ignored the frequently startling array of products on display. There were parts of the shop in fact that resembled a chic lingerie store with racks full of wispy creations and items of underwear quite clearly designed more for the purposes of titillation than practical use. God in heaven there were even changing rooms. Sarah experienced a sense of disbelief. Would you seriously want to change into an item of underwear that somebody else had possibly already tried on? She glanced quickly at the price tags on some of these items and was truly appalled. How anybody could justify prices as astronomical as these for items of clothing that could quite easily have been folded up and fitted into a small handbag beggared belief.

Even the shop assistants were a surprise. In her mind's eye she had imagined a rather grubby paunchy man behind a counter surreptitiously handing over the shop's wares in plain brown paper bags to shifty looking customers glancing nervously over their shoulders. In fact the shop was attended by two very smartly dressed young ladies with friendly smiles and an efficient air about them. They could have been assistants in a bank for all the evidence to the contrary. In fact the presence of these two attractive girls very nearly broke Nicole's resolve. She might just have been able to deal with a man but telling a pretty girl that she wanted a strap-on dildo for her girlfriend didn't bear thinking about. She stood in the middle of the shop in an agony of indecision. "Oh the hell with it!" she whispered fiercely to Sarah. "I guess I don't really need a new handbag after all. Let's get the fuck out of here."

"Pussy!"

"How the hell am I going to ask a bloody lass for an artificial dick Sarah?"

At this point one of the shop assistants walked over. "Can I help you ladies?" she inquired with a pleasant smile.

Nicole jumped. "Er we're.. er just looking." she informed the girl in a voice that sounded unnaturally high and squeaky.

"Well please let me know if you require any assistance."

"Yes... er yes of course."

The girl drifted away and Nicole leaned heavily against some shelving. "Oh God! How the hell have I talked myself into this?" She glared at Sarah fiercely. "You're not bloody helping here Sarah."

Sarah had half collapsed against a rack full of bondage wear, holding her side and trying to muffle her laughter. "I... I can't help it. Your face was a picture when she told you to call her if you needed assistance. I wonder what she would have said if you'd told her you needed help with a strap-on. God above she might have demonstrated one for you."

"Well what the hell am I supposed to do?"

"Well just look among the shelves until we find what we're looking for and then just take it over to the counter, pay the money and run."

It was a good plan but it very quickly came unstuck. There was such a bewildering collection of sex aids in the shop that they frankly had no idea where to start. Nicole regarded the array in desperation. "What the hell is a rampant rabbit for fuck's sake Sarah?"

"No idea but it comes with batteries included according to the box."

"Oh God! This is hopeless. I've not the faintest notion of what half of these things are for let alone anything else. You're going to have to ask that girl Sarah."

"No bloody way! You're not squirming out of it like that Nicole Richardson. This is *your* bloody problem. *You* ask the girl."

"Oh hell!"

Sarah examined her fingernails distractedly. "And Tempus Fugit Nicky. It's nearly ten past six so I'd hurry it up if I were you."

"Shit!"

Evidently the shop assistant had been observing them closely and noticing that they were flummoxed. She reappeared at their side. "Were you ladies looking for anything in particular?" she asked helpfully.

Nicole swallowed and stared at her in abject terror. Sarah nudged her. "Well go on. Ask the lady."

Nicole struggled to articulate for a few seconds. "Well er yes.... I mean we... er were looking for something." she ground out at last.

"Well possibly I might be able to help."

Nicole clenched her fists and took a breath. "Well we were looking for a slap on." she bleated pathetically.

The girl raised her eyebrows enquiringly. "A slap on? Oh do you mean a strap on?"

"Yes! Yes that was it." Nicole squeaked desperately before turning to shoot a poisonous glance at Sarah who seemed to be choking on some obstruction in her oesophagus.

"Well if you'd like to follow me I'll show you our range."

Nicole blinked. "You... you have a range?"

"Oh yes. If you'd like to step this way." They had a range all right. Sarah had no idea that strap-ons came in such a wide variety of sizes, shapes, designs and colours. There were even ones with changeable dildos; ones with odd appendages on or curious nobs on them; ones that came with their own lubricants; even, God help us, ones with batteries! There were black ones, flesh coloured ones, ones in day-glo colour schemes; even ones that lit up or glowed in the dark. There were big fat ones, little skinny ones, double headed ones and even ones with rotating heads. It was unbelievable. Sarah wondered what kind of person dedicated a career to the design of sex toys. God only knew what went on in the research and development departments of the manufacturers of these products.

Nicole was staring at the array with the air of a person suffering from severe post traumatic stress disorder. Once launched into her spiel, the shop assistant could not have been more helpful and informative and she was pulling one line after another off the shelves and extolling their various virtues and advantages. Nicole had turned a delicate shade of green and was making a passable imitation of an asphyxiating goldfish. "I er... I don't know." She conceded helplessly.

Sarah poked her in the ribs. "Maybe you'd like to go to the changing rooms and try a couple on." She suggested malevolently.

"Why don't you just fuck off?" Nicole growled between clenched teeth.

"I'd recommend this model." the shop assistant told

her briskly. "It has adjustable straps, it's a good make and, although a little more expensive than some of the others, it does have..."

"We'll take it!" Nicole yipped, cutting the girl off in full cry.

"Are you sure? I mean this model here for instance..."

"No, no, no! We'll take that one."

"As you wish. Do you want it wrapping?"

"Look just put it in a bloody bag all right."

At the counter the girl placed Nicole's purchase in a bag. There was nothing surreptitious about this shop. The bag was a branded carrier bag bearing the store's logo. Hastily Nicole concealed it inside one of her other shopping bags as Sarah handed over the credit card. As the girl processed the card Sarah whispered to Nicole. "God knows what Danny's going to say when she finds that little item on her balance."

The girl handed back Sarah's card. "Have a nice day now."

"Yes... er thank you." The two girls fled from the shop with their tails between their legs.

"Well mission accomplished." breathed Sarah out on the street outside.

"God I need a stiff drink now." declared Nicole feelingly.

Sarah consulted her watch. "No time Nicky. It's nearly half past. We're going to have to run if we want to catch those other shops."

Chapter Nineteen

They made it back to the jewellery store with literally a couple of minutes to spare. Nicole's morale was somewhat restored, now she had her precious handbag firmly in her possession, but they were out of breath having made the last dash at a dead run. The shop girl looked at them in amusement. "Hey I didn't think you were coming back today." she told them. "We were just about to close up."

"We were pushed for time." Nicole gasped out. "Is my pendant ready?"

"Sure. Do you want to see it before I wrap it up?"

"Yes please."

The engraving was tastefully done discreetly on the back of the pendant. Nicole seemed pleased. Sarah patted her fondly on the bottom. "I'm quite proud of you Nicky."

"What do you mean?"

"I mean having your initial engraved on a present to Charlie. I didn't think you were so sentimental. If I didn't know any better I'd say you were quite sweet on Charlie."

"I'd button my lip if I were you Sarah unless of course you want my last purchase but one shoving up your rear orifice. I've taken enough grief from you for one day."

The shop girl wrapped Nicole's present and handed it over with a smile. "Well are you girls still on for that drink?"

Nicole nodded. "After the day I've had I could use a drink."

Sarah agreed too. The girl had been so helpful and friendly that it seemed churlish to refuse the offer of a drink together although sooner or later they were going to have to tell her and her colleague that they were spoken for. The shop girl brightened visibly. Inwardly she was jubilant. She had Sarah and Nicole pegged down as a pair of beautiful but unsophisticated country girls. Well she and her friend were just the two to corrupt this pair of innocents with their decadent, city charms. Of course she would have been rather less confident of their chances had she been party to the identity of her prey's girlfriends. "Well we have to close up the shop first." she told them. "Why don't we meet you down there in about twenty minutes?"

"Er we didn't catch your name I'm afraid." said Sarah politely.

"I'm Petra. My colleague's called Kim."

"Well I'm Sarah and this is Nicole. That sounds like a plan. We'll see you there then."

"I'll look forward to it."

As soon as Sarah and Nicole had left the shop Petra collared her friend. "We're in Kim!" she exulted. "We're meeting up with those two chicks as soon as we close the place up."

Kim punched the air gleefully. She and Petra were old friends and they even shared an apartment together although they were not a couple. They had once been lovers some years ago but it hadn't worked out and they'd simply settled into a relationship of close friendship. It suited them both for they were too busy playing the field to settle in serious relationships and together they were a formidable combination. They hunted in a pack. Kim was a contrast to Petra in that she was very feminine in a hot pink short skirt and long blond hair. She wore high heeled shoes, very girly make-up and delicate earrings. Coincidentally, in one of those strange connections that often occurred among the lesbian community, she was close acquaintance of Rozella Fangio and had even modelled for her. Rozella's tentacles spread far and wide among the gay women of

Switzerland. "I like the chestnut haired one." she told Petra. "You can have the little blond piece."

"Hey they said they have to go back tonight."

"Where do they live?"

"Somewhere out in the sticks near St Gallen so they said."

"What are they; pair of farmer's daughters or something?"

"Something like that I guess. They seem out of their depth in town."

"Well we'll just have to ply them with alcohol and persuade them to stay the night won't we?"

"They might be up for it. They look like they're in town for fun and games; buying Lez jewellery and all. Looks like they've slipped the leash for the day and up in town for mischief where mummy and daddy can't see what they're up to. I'd guess they're not out. The blond girl was terrified of asking for something with a Lez theme on it."

"It's a sure fire winner by the sound of it Pet. If we can't lure those two back to our place we're losing our touch."

"Well come on... let's get this place shut up and the game is on."

Sarah and Nicole found the bar easily enough. "I wonder if they do food." Mused Sarah wistfully. "We haven't eaten yet."

Nicole glanced around the interior. "It doesn't look promising Sarah." It was true. The bar looked more like a pure drinking establishment. "Looks like we'll have to make do with a packet of crisps." In other respects however the place fitted Nicole's expectations for it was clearly gay and had a mixed clientele of gay men and lesbians. There were quite a number of people in the bar but you had the feeling that it would get very busy later on. Feeling a little shy, the two girls opted for a corner table in a little alcove where they hoped to be relatively unnoticed. It was a forlorn hope. The two attractive girls had aroused interest the moment they walked through the door. Nicole's eyes flitted about nervously. "It looks like they don't have table service Sarah. One of us is going to have to go to the bar."

Sarah pulled a face. "Well I'm not going to sit here like a spare part. I'll go. What are you drinking?"

"Get me a vodka orange."

"Don't get bloody canned Nicky. You've got enough of a list of sins to explain to Charlie today without being blind drunk as well."

"Stop being such a mother hen Sarah. I'm not going to disgrace myself."

At the bar Sarah was acutely conscious of eyes on her from several directions but it was not this that arrested her attention. The bar was evidently proud of its gay character for the back of bar was covered in a motif of gay imagery; posters and photographs of gay icons, a melange of photographs obviously taken at the Zurich gay pride festival that summer and numerous camp pictures of the bar's staff and clientele. Sarah was not surprised to see a large poster of Daniela holding pride of place among this collection and some other pictures of her. Daniela after all was just about the country's most famous lesbian. However it was not this picture that brought her to a grinding halt. A rather startling collection of pictures were an obviously new addition and Sarah stared at them in horror. "Can I get you something Miss?"

Sarah was startled out of her transfixed gaze by the bar man. "Oh! Oh yes! Er a vodka orange and a white wine please."

"Coming up." The bar man turned to attend to her order.

"Are you together with that blond girl honey?"

Sarah spun around. She was being addressed by a large rather masculine dressed woman who was eyeing her with obvious interest. "Oh er yes. Yes I am." she told the woman hastily.

"Shame. You're cute honey."

"Er thank you." Sarah looked for the bar man desperately. He seemed to be taking his time with their drinks.

"Why don't you and your friend join me for a drink?"

"Er well we're waiting for somebody actually."

"Let me know if you change your mind."

"Yes... er thank you." The bar man finally arrived with her order. Sarah paid quickly and beat a hasty retreat. Back at the table she placed their drinks down and then bent to lift Nicole's chin and kiss her tenderly on the lips.

Nicole was taken aback. "What the hell was that for?"

"Camouflage. There's a big butch girl trying to hit on me."

Nicole giggled. "Well we *are* proving popular."

Sarah took a seat looking worried. "It could get worse Nicky. I'm not at all sure it's a good idea to stay in this bar."

"Why the hell not? It seems ok."

"We might end up attracting rather too much attention Nicky."

"Chill Sarah. We're only here for a quiet drink. We're not on the pull or anything."

"So why have we got a date with two shop girls?"

"Sarah we're only meeting them for a friendly drink. Whatever you think about my morals I do have a girlfriend and I'm not about to drop my knickers for some shop girl I barely know."

Sarah snorted. "Hmmph! Well if you do drop your knickers for her you won't be showing her anything that everybody else in this bar hasn't already seen."

"What the hell are you talking about?"

"You might want to check out the picture collection behind the bar."

"What do you mean?"

"Well among the extensive collection of gay personalities of Switzerland depicted among the collection is a montage of the latest works of a certain well known Swiss photographer known as Rozella Fangio, taken from the last issue of L-Mag, entitled, if memory serves me correctly, as "Sapphic Switzerland; the gay girls of the Helvetian Republic". Holding centre spot in pride of honour is a well-known blond girl disporting herself among the alpine flowers wearing a daisy chain and a satisfied smile."

Nicole sat bolt upright. "You're taking the piss!"

"Go take a look yourself if you don't believe me. They might even ask you to sign it for them."

"Oh God! Let's get out of here."

A movement at the door caught Sarah's eye. "Too late Nicky. Here comes our date."

Petra and Kim were quite obviously at home in the bar for they turned to acknowledge the greetings of several of the bar's patrons as they crossed the room towards Sarah and Nicole. Arriving at the table they smiled in welcome. "Hey girls! Glad you turned up." Petra told them. "What's that you're drinking?"

Nicole answered for them. "I'm on vodka orange and Sarah's drinking white wine."

Petra nodded. "Ok we'll get a round in."

"Oh really there's no need." Sarah protested. "We've only just got these."

Petra winked at her. "Hey you're in the big bad city now honey. Let your hair down and live a little."

"But really we can buy our own drinks."

Kim shook her head. "You girls save your money. Zurich's an expensive town sweetheart." She turned to Petra. "Come on Pet let's go to the bar."

As they left to organise drinks Nicole turned to

Sarah indignantly. "Cheeky bitch! Does she think we're a pair of poverty stricken peasants or something? We've probably spent more than their entire monthly salaries combined between us today. We blew two grand in their shop alone for fuck's sake."

Sarah grinned. "I think they've got us down as a pair of naive country girls ripe for plucking with their city slicker wiles Nicky."

Nicole snorted in amusement. "They're in for a right sharp reality shock when our girlfriends turn up then aren't they."

"We'd better tell them that we're accounted for Nicky. It could get embarrassing otherwise."

"It's going to get embarrassing anyway as soon as they spot that bloody picture of me. Is it really noticeable Sarah?"

"It's pretty hard to miss Nicky. You're the pin-up girl of the month in this place."

"Oh for heaven's sake. Sodding Rosy. She's a fucking menace."

Sarah nodded sympathetically. "She's certainly a girl with a high impact value I'll grant you that. She seems to land in the middle of people's lives with all the subtlety and finesse of a nuclear strike." Sarah chuckled softly. "There is one thing though."

"What's that?"

"Well our simple country bumpkin façade is going to start looking a bit thin when they find out that you're a nude model centre spread in the biggest lesbian magazine in the German language. That'll shake a few of their preconceptions."

Sarah's analysis was pretty close to the mark in fact. Kim was dealing with the bar man when Petra's eye caught Nicole's picture behind the bar and it began to dawn on her that there was more to the pair of girls they had such high hopes for than met the eye. She shook Kim's elbow urgently. "Kim... Kim! Look."

Kim peered uncertainly at the picture Petra was pointing out. "What about it?"

"It's her... the blond piece... on that photo spread."

Kim squinted hesitantly. "Are you sure?"

"Of course I'm sure. Put your bloody glasses on you vain bitch." Petra leaned forward to look more closely. "Christ isn't that a set of photos from Rosy Fangio... your ex?"

"She's not my ex."

"You've slept with her."

"Well so what? So has everybody else. Doesn't make her my ex. Rosy doesn't do relationships."

"Well how the hell is there one of her photos of that blond girl hanging on the wall here?"

"I dunno. I thought you said they were a pair of farmer's daughters from the sticks."

Petra shook her head. "This doesn't make sense. When that girl asked to see some Lez jewellery she looked as if she wanted the ground to open up and swallow her. She couldn't even spit the word "lesbian" out she was that embarrassed. Yet here she is posing bloody nude for L-Mag. What the hell's all that about?"

Kim's curiosity had finally overcome her vanity and she reached into her bag for her eyeglasses. "Hey! Hot photo. Looks like you're in for fun and games tonight Pet."

Petra seemed unconvinced. "I don't know Kim. I'm starting to wonder about these two. They're not all they seem to be."

"Hell I wouldn't take too much notice of that Pet. Rosy's a genius at finding little innocent girls in all sorts of unlikely places. Probably just met her out in the country somewhere and did a number on her. Girl wouldn't have stood a chance. Anyway look on the bright side. The chick's no blushing virgin. Anybody Rosy's had her claws into you can regard as well and truly corrupted."

"Yeah maybe." Petra conceded but nevertheless a seed of doubt was germinating within her.

Somewhat wary by now they took their drinks. The bar man winked at them. "Well girls I see you've remained true to form and arrowed straight in on the two best looking baby dykes in the place."

Petra grinned. "Hey we picked them up earlier. They came in the shop and we offered to take them out for a drink."

"I haven't seen them in here before. They in the family?"

"Sure... newbies we think."

The bar man nodded sagely. "I wasn't sure. I thought they might be straight."

Petra shook her head. "Nah. You're not looking close enough Max. They've both got double Venus pendants hanging in their cleavages if you'd taken more notice. They bought them in our shop."

The bar man affected an air of affront. "Hmmph! As if I'm going to look at some chick's cleavage. I know I'm not fussy who I sleep with but I draw the line at women. Who are they anyway?"

Petra shrugged. "We don't know really. They're from out of town; a pair of country girls from out in the sticks, come to town for the day."

Kim grinned wickedly. "Me and Pet are going to show them the bright lights of the big city."

The bar man looked down his nose at them. "Oh yes? Have you actually fixed the light fittings in your digs then? The last time I was round your place the sole illumination was a single forty watt bulb and a pair of candles. Hardly the place *I'd* go looking for bright lights."

Petra laughed. "Hey sure we fixed the lights. Kim pulled a chick in the Predigerhof in August who turned out to be an electrician. We got the whole flat rewired. We even got dimmer switches on the lights."

The bar man shook his head admiringly. "You two are even more ruthless than I am. Well best of luck with your two farmer girls. I warn you though. I'll throw the lot of you out if they start yodelling."

Kim grinned at him. "Don't worry Max. We'll wait till we get them home before we make them yodel."

They returned to the table with the drinks. Petra took a seat and turned to Nicole. "Hey Nicole is that a picture of you behind the bar?"

Nicole swallowed but faced up to Petra; determined not to be taken for an unsophisticated yokel. "Yeah sure." She said with all the nonchalance she could muster. "Just a modelling contract I took for L-Mag."

Petra blinked in surprise. "You're a model then?"

Nicole waved a hand airily. "Well a girl's got to make a living somehow you know."

Petra was taken aback. "Wow! You been a model long?"

"A fair bit. I like to keep my eye in." Sarah pretended to be absorbed with her drink while keeping a straight face over Nicole's outrageous lies."

Kim leaned forward eagerly. "Hey those pics are by Rozella Fangio. Do you know her well then?"

Nicole leaned back with an air of worldliness. "Sure I know her well. I usually use Rozella for my photo shoots."

Kim looked excited. "Hey we know Rozella too. She's often up here in Zurich. She gets about that girl."

Nicole allowed herself a smugly indulgent chuckle. "Yes she sure does." The name of one of the products in the sex shop came unbidden to Nicole's mind. "Sarah and I call her "Rampant Rosy.""

Kim span around to address Sarah. "You know her too?"

Sarah choked slightly over her drink. "Oh er... yes quite well."

"Jesus! Do you model for her as well?"

334

Sarah shook her head hastily. "Oh no. I'm no photo model. Well she did take the pictures for my graduation but I don't think that counts."

Petra sat up in surprise. "Your graduation?"

"Yes. You know... my university graduation.... I got a BA in Bern."

Petra brushed a lock of hair back from her face. "Jesus. I thought you two said you were from the country."

"We are." Sarah told her. "We live up in the mountains."

Nicole interrupted smoothly. "Just because we live in the country doesn't make us a pair of peasants you know. Did you think we were a pair of milkmaids sucking grass blades or something?"

Sarah laughed and spoke in English. "Ooo Arr! Bain't they be a heap o' folk here in the big city."

Petra looked at her in astonishment. "What was that?"

Sarah smiled. "Oh just English. To be more precise it was a poor imitation of a Somerset accent."

"You speak English?"

"We *are* English. Well we're half English anyway. We both have English mothers and Swiss fathers; well half Swiss father in Nicky's case."

Petra had the good grace to look sheepish. It was clear that she and Kim had underestimated their two new friends. "Ok so what are you doing in Zurich today then?"

"Just a bit of shopping and a look around."

Kim looked hopeful "Are you girls trying to pull then?"

To Sarah's surprise it was Nicole that answered. "Not really. Our girlfriends would kill us. We just wanted to come to town and see a few gay places and so on. We don't have much of a gay scene where we come from so it's nice to be able to come to town and meet other gay people."

Kim looked deflated. "Oh hell! You've got girlfriends?"

Sarah nodded. "Yes we do. I'm sorry. Are you disappointed?"

Petra rubbed her chin ruefully. "Well yes actually. When you told me in the shop that you weren't together I just sort of assumed you were both single."

Sarah looked contrite. "I am sorry Petra. I do hope you're not affronted and leave us. As Nicky says we don't get many chances to meet and talk to other gay girls. We'd love your company and to share a few drinks with you."

Sarah's natural charm was so disarming that Petra grinned in capitulation. "Hell honey I think we can manage that. You two are the hottest pair of girls we've seen in here for ages so I think we could just about bear your company. Even if we can't touch, you make pretty good eye candy. Anyway you sound like an interesting pair. Where are your girlfriends anyway? You left them at home?"

Sarah shook her head. "No they're in Zurich as well actually. They're coming to pick us up later."

"They're practising actually." Nicole told her.

"Practising?"

"Yeah they're in a band and they have their practice studio here in Zurich so they dropped us off to go shopping while they work in the studio."

"No shit!" declared Kim. "Your girlfriends are musicians?"

"That's right." Nicole told her smugly. "We're just a pair of high class groupies."

Sarah glared at her. "I'll tell Charlie you said that. She'll be highly amused.... I don't think. It's not as if you're not in enough trouble as it is."

Nicole poked her tongue out at Sarah and laughed. "Don't take me seriously Kim. We're not really groupies."

Petra leaned back in her chair with a laugh. "I'm getting to like you two. You interest me more and more every minute. It's a damn shame you're both spoken for."

Sarah smiled at her disarmingly. "Well the least we can do to alleviate your disappointment is let us buy you another drink. We can afford it you know."

Petra scratched her head with a sheepish grin. "I'm sorry honey. I didn't want to sound like we were being patronising. It's just that you said you were from the country and the prices in Zurich can be expensive when you're not used to them."

Nicole snorted. "Well we've blown close on five grand between us this afternoon so I think a couple of drinks isn't going to break the bank."

Sarah grimaced suddenly. "Actually though, now that I've said it, I'm not actually sure that we *can* afford it. Do you have any cash on you Nicky? I've only got some loose change left. I should have stopped at the cash machine on the way here."

Nicole frowned. "Er not much. Maybe they take card here."

Kim nodded. "Yeah they take card as long as you're spending more than twenty five francs I think."

Sarah gave a wry laugh. "I think if we're having four drinks at the prices in this place that shouldn't be any problem. I'll go see to it."

Sarah picked up her handbag and walked to the bar. Before she could attract the barman's attention however her mobile telephone sounded from the depths of her bag. Sarah fumbled in her bag and extracted the apparatus. It was Daniela. "Hi sweetheart where are you?"

"Oh we're in a bar in the old town."

"Okay we'll come and get you. We've wrapped up for the evening and we're heading into town."

Sarah was puzzled. "Oh I thought you said you'd be there at least until nine o'clock. It's barely eight."

Sarah heard Daniela sigh. "Well we planned to work later but something came up and I didn't feel like playing anymore."

Sarah frowned. "What happened?"

"Oh just me being a prima donna honey. Nothing to worry about."

Sarah's concern deepened. "Is something the matter Danny?"

There was a pause on the other end. "Well... I don't know really. It's... well it's something we have to talk about."

"You're worrying me Danny."

"I'm sorry honey. I don't mean to. Look what's the name of this low life bar you're in?" Sarah told her the name. "Ok then we'll be as quick as we can."

"Do you want us to meet you outside?"

"No honey. We could do to sit down for a drink." Daniela chuckled. "I know the bar actually. What made you and Nicky end up in a gay bar? Are you up to mischief?"

"Hey it was Nicky's idea to go find a gay bar."

Daniela laughed. "God! Talk about burning your closet doors behind you."

"Actually we met up with a couple of girls for a drink. They were working in a shop we went into today and asked us if we'd like a drink when the shop closed."

"I might have known it. As soon as Charlie and I take our eyes off you you've picked up a couple of girls."

"We haven't picked them up although I think that was what they intended. I think they thought we were a pair of country bumpkins beglamoured by the big city and an easy pull. We've disabused them of the idea. We've told them in no uncertain terms that our girlfriends are on the way." Sarah hesitated for a moment. "Look are you sure you want to come to this bar Danny? You're probably going to attract attention. I mean there're bloody pictures of you all over the sodding bar."

"I think it will be all right Sarah. Zurich gay bars get a lot of high profile guests in them and they tend to be discreet."

Sarah giggled. "I suppose so. There's another high profile lesbian celebrity who's got her picture plastered across the bar as well."

"Oh yes?"

"Yes! Nicole Richardson, Switzerland's newest hot, lesbian pin-up girl no less."

"You're joking!"

"Straight up. It's priceless. Nicky's been trying to melt into the woodwork one minute and posing it up something rotten the next."

"That settles it. We're definitely coming to this bar. This I've got to see. Anyway we have to come just to catch you two red handed flirting with the local talent. Must be worth a spanking."

"Promises, promises."

"Ok honey we have to get going. We'll be there as quick as we can. Try to stay out of trouble. Love you."

"Love you too." Sarah put her phone away and caught the barman's attention. She handed over Daniela's credit card. "Would it be possible to open up a tab?" she asked. "We might be having a couple more drinks on our table and we have some friends joining us shortly."

"Yes of course."

Sarah ordered another round of drinks. They were too much for her to carry. "Er do you have a tray I could use?" she asked.

"Please don't concern yourself. I'll bring your drinks over."

Sarah granted him a gracious smile. "That's very

kind of you!"

"My pleasure."

Sarah returned to the table. Nicole looked at her in surprise. "Where the hell are our drinks?"

"The barman is bringing them over. I couldn't carry them on my own."

Petra whistled softly. "Whee you are privileged. Takes a lot to get table service in here."

"I think he was just being friendly."

"Did you use your card?" Nicole asked.

"Yes I opened a tab so if anybody wants something to drink just put it on the tab."

Nicole grinned. "So you handed him a platinum card with an astronomically high credit guarantee on it Sarah. I should imagine he'll be expecting a fat tip."

Kim frowned. "Are you girls loaded or something?"

Before Sarah could protest Nicole had waved a hand nonchalantly. "Oh we're not hurting." she stated in a matter of fact manner ignoring Sarah's fearsome glare.

Kim pulled a face. "Damn it; drop dead gorgeous and rich to boot. Just our luck you're spoken for."

Sarah fixed her eyes on Nicole in exasperation. "Oh I'm sure Nicky would love to share the fruits of her personal fortune with you Kim." Nicole squirmed. Her current "personal fortune" added up to the sort of irritatingly persistent overdraft that inspires bank managers to assume looks of patronising reproof.

In spite of their disappointment, Petra and Kim turned out to be good company and the conversation was relaxed and agreeable when Charmaine walked into the bar sometime later. She was carrying her guitar in its case as she stooped to kiss Nicole fondly. Sarah politely introduced her to Kim and Petra, amused to note the searching appraisal Charmaine subjected them to. "Where's Danny?" Sarah asked.

"Just finding somewhere to park the car. It's mostly pedestrian precincts and no parking zones around here."

Nicole pointed to Charmaine's guitar case. "Why the hell have you brought your guitar in with you?" she asked in bafflement.

"The boot's full. Danny's got a load of sound equipment she's taking home in the boot."

"Well couldn't you have just left it in the back?"

Charmaine regarded her pityingly. "Are you taking the piss? We're not in the Toggenburg here you know. I'm not about to leave three or four grand's worth of guitar lying about in plain view in the back of the car. That's just asking to get the car broken into." Sarah could have pointed out that there was extra storage under the seats but she held her tongue. She guessed that Charmaine just couldn't bear to let her beloved new guitar out of her sight.

"How was practice anyway Charlie?" Nicole asked.

Charlie nodded thoughtfully. "Good I think. I still have a hell of a lot to learn but we're getting there."

Petra leaned forward over the table. "I'm sure I know you Charlie. Don't you play with that band from Winterthur.... what's the name again... Weisse Stern...that was it."

"I used to. We split up nearly a year ago. I'm filling in with another band at the moment."

"Oh yes? What are they called?"

"Well it's Danny Devin's backing band actually." Charmaine mumbled with a somewhat self-conscious blush but Sarah could see the deep pride in her."

Petra and Kim were staring at her in astonishment. "Danny... you mean *Daniela Devin*?" gasped Kim. "You play with Daniela Devin?"

Charmaine held up a hand. "Hey I'm just a fill in while her regular bassist takes paternity leave."

Kim looked shell shocked. "Wow! We gotta get an autograph." then her brain made lightning connections. "Wait a minute. Is this the Danny you were asking about Sarah? She's not coming in here is she?"

341

Charmaine nodded an affirmative. "She will be doing as soon as she finds somewhere to park Sarah's car."

Kim stared at Sarah. "You... er ... your car... you mean?" She took a deep breath. "Please don't tell me that you're Daniela Devin's girlfriend."

Sarah swallowed but nodded sheepishly. "Yes but please don't shout it around. We don't want to advertise it to the whole world."

"Oh...My....God!" Kim shook her head vigorously and turned to Petra. "Remind me never to follow up one of your hot tips again you dozy bitch. Just a nice pair of farmer's daughters from out in the sticks you told me. Easy pickings. We can't go wrong. And there we are, like a pair of idiots, trying to pull Daniela Devin and her bass guitarist's girlfriends. We'll never live this down."

Charmaine narrowed her eyes. "I see. So you and Sarah *have* been up to mischief have you Nicky?"

Nicole swallowed hastily. "Of course not Charlie. We just met Kim and Petra in a shop they work in and they invited us for a drink. Our behaviour has been beyond reproach hasn't it Sarah?"

Charmaine was unconvinced. "So you've not been out on the pull?"

"Of course we haven't!"

Charmaine leaned forward and lifted Nicole's pendant on her fingertips. "So why are you suddenly wearing a double Venus pendant around your throat if you're not out advertising your wares?"

Sarah jumped in quickly. "We both bought one Charlie. We just wanted to something to share together and declare our sexuality. Actually Nicky bought you something in the same shop. Show her Nicky."

"Oh er yes!" Nicole fumbled in her bags and produced the gift wrapped box.

Charmaine was deeply touched by the little present and she let Nicole fasten it about her neck. She kissed her warmly. "Thank you Nicky." She seemed choked. "It's... it's lovely." Suddenly she laughed ruefully. "That's taken the wind out of my sails."

"What do you mean Charlie?" asked Nicky somewhat nervously.

"I mean after finding you picking up stray girls in town I was going to bend you over my knee and give you the thrashing of your life when we got home. It looks like I'll have to forgive you after all."

Nicole's face was a picture of wounded innocence. "You know I wouldn't go around cheating on you Charlie."

"Yeah... I suppose not." Charmaine stood up. "I need a beer. Anybody else?"

"Oh we've got a tab open at the bar Charlie." Sarah told her. "Just tell the barman that you're at our table."

"Cool."

Charmaine left for the bar. Sarah leaned across the table and stabbed a finger at Nicole. "You owe me big time Nicole Richardson."

Nicole attempted to look penitent; an entirely unsuccessful pose, but before she could think of a retort a sudden stirring of excitement among the clientele of the bar announced Daniela's appearance among the company. The bar was not an establishment liable to fawn over visiting celebrities. Chic bars and clubs in Zurich saw more than their fair share of seven day wonder celebrities and the people who frequented them tended to become somewhat blasé about them to the point of cynical familiarity. Certainly any star full of their own importance and putting on airs and graces was unlikely to impress a thoroughly modern and worldly public who had seen it all before. Any noted celebrity who did not try to impress would be shown respect and welcomed but excite little more than covert curiosity, especially in gay bars with their long tradition of egalitarian discretion.

Daniela was different. For one thing a non-professional visit from her was a very rare occasion for she was not noted for frequenting city bars and nightclubs except when called upon to perform in them. It wasn't that she was aloof in any respect. It was just that she was essentially a home loving person; private and of simple tastes who was not especially attracted to socialising away from her close circle of friends. When she did appear in such public manner she was famous for her warm charm and charismatic good nature. Sarah had seen, very early in her relationship with Daniela, how her beloved could enter a room and light it up in dazzling fashion without seeming to do anything other than merely walk through the door. Daniela just seemed to radiate an aura that could penetrate even the most jaded cynicism and reduce the most indifferent of observers to a condition bordering dangerously close to love struck. This capability continuously amazed Sarah and she was always astounded by people's reaction to Daniela. There was nothing remotely patronising about Daniela. She just had what Sarah could only describe as grace; a serene warm gentleness, completely natural and unassuming that made her irresistible. People just fell in love with her on sight.

Sarah, with her own frequent inability to see the merits of her own worth, was often puzzled why Daniela, among a choice of so many people who would have thrown themselves unreservedly at her feet, had chosen her to love. Those who knew Daniela well would have smiled to themselves and noted that Sarah was just *exactly* the kind of person Daniela would have fallen in love with. It may sound clichéd but they truly did seem custom designed for each other. Daniela was not beglamoured by her fame. It was typical of her that she would find a soul mate in a beautiful but entirely modest and self-effacing country girl of simple tastes and warm good nature who, as Daniela frequently recalled, had not

344

even been able to remember her name when they had first met. That had been just adorable to Daniela. She had been smitten from that moment on and in return she had found a partner who truly loved her as the person she was rather than some nebulous celebrity image. Sarah indeed made Daniela occasionally regret her fame and wish for anonymity. She fantasised frequently about how it would have been had she not been famous and rich and had met Sarah. She imagined a life with her in a little humble cottage or apartment forging a destiny with their own hands together, beholden to nobody but themselves; a life of simple needs, shared burdens and triumphs and the deep fulfilment of commitment. It sounded like heaven to Daniela.

But of course she *was* famous and her fame went beyond the trappings of commercial musical success. In any location Daniela would have been noteworthy. The recognition of her extraordinary talent married to her charismatic charm would have guaranteed that. In a gay bar, and particularly a Swiss gay bar, however, she was something much more. Many famous performers and recording artists have become iconic personalities in gay sub-culture. Indeed many artists have their gay fan base to thank for their success for the gay community can be fiercely loyal to those it calls its own and it is a commercially significant segment of society of high disposable income; the so-called "pink pound", that rewards its adopted stars handsomely. In Daniela's case however there was no sense that she deliberately targeted her gay audience. Her music had a wide appeal across many different strata of society. On the other hand, she nevertheless embraced the gay community. This embrace was perhaps not flamboyant or aggressive but rather a complete solidarity and empathy with her gay peers. She quietly but firmly endorsed gay rights and culture, was a reasoned and convincing advocate for that culture and an admirable role model to and champion for her community. She was gay; saw no reason to flaunt that but yet no reason to conceal it either and when she spoke of it people listened. Above all she was deeply caring and compassionate; in spite of her years, almost a wise mother figure or elder sister to the young gay community; a figurehead that stood for compassion, reason and understanding for a community sensitive to its social isolation and vulnerable to bigotry and vilification. As such she was deeply loved and almost universally respected among Swiss gays. She was, to all intents and purposes, the uncrowned queen of the Swiss gay community. It was small wonder, therefore, that her appearance in the bar afforded such a buzz of excitement. This was no appearance by some mere celebrity. This was very nearly a Royal visit.

Daniela wasn't mobbed. The clientele of the bar had a far better sense of propriety than that but certainly all eyes were upon her from the moment she arrived and the bar staff were almost fawningly attentive to her needs. Sarah had thought that the bar was rather subdued and quiet up until this point but there was a discernible excitement in the place now. Daniela kissed Sarah and took her place at the table with easy charm and endured the inevitable stream of autograph hunters good naturedly for all the world like a reluctant monarch holding court and receiving delegations from her subjects out of a sense of duty. Sarah introduced Kim and Petra to her and the two girls were so obviously in awe of Daniela that Sarah found it almost comical. Charmaine of course already idolised Daniela and her pride in being her bass guitarist, however temporary, was glowingly evident. Nicole was milking the situation outrageously and Sarah narrowed her eyes at her best friend's posturing determined to have words with Nicole over her newly acquired lesbian snobbery. In fact the only person other than Daniela at the table who didn't seem delighted by the public reaction to her was Sarah.

Sarah always felt slightly protective of Daniela in public situations for, while Daniela inevitably handled them with enormous grace and charm, Sarah nevertheless felt it incumbent on her to deflect the attentions of the public in deference to Daniela's privacy.

There was something else as well. While it was not evident to the public at large Sarah knew her girlfriend well enough by now to discern that she was troubled and uneasy about something. Even if the enigmatic phone call she had received earlier was not evidence enough, there was an air of distraction about her; an air of somebody with something on her mind. She was sat next to Sarah and clutched her hand almost as if fearing to let her go.

Characteristically Sarah was so concerned about Daniela that the significance of Daniela's obvious attachment and affection for her escaped her notice. It hadn't escaped anybody else's notice however. By now the entire bar knew that the beautiful girl with the chestnut hair, who had already attracted much admiration, was Daniela Devin's consort. It was a minor sensation and the source of wild speculation. Who was this girl? Nobody seemed to know her. There was a rumour going round that she was one of Daniela's backing vocalists; a rumour fuelled by the intelligence that Charmaine was a bass player in the band and it seemed logical that Daniela had members of her band in company with her. Even Nicole was by now feeding the rumour mill. It was now common knowledge that the picture on the wall behind the bar was no less a person than the blond haired girl in the company. She was another unknown whose identity was already generating speculation. Gay people, both male and female, can be the world's most incorrigible gossips and there was enough material here to keep everybody amused for months on end.

Kim and Petra, at the epicentre of all this

conjecture, were clearly relishing the situation. They were well known locally and liable to be grilled assiduously concerning their guests over the coming weeks. There wasn't much in the way of hard information coming their way but they were eagerly absorbing enough tit-bits to hold their future prospective audiences enthralled. Kim, a girl, it must be said, of somewhat materialistic concerns, was privately expecting to not have to pay for a drink for at least a fortnight in here and intended to bask in the reflected glory for as much as the market could be squeezed. Petra had similar thoughts although her ambitions were a little greater. She worked on commission in the shop and it hadn't escaped her attention that, with a bit of clever marketing, the pendant designs that Nicole and Sarah had bought could be seriously in demand. If Daniela Devin's girlfriend was wearing those designs then every dyke in Zurich would want one. God she'd even bought a pendant for Daniela. That much was obvious. Sarah had jumped at the design with Daniela's initials on them. Good God they'd *fly* off the shelves assuming they could get enough stock in. She'd have to have words with the proprietor. They could be on a gold mine here. Daniela Devin's name was like money in the bank.

Sarah's concern was mounting. She had scarcely seen Daniela looking so nervous and on edge. She leaned forward to whisper. "Are you all right Danny?"

"Yes... I mean.... well I'm ok. I'll be all right Sarah honey."

"Are you sure?"

Daniela sighed. "I don't know. I'm having a bit of a day Sarah."

"Do you want to get out of here?"

Daniela glanced up at Nicole and Charmaine clearly enjoying themselves and shook her head slowly. "No we'll have a last drink and then we'll go." She sat upright and addressed the company. "Anybody like

348

another drink before we have to get going?"

Charmaine lifted her beer bottle and regarded it critically. "I could do with another one. Shall I call the barman over?" Bar service had been suspended in their honour. The barman had been hovering over them ever since Daniela's arrival.

Daniela lifted a hand. "No I'll go to the bar. Same again everyone?" There was a chorus of approval and Daniela stood up and turned to Sarah. "Can you help me honey?" Sarah, perceiving immediately that Daniela wanted a private word, rose and accompanied her to the bar. At the bar, after ordering their drinks, Daniela placed a hand around Sarah's waist and grinned. "So where's this picture of Nicky then?" Sarah pointed out the offending portrait and Daniela bit her lip in amusement tinged with consternation. "Oh God! Bloody Rosy has a lot to answer for. What did Nicky have to say?"

"Oh she was well pissed off at first but since then I think she's been quite enjoying her new found celebrity status. Everybody's been crooning over the picture and telling her how gorgeous she looks. I think she rather likes all the attention and she's not averse to a whiff of scandal."

"Well she *does* look gorgeous. Mind you if she's going to have this sort of impact we'd better see about getting her a proper agent. Rosy's got loads of contacts. We ought to have a word with her."

Sarah groaned. "Oh God! Nicole Richardson... lesbian supermodel... where did it all go wrong?"

Daniela smiled. "Well let her enjoy it Sarah. It looks like she's come out with a vengeance. I'm glad that it's been such a relatively easy transition for her." She chuckled quietly. "Mind you, now that she's discovered the delights of girls, Charlie's going to have the dickens of a time keeping an eye on her."

"Do you think Charlie's pissed off with her because she found her with two other girls?"

Daniela shook her head. "No I don't think so. In fact I think she was rather expecting it. Apparently Nicky was even canvassing her opinion on the best gay bars in Zurich to visit. Charlie's not dumb Sarah. She likes Nicky a lot but I don't think she's under any illusions about her. It's normal that a girl like Nicole having just come to an acceptance of her sexuality is going to want to play around a bit. When you first come out and discover all these lovely lesbian girls in the world.... well it can be pretty exciting."

Sarah snorted. "Yes well she admitted as much to me today. She said it was loads more fun being lesbian than straight."

"Well it *is* fun. It's a whole new exciting world opening up for her. It's normal she feels like going a bit crazy at first. She's never seen this side of things before."

"What about Charlie?"

"I think Charlie's smart enough to handle her Sarah. I think she probably realises when to let her slip the leash and when to rein her in. Charlie's pretty savvy about things like that. She was very touched that Nicky bought her that pendant. I don't think she expected that."

Sarah grimaced. "Well to be honest Danny that was *my* idea."

Daniela laughed and kissed her. "I guessed as much. You're precious Sarah."

"Don't tell Charlie it was my idea Danny."

"I wouldn't dream of it."

"In her favour Nicky bought that pendant out of her own money Danny. She didn't use your card."

"Well that was very naughty of her then. I wouldn't have minded."

"Yes but she wanted it to be something personal to her and she had it engraved as well."

"My word. Nicole getting all romantic. Who would have thought it?"

"Yes well don't be getting too pleased by her considerate self-sacrifice Danny. She managed to blow enough of your money on purchases for herself. You'll blow a cylinder when you see the hole we've made in your bank account."

"Have you spent more than fifty thousand?"

Sarah staggered visibly. "Good God! No!"

"Well then I won't even blink." Sarah looked so shocked that Daniela burst into laughter. "Come on Sarah! You don't even know *how* to spend money. I've seen you in Migros agonising over the bargain offers when we've enough money to buy the whole bloody shop and the shop girls as well. I'll bet you've spent a trifling amount of money today and you're agonising over the thought that you've been extravagant. You're just adorable."

Sarah frowned. "I'm not quite sure whether I've been complemented or not."

Daniela laughed in pleasure before reaching up to turn Sarah's face to her own and stare into her eyes. The great blue eyes were so full of love that Sarah felt her words choke in her throat. "Oh Sarah." murmured Daniela softly. "What did I do to deserve to find you? Why am I so blessed that the only girl in Switzerland who couldn't care less about my fame and riches loves me. God must truly love me to grant me such a gift."

Sarah blinked. "Stop it Danny! You'll make me cry."

"Not all tears are sad Sarah."

Sarah took a deep breath. "What is the matter tonight Danny? You seem upset by something. You said there was something we have to talk about."

Daniela lowered her eyes. "Yes there is. I... I don't know how to begin."

Before she could even start they were interrupted by the barman with their order. He seemed embarrassed about something. "Erm excuse me Miss Devin but..."

Daniela turned her full charm on him with a radiant smile. "Please call me Danny. It's Max isn't it?"

"Yes. Yes that's right."

"You seem to have something on your mind Max."

"Well er... Danny it's kind of embarrassing and I don't want to impose on you or anything but..."

"Spit it out."

"Well the staff were wondering if you'd... well if you'd be kind enough to sign our poster of you for posterity."

Daniela smiled warmly. "I'd be delighted to."

Max grinned triumphantly. "Hey thanks. I... er... I suppose a photograph of you for our celebrity collection would be out of the question."

"Of course you may take my photograph."

"Oh wow! Thank you."

Daniela raised her hand. "On one condition however. I would prefer it if you didn't include my girlfriend in the shot. We're trying to keep our private life out of the public domain."

Max held his hands up. "Naturally. I understand completely."

Daniela posed for the camera obligingly. Max was exultant. This was a picture destined to become the most prized possession among the bar's décor. As he thanked Daniela Sarah saw a wicked glint of amusement in Daniela's eyes. "You have other celebrities present in the company. My new bass guitarist is here as well. I'm sure she would let you take her photograph as well if you ask her nicely."

"Yes. Thanks. I'll do that."

"Oh yes and we have a new hot gay model with us. You have a picture of her as well on your wall."

"Is that the blond girl with you? I wasn't sure if it was her."

"Oh it's her all right. She's an up and coming new modelling star. Why don't you ask her to sign her picture and maybe see if she'll let you photograph her."

"Hell yes! Every lesbian in the bar has been drooling over that picture since we put it up. Do you think she would?"

"Oh I'm sure she would if you told her how popular she is. You'll have to ask her nicely though. She's a bit shy."

"Yes thank you. I'll do that. Er do you want me to carry these drinks over for you?"

"No that's fine. We can manage."

"Ok I'll go and talk to your companions then." He left eagerly.

Sarah wagged her finger under Daniela's nose. "Daniela Devin! You are a wicked, wicked woman."

Daniela laughed delightedly. "I couldn't resist. This is going to be priceless when he asks Nicky to sign her nude portrait."

"You're a bad, bad girl, putting Nicky on the spot like that."

Daniela grinned incorrigibly. "Hey I'm just helping remind Nicky of her duties. She's got her public to think about now."

Sarah shook her head in exasperation. "Oh God! Anyway you never answered my question."

"Your question?"

"Yes. I want to know what's bothering you today. What is it we have to talk about?"

The mischievous twinkle faded from Daniela's eyes and she became serious. "This isn't really the place to talk about it Sarah. It's better we leave it until we get home."

"You can't just leave it like that. You'll have me worried sick all the way back to the Toggenburg. At least tell me what it's about."

Daniela sighed heavily. "I had a phone call during our rehearsals Sarah. It's kind of thrown a spanner into my works."

353

"What about?"

Daniela hesitated. "Sarah you know I love you more than I can say but now I feel torn and I don't know what to do."

"Torn about what?"

Daniela took a deep breath. "Sarah you're not the only girl in my life."

Sarah felt the room spin. She stared at Daniela in shock. "There... there's another girl?"

Daniela nodded solemnly. "Oh yes! There's another girl all right."

Sarah had trouble speaking. "I... I thought you loved *me*."

Daniela grasped her hands urgently. "Of course I do. You're the only woman in my life."

"But, but this... other girl..."

"I love her very much as well."

"You love her?"

"Yes Sarah, although I've not done a very good job of it. But I must love her. I must love her even if it costs me *your* love."

"But...but why?"

"Because she's only nine years old and I am her mother."

Chapter Twenty

It was late by the time they arrived home. Under normal circumstances, after such a long day, Sarah would have been happy to retire straight to bed. Tonight however she was determined not to sleep until she had had it out with Daniela as to exactly what was worrying her. Daniela had not elaborated any further in the bar in Zurich, deferring the matter until such time as they could talk alone. They had left the bar in triumph eventually. Daniela had posed for photographs with Charmaine and her new guitar and Charmaine's embarrassed pride had been almost comical. As far as the Zurich gay scene was concerned, Nicole was by now well and truly out and already in possession of a small but deeply devoted fan club. She had been coerced into signing the bar's copy of her picture spread in L-Mag and had even allowed herself to be photographed alongside a number of the bar's regular lesbian clients. Charmaine had been deeply proud of her girlfriend. Nicole for her part had been tipsy enough to relish all the attention and she had handled her new found mini celebrity status with modest charm. She had enjoyed herself although doubtless she would experience deep misgivings about such a public exposure in the cold, sober light of day. As far as the bar was concerned, the one big disappointment was the refusal of Daniela's strikingly beautiful new girlfriend to pose for a photograph as well or even to surrender much in the way of information about herself. Daniela had been fiercely protective of Sarah's privacy and it had merely fuelled the storm of speculation about the new love in the life of Switzerland's favourite gay celebrity. She was a mystery girl and destined to become the hot gossip topic of the month.

The excitements of the Zurich gay scene had been

abandoned, however, on the road home. It is true that Charmaine and Nicole were still chattering away happily but Daniela had retreated into worried introspection. Sarah, with too much alcohol on board, had surrendered the wheel of the BMW to Daniela and she had driven them back in uncharacteristic silence, rarely venturing to initiate any conversation. Sarah had been equally quiet as she watched her distracted girlfriend with mounting concern. Charmaine was staying over in the Toggenburg again, it seemed, and it appeared as if she had moved sufficient of her clothes into Nicole's wardrobes to facilitate a protracted stay. This appeared to be eminently agreeable to Nicole. She was tipsy enough by now and, after the excitement of the day, more than a little frisky. Sarah hoped that Charmaine wasn't too tired after her day in the studio because, judging by Nicole's mood, she wasn't going to be getting much sleep tonight.

Sarah and Daniela arrived home alone after dropping Nicole and Charmaine off in the Alpli. Daniela collapsed onto a sofa in the big living room, looking, Sarah thought, downright upset. "Are you tired honey?" she asked Sarah considerately.

Sarah shook her head. "No. I want to talk. I want to know what's bothering you."

Daniela nodded and wrung her hands together. "Yes I need to get this off my chest."

Instead of taking a seat Sarah inclined her head in the direction of the kitchen. "Well why don't I make us something to eat? I don't know if you're hungry but, what with being dragged around by Nicky all day, I haven't had a bite since lunchtime."

"I could eat something but don't go to a lot of trouble sweetheart. It's too late to start cooking."

"No need. We've plenty of cold stuff in the house. We've still got the rest of that tuna, rice and bean salad left over and I could put out some cold meats and cheese. We've plenty of fresh bread from this morning and there's a flipping great blackberry tart from Elrika that needs eating up."

"Sounds fine to me. Have we got any wine to wash it down with?"

Sarah frowned. "Well we've got that bottle of Chablis Grand Cru if you wanted white wine but I was saving that for something special because it's a really good wine and expensive. It seems a shame to waste it on a late night snack. Otherwise we're out of white. We drank the last bottle of Fendant yesterday."

"Have we got any red?"

"Oh yes. There're a couple of bottles of Shiraz and a Merlot."

"Well the Shiraz might be a bit heavy for light food. Why don't we crack open the Merlot?"

"Ok. Why don't you jump under the shower while I'm getting stuff ready?"

"Yes I'll do that. It's amazing how grubby you can get messing around in a studio."

Sarah laid out the food on the big coffee table as Daniela showered. She dimmed the lights and lit a pair of candles to make the room more intimate. She opened the wine to let it breathe and then was obliged to shoo away one of the cats who was taking an interest in the magnificent spread of food, apparently under the misapprehension that this largess had been laid out for his own benefit. Sarah loved these late night little feasts she and Daniela shared together. The very first night she had come to this house; the same night she had become Daniela's lover, they had enjoyed such an intimate repast. It was one of the happiest memories in Sarah's life and tucking into a table full of assorted nibbles over a bottle of wine late at night had become a custom between them ever since, nearly always ending up with their clothes scattered around the room and a happy roll on the hearth-side rug.

Daniela returned from the bathroom dressed in a

very short cream robe over a pair of tiny lacy briefs and looking so enticing that Sarah had to remind herself that a serious discussion was the order of the day. They ate quietly and for once Daniela seemed distracted while eating. This was highly unusual. Daniela normally took a nearly hedonistic pleasure over her food, savouring it almost sensually. It was very unlike her to merely consume it without appearing to enjoy it. Sarah's disquiet grew. Finally she could take no more and pushed her plate aside. "Ok for heaven's sake tell me what the matter is."

Daniela placed her plate down slowly while she gathered her thoughts. "I... I hardly know where to begin."

"You said something about your daughter."

Daniela nodded miserably. "Yes." She paused for a moment and wrung her hands in anguish. She seemed near to tears. "Oh God Sarah! I don't know what to do. I didn't expect this problem to come up at least until next year; the summer at the earliest. Now it's right on me and I'm scared to death."

"What the hell is it?"

Daniela took a deep breath. "I got a phone call from my dad while we were in the studio today. You know he's an architect."

Sarah shook her head surprised at this information. "No. No I didn't know that. You've never mentioned what your parents do for a living."

Daniela took a sip of wine. "Well he is and a very accomplished and senior one too. Well he's been involved in this big project building some massive great holiday complex in Saudi Arabia. Initially he thought the project wouldn't be going ahead until sometime next year but the thing's been brought forward and they've got a go ahead to start right away. It's a big deal for my dad. There's a shed load of money in the project and he's the senior architect on it. This one big project and he can retire comfortably for life. That's appealing to him. He's been talking for years about winding up his affairs in California and coming home to retire in Switzerland or England."

"Well that's good for him but what has this to do with your daughter?"

"Elizabeth lives with my parents in California now."

"Elizabeth?" Sarah stifled a giggle.

"What's so funny?"

"I'm sorry Danny. It's just... well Elizabeth sounds such an old fashioned sort of name for a pop singer's daughter. I thought she'd be called Moon Dancer or something like that."

"It was my Grandma's name Sarah."

"I'm sorry Danny. I shouldn't be making fun. I can see that you're upset but you still haven't told me why. I mean why is an upturn in your dad's career something to worry about your daughter over?"

"Because now the project is going ahead it means dad will have to move to Saudi Arabia to consult on and oversee the project. He could be there two, three years or even more. What's more he'll be taking my mum with him."

Sarah bit her lip. "I think I see. What will happen to Elizabeth then? Will she go as well?"

Daniela lifted her head and looked Sarah in the eye. "Not if I have anything to say about it and my parents don't think it's a good idea either."

Sarah was puzzled. "But why? I thought your parents doted on your daughter."

"They do but they agree with me that Saudi Arabia is not a place for her to grow up in."

"I thought Saudi Arabia was a rich country though and pretty safe."

"Oh it's rich enough although a lot of that wealth is mainly in the hands of a privileged upper class. It's dripping with oil money. As to being safe well generally speaking it is for the most part. Riyadh almost certainly has a lower rate of violent crime than Los Angeles. There is a terrorist problem though. There's an awful lot of fundamental Islamic nutters in the country and security is always going to be an issue for any westerner there and especially ones with American connections. This is going to be a big high profile project my dad's working on and an obvious target for terrorists. There could be a lot of crazy bastards who will think their fucking evil agenda would be benefit from harming the project and the people and their families involved with it. You know after nine eleven the last American administration made war on Iraq and Afghanistan and people tend to forget that, out of the nineteen terrorist hijackers on those planes, fifteen of them came from Saudi Arabia." Daniela snorted. "I suppose the US was hardly likely to attack Saudi Arabia when American oil depended on it."

"So you're frightened about terrorists harming your daughter?"

"Well obviously I'm concerned. After all is said and done my little girl has been largely brought up in America although she has multiple nationality. She is, however, visibly a little American girl and the sort of bastards that do these kind of things aren't in the slightest bit concerned that she's only a child. These people don't have a conscience about things like that."

"But surely lots of westerners, Americans and others, live and work in Saudi Arabia. Surely there is security provided for them."

"Oh yes. In fact most of the professional westerners employed in Saudi live in enclosed compounds; enclaves where they live a more or less western life separate from the rest of Saudi society. Foreign workers from Third World countries are another matter of course. Rich Saudis employ a lot of domestic workers from overseas and their treatment of them is a scandal. They are often treated as little more than indentured slaves and subject to all kinds of abuse and mistreatment."

Sarah frowned. "That wouldn't be the case with your family though would it?"

"Oh no. My parents will be housed in a luxurious compound with all the amenities where they'll be permitted to adhere more or less to western customs and which will be heavily guarded with its own security force."

"So wouldn't your daughter be safe there?"

"Most probably yes. But you can't raise a kid completely within the walls of a secured compound Sarah. I don't think it's healthy for one thing. Once she leaves the compound then she's exposed. Oh she'd doubtless go to an exclusive English speaking school where she hopefully would be well looked after but it goes beyond merely the security risk Sarah."

"What do you mean?"

"I mean I'm damned if I want my child brought up in a backward, medieval repressive nation with a civil rights record stuck back in the fucking dark ages."

Sarah blinked at Daniela's sudden vehemence. "Is it so bad?"

"God you've no idea. My daughter is not only a child and partially American and vulnerable on that account, she also happens to be female. Do you know much about women's rights in Saudi Arabia Sarah?"

"Well no. Not much anyway. I think I read somewhere that they have to cover their whole bodies or something."

"You don't know the half of it. Saudi Arabia is one of the most patriarchal societies in the world. The Global Gender Gap Report of the World Economic Forum has placed Saudi Arabia 130th out of 134 countries in gender parity. Women are not allowed to vote. They are not allowed to hold political office. They have effective zero empowerment. You were telling me about Appenzell's somewhat retarded attitude to female political rights. Well you can take it from me that Appenzell is positively a hotbed of revolutionary feminism compared to Saudi Arabia. Did you know that all women in Saudi Arabia are obliged to have a male guardian?"

"You're joking."

"Not at all. Oh the Saudi's insist that the system is there to protect women but the practice is incredibly restrictive. Any woman, regardless of her age or marital status, is obliged to have a male guardian. It might be her husband, her father, her brother, uncle or other family member. It can even be her son. Whoever he is she can't do diddly squat without his permission. She can't get married without his permission or get divorced, travel, get an education, get a job, have elective surgery or even open a fucking bank account. Ownership of a woman under the guardianship system is passed on from one man to another. That's why a widow can end up becoming the chattel of her own son. If she wants to remarry she has to go to her own son and humbly beg permission."

"And this is a legal requirement?"

"The Saudi government says not. The reality is a different matter. In fact Saudi Arabia is a theocracy and therefore comes under Sharia or Islamic law. In Saudi the form of Sharia law is a strict version of Sunni Islamic law known as Salafi. Because it is religious law it is mostly not written down and is open to the discretion of strictly conservative judges who usually interpret the law according to outdated custom. Thus the Saudi government can protest that such a system is not written into the country's law even though it is universally practised. Then there is Namus."

"What the hell is that?"

"Honour, roughly speaking. In return for their "protective" guardianship men expect women to guard

362

their honour since her misconduct would reflect on his personal honour. That misconduct could be something like talking to a strange man, showing her face in public or something equally trivial. Since his honour is adversely affected by her misconduct he is expected to control her behaviour. This means he is expected to punish her should she do anything which might be construed as contrary to his honour. He may beat her for example and it is very unlikely that he would be taken to task by the legal system for doing so. In extreme cases women have been murdered for bringing dishonour on their guardian. There was a frightful case a few years ago when a father murdered his own daughter because he caught her chatting to a man on Facebook. Did that murder lead to an outcry over the barbarity of Namus? Not noticeably it has to be said. In fact the major initiative to come out of the case was a conservative call for the government to ban Facebook because it encouraged gender mingling and incited lust among women."

"Surely that's a rare case though."

"I don't know Sarah because statistics specific to Saudi Arabia are hard to come by but thousands of women are killed under the code of Namus where it exists every year around the world. Honour killing is not specifically a Saudi trait or an Islamic one but an ancient barbaric cultural custom which pre-dates all the monotheistic religions. Even a woman being raped is considered grounds for killing her to restore honour under this custom."

"Surely not."

"Oh yes."

"But that doesn't happen in Saudi Arabia surely?"

"Well I can't quote you specific cases of murder in those instances in Saudi Sarah but it is documented fact that women are frequently punished by law for being raped."

"I can't believe that."

"It's true. Actually rape cases rarely come to trial in Saudi Arabia because the victims are afraid to report them because of the fear of Namus, accusations of adultery, the reduction of her marriage rights or because the woman fears that she will be punished as well as her attacker. In point of fact there is no specific written law criminalising rape in Saudi Arabia because the penal code is unwritten. It is entirely at the discretion of the Sharia law. In any case there is no prohibition against statuary rape or being raped by your own husband."

"They surely can't punish a woman for being the victim of a rape."

"Oh No? In 2006 a young woman, nineteen years old, and a male companion from Qatif were kidnapped and gang raped by seven men at knife point. She insisted on taking the case to the authorities who caught the men and sent them to trial. They all got between two and ten years imprisonment. She on the other hand was sentenced to ninety lashes because she was alone with a man who was not a relative."

"Oh no."

"It gets worse Sarah. The case went to an appeal and unfortunately the girl admitted having an affair with the man she was with. Now this was no steamy clandestine meetings in a hotel room you understand. This "affair" had been conducted solely over the phone when they were both sixteen and the man in question had blackmailed her into giving him a photo of herself by threatening to tell her family about their phone conversations. In fact after she married she only agreed to meet the man in order to recover this photograph which he said he would let her have back only in person. Nevertheless the appeal court interpreted this rather childish silliness as adultery and increased her sentence to two hundred lashes and six months in jail."

"Oh God! No!"

"It's true. She was further prosecuted for attempting to use the media to gain support for her case and, just to add further disgrace to an already sordid tale of barbarity, her lawyer was hauled up before the judiciary for the same offence and had his licence revoked. Conservative critics branded him an infidel and a lawyer of homosexuals. He's been jailed and banned from travelling abroad before. So much for "justice" in Saudi Arabia. The Minister for Justice in the country even publicly defended the sentence against the girl saying she had committed adultery and provoked the attack on her by dressing indecently."

"Good God!"

"It's not an isolated case Sarah. Rape victims are routinely prosecuted for adultery in Saudi Arabia. In 2009 a 23 year old unmarried woman was sentenced to one hundred lashes and a year in jail for adultery. Her crime was to become pregnant after being gang raped and trying desperately and unsuccessfully to abort the foetus after becoming pregnant. Magnanimously the court postponed her whipping until after she'd delivered the baby."

"Bastards!"

"Those are just the extreme cases Sarah. There are no end to the lists of things that women can be punished for in Saudi Arabia. Purdah is the enforced segregation of men and women. A woman is obliged to avoid all contact with men other than close relatives or her husband. She has at all times to be covered from head to toe with an abaya which is the long cloak they wear and the hijab which is the head covering. The only parts of the body they can expose are their hands and eyes. The Mutaween, which are a sort of clerical police, rigidly enforce these rules and can apprehend any woman on the street not adhering to strict dress code. They will arrest any woman on the street socialising with a strange man and charge her with prostitution or arrest her for just appearing in public without her male guardian. Furthermore they can administer floggings to offenders. They are a right bunch of thugs. The most notorious case involving them came in 2002 when a girl's school burned down in Mecca. They prevented the girls from leaving the burning building because they weren't wearing full abayas and hijabs or accompanied by a male guardian. As a result fifteen girls burned to death and another fifty were injured."

"Oh my God!"

"Even many conservative Saudi people created an uproar over that one. Some people pointed out that many Mutaween were recruited in jails and their only qualification was that they had learned the Qur'an, by heart, to get their sentences reduced. The force came under pressure to regulate its activities in 2007 after two people died in their custody in less than two weeks. But they control everything from dietary law to segregation in restaurants."

"There's segregation in restaurants?"

"Hell yes. Women have to eat in separate rooms in restaurants because they might show their faces when lifting their veils to shove food in their mouths. The sexes are segregated everywhere Sarah. A woman can't even show herself unveiled to a male guest in her own house unless he's a close relative. If a man invites his male friends around then she has to stay out of sight. She even has a separate door to the males of the house to enter and exit. Segregation is everywhere between the sexes. It's worse than Apartheid was in South Africa. Women are discouraged from using public transport because they might mix with men. That's a problem because Saudi Arabia is the only country in the world where women are forbidden to drive. You might say that that limits your mobility somewhat and especially since you're not able to even leave the house without the permission of your guardian or travel anywhere without it. It's already hard enough for women to get jobs but even harder when they have no way of getting to work. They generally have to take a taxi which is, strictly speaking, forbidden although it's one area where the rules are generally not enforced. Maybe they're expected to walk as long as they have a guardian in tow. They probably need the exercise because women's sport is strictly discouraged. Saudi Arabia is one of a handful of countries in the world which doesn't have a female Olympics team."

"My God I had no idea the place was so rigid."

"Oh Sarah I could go on and on. In 2008 a woman called Khamisa Mohammed Sawadi was sentenced to forty lashes and imprisonment for allowing a man to deliver bread directly to her in her home. Now you might think the court interpreted this as lewd behaviour or something. Well it would take a pretty twisted court to think that. Khamisa was seventy five years old for fuck's sake."

"Oh Jesus!"

"Then there's marriage. Officially Saudi Arabia bans forced marriage but in reality nearly all marriages are a contract between the husband to be and the father of the bride and the woman has virtually no say in the matter. There's no law for the minimum age for marriage and many girls are married off as early as nine years old although they might be excused from having to consecrate the marriage by having sexual intercourse with their husbands until they have reached puberty. I read of one case where a ten year old girl was married to an eighty year old man as part of a financial deal."

Sarah pulled a face. "Christ and I thought I had it rough."

"Oh yes and a woman doesn't own her own children. The father has full legal ownership of all children or, failing him, another male member of the family. That's of all his children by all his wives of

367

course. Naturally polygamy is practised in Saudi and a man can have up to four wives. In case of divorce or if she is widowed a mother might be granted custody of her children but only up till the age of seven when legal custody devolves on the father or her grandfather or somebody. If my daughter was in Saudi I wouldn't even be able, under the law, to claim ownership of her. And that brings me to another problem. If Lizzie lived in Saudi Arabia it is possible the authorities could prevent me from going there to visit her."

"Surely not. I mean they wouldn't enforce that law on foreign nationals would they?"

"They might well do. For one thing I am not under their law the legal guardian of that child and for another I might be refused entry to the country."

"Why?"

"Because I'm gay."

"Oh! Is that forbidden too?"

"Sarah do you know the maximum penalty under Sharia law in Saudi Arabia for homosexuality?"

"No but I'm guessing it's something serious."

"It's *death* Sarah. Death! Homosexuality carries the death penalty."

Sarah gasped in shock. "Oh my God! Please don't go there Danny."

"Oh I'd have to actually go there and commit a homosexual act to be prosecuted I suppose and it is extremely unlikely that a prominent foreign national would be executed for that offence because the international outcry would be horrendous. Nevertheless I'm gay and not only am I gay but I'm also publicly gay, well known and a high profile advocate for gay rights. I'd be persona non grata with a vengeance in Saudi Arabia and my chances of obtaining a visa to visit my daughter are likely to be slim to remote. I don't particularly want to visit their fucking backward retarded country until it finally drags itself into the twenty first century of course but I don't want my daughter in any place where I feel she is unsafe, where her basic human rights as a female are denied to her and where I, as a mother, risk being denied access to her because of my sexuality. They can keep their archaic customs. My daughter will be raised in a civilised country which at least shows some respect for justice and human rights."

Sarah blinked, taken aback by Daniela's vehemence. It was unlike Daniela to be so vocally condemnatory or sound so outraged. She normally took a more balanced view and was able to understand the viewpoints even of people she strongly disagreed with. Her anxiety over her daughter was evidently putting a great deal of strain on her that she should so lose her normally tolerant understanding. "I take it that you're a bit down on Islam then."

Daniela took a deep breath and shrugged. "Not particularly as it happens. Generally speaking I couldn't give a monkey's about a person's religious beliefs. In any case most of the more repressive aspects of Saudi Arabia are more to do with ancient outmoded custom than religion. They date back to the days when the population consisted of wandering nomads with camels long before the Prophet was even born and have bugger all to do with Islam. Most of their so-called laws and restrictions under Sharia law are just a means of a patriarchal reactionary male dominated society maintaining the status quo and interpreting the Qur'an to suit itself and citing it as justification.

"In fact leading female advocates for women's rights in Saudi aren't opposed to Islamic teachings. On the contrary, they argue vociferously for the rights they believe they are entitled to under Islamic law, as they see it, and which they think they are being denied by the male dominated clerical and secular authorities of the country. They state that there is no evidence that the prophet practised segregation of the sexes or denied women political power. They state that several of the Prophets wives were active politically; even becoming generals in the army. They also state that the abaya and hijab have no authority anywhere in the Qur'an, which contains no rules concerning women's dress other than advice to dress modestly which could mean anything. Indeed some authorities argue that wearing a veil was only mandatory for the wives of the Prophet himself as holy women. There was even one noted first century female Islamic scholar, who was a pupil of one of Mohammed's wives, called Aisha bint Talha who refused to wear a veil saying that "Since the Almighty hath put upon me the stamp of beauty, it is my wish that the public should view the beauty and thereby recognize His grace unto them. On no account, therefore, will I veil myself."

Sarah smiled at Daniela. "I think I know where she's coming from. I look at you every day and thank God for your beauty."

"Flatterer."

"Not at all. Simple statement of fact."

"Anyway my point is that you can interpret Islam any which way you want. That's pretty much true of any religion. Islam certainly isn't alone in being used as a justification for suppressing people's rights. Look at some of the atrocities carried out under the supposed authority of the Bible. Humanity has a long history of repressive actions that somebody insists are the command of Holy writ. It's the easiest thing in the world to selectively point to some obscure passage in an ancient text and claim it justifies your bigotry and tyranny because it represents the word of God whilst ignoring every other passage in the same text that contradicts it. Bible bashers in the United States do it all the time. Religion isn't the problem... it's what people do with it, how they manipulate it to their own ends and corrupt it to make it say what they want to hear."

Daniela paused for a sip of wine. "You know Sarah I actually have no issue whatsoever with a person's religious beliefs. I don't care if they're Christian, Muslim, Buddhist, Jewish, Hindu or if they dance around bonfires naked under the full moon for that matter. I believe that a person's spiritual and religious beliefs are entirely private to them and should be respected. Many people may decide that their religious belief places certain restrictions and obligations upon them such as praying six times a day or not eating pork or meat on Fridays or something. Well that's just fine. I respect that. That's their problem. What is not fine is when they make it *my* problem. Just because your religious belief forbids something you have no right to impose that restriction on me. Your belief should be personal to you. I am not going to tell you what to believe in so therefore don't try to impose your religious sense of morality on me. I have my own spirituality and beliefs and they are no business of anyone else as long as I keep them to myself and don't use them to manipulate the behaviour of others or suppress their own beliefs."

Daniela pulled a face. "The trouble is that people do that all the time. Look at the trouble gay rights gets into every time somebody raises the spectre of religious authority. Every time gay rights is discussed in America some bloody Bible thumper stands up and says the book of Leviticus condemns homosexuality as an abomination. Great! So you are going to deny me my basic human rights on the authority of a single sentence in an obscure backwater passage of the Bible thousands of years old which has probably been mistranslated from the ancient Hebrew in any case and been even more subject to creative misinterpretation and revision ever since?

"In fact" Daniela continued, "Homosexuality is hardly mentioned at all in the Bible and then only in passages you could spend the rest of your days arguing over the interpretation of. St Paul apparently condemns lesbian homosexuality in his letter to the Romans. Well maybe he did but then again he was also a strong advocate for the oppression of women and the institution of slavery so forgive me if I decline to accept his bloody opinion as the moral authority of God. You can bet however that he was quoted heavily by the deniers of women's rights or by South Carolina plantation owners in the 19th century. Nearly every time somebody is trying to trample all over human rights there's some blasted bigot waving a Bible aloft and claiming verse and passage in a thunderous voice to argue in favour of it. Apparently when Jesus was saying "do unto others as you would have them do unto you" these idiots weren't listening."

Daniela heaved a long sigh. "So it's not just Saudi Arabia where people's rights are crushed under the questionable authority of clerical interpretation. It happens all over the place to a lesser degree. Even California, where my daughter lives now and you would have thought was a model for liberty and tolerance, is not blameless. Ever heard of Proposition 8 Sarah?"

Sarah frowned. "I think I've heard something about it but I'm not sure of the details. Wasn't it something to do with gay marriage?"

"That's right. Gay marriage as an issue has a bit of a strange history in America actually. In the early days of the gay rights movement; its more radical and revolutionary days, activists were arguing in favour of a complete overhaul of traditional sexual mores and relationships. To them the institution of marriage was an outdated oppressive dinosaur imposed by a patriarchal and heterosexual society to control the sexuality of the masses. This was back in the sixties and seventies you understand; days of free love and a population liberated by birth control and the old ideals of love and marriage of the fifties seemed hopelessly antiquated and nobody had ever heard of AIDS. Marriage was a conservative agenda and indeed the conservative right wing actually *favoured* gay marriage as an answer to what it perceived as rampant promiscuity and the undermining of traditional values. Oh how things have changed. After those first heady days when everyone had settled down and gay people decided that they just wanted the right to loving relationships the same as every bugger else the moral right wing changed its tune right sharpish. Now that gays *wanted* the right to marry they were no longer conforming to traditional values but, on the contrary, undermining them. So it was time to roll out the preachers and start thumping the Bible."

Daniela shook her head despairingly. "Proposition 8 was a bloody disgrace Sarah. After years of trying, the gay community actually won the right to marry under Californian state law. Thousands of committed gay couples instantly rushed into marriage. The ultra-religious right wing was appalled and led a furious counter attack. Right wing organisations and reactionary church authorities introduced Proposition 8; a referendum on an act to alter the State Constitution introducing a clause to ban gay marriage within California. They then poured fortunes into a massive publicity campaign to persuade voters to back the Proposition. The Mormon Church alone poured millions into the campaign. That really stuck in my craw. The bloody Mormon Church, with a history of forced marriage, child marriage and polygamy suddenly has the effrontery to dictate the morality of somebody else's marriage vows. How dare they! But the campaign was successful and the voters, by a slender majority, voted to outlaw same sex marriage. Gay couples had only had a few months to marry in before being once again denied the right and all this allegedly under the moral authority of Holy scripture. It was a shambles. If I was Californian, I'd be thoroughly ashamed of my state."

Sarah frowned thoughtfully. "But if a majority of people voted against it don't you have to accept it?"

Daniela shook her head decisively. "Not at all. You *can't* quash the rights of a minority by the decision of the majority. That's simply immoral. That's like saying that because Hitler ascended to power with the approval of a majority of Germans for his racist policies that he had a mandate to suppress and ultimately murder millions of Jews. State elections in the Confederate States prior to the civil war were overwhelmingly in favour of the retention of the institution of negro slavery. That doesn't make it right. You can't justify holding millions of African Americans in odious bondage just because of an electoral majority. Human rights are exactly that...*rights*...not something open to negotiation or haggled over through your own personal prejudices. That's why I don't want my child to grow up in a land where her basic rights are subject to whim of state interpretation of religious and cultural morality. My child's rights should be inviolate regardless of her gender, ethnical background, nationality, religion, sexuality or political and social persuasion and not to be disregarded at the whim of some priest, mullah or government official with their own moral hobby horse."

Sarah smiled at Daniela's passion. "Which brings us back to where we started. We seem to have got side-tracked. If you don't want your daughter to live in Saudi Arabia then what are you going to do with her."

Daniela lowered her head. "That's the problem. I don't know."

"Well your parents have been her guardians up until now so what do you think they want to happen."

"I *know* what they want. That's sort of a problem though. They don't think that Saudi is a place for Elizabeth either. My mum's not at all happy about moving to Saudi herself. She's even more outraged about the Saudi human rights record than I am and she's not

374

relishing the thought of living for a couple of years in a country where she's a second hand citizen. However she's prepared to make that sacrifice because she couldn't bear to be separated from my dad and because she sees it as a means towards an end. What she really wants to do is come back to live in Europe. It's not that she doesn't like California but it's been a bit of a rat race for them out there and the thought of retiring back to Europe with enough money to live on the fruits of their labours is very attractive to her. She's always been more European in outlook and she misses the European culture and lifestyle. Now she loves my daughter but she's downright adamant that she wants her to grow up in a safe country compatible with her own cultural heritage. Dad agrees with her. He sees Saudi Arabia as a case of taking the money and running. It's all very well for them as adults to make the decision to risk a couple of years in Saudi Arabia but quite another thing to subject a young girl with all her needs of the right environment and education to that same risk."

"So they don't want to take her to Saudi, and I'm presuming that leaving her in America isn't an option, so now what?"

"Well if there wasn't a third alternative I don't think they'd even consider going to Saudi Arabia. But there is another alternative. They think Elizabeth belongs with her mother."

Sarah nodded thoughtfully. "I see."

Daniela sighed heavily. "They're right as well Sarah. I haven't been much of a mother I'm afraid. It's all very well for me to pontificate about what I consider best for my daughter but it's not as if I've taken much responsibility for her up until now. One of the main reasons I took this house in the first place was because I knew that sooner or later this was going to crop up and I needed a place for my daughter. I just didn't expect it to happen so soon and secondly I didn't expect you."

Sarah held a hand up. "Leave me out of this for the moment. What do *you* want to do?"

Daniela's face was anguished. "I don't know Sarah. I'd love to be the mother to my child that I've never managed to be but how is that possible? I'm committed now to major tours this year and next year too. I can't cancel them now and nor can I leave my child to fend for herself why I go swanning off on tour. Then, of course, there's you. I can't leave you out of the equation."

Sarah picked up the wine bottle, deep in thought, and replenished their glasses. "So you want Elizabeth to come here..."

"I said I would like her to come but I don't see how it's possible."

"Wait a minute Danny. If it *was* possible, would that be what you wanted?"

"Yes of course but how..."

Sarah held up her hand once more. "Bear with me on this Danny. So you want her to come here and your parents want her to come here. There's another person who you need to ask though."

"Sarah I don't have the right to ask you if that would be all right."

"I'm not talking about me Danny. I'm talking about Elizabeth. Everybody seems to be talking about what is best for her but has anybody actually asked her what *she* wants to do? You're right about one thing; child or no child, she does *have* rights."

Daniela had the grace to look chagrined. "You're right of course Sarah. Actually though I don't think that would be a problem. I think she would love to come and live with me."

"But why Danny? I mean she has been brought up by your parents mostly so won't she miss them?"

"Yes she will but she always misses me terribly too. In spite of my being such a lousy mother she loves me very much... God knows why."

"What about her life in California? Won't she miss that, her school and all her friends? It can be a big wrench for a young kid to just up and move across the world away from all she knows."

"I take your point Sarah but it might be less of a wrench than you think. When they first moved to California my folks had a place out of town out in the backwoods. Lizzie loved it there. She's a kid that needs the outdoors and the wind in her hair. But a bit over a year ago mum and dad moved into a house closer to down town LA so that dad didn't need a three hour commute into work every morning and she's not been properly settled since. She had to change school too which she hated. She's always been very bright and ahead of her grade but the new school is a big public elementary school which doesn't challenge her as much and she started to lose interest. I was going to pull her out of that school and enrol her in a private school in any case. Her present school is pretty rough as well and, although she can look after herself among her peers, my parents weren't happy about it. All in all though I think she'd be happier here. The Toggenburg is just the kind of place she'd love. She was over here in the summer last year and we spent two weeks around here and she adored it. She's always asking when she can come back. In fact my parents have already sounded her out on the possibility of her coming over here to live; tactfully of course; they didn't want to promise anything. She was ecstatic about the idea. So I don't see any problems there."

Sarah rubbed her chin. "You say she's ahead of her grade. She might have to drop a grade or two here Danny... I mean the language barrier and all that. It won't be so easy for her in school."

"Oh I don't think that will hold her back Sarah. You forget. My dad is Swiss and he's brought her up pretty much bilingual. She speaks a sight better German than *I* do, albeit with a Californian accent."

Sarah leaned back in the sofa and swilled her wine about in her glass. "So where's the problem then?"

"I've told you the problem. I have commitments. I have a career. Yes I would give it up for my daughter if necessary but that means letting a lot of people down Sarah. I may yet have to do that but it's not going to be easy."

"If you could have both your career and your daughter without harm to her would you go for it."

"Well of course but I can't."

"No you can't... *alone*."

"What are you saying?"

"I'm saying that you're *not* alone Danny. *I'm* here."

"Sarah I can't do that. I can't ask you to take on my daughter. It wouldn't be right."

"Why not?"

"Because it wouldn't. God we've only been living together for a couple of months. I can't ask you to take on the responsibility for my daughter. For heaven's sake you only just escaped from one stultifying commitment to that prat they were going to marry you off to. I can't now ask you to start an instant family and become a second mother to my kid."

"So Elizabeth can't go to Saudi Arabia, she can't stay in the States and so she *has* to come here. What are you going to do when she arrives? Chuck me out of the house?"

"Of course not... I mean....Oh God I don't know what I mean. I don't know *what* to do. If it was just a choice between my career and my daughter I'd figure something out. But it isn't. I can't bear the thought of losing *you*."

"You can have your career, your daughter *and* me Danny. There's no conflict at all there. On the contrary the three things are mutually supportive."

"But how can I possibly expect you to do that

Sarah?"

"That's not one of the questions you should be asking Danny. The two questions you *should* ask, the *only* two questions are; a) is Sarah the right person to help bring up my child and b) is my daughter going to get along with Sarah? Those are the things you should be asking yourself. If the answer to those is yes then this conversation is at an end and we can start tomorrow redecorating one of the spare bedrooms and buying some kiddy furniture to put in it."

"But Sarah..."

"Stop finding bloody buts and answer the question. Would you trust me with your child?"

Daniela looked her deep in the eyes. "I couldn't think of anybody better Sarah." she said softly. "There's nobody I can think of more loving and caring."

"And Elizabeth?"

"She'll just love you. I know she will."

"Are you sure? I mean will she be ok about us being a couple? Is that something we'll have to tip toe around?"

"Oh God no! Lizzie's perfectly aware that her mom is gay and has a girlfriend. She's got no problems with that. She's very precocious and anyway she's been living in West Hollywood for the past year and a half for God's sake so she's hardly been raised in a homophobic environment. Over forty percent of the population is gay in West Hollywood. There are nearly as many same sex couples sharing households as there are heterosexual ones according to the last census."

Sarah grinned. "Maybe it's a good idea to get her out of there then. She might be straight."

"Oh God! Don't say that. My daughter's straight! Where did I go wrong?"

"You should never have let her watch all those nineteen sixties sitcoms on the television. It'll have corrupted her mind."

"I should have known something was wrong when she didn't want to play with her Xena action doll anymore."

Sarah grinned. "So what about giving her that big attic room then? It's a big space so she'd have loads of room and there's loads of closet space for all her toys and everything. It's right at the top and back of the house too so she can make plenty of noise up there without disturbing us. I know it needs bit of work but it's a lovely room and it's so big we can put extra bunk beds in there so she can bring her friend's home for a sleep over."

Daniela was serious again. "Sarah I can't ask you to make this commitment."

"Too late. You already did."

"What do you mean?"

"Danny do you remember the day I came back from the Ticino; the day I told Alan I wasn't going to marry him and told my parents I was gay?"

"How could I forget?"

"Well I committed myself to you then and you committed to me; completely; unconditionally. Did we say anything then about just moving in together for the time being; see how it worked or whether or not it would prove to be convenient?" Daniela shook her head. "No we didn't." Sarah continued. "We committed for good; for life; through thick or thin; for better or for worse. I threw away everything for that commitment Danny. I abandoned my marriage; lost my family; threw away the habits of a lifetime all on that one mad hope of happiness. I went into it with my eyes open. I knew there would be rocky shoals ahead. I knew there would be times we would be separated because of your career. I knew we risked the attention of the media and all the pressure that could come with that. But I did it anyway. Nothing, but nothing, has happened since then to make me regret my decision one iota and certainly not the news that I'm going to be sharing my life not only with the woman I love but also with her beloved daughter and I'm guessing that any daughter of yours is going to be a pretty remarkable person. Do you seriously think that suddenly finding that I'm going to have a family is onerous to me? Nothing could be further from the truth. I'm deliriously happy about it. I love kids. I've always wanted my own family. That was about the only bright side of my late and unlamented future marriage I could see. Well now I *can* have a family. With you." Sarah grinned happily. "I warn you though. I want more than one kid. I want a *big* family. We've both got plenty more years of baby production potential in us so I want lots of kids."

Daniela was overcome with love. With tears spilling down her cheeks she grasped Sarah to her. "Oh Sarah I love you so much."

"I love you too mom."

"But Sarah what about all the things you wanted to do? I mean like your PhD for instance?"

"Oh I'm still going to do all that. It's not as if you'll be away all the time and most of my study work and research I can do right here in my own living room while the kids are at school. I once bought into the bloody lie that I'd have to abandon all my dreams just to become a housewife and mother. I know better now. I feel invincible. I can do anything. Together *we* can do anything. With your looks and my brains we're unstoppable."

"Are you suggesting I'm deficient in the brains department?" demanded Daniela in outrage.

Sarah patted her on the knee. "Well you're just a dizzy little blond after all."

"You cheeky bitch!" She tried to push Sarah away but Sarah grinned, grasped her wrists and held her firmly. Daniela squirmed. "Let go of me! I've never been so insulted." But Sarah had learned that she was stronger than Daniela and she wrestled her down onto the carpet where she managed to pin her. "Let go you brute!" Daniela squealed.

Sarah grinned in triumph. "Shan't." Sarah managed to grasp both Daniela's wrists in one hand. With her other hand free she managed to pull open the sash holding Daniela's wrap about her and ease the garment open. "Hah! I've been wanting to get this thing off you ever since you got out of the shower. I bloody know you put it on just to tease me you little vixen."

Daniela lay back on the carpet and called, "Help! Rape!"

Sarah laughed at her. "You could have at least *tried* to make that sound more convincing you shameless hussy. I doubt if even the cats heard that."

"I tried my best but I was too overwhelmed."

"Well you'll have to do better than that. The nearest house to us is over five hundred metres away and that feeble plea wouldn't have carried as far as the kitchen. Then again the nearest house is Elrika's cottage so I'm not so sure how much help you could rely upon. Even if she happened to hear you I'm sure I could have violated you long before she managed to hobble over here to render assistance."

Daniela regarded her quizzically. "Look are you going to get on with this job or not? Bloody typical. Only you could stop in the middle of violating somebody to conduct a critical analysis of her chances of being rescued. What kind of rapist do you call yourself? Do you want your victim to fall asleep in the middle of the act?"

"Oh I'm sorry. Am I neglecting you?" Sarah reached down and pulled Daniela's knickers away from her hips fiercely.

Daniela sighed and lay back in deep contentment. "That's better." she murmured.

Chapter Twenty-One

When Nicole and Charmaine turned up at the house the following day, they found the place apparently deserted, despite having phoned a little earlier to assure themselves that Sarah and Daniela were present and to announce that they were on their way. Nicole stepped up to the staircase and called out loudly. "Yoohoo! Anybody home?" She was rewarded by a distant call from upstairs.

"Maybe they're still in bed." Charmaine suggested.

"It's nearly eleven o'clock, for crying out loud." Nicole protested. "What would they be doing in bed this late?"

Charmaine grinned happily. "Much the same as we were doing about an hour ago I suppose."

Nicole blushed. "They can't spend the whole day shagging." she mumbled.

Charmaine chuckled and took her around the waist from behind, nuzzling at her neck. "I don't see why not. It's what *you* would do if I let you."

Nicole disentangled herself hastily. "Stop it Charlie. I can hear somebody coming."

"Oh my! Silly me. We mustn't let Danny and Sarah come to the wrong conclusion must we? They might think we're on intimate terms or something." Nicole glared at her but Charmaine just laughed happily. And Charmaine *was* happy. It had taken weeks of gentle seduction since she had met Nicole at Sarah's graduation to entice Nicole into becoming her lover but she was reaping the rewards for her patience now. Nicole was apparently attempting to make up for a lifetime in the closet as quickly as possible. To her delighted surprise, Charmaine had discovered that her little blond girlfriend, once teased out into the open, was proving to be an eagerly enthusiastic lover of apparently insatiable appetite. Charmaine was completely smitten with her. Life was good: a place in Daniel Devin's band, exciting live concerts to look forward to and a gorgeous little, crazy but captivating, new girlfriend to boot. It didn't get better than this.

Sarah skipped down the stairs looking, Nicole thought, like a kid on Christmas morning. She was clearly excited about something as she embraced Nicole and Charmaine fondly. Daniela followed closely on her heels and she looked happy and animated as well. Charmaine's possible explanation for this scene of domestic bliss seemed ungrounded however for they were both fully dressed albeit in rather old and dusty clothes. Nicole frowned. "What the hell are you two up to?" she asked. "You look like the cats that got the cream."

Sarah grinned. "Oh just clearing out one of the spare rooms." She informed Nicole happily.

Nicole raised an eyebrow. Of all the reasons for looking flushed and excited she could think of, rummaging around in a disused old room came fairly low down the list. She began to suspect that they might have interrupted Sarah and Daniela after all. "So er... you've been... er clearing out a room?" asked Nicole for puzzled confirmation.

Sarah beamed and wrapped an arm around Daniela's waist. "Can I tell her Danny?"

"Sure. Go ahead."

Sarah grinned at Nicole. "We're shortly about to have an addition to the family." she declared joyously.

Nicole blinked in astonishment. "Oh! Er right! Well...er...congratulations... I suppose. Er... like which one of you is it if you don't mind me asking?"

Sarah laughed merrily. "Neither of us you muppet. We're not pregnant. Well at least not unless there's been a second immaculate conception. It's Danny's daughter.

She's moving from America to come and live with us here next month some time. We're just trying to sort out a room for her."

Nicole was taken aback by this intelligence. "Oh wow! That's a pretty serious move isn't it?"

Sarah nodded. "It certainly is. We've got loads to do. We've got furniture to buy, redecorating to do, paperwork to organise: all sorts of stuff. We haven't even thought about which school we're going to place her at. We're going to be busy."

Daniela smiled. "Come on let's all go in the kitchen and grab a coffee and we can tell you all about it. Have you girls eaten yet?"

"Er we had a roll and a cup of coffee before we came out." Charmaine advised Daniela hopefully. In spite of her slender figure Charmaine had a healthy appetite generally and the quick bite to eat they'd snatched before leaving the house had left her woefully short on calories for the morning.

Sarah took their arms and steered them toward the kitchen. "Well come along then and I'll fix you something to eat. We've got loads to tell you."

They certainly did. Sarah cut them some slices of honey roasted ham and topped them with fried eggs. They had fresh bread and butter, some potato salad, some cherry tomatoes which Nicole was greedy about and they finished the last of Elrika's blackberry tart with some fresh cream and, all throughout this, Nicole and Charmaine listened in astonishment as Sarah and Daniela chatted away garrulously about the impending arrival of Daniela's daughter and their plans for her.

In fact Sarah and Daniela were somewhat short of sleep. After making love in the living room they had lain awake half the night in bed continuing the conversation they had begun earlier. Even after they had fallen asleep they had not slept long but jumped from bed early to snatch a hasty breakfast and then rush upstairs to examine the big spare attic room that Sarah had suggested would make a fine room for Daniela's daughter. They had spent most of the morning rummaging about up there, discussing furnishings and decoration happily and making endless lists of requirements.

The pair of them looked, thought Nicole amusedly, even more like a pair of cooing love birds than ever. There was a definite air of nest building about the household. In a sense Nicole could understand why Sarah was so happy. For all her outdoor life Sarah had always had a somewhat homely side to her; a certain satisfaction with the mundane trappings of domesticity. In their life together in the Alpli it had been almost invariably Sarah, when not away at university, that had attended to the running of the household and the necessities of domestic life. Nicole was something of an indifferent housekeeper and generally the major source of friction between them had been Nicole's neglect of her domestic duties.

Even now, after Sarah had moved out to set up house with Daniela, whenever Sarah came around to visit she would cluck her tongue at the state Nicole was allowing the house to degenerate into and start tidying up. Nicole was happy to let her, not because she was too lazy to attend to the matter herself, but because it maintained some sort of connection between them; a continued presence of Sarah about the house. Sarah grumbled that she seemed to be keeping two houses at once sometimes but her moans were transparent and entirely unconvincing. In fact she relished the situation. She was a girl that liked to be busy and, in truth, the maintenance of Daniela's house did not tax her greatly because much of the general cleaning devolved on their housekeeper Elrika. Sarah often had to sit on her hands to avoid impinging on Elrika's areas of responsibility and even daily chores about the house were not onerous for Daniela herself was fastidiously tidy and insisted upon sharing the burden of cooking and housekeeping whenever her work allowed.

In a sense, however, Sarah, by going to live with Daniela, had moved into what was to all intents and purposes a finished product. It always felt as if she was living in Daniela's house. It still did not feel like her own home; as if she had placed her own personality into it. Of course she shared the place entirely with Daniela but most of the furnishings, decorations and colour schemes were Daniela's. Sarah felt like a lodger. She had not even moved all her things into Daniela's house. A lot of her possessions were still in her old room at the cottage in the Alpli as if she kept a foot in both houses.

Now, however, things were different. If Daniela's daughter was coming to live with them then Sarah had a proactive role in the process. For the first time she would be joining with Daniela in creating something about the house. This would be something they would do together; a very real sense of building their own family nest. Although ostensibly they were making a home for little Elizabeth they were also making a home for themselves. Sarah finally had her own house; her own family.

With an inward smile Nicole had to concede that few people she knew were so qualified for the role of housekeeper and parent. It was Sarah's ex fiancé, Alan's, loss that Sarah had discovered she was gay and that in any case she was rooted in her beloved valley. Nicole had sometimes detected a sense of regret in Sarah that her sexuality seemingly precluded her from having her own family. Sarah adored kids; always had done. Sarah was born to be a mother and now it appeared as if she was about to become one. Nicole suspected that Daniela realised that too. Daniela it seemed had looked for a home for her child and, with Sarah, it appeared as if she had found one. She looked profoundly happy. They both did.

For her part, it would not have appealed to Nicole. She wasn't ready to settle down and think of serious things like families. In a way she was even less settled than ever. Before coming to an acceptance of her own sexuality Nicole had sort of drifted from one boy to another without any real pleasure or any thought of commitment. In fact the only person she had felt at all settled with had been Sarah. Secretly Nicole wondered what her life would be like had she not been so afraid and repressed as to express her feelings for Sarah. Sarah was the one person that Nicole could have happily settled in for the long haul with. But that was water under the bridge. Daniela had come along and taken her Sarah's heart and made Nicole a free agent. That freedom was not entirely regrettable for the process had liberated Nicole from her sexual repression. For the first time it had forced Nicole to face her own sexuality. That was an exciting new experience for her. She now officially had a girlfriend and yesterday, in Zurich, she had realised for the first time just how exhilarating and liberating it was to openly embrace your true sexuality. She had a whole new world to explore before she thought of settling down into domesticity.

Of course Nicole had some familial problems of her own to clear, however, and that brought her to the reason for her visit. "By the way Sarah," she interposed when she could get a word in edgeways between Sarah and Daniela's effusive outpourings. "My mam phoned this morning."

Instantly, Sarah became serious and attentive. "Oh. Oh I see."

Nicole nodded. "Yeah she wants to know if we're still on for this evening."

Sarah had been stood up and fussing around putting dishes into the dishwasher but she paused to come and sit at the kitchen table. She looked at Nicole soberly. "What did you tell her?"

"I said I'd have to ask you. I'm now asking."

"Where does she want to meet?"

"At the Toggenburg she says but I said I'd have to run that past you. I thought you might feel awkward about that."

"No I'd be fine with that Nicky but what about you? I mean what are you going to say to her?"

Nicole took a deep breath. "I'm going to tell her the truth Sarah."

Sarah blinked. "Christ! That's a turn up for the books. You bloody well refused to even consider the idea yesterday."

"Yes well Charlie and me had a long talk about it last night. She's going to find out sooner or later and it sounds as if she pretty much knows in any case so there seems no point in further denial. I suppose it's something I have to face up to sometime or other so it might as well be tonight."

Sarah regarded her compassionately. "Are you sure you're ready for this Nicky?"

Nicole grimaced. "I don't know. I'm bricking it to tell the truth. It's something I have to do though."

Daniela nodded seriously. "I think you're being wise Nicole. It's something we all have to go through. I don't think it will be too bad though. From what Sarah says, it sounds like she's already figured it out."

Nicole pulled a face. "Well yes to a certain extent Danny. The trouble is that she seems to think that Sarah and I are a couple. She was dropping some pretty heavy hints on the phone. I'm going to have to disabuse her of that. What I wanted to say was that you don't have to come if you don't want Sarah. This is really my business and it could be an uncomfortable evening."

"Do *you* want me to come?" asked Sarah uncertainly.

"Well it would be nice if you did Sarah because she's asked to see both of us but it's not something I can really ask you to do because it's my business."

"She asked me to come because she thinks I'm your girlfriend Nicky. Are you going to tell her about Charlie?"

Charmaine spoke up. "I've already offered to come along Sarah but Nicky's scared to death it will be embarrassing for me. I've told her that I'm not frightened about it." Charmaine grinned. "I'd kind of like to meet Nicky's mum in any case. She sounds like a hell of a woman."

Nicole threw her hands up in despair. "She's barking mad Charlie. I can't put you through the trauma of me coming out to my mam."

"You were willing to put Sarah through it." Charmaine pointed out.

"Hey I've just given her an opt out clause. I'll go on my own if necessary."

Daniela raised a finger. "Here's a thought. Why don't we *all* go?"

Nicole regarded her in shock. "What you mean you as well Danny?"

"Exactly. Look if you go on your own it looks as if Sarah's deliberately snubbed your mum because she specifically asked her along. But if you go with Sarah you're going to have to say that Sarah's not your girlfriend and that you have another one. Then your mum's going to want to know who *is* your girlfriend and why she isn't there. So you could take Sarah and Charlie but that leaves Sarah looking like a spare part. So Sarah brings *her* girlfriend and we turn up as two couples."

"Christ I don't know." said Nicole worriedly. "It'll seem like a bloody delegation."

Daniela leaned across the table. "Look I wanted to take Sarah out to dinner in any case to celebrate my daughter coming to live with us. We can just turn up together and say hello to your mum and let her know what the situation is. If after that you want some privacy to talk to your mum alone or with Charlie or whoever we can always take another table. We'll just see how she reacts and take it from there."

Charmaine looked concerned. "I'm not sure. I mean it would mean outing your relationship with Sarah publicly Danny. I thought you were trying to keep that under wraps for the moment at least until Sarah gets around to telling *her* parents about it."

Sarah shrugged resignedly. "I suppose it won't matter. I guess half the gay population of Zurich is speculating about my identity by now."

"They don't know you Sarah." Charmaine pointed out. "You're just some mysterious girl Danny turned up with. You could be anybody. Nicky's mum's known you most of your life though."

Nicole shook her head. "No. I'll say one thing about my mam. She might have the odd screw loose but she's no tittle tattle. If somebody tells her something in confidence she wouldn't dream of spreading it around." Nicole allowed herself a wry smile. "Her discretion isn't entirely altruistic of course. She's got enough skeletons rattling about in her *own* cupboards and you know what they say about people who live in glass houses."

"What about if you go and meet your mum on your own first Nicky then we turn up later." suggested Sarah.

Nicole thought for a moment. "No maybe it's better if we do it Danny's way after all. I mean this is only supposed to be a casual dinner meeting even though we know it's anything but. I'll just say to mum that I have a couple of friends I'd like her to meet and we'll take it from there." Nicole grimaced. "At least once she meets Danny I don't think there's going to be any further question about where the conversation's heading. Even my mam's going to recognise the most famous lesbian in the country. I think she'll be thrilled."

Daniela clapped her hands together. "That settles it then. We're all going out for dinner tonight." She grinned and waved a finger at Sarah and Nicole. "At least we'll have these two well chaperoned tonight Charlie so they won't be getting up to any more mischief such as picking up the first two available shop girls they lay eyes on."

Charmaine laughed. "Yeah or disgracing themselves in a Zurich sex shop."

Daniela raised an eyebrow. "Sex shop? Sex shop? What's all this about? First I've heard about a sex shop."

Charmaine grinned mischievously. "Oh didn't your girlfriend mention our two little darlings' escapades in the Magic X Erotic Megastore in Zurich yesterday then Danny?"

"No she bloody well did not."

Sarah swallowed hastily. "Er we just went in because Nicky wanted to buy something Danny."

Nicole jabbed a finger at Sarah furiously. "Don't try laying the rap on me Sarah Fuchs. It was your sodding idea."

Daniela leaned back in her chair and rolled her tongue about on the inside of her cheek. "I see. Well this is all very interesting. Pray tell more. What exactly was this idea of yours Sarah?"

"Yes girls," urged Charmaine wickedly. "Do tell Danny exactly what it was you went looking for in that shop."

"It was only a bedroom accessory." remarked Sarah austerely although she was blushing crimson.

Daniela's amusement grew. "A bedroom accessory?"

"Nicky only brought back a deluxe strap-on dildo Danny." Charmaine informed her.

"Oh!" said Daniela in mock outrage, "So this is what you two were spending my hard earned cash on is it? That's going to make a pretty little item on my credit card account isn't it?"

"It was only a bit of fun." protested Nicole. She

turned to glare at Charmaine. "Anyway I didn't hear you moaning about it last night."

"No it was *you* who was doing the moaning if I recall."

Daniela burst out laughing as Nicole turned pink and folded her arms. "Do you think we could maintain a little decorum around this table?" she demanded indignantly."

Daniela wiped a tear from her eye and mastered herself. "I bet that's one little heart felt confession you won't be sharing with your mam tonight Nicky." she wheezed. "Oh my! You two are something else. I should have known better than to let the pair of you off the leash together."

Nicole and Sarah were spared further embarrassment by the bell; literally by the bell for there was chime from the front door. "Was that the doorbell?" asked Charmaine.

"Er I'll go see to it." said Sarah rising hastily.

Sarah was surprised for, stood at the door, were Simon and Peter. They'd evidently been working; decorating the pub for, while they had both changed out of their old clothes, there was still evidence of spots of emulsion adorning their hair. "Hi Sarah." Simon greeted her. "Is Danny in by any chance?"

"Sure. Nicky and Charlie are here as well. We're in the kitchen. Come in and have a coffee with us."

Simon ran a hand through his hair. "Well actually I could kill a beer if you've got any in the fridge Sarah."

"Sure we have. Come in. I'm glad you've popped round actually. I wanted to talk to you about something."

Once the two boys had greeted the company and were installed around the kitchen table with bottles of beer in front of them Simon glanced at Peter and addressed Daniela. "This isn't just a social call Danny we've come around to ask your advice on something."

"Well I hope I can help you. What's bothering

you?"

"We need a bit of business advice actually. Since you're our partner in the pub we didn't want to go ahead without your ok on this one."

"Well actually Sarah and I are joint partners in the pub Simon so anything you need to ask my advice on you should consult Sarah too. I thought we were leaving most of the business decisions up to you two though."

"Well yes except we can't agree on this one so we thought we'd ask you to arbitrate."

"So what's the problem?"

"Well somebody came around asking for a job yesterday."

Daniela frowned. "Surely you don't need me to advice you on recruitment. Anyway isn't it a bit early to be employing staff? I thought you weren't opening until December."

"A bit earlier Danny." Peter told her. "We're opening up for the winter season which starts around the twentieth of November. So we need to think about getting staff in now."

"So have you been advertising then?"

"Well actually no." Peter confessed. "We were going to put in an ad next week sometime."

"Yes," Simon continued "In addition to Nicky we reckoned we needed at least one more waiter or waitress and possibly two, maybe even three if they're part time. But, until we start turning over a profit, you're more or less going to paying them so we thought that it was best if we ran any candidates past you."

"I don't understand boys." said Daniela with a frown. "I thought we'd more or less covered all this. I said I'd cover the expenses and staff salaries until the place was able to pay its way. I'm sure I trust your judgement on suitable staff."

"If you haven't advertised for staff yet how did this person you're talking about know about the job?" asked

Sarah in puzzlement.

Simon answered her. "Well she's new in the valley. She's just moved here from Graubunden and she's been looking for work locally. Apparently she was asking around in Wildhaus and somebody happened to mention this new place that was opening and she wandered across on spec."

"So this woman," asked Daniela, "Does she appear to be suitable?"

Simon nodded. "I think so but Peter's not so sure and his misgivings are not without foundation. On the face of it she appears ideal. She's Swiss and got good diplomas in catering and hospitality management. She's got plenty of experience and glowing references and she's full of good ideas. Also she's experienced on the accounting and paperwork side. Pete and I are both a bit wet behind the ears on that side of things so it would be a real boost to have someone who knows what they're doing with all the tax returns, invoices, acquisitions and what have you. On the face of it she seems like a real asset."

"So what's the problem? Is she a psychopath or something?"

Simon shook his head with a chuckle. "No. Well not as far as we can tell. Actually she seems like a really nice lady; a bit timid and introverted perhaps but perfectly personable and pleasant when you get talking to her. There's a touch of sadness to her but I think she's gone through a few problems and life's dealt her some bum hands."

"Is this the reason for your uncertainty about her?" asked Daniela.

Simon nodded. "Well maybe. You tell her Pete."

Peter hesitated. "Well it's a bit awkward Danny. Don't get me wrong. I like her too and she's certainly got all the qualifications. But she's looking for a full time job and I'm worried that in our line of business she wouldn't be able to commit herself full time to the position."

"But why?" asked Daniela.

"Because she's a single mother." Peter told her. "She's only twenty nine but she's got a young child of seven or eight years old. Raising a kid that age is hard enough on your own without having a job with such unsociable hours as working in a pub entails. I mean she might be expected to work late into the night and so on. How the hell is she going to look after the kid as well?"

"Just a moment." said Daniela thoughtfully. "You said she's got experience and references. She must have handled her childcare problems and work before."

"Yes and she assures us that she will be able to do so again. But her previous experience is in Graubunden where she knew people and had people who could babysit for her and everything. Here she knows virtually nobody. If she had a day job she could work her hours around the kid's school times but working at night is another matter."

"Why did she leave Graubunden?"

"Personal reasons she tells us. Apparently her parents more or less threw her out of the house when she had an illegitimate child and the father refuses to acknowledge his parentage and doesn't help her."

Daniela snorted. "That's easy enough to handle. He can be legally required to take a paternity test and if it's proven that he's the father then he's liable to pay maintenance on the kid whether he likes it or not."

Simon nodded. "I agree but I don't think it's as simple as that. Reading between the lines it sounds as if the guy's a real asshole and his family wield a lot of clout where she comes from. She sounds scared to death of him and her own family have disinherited her and cut her off. I think she was running away from Graubunden; trying to make a new start among people that don't know her. She's wound up in Wildhaus because she knew it as a child and liked it. But she's on her own and trying to raise a kid on a pittance. She sounds like she's desperate for a job. Life's pretty hard for her."

Daniela shook her head wonderingly. "I find it incredible that even in this day and age people can be so marginalised and repressed and so frightened as to not be able to stand up for their rights. It sounds like this girl needs help."

Peter looked uncomfortable. "I think she needs help as well Danny. I'm just not sure that we should be the ones to give it to her. I mean I feel sorry for her. She very nearly begged us for the job but we can't afford to let sentimentality get in the way of business decisions."

Daniela looked even more thoughtful. "Sentiment is not without its plus points Peter. Even in business it sometimes pays to put the purely clinical business considerations to one side and go with what your heart tells you to be right. I've taken on a lot of people over the years that had no place else to go and were just looking for somebody to give them a break for once. I've never regretted it yet. The most fiercely loyal and dedicated people I have working for me were all people that had the talent but were never given the opportunity. They're so thankful that somebody put cold calculation aside to give them a chance to prove themselves that they'll follow you to hell and back. You might do well to give this girl a break."

Charmaine who had been quiet up until this point raised a hand. "I agree with Danny. I know it's none of my business but what she says is true. I'm a case in point. Look at me. I was an out of work bass guitar player living in a run-down bedsitter in Winterthur. I had no money, no reputation other than a local one through my ex band, no future, a clapped out old guitar, old clothes I bought in second hand shops and a family that was barely on talking terms with me. There was no earthly logical reason why Danny should even consider me to play in her band except for the fact that I'm a good guitar player and I'm prepared to grab the best chance I've ever had and never let her down. If Danny told me to go run up the Chaserugg right now in my birthday suit I'd do it because I owe her so much. I know what it feels like to be thrown out by your family and loved ones without a friend in the world and knowing you can do it if only somebody would give you the chance to prove it. If this girl has the qualifications then let her have a go."

Peter wrung his hands in anguish. "That's more or less what Simon says but I still don't see how she's going to manage it. There's more to it too. We think there's something wrong with her kid."

Daniela frowned. "Yes?"

"Well it sounds like the kid has some sort of special needs. Apparently she had to pull him out of his last school because of behavioural problems and because he wasn't fitting in and the other kids were bullying him. He's got some sort of emotional and psychological problems. She wouldn't go into details. I think she was a bit embarrassed by them. My point is that it would be hard enough for her to manage the job with any child of that age. It's going to be doubly difficult for her to cope when her kid has serious problems."

"Do you think he might be autistic or something Peter?" asked Sarah.

"I've no idea Sarah. As I say, she didn't want to go into details so I didn't press her. But if the kid has got problems then who the hell is she going to find to take care of him while she works? He might require specialist care or something. It's not just like you could ask the neighbours to take him in or something."

"It sounds even more as if this lady needs some real help." Sarah remarked.

Daniela held up her hands. "Look Peter. If this girl can do the job as she insists and Simon is right about the fact that her talents make her an asset to the business then these are details we can work out. We know enough people in the valley surely to find the help and care she and her child need. We can't humanely discriminate against this lady on the grounds that she's the single mother of a special needs child. For one thing I'm not even sure it's legal. There are all sorts of cantonal and federal programmes to assist single working mothers with care for their children and even more so when the child has special needs. These are problems we can help her with. If this lady has the talents you say she has then she deserves the chance to show us them. Don't you agree?"

Peter looked worried. "Well yes but... hell I don't know. You can understand my concerns."

"Of course I understand. What have you told this lady?"

Simon answered. "We haven't said yes or no Danny. We told her that we had to consult with our business partner before making any decisions regarding staffing."

"Does she know who your business partner is?" asked Daniela hesitantly.

Simon shook his head decisively. "No. She hasn't a clue. We haven't told anybody that Danny. We've respected your confidentiality completely."

"Well I didn't insist on confidentiality Simon. I have enough faith in you and Peter to make this business work and I'm not ashamed to have my name associated with it. Still perhaps it's a good thing that this lady doesn't know about my connection. At least we know that she's not some gold digger after the job because of its connection to me."

"Oh no. I may not be the best judge of character Danny but I'm certain she has no ulterior motive. She seems a genuine and honest person. To be frank I like her. I understand Pete's concerns but I think we can make this work. I think she'll be good for the business

399

and I think we'll be good for her."

Daniela nodded. "When have you said you'll give her a decision?"

"We said we'd call her sometime this week."

"Well I want you to call her this evening and ask her to attend a second interview... with *me* this time; or, to be more precise, with me and Sarah."

Simon blinked. "You want to see her?"

"Yes Simon. With all due respect Simon I have rather more experience in employing people than you and Peter have."

Simon grinned ruefully. "I'll not argue that with you. We're out and out novices when it comes to things like this."

"Well then I'd like to see her."

"Why me though?" asked Sarah somewhat perplexed. "Why do you want me to be there?"

"Yes why Sarah?" Peter also wanted to know.

"Because I have unshakeable faith in Sarah's instinctive empathy Pete, even if Sarah doesn't know she has it. If Sarah takes a liking for this lady, then that's good enough for me. I have yet to meet anybody that has a place in Sarah's heart who isn't special." Daniela pondered for a minute. "It'll have to be tomorrow because we're back in the studio the day after. Shall we say two o'clock in the afternoon?"

Simon nodded. "Ok. If she really wants this job she'll be there. Thanks for doing this Danny. You've taken a weight off our shoulders."

Daniela turned to Peter. "And you Peter? Do you agree this is the best way?"

Peter nodded quickly. "Yes Danny. I admit I'm a bit out of my depth here. I've never had to employ anybody in my life before. I'm worried sick about making a cock up of it. I trust you implicitly to make the right decision."

"Excellent. Don't worry about making a cock up

though Peter. It's the first time you and Simon have been in business like this and you're bound to make a few mistakes. It'll come in time. I wouldn't be putting money behind this venture if I didn't think that you and Simon could make a go of it."

Peter smiled bashfully. "I'm pleased you have faith in us Danny. I hope you won't be disappointed in us."

"I'm sure I won't."

"Where do you want this interview to take place Danny?" asked Simon. "Do you want to meet her at the pub?"

"Not if we can help it. For one thing she's already seen it and for another it's a bloody bomb site at the moment. Has she got a car?"

"Well yes, of sorts. She drove over yesterday in one anyway although it's a bit of an old banger."

"Well then tell her to come here. We can rustle up some coffee and nibbles and put her at her ease."

Peter snorted. "Put her at her ease. Being interviewed by Switzerland's most famous pop artist and you think she'll be at her ease. I don't think so. She'll probably shit herself."

Daniela ignored him and turned to Nicole. "Oh Nicky could you be there as well please?"

"Eh? Me? Why?"

"Because you're going to be working with this girl so it would be nice to introduce her to her future colleague and see if you two can get along together. You only have to pop in briefly. She'll need to know the sort of people she's going to be working with though."

Sarah grinned. "As long as you don't tell her that you're a ruthless predatory lesbian who chases anything in a skirt to threaten them with her strap on dildo Nicky."

"Fuck you Sarah!"

Charmaine laughed. "Yeah you'd better hide your copies of L-Mag Nicky. One look at your photo spread and she'll think we're luring her into an iniquitous den

401

of raving poufs and dykes."

Nicole snorted. "Well she won't be far off the mark will she? If you do take this poor girl on she'll probably be the only straight person in the fucking establishment."

Simon grimaced. "You know that's a point. I don't actually know if she realised that Pete and I are a couple. Then again if she meets Danny and Sarah she really is going to see that she's working with nothing but gay people. She might not be comfortable with that. I never thought to ask her."

"You shouldn't have to ask her Simon." Daniela was quick to point out. "Our sexuality has no bearing whatsoever on her job. We're not discriminating against her because she's straight. If she's got anything about working with gay people well there's the door sweetheart.... use it."

Peter shook his head. "I don't think there's a problem there Simon. I think she pretty much figured out that we were more than just business partners. It didn't seem to faze her. If anything she seemed quite interested."

"Maybe she's gay as well." suggested Charmaine. "I mean she's twenty nine and not married after all. Having a kid doesn't mean anything. I know loads of lezzies with kids."

Daniela rolled her eyes. "Oh God! I hope not or we'll have to keep Nicky on a leash."

Nicole donned her indignant face. "I don't see why I have to sit here and take all these unwarranted slurs on my character."

Peter shrugged. "Maybe it's just me but she did seem a bit interested in a wary sort of way. Maybe she's in the closet."

Sarah laughed. "Well we've got Rozella coming along to take the photos at the opening party. If she's gay, Rosy will soon winkle her out."

Nicole snorted cynically. "As if Rosy could give a

flying fuck about whether she's gay or not. As long as she's got XX chromosomes and a body temperature of thirty seven degrees, Rosy will be in there like a truffle pig on a hot scent."

Daniela rapped on the table. "Can we bring this meeting to order please?" She looked around. "So is it all settled then?"

"Er one problem Danny." Peter brought up. "What if she can't get a babysitter on such short notice?"

Sarah looked at him in puzzlement. "Why should she need a babysitter? The kid will be in school won't he?"

Peter rubbed his chin. "Well no. That's the problem. Apparently she hasn't got him into a local school yet. She has to see social workers and psychologists to assess his learning difficulties first or something. I told you there was a problem there."

"Well that's just perfect." declared Daniela. "It's even better. Tell her to bring her little boy with her. That way we can see what exactly might be the challenges she has with her child and see what kind of solutions we would need."

Simon looked dubious. "Is that appropriate Danny; I mean asking her to bring her son along on a formal interview?"

"So don't couch it as a formal interview Simon. Tell her that this is just an informal meeting to meet the other people she'll be working with; which it is really. Tell her we'd love to meet her little boy. We might even be able to help her with babysitters or something. She'll soon read between the lines, but what of it? She might in fact be reassured that we're taking the concerns about her child seriously. At least it shows we're serious about her candidacy."

Simon shrugged. "Ok then but she might think it a bit weird. I'll tell her two o'clock then. I should imagine the poor brat will be under the direst warnings of good behaviour or woe betide him though; bless his little cotton socks!" Simon straightened up. "So if that's all settled then, what was the other thing you wanted to talk to us about Sarah?"

Sarah looked at him coyly. "Well boys I know you have quite a bit of work still to do in the pub."

"Yes? And?"

"Well I thought I might be able to give you a hand now and then."

Simon nodded. "Well we could always use some extra help Sarah."

Sarah smiled eagerly. "Yes of course. I'd always be willing to help out. I mean that's what friends are for after all... to help each other out when they need it."

Peter narrowed his eyes and squinted at her. "What are you after Sarah?"

"What do you mean?"

"Don't be coy with me! I've known you too long. There's a conditional clause in this generous, selfless offer of help I could throw a cow at."

"Well there are a couple of little things you could help us with in return."

"Oh yes?"

"Yes we have to buy some new furniture; beds, chests of drawers, chests, bean bags that sort of thing. Well my BMW is roomy but I can't get that much in it. I thought perhaps if you had some spare time you could help us out with your pick up. Also of course the stuff might be heavy so we need a pair of big strong men as well."

Nicole guffawed. "But since there aren't any available they'll have to make do with a pair of mincing queens instead."

Simon picked a handy wooden spoon off the kitchen top and brandished it under Nicole's nose. "One more crack like that Nicole Richardson and this baby has got your arse's name on it."

404

"Why the hell are you buying new furniture Sarah?" asked Peter.

Sarah beamed happily. "We need to furnish a bedroom for Danny's daughter Pete. We're going to start a family."

Chapter Twenty-Two

Later that evening, after returning home in the afternoon, Nicole and Charmaine arrived back at Sarah and Daniela's house prior to venturing out together to the anticipated confrontation with Nicole's mother. Sarah and Daniela had dressed up for the occasion; prettily but conservatively. Daniela had donned a soft floral knee length print dress in aquamarine and white whilst Sarah had opted for a slightly shorter dress but of more subdued tones of creams and autumnal colours. Both dresses were of soft material that flowed over their figures attractively but without too much in the way of suggestion. They were dresses to look pretty in at church or, for that matter, for meeting your best friend's mother for dinner.

They were not the only ones to have made a special effort to dress nicely for the coming showdown. Nicole stepped into the house looking the perfect image of any proud mother's pretty daughter in a lovely knee length, printed dress of pinks and whites. Sarah recognised the dress. Nicole had bought it only the previous day in Zurich. The choice had surprised Sarah at the time although she had been very pleased about it. Nicole looked lovely in it although it was far more grown up than some of her usual ensembles. She had matched it with pretty shoes, a broad belt, some understated costume jewellery and, clutched possessively, her new and expensive handbag. Mrs Richardson would doubtless be delighted with her daughter and Sarah thought wryly that Nicole had bought it with exactly that aim in mind. She was facing after all what promised to be a fairly torrid encounter with her mother. She'd wanted to power dress for the occasion.

It wasn't Nicole's ensemble that really brought

Sarah to a grinding halt however. Charmaine looked very pretty, very feminine and thoroughly fed up. Sarah blinked in astonishment. "Charlie!" she exclaimed, "You're wearing a *dress.*"

"I *know*!" Charmaine ground out between her teeth. "Little madam here fucking insisted. She wants to turn me into a damn lipstick lesbian to meet her bloody mother." Charmaine looked so comically disgruntled that Sarah and Daniela burst into laughter. "It's not funny." Charmaine protested indignantly. "If the fucking dykes at the Planet hear about this I'll never live it down."

Sarah stifled her laughter. "Well I think you look very nice." she told her. It was true although it was strange. She had never seen Charmaine in anything other than trousers or jeans. It was almost incongruous to see her in one of Nicole's nicer dresses and she managed to look both very pretty and downright ill at ease simultaneously.

"I think I look like a complete arse hole." was Charmaine's verdict.

"Oh come on Charlie." Daniela chided her with a grin, "Get in touch with your inner woman for once. You can't be a butch bass guitarist all the time."

"I *like* being a butch bass guitarist thank you."

Daniela grinned mischievously. "Well you look lovely or rather you would look lovely if you could stop scowling for a minute. Lighten up Charlie. You're supposed to be meeting the girlfriend's mother so try to look as if you're not there to frighten the children."

Charmaine's scowl deepened. "Well I'm damned if I'm going to do this without a stiff drink first. I hope you girls have some liquor in the house with a bit of authority behind it."

"That goes for me too." remarked a visibly agitated Nicole. "I'll have a double."

Daniela frowned uncertainly. "Is it wise do you think to meet your mum all reeking of alcohol?"

Nicole patted her handbag. "I've come equipped for all eventualities; to wit one packet of mints. Anyway whether my mam thinks I've taken to strong drink or not is the least of my worries."

Sarah took a deep breath. "I think we could all do with a drink. We've got Scotch, brandy or vodka in the house. Name your poison."

"A stiff draught of hemlock sounds like a good idea at the moment." noted Nicole acerbically.

"Make mine a Scotch; no ice and easy on the soda." said Charmaine. "Just because Nicky's misguided sense of protocol demands I have to dress up like a fucking prom queen doesn't mean I have to *drink* like one."

Sarah busied herself preparing drinks. It was true that they all needed a drink. Nicole was a bundle of nerves and Charmaine was little better. Up until this moment Charmaine had considered the prospect of meeting Nicole's mother with a certain equanimity but Nicole's anxiety had reached contagious levels and now she looked thoroughly discomfited about the whole mad idea. Sarah herself was looking forward to the encounter with a good deal of trepidation. It promised to be highly embarrassing at the very least. Only Daniela was anticipating the evening with her customary tranquillity. She had an announcement to make. "Oh by the way," she began, "Simon and Peter said they'd be coming along later as well."

Sarah raised an eyebrow at this intelligence. "Why the hell are Pete and Simon coming?" she wanted to know.

"For a celebratory drink of course." Daniela wrapped an arm around Nicole fondly. "I mean this is like Nicky's official coming out party."

Nicole groaned comically. "Oh for fuck's sake! With Elke and Angelica there this is going to be like the gay elite of the whole fucking valley present. My mam's not going to know what hit her."

Sarah glanced at the clock. "Your mam said seven o'clock didn't she Nicky? It's nearly that now so we'd better get going. Are we going to walk or take the car?"

"We'll take the car." growled Charmaine. She pointed accusingly at Nicole's choice of footwear for her. "I can barely stand up in these fucking heels let alone walk all the way over to Schwendi."

So they took Sarah's car. It was only a short drive along the little road perched high on the hillside above the valley below before they pulled up at the Hotel Toggenburg in the little hamlet of Schwendi. This was the hotel where Sarah had worked part time during the summer and a place of fond memories for her and Daniela. It had been the devious manipulations and gentle coaxing of the hotel's mercurial proprietress, Elke that had engineered the hesitant flowering of Sarah's relationship with Daniela in the early days and Elke had remained Sarah's mentor and, together with her partner Angelica, numbered among Sarah and Daniela's closest friends. The sun had already set behind the mountains and lights were beginning to twinkle about the valley. The hotel was ablaze with light and, under normal circumstances welcoming, but Nicole cowered down into the back seat as they drove around the corner, before Schwendi, to see it glowing on the mountainside.

It took several minutes of wheedling and sympathetic urging to extract Nicole out of the car outside the hotel. Now that the moment of truth was finally imminent what little remained of her nerve had deserted her completely. "Come on Nicky!" Sarah exhorted her. "You can't wimp out now."

"I can't do it. Look Sarah just go in and tell my mam I've contracted Ebola and I'm shut up in an isolation ward in a tropical diseases clinic or something."

"Stop being such a pussy. We all have to do it."

Nicole glared at her. "Oh right! I seem to recall you only told your mum and dad in a fucking letter and then legged it out of the house before they had chance to open it."

Sarah conceded the justice in the remark. "All right so I was a coward too but let's face it your mum's liable to be a sight more sympathetic than my parents were."

Daniela reached over and took Nicole's hand gently. "Look Nicky nobody's trying to force you to do this if you're not ready. But Sarah's right. I think you'll find your mother quite understanding if what you've told me is correct about her. Sooner or later we all do have to go through with this. It's either that or continuing living a lie. It's a relief to get it off your mind. You know your mother loves you Nicky. She might even feel hurt that you felt unable to confide in her. Maybe you owe it to her to tell her the truth."

Under Daniela's soothing persuasion they finally managed to coax Nicole out of the car and into the foyer of the hotel. There a new crisis emerged. Elke was behind the front desk with her receptionist when they walked in. She emerged to greet them looking puzzled. "Well, well this is surprise. What the hell's going on?"

"What do you mean?" asked Nicole nervously.

"I mean what are you doing here with Sarah, Danny and this young lady here when your mum and dad are in the restaurant Nicky?"

Nicole turned ashen and staggered back against a table. "My mam *and* dad?" she whispered hoarsely.

"Why yes they've been here for twenty minutes or so. Didn't you know?"

Nicole shook her head feebly. "I knew my mam was going to be here but not my sodding dad." she squeaked in agitation.

"Are they expecting you?" asked Elke. "They said they were expecting company."

Nicole span on her heel. "That's it! I'm out of here."

Sarah grasped her firmly by the shoulders and

turned her around. "Nicky sweetheart. It's too late to back out now. You can't stand your mum and dad up."

Nicole looked terrified. "What... what the hell am I going to say?"

Daniela put an arm around her. "Take a deep breath Nicky. Bite the bullet and get it over with. Do you want us to come in with you?"

Nicole fought for control for a few moments mastering her rising panic. Finally she took a deep breath and shook her head. "No. No I'd better go in alone. I'll see what they have to say and see what the lie of the land is. If I don't have to make a bolt for the door then I'll call you in later."

Daniela nodded. "Ok honey. We'll wait for you in the bar in that case. Don't be worried. It'll be ok."

Nicole drew herself up with renewed fortitude. "Right then. Here goes."

Sarah patted her on the bottom. "Atta girl! Into the valley of death and all that."

Nicole shot her a poisonous look. "I'd ten times rather face a sodding Russian battery than what's waiting for me in that bloody restaurant!" Nevertheless she strode purposefully out of the foyer toward the restaurant.

Elke placed her hands on her hips. "Will somebody please tell what the hell is going on!" she demanded.

Daniela pulled a wry face. "Coming out nerves Elke." Daniela held a hand towards Charmaine. "You've not met Charlie have you Elke? She's my new bass guitarist and incidentally Nicky's girlfriend; a fact of which Nicky's unsuspecting parents are about to be apprised."

Elke drew in a sharp breath. "Oh Christ!"

"Exactly."

Elke subjected Charmaine to a searching appraisal. She liked what she saw. "So you girls are here for what... to lend moral support or something?"

411

"Yes. We'll be joining them for dinner if all goes well or here to hold Nicky's hand whilst she has a good cry if it doesn't." Sarah told her.

Elke thought for a second. "I think it'll be ok. I know Nicky's parents quite well and they've always struck me as tolerant sort of people. I think she'll be all right."

"That's what I think too." said Daniela. "By all accounts her mum's already pretty much figured it out anyway. The only fly in the ointment is that she seems to be under the impression that Nicky is together with Sarah. That's why Charlie and I are here."

Elke shook her head wonderingly. "Oh my. This promises to be an interesting evening. Come on you girls. Let's go in the bar and get you all a drink. I'll keep a weather eye open on developments at the Richardson table."

Chapter Twenty-Three

Nicole's parents had taken a table by the window overlooking the darkening valley below. Walking across the restaurant to greet them was, in Nicole's opinion, one of the bravest things she had ever done. Her parents rose to greet her with a smile but her mother looked puzzled. She kissed her daughter fondly. "Nicky. I'm so pleased you made it but where is Sarah? Couldn't she come after all?"

"No... er no she's here. I... I just wanted to see you in private first."

Mrs Richardson regarded her daughter keenly. "Are you all right Nicky? You seem a bit pale."

"Er fine... fine. Look could we sit down please?"

"Of course. Come and take a seat."

Once they were all seated Nicole turned to her father. "Mam didn't say you were coming as well dad."

Nicole's father was a quiet and gentle man with a receding hairline and a stubbornly persistent middle aged paunch. Nicole loved him but had never been able to confide in him completely. It was a mistake for, beneath his quiet reserve, Mr Richardson was a warmly compassionate and understanding man. He nodded slowly. "I'm sorry to surprise you by coming unannounced Nicky but your mother and I had a long talk and we decided it was better if we all got together as a family to talk to you."

Nicole took a deep breath. "And just what was it you wanted to talk to me about dad?"

Her parents glanced at each other before her mother intervened smoothly. "It's not so much what we wanted to talk to you about Nicky. We thought more that perhaps there was something you'd like to talk to *us* about."

Nicole swallowed. It was obvious which way the

413

conversation was heading. She stalled for time. "I'm not sure I follow you mam."

Her mother leaned across the table and took her hand. "Nicky darling we, your father and I, want you to know that if there's anything, anything at all, that you want to tell us then we're ready to hear it. We want you to feel that you can always talk to us about anything. We love you very much and you can tell us anything freely and it won't change how we feel about you one bit."

Her father nodded in agreement. "That's right Nicky. We thought you might have something on your mind that's been bothering you; something that you might be frightened about telling us. We're just here to reassure you that there's nothing to be frightened of. We're not here to sit in judgement. I know your mother and I are a pair of old wrinklies but..."

"Speak for yourself!" his wife interrupted.

Mr Richardson ignored her, "but we're not so old that we're hide bound and intolerant. We understand that there are things which a daughter may find very hard to tell her parents but we want you to know that we won't love you one iota less because of them. You're still our darling little Nicky and always will be. There's nothing you can tell us that will alter that."

Nicole felt tears pricking at the back of her eyes but she mastered her self-control. "So what is it that made you think I was not telling you something dad?"

Mr Richardson removed his glasses and rubbed his eyes before replacing them. "Well Mrs Fuchs phoned us Nicky."

Nicole swore under her breath. "I see. So what did she have to say?"

Nicole's mother snorted. "Not a lot that made any sense. I answered the phone as it happens. I thought she'd finally come adrift of her marbles. I never did have much time for Sarah's mother."

That was putting it mildly thought Nicole. Her

mother and Mrs Fuchs were sworn enemies. "But what did she say?" asked Nicole insistently.

"Oh she was blathering some nonsense about how our daughter had corrupted her daughter and led her astray. I asked her what the devil she was babbling about and all I got was a load of incoherent ranting about how she'd always thought that you'd been a bad influence on Sarah. She ended up by declaring pompously that although we might tolerate that sort of behaviour in our daughter she was damned if she'd allow her to lead their daughter into that sort of thing. I demanded to know the hell she was referring to and she just declared that *her* daughter hadn't been brought up to be one of those and slammed the phone down. Well I wasn't just furious, I was perplexed as well so I talked to your father about it."

Mr Richardson nodded and continued the story. "Yes and I was understandably annoyed about it, Nicky, although I was as puzzled as your mother. To get to the bottom of the matter I phoned up Sarah's father to demand an explanation."

Nicole paled. "Oh Christ! What did *he* have to say?"

"Well to give him his due he was very diplomatic and apologetic about the whole thing. I've had business dealings with Sarah's father and always found him a reasonable man. He apologised for his wife's accusations but said in her defence that she was distraught and apt to jump to erroneous conclusions. He told me that Sarah had recently broken off her engagement virtually on the eve of her wedding and her mother was naturally deeply upset. I asked him how the blazes his wife could get it into her head that you had anything to do with it. He sort of hummed and hawed a bit and seemed reluctant to elucidate but I pressed him on the matter and demanded to know what his wife had meant when she talked about your behaviour and what she meant by "one of those". Finally, although he swore me to strict confidence, I got

415

the full story out of him. He told us that the day Sarah had broken her engagement and run away from their house she had left them a letter."

Nicole groaned. "I think I know what's coming next."

"Well yes. In it apparently Sarah told her parents that she was well... a lesbian and in love with another woman. Mrs Fuchs had apparently convinced herself that this other woman was you. I told him that was absurd. I knew for a fact that you'd had several boyfriends for instance and just because you shared a house with Sarah it didn't conclude that you were this other woman Sarah was seeing. I told him that I'd never had any reason to suspect that you were so inclined. He was most apologetic about it. He seemed to think that this was only some phase Sarah was going through in any case and possibly just her petulant way of striking out for independence. He even went so far as to assure me that he didn't share his wife's belief that you were the person responsible for leading his daughter astray. Apparently Sarah had told her sister that it wasn't you she was seeing but somebody else entirely. I thanked him for his candidness and he in turn assured me that there would be no repetition of these accusations and we left it at that."

Mrs Richardson squeezed Nicole's hand. "I was shocked when your father told me the story Nicky. It wasn't because I'm homophobic or anything but I'd just never imagined that Sarah was that way inclined. I've always liked Sarah. She's a lovely girl but I'd always thought she was perfectly heterosexual. Don't get me wrong. I'm not saying that learning that she's a lesbian will make me think the less of her but I just didn't see it in her. I always thought she would end up marrying that boyfriend of hers. When I got over my surprise in fact I was actually quite impressed. Lovely girl though she is, I'd always had the feeling that she was a bit well...

boring I suppose and a bit of her parents' pet lamb. When it turned out that she'd upset the apple cart in no uncertain fashion, declared herself a lesbian and told her boyfriend and her parents to shove the marriage they had planned for her I realised I'd underestimated her. I didn't know she had so much spirit and independence in her."

Nicole's father cut in. "Are all these facts that Mr Richardson told me correct Nicky?"

Nicole bit her lip. "Well yes dad... up to a point anyway."

"Up to a point?"

"Yes. I think Sarah might take issue with her dad's belief that she's just going through some phase dad. She seems pretty adamant and serious about it to me."

Mr Richardson looked grave. "Yes I thought that might be the case. It sounded to me as if he was unprepared to accept his daughter's declaration that she was a lesbian. I understand that it's a common reaction for parents confronted with er... their children's homosexuality."

Nicole took a deep breath. "What about you two? What I mean is did *you* accept Mr Fuchs' explanation?"

Mr Richardson blinked. "What do you mean Nicky?"

"Well according to your account he assured you that he didn't believe I was the person that Sarah was seeing. Right now you don't seem so sure otherwise you wouldn't be giving me all this guff about my being able to tell you anything whatever it is. Sarah says you damn as near it came straight out and said you thought that we were together when you came round yesterday mam."

Mrs Richardson squeezed Nicole's hand once more. "Are you Nicky? I mean *are* you having a relationship with Sarah? You can tell us you know."

Nicole took a deep breath. "No mam I'm not. Sarah is my oldest and dearest friend and I love her to bits but I'm not the woman Sarah referred to in that letter. I

417

know Sarah's girlfriend. In fact she's here tonight. Sarah doesn't even live in the cottage any more mam. She's moved in with her girlfriend."

Mr Richardson looked uncomfortable. "I see. Well perhaps we, your mother and I, well... perhaps we might have been jumping to conclusions prematurely."

Nicole looked at her parents levelly. "There's more to this story isn't there. I mean if Sarah's dad assured you that the person Sarah was seeing wasn't me there must have been some other reason for you to believe otherwise."

Mrs Richardson shuffled awkwardly. "Well yes there was. A couple of days ago a friend of mine showed me this magazine she'd come across."

Nicole closed her eyes and issued a silent prayer. "Oh God! I knew it."

"Well it had this photo spread of you in it Nicky."

"I *know* mam."

"Well I must say I thought the pictures of you were wonderful; a bit bold of course but very artistic."

"God I'm sorry mam. I should never have agreed to do that photo shoot. You must have been mortified when your friend showed you them."

"Not at all. I thought the pictures were lovely. I never knew you had aspirations to be a model."

"But I wasn't wearing a bloody stitch in those photos mam."

"Well so what? You're not the only one in this family to model in her birthday kit you know."

Nicole stared at her mother in shock. "What do you mean?"

"Well I used to do a bit of nude modelling when I was younger as well you know. Helped to pay my way through college that did."

"You're pulling my leg."

"Nothing of the sort. I was just as good looking as you when I was your age I'll have you know."

Mr Richardson chuckled in reminiscence. "I first fell for your mother when I saw her pictures in a glossy magazine Nicky. I've still got the pictures to this day."

Nicole flopped back in her seat helplessly. "Well I'll be damned!"

Mrs Richardson smiled. "Of course I didn't quite have the bottle to have *my* pictures published in a magazine for lesbians of course. That was pretty radical of you. Still I suppose you have to take work where you can get it."

"Yes." Mr Richardson agreed. "Still, because of the nature of the magazine you can see why your mother and I jumped to conclusions about you and Sarah."

Nicole was starting to feel her head swim. She rubbed her temples and decided to leap off the cliff. "Mam, dad, it's no accident that I'm in that magazine."

"What do you mean?" asked her father.

"Those photos were a study of gay women in Switzerland dad. That includes me. I'm gay."

There was a long pause. Mr Richardson looked confused. "But...but you just said that you and Sarah were not together."

"And I was telling the truth dad. I didn't say that I was *straight* though. Sarah's gay and so am I. Sarah has a girlfriend and so have I. I'm sorry. Your daughter is gay." Nicole was close to tears.

Mrs Richardson grasped Nicole's hand. "Don't say sorry Nicky! We meant what we said when we told you that it was safe to tell us."

Mr Richardson was quick to agree. "Yes Nicole. I'm sorry but you threw me when you told me that you weren't Sarah's girlfriend and I thought we'd got it all wrong. But no your mother is right. We don't want you to feel sorry about it."

Mrs Richardson hugged Nicole suddenly. "Oh Nicky! We came tonight because we thought you might want to tell us this. It's all right. Really it is. Don't cry

419

honey."

It was too late. Nicole's eyes welled up and tears ran down her face. "I... I can't help it. Oh mam I was so scared to tell you. I... I'm sorry."

"Hush now sweetheart. We understand. We *do* understand. You've done nothing to be ashamed of. We love you Nicky."

Mr Richardson came around the table to hug his daughter fiercely. "Of course we love you. You're still my little baby whatever else you are."

Nicole snivelled miserably. "Thanks dad. You make me sound like a convicted murderess."

"I didn't mean it like that honey. I mean we are still behind you and support you. We know this can't have been easy for you."

Nicole nodded grimly through her tears. "That's an understatement if ever there was one." she mumbled abjectly.

"Her mother lifted her chin to look into her eyes. "Your father and I are not stuck back in the dark ages Nicky. We're not going to start quoting scripture at you and tell you that you're an abomination or something. We know it's not something you chose to be. God knows it can't be easy being different. Why would anyone ever *choose* to be gay and have to face all the bigotry and ostracism that goes with it? But whatever anyone else says you know you can always rely on your father and me to stick by you no matter what."

"That's right Nicky." Her father agreed. "Our love doesn't come with conditions attached. Personally I think it's disgusting that some parents throw their children out and refuse to have anything more to do with them because of something those children have no control over. I'm not one of those kind of parents and neither is your mother."

"But dad..." bleated Nicole pathetically, "What about all the things you used to say about looking forward to walking me down the aisle and being proud about seeing me married one day?"

Her father shrugged. "So maybe you'll marry a nice girl some day. The times are changing honey. When we had to face up to the fact you might be gay your mother and I went to some trouble to inform ourselves about the issues. We know that gay couples can already form legal civil unions in this country and I'm sure that full marital status is just around the corner. It's a matter of complete indifference to me who you decide to live the rest of your life with Nicky, be they man or woman. As long as they make you happy I'll still be proud to give you away and the devil with what anybody else might think about it."

"But what about the grandchildren you always wanted dad?" asked Nicole in a little voice.

Her father smiled and ruffled her hair playfully. "I don't know a lot about the issues involved Nicky but I *am* aware that a lot of gay couples find a way around that particular problem. I'm sure that if you ever decide you want to have children you'll find some way of doing it and we'll support you in that as well. We're not Mr and Mrs Fuchs Nicky. I was horrified to learn that Sarah is estranged from her parents because she told them she was gay."

"Yes." Mrs Richardson agreed. "God knows I'm not perfect but I would hope that I'm more open minded and understanding than Sarah's mother. To hear her talk you would have thought that Sarah was damned beyond salvation. It must be rotten for the poor girl. Where is she anyway? She's not too frightened to see us is she?"

Nicole shook her head. "No mam I just wanted to see you alone first so she's waiting in the bar."

Her father smiled at her. "Well we'd like to talk to her so why don't you bring her in? Whatever her parents are saying about her we'd like her to know that we at least won't condemn her or be judgemental."

Nicole stared at her parents as if seeing them for the first time. "Mam, dad.... I... I love you!"

"We love you too Nicky." said her mother with a kiss "Now dry your eyes, get Sarah in here and tell us all about this young lady you say you're seeing."

"Er mum she's here. I'm sorry but I came with Sarah and her girlfriend and my girlfriend too. They're all here to lend me support."

Her father beamed at her. "Really? Well this is just perfect. I'm dying to meet her. Get them all in here and don't keep them kicking their heels in the bar. We'll need to pull another table up if we're going to sit six down for dinner though."

"Er eight dad. I've got another couple of friends coming as well. Peter's coming with his boyfriend Simon. Peter and Simon are giving me a job this winter."

Mrs Richardson was taken aback. "Peter? You don't mean the Peter who is Sarah's friend do you?"

"Yes mam. He's my friend too you know."

"He's not gay as well surely is he?"

Nicole nodded. "Yes mam. There're a lot of us about nowadays."

Mrs Richardson shook her in wonder. "My word. This *is* a night for revelations."

Nicole managed a watery smile. "You don't know the half of it mam. Wait until you meet *Sarah's* girlfriend."

Mr Richardson wrung his hands together delightedly. "Well the more the merrier I say." Mr Richardson lifted a hand to attract the attention of Elke who was loitering in the background and observing developments at the Richardson table with increasing satisfaction. She walked over with a smile. "Ah Frau Fritzl." Mr Richardson boomed at her. "I wonder if we could push another couple of tables together. We're expecting eight altogether for dinner now. You can put them all on my bill."

"Dad." protested Nicole. "You don't have to go to all that expense. My friends can afford to pay for their own dinners."

"Nonsense! I won't hear of it."

Elke cleared her throat. "None of you will have to pay Mr Richardson. Dinner is on the house tonight."

Mr Richardson blinked in surprise. "Good heavens! Whatever for?"

Elke smiled at him. "Forgive me for intruding Mr Richardson but I know why Nicole is here to meet you tonight and I couldn't help but overhear snippets of your conversation and see your reactions. I didn't want to be nosy you understand but I've known Nicky since she was a little girl and I've always been fond of her. I think she's very lucky to have such caring and understanding parents as you and Mrs Richardson. I am delighted and honoured to have you and Nicole's friends as my guests tonight and I won't take a single rappen of your money."

"Really Frau Fritzl...." Mr Richardson protested.

"Please call me Elke and not another word now. When it comes to being stubborn I wrote the book. Dinner is on the house tonight and I'll not hear another word about it. Come along now Nicky and help me move these tables and then I'll go tell the others to join you."

"Are Pete and Simon here yet Elke?" Nicole asked.

"Yes they just arrived. Now lift this table cloth up."

Chapter Twenty-Four

Tension was mounting by the minute in the bar and conversation had descended to muted and worried whispers. When Elke strode into the bar, five pairs of eyes turned on her questioningly. "Ok ladies and gentlemen." She announced, "Your table is set. You can go in now."

"Is...is everything all right Elke?" asked Sarah in agitation.

"Sure it is." Elke reassured her. "Job's done as far as I can see; hugs and kisses all round. There were a few tears perhaps but nothing tragic. Nicole's mum and dad seem completely happy about it all."

Daniela looked unbearably smug. "I thought this was going to be relatively painless." she remarked. "Nicky was just getting herself into a state about nothing."

"Do they know that Nicky's girlfriend is here?" enquired Charmaine nervously.

"Yes. Mr Richardson seems quite eager to meet you."

Sarah grinned. "Perhaps he'll want to have a man to man talk with you about his daughter's future Charlie." she suggested wickedly.

Charmaine glared at her. "I'd can it if I were you Sarah unless of course you're harbouring ambitions about *wearing* the soup course."

Come along everybody!" said Elke, clapping her hands together authoritatively. Let me escort you to your table." She grinned hugely. "I'm looking forward to this."

The arrival of the party at the table was every bit the occasion Elke could have wished for. She ushered Charmaine forward first as befitting her status as

Nicole's girlfriend. The Richardsons rose in a body to greet her. Nicole took Charmaine's hand shyly. "Mam, dad, I'd like you to meet Charmaine. Charmaine is... is my girlfriend."

Mr Richardson took Charmaine's hand warmly. "Welcome young lady. I'm very pleased to meet you."

"And me too." enthused Mrs Richardson and to everybody's astonishment, and Charmaine's slight embarrassment, she folded her in a warm embrace. She stood back holding Charmaine's hands to look at her properly. "My word what a pretty girl you are. I always said Nicky had good tastes."

"You're embarrassing the poor girl my dear." Mr Richardson admonished her. He glanced around to see Sarah. "Sarah!" he boomed delightedly. "You're a sight for sore eyes girl. Come here." Sarah stepped forward with a laugh to accept Mr Richardson's embrace. It was Mr Richardson's turn to be effusive. "Good God Sarah. It must be ages since I last saw you. What a beauty you've turned out to be."

Sarah smiled at him warmly and blushed. "Thank you Mr Richardson."

Nicole's mother folded Sarah in a hug. "She's always been a beauty Robert." she told her husband, "She just needed to grow into it a bit."

Elke was manipulating the situation ruthlessly as she ushered Simon and Peter forward, keeping Daniela in the background to introduce into the company as the piece de resistance. Mr and Mrs Richardson shook hands with the two young men. They both knew Peter somewhat but Simon was a complete stranger to them. Sarah noted with amusement that Mrs Richardson seemed quite taken with the devastatingly handsome Simon and, intelligence to the fact of Simon's sexuality notwithstanding, appeared perfectly willing to flirt with him. Finally Elke eased Daniela forward into view. Elke loved the opportunity to drop Daniela into a company like a bombshell and there was no doubt that the Toggenburg's most glamorous and famous celebrity was a show stopper under any circumstances. Sarah took Daniela's hand shyly. "Mr and Mrs Richardson," she simpered with beguiling timidity. "I'd like you to meet my girlfriend. This is Daniela."

Daniela held out her hand to Mr Richardson and turned what Nicole would later describe as about five hundred gigawatts of pure charm on him. "I'm so very pleased to meet you sir." she said with the thrilling timbre to her voice that never failed to melt whoever she addressed. "Nicole has told me a great deal about you."

It was clear immediately that Mr Richardson was no follower of the celebrity pages of tabloid journalism for, while he was quite clearly thunderstruck by the stunning beauty that took his hand, it was plainly apparent that he had no idea who she was. "Er I'm very pleased to meet you too Miss." He managed to croak gallantly. "Er sorry... what was the name again? I didn't catch it the first time."

Mrs Richardson who was rather more familiar with popular celebrities had been staring at Daniela in shock. She pushed forward now. "Oh Robert!" she groaned. "You infernal nincompoop! Surely you recognise Miss Devin."

Daniela turned to Nicole's mother with another dose of the charm offensive. "Mrs Richardson. I've so been looking forward to meeting you. I've heard so much about you from Nicole."

Mrs Richardson seemed shell shocked. "You... you're Sarah's girlfriend?" she gasped at last.

Daniela smiled. "Yes. I have that immense honour."

"Oh my God!" Mrs Richardson seemed lost for words.

Her husband was floundering in the background. "Am I missing something here?" he bleated comically.

Mrs Richardson turned to him in exasperation. "For

God's sake Robert! Please try to emerge into the twenty first century. Miss Devin here is just about the most famous pop star on the continent for the moment."

"Please call me Daniela or better yet just Danny." Daniela insisted.

Mr Richardson connected up the dots at last. "Oh! Oh yes of course. Miss Daniela Devin. I recognise the name now. My word! So *you* are the mystery lady that Sarah's father mentioned."

Sarah blinked in consternation. "What? You've spoken to my father Mr Richardson?"

Nicole intervened smoothly. "There's been a bit of underhand snooping in the background Sarah. Your mum telephoned my mum accusing her of letting *me* corrupt her precious daughter."

Sarah groaned. "Oh God!"

"Don't worry Sarah. My dad had words with your dad and smoothed things over. Your dad told mine that the identity of your girlfriend remained unknown."

Mrs Richardson shook her head in disbelief. "Are you honestly telling me that Sarah's parents have no idea that her partner is one of the most famous ladies in Switzerland?"

"Mam!" said Nicole with a warning gesture. "That is classified information okay. Please don't go spreading it around. Sarah and Danny don't want Sarah's parents to find out before they have a chance to talk to them privately which, judging by Sarah's parents' apparent refusal to have anything to do with her, could be some time yet."

Daniela nodded. "Yes Mr and Mrs Richardson. We would appreciate it if you treated the matter with a certain amount of discretion for the moment. Relations between Sarah and her parents are a little strained for the moment and it would be undiplomatic for them to learn about our relationship from a third party."

Mr Richardson nodded gravely. "Of course, of

course. I fully understand. You may rely on us for complete discretion Miss Devin."

Mrs Richardson shook her head in disbelief. "This is incredible. Bloody Alisha will lose what few marbles she has left when you bring Daniela Devin home Sarah."

Sarah fidgeted anxiously. "I would prefer to delay that confrontation until such time as my parents come to terms with my... my sexuality Mrs Richardson."

Mrs Richardson snorted contemptuously. "Well don't hold your breath Sarah. She didn't sound as if she was coming around to the idea over the telephone."

Sarah's shoulders sagged. "No I suppose not."

Mrs Richardson saw instantly that Sarah was upset. Hastily she took her hands. "There, there Sarah. It'll be all right I'm sure. Forgive me for saying so but even your pig-headed mother can't remain rooted in the dark ages forever. I'm sure she'll come around even if somebody has to drag her kicking and screaming." Mrs Richardson allowed herself a little chuckle. "My God though, I'd give anything to be there when she learns the identity of your girlfriend." She turned to Daniela. "And so you know Nicole as well then Daniela?"

"But of course. She's my girlfriend's best friend and her girlfriend, Charmaine here, plays bass guitar in my band."

Mrs Richardson span around to gaze at Charmaine in astonishment. "My God! You play with Miss Devin's band Charmaine?"

"Er only recently Mrs Richardson. I've just joined the band. We've only rehearsed in studio so far. We haven't actually gone live yet."

Mrs Richardson seemed delighted. "My word! Nicky actually has a real life rock star for a girlfriend. My God! It takes me back. When I was younger I spent three months on the road with the lead guitarist in a rock and roll band. We got into an altercation in this hotel in France and the Gendarmerie threw us out of the country.

Bloody pigs didn't even let me pick up my clothes from the hotel and I got escorted to the border dressed in a flimsy baby doll nightie in the middle of bloody February."

Mr Richardson cleared his throat loudly. "I think possibly we shouldn't be boring our guests with your reminiscences my dear."

Charmaine grinned. "Hey I'm not bored. I was just getting interested."

Mr Richardson ignored the sally of laughter. "Nevertheless I suggest we all take a seat, order some drinks and ask for menus."

Seating was achieved with a certain old fashioned formality with the gentlemen present holding chairs out for the ladies; a gallantry which amused Sarah given the sexual proclivity of the majority of the guests. Mrs Richardson smiled at Charmaine and patted the seat next to her. "Come and sit next to me Charmaine. I want to learn all about you!"

Mr Richardson took place of honour at the head of the table and beamed hugely at the assembled company. "Well this is marvellous." he declared. "I must say you four young ladies are as fine a collection of beauties seated around a single table as it would be possible to imagine. My word the lads in this valley must be cursing their luck."

"*Dad!*" protested Nicole in outrage.

Mrs Richardson chuckled warmly. "It won't be just the boys cursing their luck Robert." She told him with a grin. "I should imagine there'll be more than a few girls ruing the fact that a pair of good looking hunks, such as Peter and Simon here, have no eyes for them."

"Mam, Dad, that'll *do*!" said Nicole firmly.

Mr Richardson smiled. "Well I think we need some drinks around this table. What is everybody having?"

Whilst they waited for the waitress to fetch their drinks Mr Richardson engaged Daniela in conversation.

He was quite clearly smitten by her Sarah thought with amusement. For her part Mrs Richardson patted Charmaine on the knee. "Now then my dear I want to know all about you. When did you first meet Nicole?"

"Er well it was back at Sarah's graduation Mrs Richardson. We've been dating for a couple of months or so." Sarah forced herself to keep a straight face overhearing this. This version somewhat contradicted Nicole's official account of the affair.

"Well you seem to be a most charming young lady Charmaine." Mrs Richardson told her. "I'm pleased Nicky has shown enough sense to find a girl like you."

Charmaine seemed to be regarding Mrs Richardson with something approaching awe. "I never thought that I'd ever hear the parent of any girlfriend of mine say that Mrs Richardson. I think you're a remarkable lady. Not many parents would be so understanding and accepting of their daughter's sexuality."

Mrs Richardson shrugged. "Well dear I'll be frank. When we first had to face that Nicky was gay it was an adjustment. It still is. It was something we never expected and it's going to take some getting used to. I think that all parents are going to have to go through a period of readjustment upon learning that their child is gay." Mrs Richardson paused to tap on the table. "I'll say this though," she continued, "When you decide to become a parent you make a covenant to love and cherish your child whatever the future may bring. There's no get out clause in the parenting contract that says you're only supposed to love your child as long as they turn out to be exactly what you wanted and expected of them. There are a lot of parents in this world who might do well to remember that."

Charmaine shook her head in wonder. "You know Mrs Richardson if I wasn't so old I'd ask you to *adopt* me!"

Sarah laughed at Charmaine's reply. The evening

was turning out to be a triumph. She sighed inwardly. If only her own parents could be so tolerant and understanding. She brushed the thought from her mind with more pleasant thoughts. Nicole's family was all right and if her own was still fractured then what of it. Over the next weeks she had her own, *new* family to forge.

Chapter Twenty-Five

Sarah's new family was much on her mind the following day although she certainly did not anticipate how the events of that day would have far reaching consequences for that family. Daniela and she were happily rummaging through catalogues of children's furniture and discussing net curtains with Elrika, their house lady. The intelligence that Daniela's daughter was coming to live with them had galvanised the old lady and she was visibly excited. Elrika adored children but nature had been unkind to her. Her only daughter had died young and without bequeathing any grandchildren to her. It seemed as if little Elizabeth, when she arrived, would find herself not only in possession of a second mother but an extra surrogate grandmother as well. Sarah rather suspected that the old lady would spoil Elizabeth rotten but she hadn't the heart to dampen her enthusiasm. She'd spent the whole morning scrubbing down the attic room destined to be Elizabeth's quite oblivious to Daniela's protests that the task was superfluous since they were intending to redecorate it in any case.

Now she was laying out lengths of curtain material on the kitchen table and discussing their merits in exhaustive detail. The making and design of net curtains was something of an art form in rural Switzerland but the finer points of the mysteries of lace drapery had rather eluded Sarah. Doubtless they could have simply purchased perfectly adequate ready-made curtains for Elizabeth's room at a lower cost and a fraction of the hassle but it seemed unkind to overrule Elrika's input into the familial expansion and now curtain making was officially a part of her domestic portfolio. Elrika was deeply content.

She was not alone in that. In fact domestic bliss reigned in the household. Daniela had phoned America earlier and talked to both her parents and Elizabeth. Plans were already in an advanced state. They were provisionally looking at a date in early November for Elizabeth's arrival. That was only a few weeks away. There was a lot to do. It was exciting.

In truth Sarah would have preferred to spend the afternoon in town buying decorating materials and perhaps furnishings but that was not an option today for they had a commitment. The lady that Peter and Simon were considering employing was due to arrive at two o'clock. Simon had phoned this morning to confirm the interview, having consulted the lady concerned. Sarah had then phoned Nicole to remind her to put in a token appearance. That conversation had been amusing. Nicole's parents had seemingly taken Charmaine into the bosom of the family like a second daughter. She and Nicole were invited over the following weekend for Sunday dinner. Nicole was grumbling about it but her disgruntlement was transparent. The evening before had been a triumph and Nicole's relief and happiness were obviously apparent even while she moaned about the obligations of family duty.

Sarah felt a warm glow of satisfaction every time she thought about the evening before. Nicole's family's embracement of her sexuality, standing as it did in stark contrast to Sarah's, was deeply gratifying and the evening had been merry and full of camaraderie. At the end of the meal they'd been joined by Elke and her partner Angelica and lingered long over coffee and liqueurs. In a sense it had been more than just about Nicole's family. There had been the real feeling of an extended family; a sort of meta-family of dear friends belonging to a specific community.

Sarah and Daniela had told Mr and Mrs Richardson and Elke and Angelica about Elizabeth's anticipated arrival and there had been universal enthusiasm. Angelica had some big kiddy bean bags and wall drapes she wanted to contribute to the furnishing of Elizabeth's room and Elke was talking about throwing a kid's party at the hotel for Elizabeth's arrival so that she could meet some new friends. Simon and Peter were offering material assistance in the matter of some repairs that Daniela and Sarah had identified as necessary and even Mr Richardson had weighed in with an offer of help. Apparently he had friends in the furniture business who could do them a good price on bunk beds. Mrs Richardson had an even more astonishing offer. She was still in possession of a kid's dressing table; a sort of play version of a grown up lady's dressing table complete with play cosmetics and accessories and an illuminated mirror. It had previously belonged to Nicole and Mrs Richardson hadn't had the heart to throw it away or sell it. Nicole was slightly miffed about this offer. She'd loved that little dressing table when she was a kid and felt secretly a little aggrieved that her mother was just giving it away without her consent.

The general pulling together of all their friends in the common cause had extended even further this morning. Not only was Elrika throwing herself into the fray on behalf of young Elizabeth but Hans-Ruedi, the old handy-man that pottered about in the garden, was now talking about fixing up and repainting an old garden shed that was currently not being used and converting it into a little Wendy House for Elizabeth and her friends. There was no doubt about it... Elizabeth was going to be spoiled.

Sarah glanced up at the clock on the kitchen wall. It was just approaching twelve o'clock. She caught Daniela's attention. "If you're going to drive down to Buchs you're going to have to go soon Danny." she told her, "Otherwise you'll not be back in time for when this lady arrives."

434

Daniela nodded at the wisdom of this. She had errands to run in Buchs and she'd been putting them off all morning. Now she was cutting it a little fine, for the interview with Simon and Peter's proposed employee was at two o'clock. She pushed her catalogue aside decisively. "You're right. I'd better get going." She turned to Elrika. "Do you need anything from town while I'm down there Elrika?"

"Nein danke Fräulein."

Sarah clicked her tongue. "Don't be taking any more commissions on Danny. You'll be pushed for time as it is."

Daniela stood up. "Ok I'll get going. Where are the keys for the BMW sweetheart?"

"In the bowl on the hall table where they always are."

Daniela grinned. "I know. I just keep hoping that one day you'll let your hair down and do something completely radical like hiding them where nobody can find them."

Sarah poked her tongue out at Daniela. "I can't help it if I like to be organised."

Daniela laughed and bent to kiss her. "I think you're just lovely." She held her hands up. "Ok, ok! I'm going."

"Try to be back by two o'clock Danny."

"I will do honey. Look, if by any chance I do get delayed, just make my apologies and entertain this lady until I arrive ok?"

"Oh for God's sake don't be long. I won't know what the hell to say to her."

"I shan't be long I promise. Ok I'm out of here."

For the next hour or so Sarah busied herself making sure the living room was spotless and tidy enough to receive guests and then ran through an inventory of light refreshments in the kitchen. She was gratified to note that there was still some diet coke and a tub of vanilla ice cream in the fridge so at least she would be able to

435

offer the lady's little boy something. Despite her meticulous preparations, however, Sarah was still caught by surprise for it was only twenty to two when the doorbell rang. Sarah jumped up, flustered, and hastened to the front door.

The lady stood nervously at the front door was a slim attractive brunette with a kind but somewhat careworn face. Clutching her hand and trying to hide behind her was a young child, peering fearfully around the shield of its mother. The lady was clearly ill at ease. "I'm very sorry." she stammered, "But is this the house of Miss Devin?"

Sarah smiled reassuringly at her. "Yes that's right."

The lady held out her hand. "I'm Jacqueline Morel. I have an appointment to see Miss Devin. I'm afraid I'm a bit early though. I wasn't sure if I could find the house so I set off early. I hope I haven't inconvenienced you."

Sarah took the proffered hand warmly. She liked the look of this young woman. There was something gentle and warm hearted about her. She felt like the kind of person you would instinctively like to have as a friend. "Not at all." she reassured the lady. "I'm afraid Daniela isn't home at the moment though. She had to drive down to town for some things. She assured me that she'd be back by two o'clock so if you don't mind waiting a little while..."

The lady smiled. "Of course not. Er you must be Sarah."

Sarah nodded. "Yes that's right I'm..." Sarah hesitated for a moment. "I'm Daniela's partner."

"I'm very pleased to meet you Miss. I've heard a lot about you."

Sarah laughed. "Good things I hope."

"Oh yes."

Sarah smiled at the young child still trying to hide behind its mother. "And this is?"

The lady took a deep breath. "Er this is Chrissie."

She urged the child forward gently. "Don't be rude now Chrissie. Say hello to the lady."

Chrissie poked a hand out timidly and muttered a tentative "Hello Fräulein."

Sarah shook the hand gently. "Chrissie? Is that short for something?"

Chrissie's mother intervened hastily. "Er just Chrissie Miss." She caught Sarah's eye and flashed a warning. "It's really Christian but he doesn't like to be called that." The little boy seemed to cringe as his mother forwarded this information and for a horrible moment Sarah thought he was going to burst into tears. There was something odd and something very wrong with this little boy. It was difficult to put your finger on it. Able to see him clearly for the first time Sarah found herself fascinated by him. He was small for his age, very slender and delicate with big brown eyes full of timidity and a touch of sadness. He was clearly unhappy but he could in no way be thought to be neglected or not well looked after. He was spotlessly clean and clearly in his best clothes. The only thing about him that perhaps hinted at neglect was his hair. It was immaculately brushed and clean but it was far too long for a young boy. It fell well over his shoulders. It was not unattractive by any means for he had thick brown hair with a natural wave and a healthy gloss. "What a curious child." Sarah thought to herself. She struggled to find a word in her mind to describe him and the only one that came to mind was pretty. Pretty! The little boy was undoubtedly pretty with his delicate features and long brown hair. But little boys weren't *supposed* to be pretty. They could be amusing, endearing... cute even... but you didn't describe them as *pretty*. Sarah smiled at him. "Chrissie then. What lovely hair you have Chrissie." she ventured experimentally.

Amazingly the little boy's face lit up and he looked pathetically grateful. His mother sighed apologetically.

437

"He won't let me cut it." she told Sarah in exasperation. "Every time we go to the hairdressers he throws a tantrum because he thinks I'm going to have his hair cut off."

Sarah's antennae were up and waving by now and flashing warning signals at her. Cautiously she reached out to touch the luxurious brown locks of Chrissie's hair. "Well it's nice hair." She told the little boy. For the first time, Chrissie smiled at Sarah shyly and bit his lip. Sarah straightened up. "But please come in both of you. Let me take your coats and I'll see if I can rustle up some coffee."

Courteously Sarah ushered Jacqueline and Chrissie into the living room. Jacqueline looked around in admiration. "What a lovely house you have." she remarked feelingly.

Sarah smiled in agreement. "Yes. I love it. It's a lot of work though because it's so big. It's an old guest house originally called the Edelweiss. Some of the rooms were originally dormitories and they're enormous. Danny uses one of them as her dance studio."

Jacqueline bit her lip. "May I be honest Sarah?"

"Of course."

"I'm really nervous at the thought of meeting Miss Devin. I had no idea that Peter and Simon's business partner was somebody so famous. I nearly peed myself this morning when Simon phoned up and said that she wanted to meet me."

Sarah laughed. She found herself liking this lady more and more. "Please don't concern yourself Jacqueline. Danny's no prima donna diva. She's a lovely friendly down to earth person. You'll get on just fine with her." Sarah waved a hand at sofas and armchairs around the coffee table. "Look take a seat and I'll see to coffee." Once Jacqueline and her odd son were seated Sarah rushed into the kitchen. Elrika was still pottering about. "Elrika." breathed Sarah hastily. "Would you be an absolute darling? Our guest has arrived early and Danny's not back to greet her. I don't want to leave her alone so would you be a sweetheart and make us some coffee and biscuits or something?"

"Ja, ja. Don't you worry liebchen. I'll see to all that."

"Thanks Elrika." Sarah dashed back to the living room. "Coffee will be a few minutes." she told Jacqueline.

Jacqueline raised an eyebrow. "You have servants?"

Sarah laughed. "Oh God no. Nothing so grand. We have an old lady who helps out with the housekeeping part time is all. She's offered to make the coffee so I don't have to rudely leave you to your own devices."

Jacqueline was apologetic. "I'm sorry. I didn't wish to sound presumptuous. I don't really have much idea how the rich and famous live."

Sarah smiled at her. "Neither have I Jacqueline! At least I had no idea until this summer past when I met Danny. Even now we don't really live ostentatiously. Oh we have a big house and Danny has a Ferrari but other than that we live quite simply actually. We don't exactly live in the fast lane. We're a bit boring actually."

Jacqueline looked unconvinced. "It doesn't sound boring to me." she declared. "I mean you're the partner of one of the most famous celebrities in Switzerland." She blushed. "I'm sorry. It's none of my business how you live of course but I can't help myself being curious. I'm a big fan of Daniela Devin actually. I've got all her records. That's why I'm so nervous about meeting her."

"Please don't be. She doesn't bite."

Jacqueline grinned ingenuously. "Chrissie really likes Daniela's music as well." She told Sarah. "He keeps a poster of her in his bedroom. He's a bit shy but he's excited about meeting her."

Sarah smiled at the strange little boy. "Well if you ask Daniela nicely Chrissie I'm sure she'd love to sign a

439

poster for you. Would you like that?" The little boy bit his thumb timidly but his eyes were sparkling and he nodded eagerly. Sarah found her attention constantly wavering toward Chrissie. She still couldn't quite put her finger on what exactly was so singularly unusual about him. There was something incongruous about him, as if what you were seeing was not the whole story. There was something deeper to him; something showing superficially on the surface but not overtly recognised. This was a little boy with a secret. Even his mother seemed a little discomfited by him, in a strange way, as if she feared he might embarrass himself. Sarah was fascinated by him. There was something about his gestures; his postures; even the way he walked that just didn't fit with the image of the well-dressed young boy he outwardly appeared to be. The elusive nature of him was nagging at the back of Sarah's mind. Sarah shook the thoughts from her mind and turned to his mother. "Peter and Simon said you come from Graubunden originally Jacqueline."

"Yes I'm from the Engadin actually; not far from Sils."

Sarah was pleasantly surprised. The Engadin was the upper valley of the river Inn in the very south east corner of Switzerland. Sarah had visited the region several times. It was a beautiful mountainous region containing the famous resort of St Moritz. "Oh so you speak Romansh then?" Sarah asked. Romansh was the fourth official language of Switzerland spoken by a tiny minority of people in the Confederation exclusively in the Canton of Graubunden.

Jacqueline nodded. "Yes I speak some. My mother speaks Oberengadish or Puter but most people speak German as well. My father is from the Lower Valais though and speaks French naturally."

"A real multi-lingual family then?"

Jacqueline laughed and it lit her face up with

440

warmth. Sarah had the feeling that this was a lady who needed to laugh more often. "I suppose so." she conceded. "I was brought up with a real mix of languages at home. I suppose that's what gave me my dexterity with languages. As well as Romansh, German and French I also speak Italian. My last job was in a hotel in the Bergell where I mostly spoke Italian."

Sarah nodded. "I know the Bergell. I went on holiday there once with my father." The Bergell was a curious little steep sided valley; the upper valley of the River Mera which flowed from the Maloja Pass at the extreme western end of the Engadine into Italy. There was a forgotten feeling to the little valley cut off from the rest of Switzerland by the mountains and Sarah had found its isolation charming. Sarah grinned. "Maybe you could help me with my Italian." she remarked. "My parents live in the Ticino and I always have to speak Italian when I go down there. I can speak it somewhat but it's not my best language I'm afraid."

Jacqueline regarded her shyly. "I speak some English as well. I understand that you and your partner are both English. We can speak English if you're more comfortable with that."

Sarah laughed and shook her head. "We're only part English Jacqueline. My mother is English and my father is Swiss. I was born in England but I've spent nearly all of my life right here in the Toggenburg. As for Danny she's even more of a mixture. Her mother is part English and part Swiss German while her father is half American and half Swiss French. Danny lived a lot longer in England though so she's a bit more naturalised to England than I am. We're pretty much multi-cultural hybrids though."

Jacqueline puckered her brow inquiringly. "Is it true that Daniela has a child as well?"

"Yes she has a young daughter who lives with her grandparents in California for the moment. That's about to change however. She's coming over to Switzerland to live with us in the near future."

Jacqueline's eyebrows rose with interest. "Oh really?" Then she lowered her eyes. "I'm sorry. I'm being nosy again."

Before Sarah could elaborate on her current favourite topic of conversation they were interrupted by Elrika bearing a tray holding cups, saucers, cream, sugar, coffee pot, a glass of coke for the young boy and a plate of biscuits. Sarah politely served coffee before resuming the conversation. "So what brings you to the Toggenburg Jacqueline?" she asked.

Jacqueline pulled a wry face and took a breath. She looked sad. "Escape I suppose. Things were not good for me or Chrissie back home. There was a lot of talk about us and... well people can be pretty cruel sometimes. Chrissie had trouble at school because... well because of the way he is and I thought we both deserved a fresh start. I spent some time in the Toggenburg years ago and I always remembered it as a place where I found some peace and tranquillity. I suppose I came here to try and rediscover that peace. The last couple of years have been a bit rough on both of us. I don't really know anybody in the Toggenburg so that was a positive. I just wanted a place where we wouldn't be prejudged. Most of all, I want a safe place for my son; somewhere where he isn't known and he can make a fresh start."

"Won't he miss his friends in Graubunden?"

"He didn't *have* any friends in Graubunden Sarah. I had to pull him out of two different schools and most people who had children his age we knew didn't want to let their kids play with him."

Sarah was shocked. "That's awful."

Jacqueline nodded. "As I said people can be pretty cruel." She reached out to stroke her son's hair fondly. "I'm sure he's going to make some real friends here though. We don't need those people back home. I hope we can both make some real friends here. We deserve another chance." Impulsively Jacqueline hugged her son. Sarah found her protectiveness endearing. However odd the little boy might be there was no doubt that his mother loved him very much. Feeling a little awkward and not at all sure how to proceed, Sarah was relieved to hear the front door. She glanced at the clock. Daniela had been true to her word. It was almost exactly two o'clock.

As Daniela entered the living room Sarah jumped up to introduce their guests. Jacqueline rose courteously if a little nervously to take Daniela's hand. Sarah was watching them interestedly. As she had expected Jacqueline melted visibly under Daniela's formidable charm as she greeted her and apologised for her absence. Even more gratifying to Sarah was to observe Daniela's reaction to Jacqueline. Although Daniela was invariably charming to anyone she met, Sarah was coming to know her well enough to detect when she took a liking to somebody on first acquaintance. Daniela shared with Sarah the instinctive ability to warn immediately to somebody who was just basically a good person. Sarah was even more interested to see how Daniela would react to little Chrissie. The little boy was visibly shaking with a comical mixture of dread and excitement as Sarah introduced him. Under his mother's urging he offered a limp hand to Daniela with the curiously odd mannerism that seemed characteristic of him but he seemed too awestruck to be able to speak. "Chrissie here is one of your biggest fans Danny!" Sarah told her with a smile.

"Really?" Daniela's eyes were dancing. Triumphantly Sarah realised that Daniela was as fascinated with the little boy as she was. She took the little boy's hand and turned on her biggest and most heart melting smile. "Well I *am* lucky." she declared. "It's not every day I get to meet one of my biggest fans. I shall have to be on my best behaviour." Chrissie smiled shyly quite clearly entranced by the vision of the object of his adoration in the flesh before him.

With a laugh Sarah relieved Daniela of her shopping bags. "I'll put this stuff away." she volunteered. "Why don't you all sit down and I'll grab an extra cup for you Danny."

Daniela nodded. "Yes let's do that." She took Chrissie's hand. "Why don't you come and sit with me on the sofa Chrissie?" The little boy beamed hugely but he could only nod dumbly.

It took a few minutes to stow away the provisions in the kitchen and when Sarah returned with an extra cup she found the atmosphere considerably more relaxed. Nicole had once remarked jokingly that Daniela could put a conference hall full of paranoid schizophrenics at their ease and there was a lot of truth in the statement. Jacqueline was looking visibly more comfortable and smiling more. As for little Chrissie, sat on the sofa next to Daniela and clutching her hand, he looked as if Christmas had come early this year. Daniela was taking particular interest in him and coaxing out a few mumbled words. Jacqueline was looking deeply grateful for the interest Daniela was showing in her unusual son. Reading between the lines Sarah guessed that she was unused to such a positive reaction to him. It *was* a positive reaction as well. Daniela's interest went clearly beyond the natural kindness and sympathy of the warm hearted person she was. Daniela could barely take her eyes off him, so clearly bewitched by him she was. As Sarah put down a cup in front of her Daniela lifted a hand to stroke Chrissie's hair. "I was just saying to Jackie here what beautiful hair Chrissie has Sarah." she remarked.

Sarah suppressed a smile. Daniela had wasted no time in coming to more intimate terms. Jacqueline was now firmly Jackie. "I said so as well Danny." Sarah replied. "Apparently he won't let his mum cut it for him."

"That's right." Jacqueline confirmed. "He's a nightmare at the hairdressers. The last time we went it took me over an hour to coax him inside and even then he made me promise not to let the hairdresser do anything more than just trim the ends."

Daniela's interest grew by the second. "So you like your hair long then Chrissie?" she asked him. Chrissie nodded in reply. Daniela smiled at him and took a lock of her own hair. "Well I like my hair long as well."

Chrissie gazed in fascination at Daniela's luxurious blond mane. "C..can I touch it?" he stammered timidly.

"Chrissie!" his mother admonished quickly. "You can't ask Miss Devin something like that."

Daniela laughed. "It's all right Jackie." she reassured her. "Of course Chrissie can touch my hair." Chrissie reached out to stroke Daniela's hair shyly. He stroked it gently; almost lovingly quite plainly enraptured by its long silky texture. There was almost a sense of yearning in his fascination. "Do you like my hair Chrissie?" Daniela asked the question gently but she had turned serious and Sarah could detect that she was more than casually interested in his reply.

"It... it's beautiful." Chrissie mumbled.

Jacqueline was ruefully apologetic. "I'm so sorry Danny. He always wants to stroke ladies' hair. He's got a thing about it." Sarah frowned slightly. Jacqueline spent too much time apologising for her son.

It seemed as if Daniela thought the same for she glanced at Jacqueline and said. "Please don't apologise Jackie. There's nothing wrong with wanting to stroke people's hair. I find myself wanting to stroke girls' beautiful hair all the time but I'm grown up and people frown on it a bit, apart from Sarah, and I could stroke *hers* all day long."

Jacqueline blushed. "Yes but you're...." she stopped herself in time. "I mean I don't think it's appropriate for him to want to stroke a girl's hair."

445

"Why?"

"Well because he's a boy."

Daniela nodded uncertainly and turned her attention back to Chrissie. "When I was a little girl I used to love to stroke my mother's hair. She used to let me help her brush it out as well. Maybe you could help me brush mine a bit later Chrissie. I could do with the help. Hair like mine takes a lot of looking after."

Chrissie looked eager. "Oh! Could I?"

Daniela laughed. "We'll have to see what your mother says Chrissie."

At this moment Elrika entered the living room. She was a lady convinced that, without her constant vigilance and left to their own devices, people of her acquaintance were all too liable to starve themselves to death. She was carrying an enormous plate of Black Forest Gateau and a fresh pot of coffee. Her entrance gave Daniela an opportunity. She smiled at Chrissie. "I happen to know that Elrika has a blueberry tart and a big tub of ice cream in the kitchen Chrissie. Would you like some?"

"Yes please."

Daniela looked up at Jacqueline. "Is it ok if Chrissie has some ice cream?" she asked.

Jacqueline smiled. "As if I could stop him. He loves ice cream. Sure he can have some Danny. We only had a light luncheon and it's ages until dinner."

Daniela nodded in satisfaction. "Good. Well why don't you go off with Elrika into the kitchen then Chrissie. Your mum and I have to talk about some boring things now."

The lure of ice cream notwithstanding Chrissie nevertheless looked reluctant to be parted from Daniela. Elrika held out a hand invitingly. "Come along." She urged. "When we've had some pop and some ice cream you can help me feed the cats and the chickens." With the prospect of these further adventures in store Chrissie allowed himself to be led away.

446

Daniela's eyes followed Chrissie all the way as Elrika led him out. When he was gone she turned to Jacqueline. "You have a very singular and remarkable child Jacqueline."

Jacqueline blinked in surprise. "Oh er... do you think so?"

"Yes I do. You seemed surprised that I think so."

Jacqueline rubbed her chin ruefully. "Well to be honest Danny that's the first time anybody ever said that to me. I've heard him called a few things but never remarkable."

"Well perhaps it is about time then that people took a better look at him Jackie. I not only think he's remarkable but, and at the risk of being intrusive, I'm not convinced that you yourself are aware of just how extraordinary he is."

Jacqueline gave a wistful smile. "Mothers always think their kids are extraordinary Danny. I suppose it's nature's way of stopping us from strangling them when they get on our nerves. I love my son very dearly but I'm under no illusions about what other people think about him. Most people think he's a little peculiar at best."

Daniela laughed. "Well I can sympathise Jackie. I pretty much think my own daughter is extraordinary and she is. Some people are a little taken aback by her though. She's so intelligent, self-assured and mature that you sometimes have to pinch yourself to remind yourself that it's a little girl you're talking to and not a grown up. Nevertheless I stand by my opinion. I think Chrissie is a fascinating young child."

Jacqueline frowned and placed her coffee cup down before collecting her thoughts. "May I ask a frank question Danny?"

"By all means."

"Well I thought that the purpose of this interview today was about the job in the pub but Simon told me you wanted to meet my son as well. May I ask why? I

447

mean we haven't even mentioned the job. We seem to have talked about little else than my son."

Daniela nodded in agreement with the justice of Jacqueline's inquiry. "Yes that's true Jackie and I think you deserve an honest answer. As far as the job is concerned, from a purely practical point of view, there is no question I think that you are admirably qualified and suited to the position. Simon and Peter are more than satisfied with your qualifications and references. They are of the opinion that you are a highly talented and gifted person who will be nothing but an asset to the business. However the business is more than just the particular skills and qualifications a person brings to the job. There is also the question of whether or not the people working together can get along together. That's true in any business but it's even more so in this case because all the people involved are already a close knit community and good friends together. That's why Peter and Simon wanted me to meet you. I, in my turn, wanted you to meet Sarah. Sarah isn't actually part of the business. She might well help out part time on occasion but she has her own things to be getting along with. I'm not really involved in the day to day running of the business either. I'm just putting up the money behind it. Theoretically then, there's not the slightest reason why you should need to talk to either Sarah or myself. But we're a tight knit little family and we mutually support one another. We needed to how you'd fit within that family. That, of course, includes your family and that means your son."

"But why should he be relevant?"

"Well Peter and Simon were concerned about the fact that you are a single mother Jackie and, not only that but, that your child has special needs. That's going to put extra pressures on you regarding the job."

Jacqueline looked stubbornly defiant. "I can cope. I've done it before. I really need this job."

Daniela held up a hand. "Wait a minute Jackie. The position is not dependent on your ability to balance the requirements of being a mother with the job. I'm not here trying to ascertain whether or not you'd cope. What I'm trying to do is think of the best way of *helping* you to cope. This interview, if you can call it that, ceased to be about the job some time ago. We know what your qualifications are and I've seen all that I need to. I know that Peter and Simon think you are perfect for the job and Sarah here likes you."

Jacqueline blinked. "Oh? Does she really?"

Daniela nodded. "Yes. I know she hasn't said so as such but I know Sarah well enough to know when she's taken a liking to somebody. Well that's decisive as far as I'm concerned. You may consider yourself employed. Now all we have to do is sit down and thrash out how we're going to make this thing work. Merely "coping" isn't an option Jackie. We have to find a solution that helps everybody and that includes the needs of your child just as I have to find solutions around the needs of my own."

"Sarah said that your child was coming to live with you."

"Yes that's right and of course it means I have to make adjustments and arrangements too. I have work obligations as well with concerts, live tours, recording contracts, videos, television appearances and so forth. I couldn't possibly manage all that and attend to the needs of my child without the help of my friends and loved ones and I wouldn't expect you to balance your work and the needs of your child on your own either. That's why I wanted to see your child Jackie. I needed to know just what his needs were so that we could find a way to help you meet those needs. You've been trying to do this on your own Jackie and you shouldn't have to. We can help you."

For a moment Sarah thought that Jacqueline was

going to cry but she mastered herself and took a deep breath. "I... I don't know what to say Danny. Thank you. This means a great deal to me." She paused for a few seconds to control her feelings. "I... I really wanted this job Danny and not just because I need the money. Well I do need the money of course but there was more to it than that."

"Oh yes?"

"Yes. I found out that Simon and Peter are gay and then I learn that you're involved in the business too and I suppose all Switzerland knows that you're gay."

Daniela frowned. "Do you have a problem with that?"

Jacqueline shook her head vigorously. "No, no, no! Not at all. On the contrary it's why I really wanted the job. You've got to understand that I don't know any gay people. I really wanted to meet some and talk to them. I thought perhaps they might be able to advise me or at least be a bit more tolerant than the people I knew in Graubunden."

Daniela raised an inquiring eyebrow. "Tolerant? Are you saying that you're gay Jackie?"

"Not me Danny. My son! My son is gay."

Daniela looked gently amused. "So you believe your son is gay then Jackie?"

"Well it's obvious isn't it? You just have to look at him."

"Well I've looked at him Jackie and it's not obvious to me. I think he's a bit young to properly determine his sexual orientation don't you? I mean how can you tell if he prefers girls or boys? Most boys his age think that girls are pretty gross whatever their sexual preferences turn out to be in later life."

Jacqueline seemed puzzled. "But I thought from what you were saying that you thought he was gay as well."

"I have no idea whether your son is gay Jackie. But

tell me something. Why do *you* think he's gay?"

"Because he's so *feminine* Danny. He doesn't act like a boy. He acts just like a girl."

Sarah had been keeping an interested silence up until now but at this point she blurted out. "Of course. That's it. I've been trying to put my finger on it ever since I first met him. He looks just like a girl dressed up as a boy. It's his mannerisms; the way he talks, moves, even the way he walks. God he could easily be a little girl."

Daniela nodded thoughtfully. "Yes I noticed it straight away. It's very marked."

Jacqueline pulled a face. "Everybody remarks on it sooner or later. It gets more marked the older he gets as well although he's always been that way. The people we knew back in the Engadine used to call him a sissy or a nancy boy. He got into all kinds of trouble at school. The other kids used to bully him about it and the teachers kept telling him off for pretending to be a girl. A lot of parents wouldn't let him play with their children because they thought he was queer or something. The lady who used to babysit for me when I was at work had a daughter the same age. She found him one day putting on her daughter's clothes and she told me that she preferred it if he didn't come around to their house anymore." Jacqueline looked sad. "That was when I decided we needed to get away; make a fresh start somewhere else. The people I worked for weren't very sympathetic. They just thought I should stop him from being such a girl and tell him to act like a boy. It's not as easy as that though. I tried to make him behave like a boy but he just got more and more miserable. It got to the stage that he was just unhappy all the time and it was breaking my heart."

Daniela was looking at her with gentle understanding. "I can well imagine it Jackie. I'm sorry for saying so but it sounds as if you knew some pretty

451

ignorant and bigoted people."

Jacqueline nodded sadly. "I was desperate to tell the truth Danny. I didn't know what to do. He used to cry whenever I made him dress in boy's clothes. It was ok if I let him put a pretty top on that was a bit girly but people either frowned at that or laughed at him. I had the devil of a job dressing him this morning. It was only the chance of meeting you Danny that helped me to persuade him."

"Does he like dressing as a girl then?" asked Sarah in fascination.

"Hell yes. He's always playing with my clothes. A lot of the time at home he'll wrap a piece of cloth around his waist so that it looks like a skirt. He likes to play with my make-up and things as well. I have to hide my nail varnish or he starts painting his nails. That's why he won't let me cut his hair. He wants it long like a girl's. He even plays with dolls. I have my old dolls from when I was a kid and they're his favourite toys. All the boy's toys I buy him, like trucks and things, he's not interested in." Jacqueline sighed deeply. "One day at school they were staging a dance for the kids to perform in front of their parents. They had all the girls dressed up as little ballerinas in pink and the boys in blue shirts and pants. Chrissie was so upset that he couldn't put on a tutu with the girls I had to take him home." Jacqueline pulled a wry face. "It's not the only time he's had that sort of trouble at school. He likes to draw a lot and one day at school he drew a picture of a girl in high heels and a dress. The teacher asked him who the picture was of and he told her that it was him. Well she told him that it couldn't be him because he was a boy and he threw such a tantrum that they told me to come and collect him from school. I got called into the headmistress' office and she recommended that I see a doctor; a psychiatrist about him."

"And did you?" asked Daniela.

"Yes I did. It didn't do too much good though. The doctor thought it was some kind of childhood phase he was going through and had me follow this program of rewarding him for masculine behaviour and penalising him for being feminine. He told me that the likely cause of my child's behavioural problems was that he'd been raised by a single mother without a male role model in the form of a father."

Daniela looked shocked. "Please change your doctor at your earliest convenience Jackie because you can take it from me that the one you've been seeing is a quack."

"Well I have changed now Danny because we've moved here. I still have to see a doctor though because of the problems Chrissie has had. I can't put him into a new school without an assessment because he's been diagnosed as special needs because of this problem."

"Does he have any other learning difficulties or clinical problems other than this characteristic of his?" Daniela wanted to know.

"No. Not that I'm aware of. He's actually very bright and generally in advance of the other kids at school although his progress has been a bit reduced of late because I've had to keep him out of school so much. But no, he's an intelligent kid."

"He just wants to be a girl then?" asked Sarah.

It's worse than that Sarah. It's not just that he wants to be a girl he actually seems to think he *is* one. He doesn't even like to be called by his real name of Christian. He wants to be called Christine. Calling him Chrissie is a sort of neutral compromise."

Sarah frowned. "How does he think about not being anatomically a girl though Jackie. I mean presumably he knows that he looks different between his legs than girls do."

"Oh yes and he hates it. He loathes the fact that he has a penis. He seems to think it's a big mistake; that

453

God made a mistake or something by giving him one." Jacqueline shuddered. "God one day I found him in the bathroom. He'd got hold of a pair of scissors and if I hadn't come in at that moment I swear he would have tried to cut it off."

Sarah covered her mouth with a hand. "Oh my God! That's terrible."

"Yes I hid anything he could harm himself with after that but it scared me to death. That's when I knew we had to get away and make a fresh start. I needed to find someone who could advise me Sarah. That's why this job seemed perfect. I thought perhaps gay people would be more understanding and able to help me understand what is happening to my son who just has to be gay."

"I don't think you've got a gay son Jackie." said Daniela quietly.

Jacqueline looked taken aback. "I beg your pardon?"

"I said I don't think you've got a gay son. In fact I'll go further than that. I don't think you've got a son at all. I think you've got a *daughter*."

Chapter Twenty-Six

There were a few moments silence following Daniela's startling remark; a few moments whilst the significance of her words sank in. Sarah stared at her in astonishment but with a tinge of excitement. She realised almost immediately what Daniela was trying to say and she felt a thrill of discovery. This was something she had never encountered before; something that was truly special; one of nature's more intriguing if somewhat mischievous variations. Sarah, since Daniela had come into her life and forced her to reassess her sexuality, had researched widely into the sub-culture of the LGBT community and found the field fascinating. Among her researches she had come across this very subject and she had read some of the rather thin body of literature concerning it as well as watching some documentaries about it on-line. Daniela with her deeper background knowledge had recognised Chrissie for what he truly was a lot earlier but Sarah, the more she looked at it, was increasingly sure that she was right. Chrissie was something very special.

Of course being special was as much of a curse as it was a blessing. Most people don't want to be special. Society was very good at imposing mundane uniformity and often cruel to those who didn't fit into its categories of "normality". There was even a Japanese saying which summed it up; the saying that the nail that stood up was hammered down until it was level with the rest. Gay people of course were all too aware of this. They, most demonstrably, didn't fit into society's definition of normality. They were the ones that stood out as different and, as a result, suffered from the bigotry towards and fear of the different. Sarah remembered the conversation she had had with Daniela on the day they had hiked over to the Voralpsee. Daniela had argued that day that people didn't fit into boxes neatly. Society was forever trying to fit you into acceptable boxes. Gay people themselves had even bought into the idea by arguing that they were in fact *normal*; that there was a perfectly simple box into which they could step and be just as ordinary as everybody else. They sought no celebration of their difference but the obscurity of their normality.

Sarah felt slightly troubled by that and she suspected that was not the way that Daniela looked at the world either. Why shouldn't society in fact glory in individual difference; revel in the vast complexity of humanity? There were seven billion people on the planet and every single one of them was *different*. You were going to drive yourself mad trying to impose standards of normality on seven billion individuals. Not only could it not be done but it was a miserably depressing thing to even want to. It was the incalculable variation of humanity that kept the species so infinitely dynamic and creative. Why would you even *want* to reduce that dynamism to a flat level of mundane conformity? How dull and grey life would be.

Were gay people even making a mistake by demanding normality? Were they too ready to accept a definition of themselves as "gay" and therefore trapping themselves into an ordained category which they would be expected to conform to? Daniela had pointed out that even gay people on occasion were far too comfortable in accepting such simplistic definitions of themselves. They too had their problems when it came to categorisation; their own difficulties in squeezing people into boxes. The obvious one was the bisexual person. Life would be a lot simpler if people could be defined as either gay or straight. The bisexual was an irritating variable; so irritating that you had to invent a whole new box for them; a sort of catch all repository for all the people who didn't fit neatly into the two main categories. The problem was that once you started sub-dividing all the categories then there was no end to it and you ended up where perhaps you should have started in the first place; i.e. the notion that everybody was in fact different from everybody else and the only box you could put them in was ultimately the one that was uniquely theirs. Nobody's sexuality was going to be the same as anybody else's so why on earth try to define a normality about it? Humans were not clones. *Difference* was normal. Who you slept with should not be a definition of you. It should be an irrelevancy.

But if ever there were two categories that were regarded as holy writ; set in stone, then they were the categories of gender. If people were beginning to explore the notion that sexuality was far more fluid than had been previously accepted there was, as yet, only the glimmer of suspicion that one's gender might be equally open to variation. You were either a man or you were a woman. There seemed little compromise with that bi-polar view within contemporary society. It was a fundamental bedrock of belief within society; male or female. Anybody who challenged that simplistic view in some respects challenged humanity's very definition of itself and Chrissie was just such a person. Of all the differences that society might abhor then this was one of the most threatening for it questioned even the most basic premise that people came in but a simple two genders. Life threatened to be difficult for Chrissie but there was an excitement about the challenge that Chrissie and like people presented; an excitement simply because they introduced entirely different ways of looking at human beings; radical concepts calling into question the very philosophy of humankind and how we view ourselves as living beings. Chrissie was a challenge that asked every open minded person to stand back and think again. Chrissie was special.

Jacqueline seemed momentarily shocked by

Daniela's assertion. She seemed to have accepted gradually that her son was most likely gay but Daniela had raised the bar and was suggesting something even more startling. Finally she found her voice. "But... but he's a boy." she protested at last.

Daniela raised an eyebrow questioningly. "Is he? Is he really?"

"Well yes... I mean that's what it says on his birth certificate."

Daniela laughed shortly. "Which, of course, is a sacred document entirely free of any possibility of error or misinterpretation." Daniela smiled ironically. "Jackie have you any idea of the prevalence of ambiguity in gender assignment at birth. It's a lot more common than you would think. Generally speaking a physician or mid-wife upon delivering a baby will examine the external genitalia of the child and assign gender on the basis of that examination. Unfortunately that's not always possible. In a significant minority of cases there is enough ambiguity about the genitalia to call into question the gender. In such cases it's necessary to conduct an examination of the internal anatomy and sexual characteristics such as gonads, internal ovary structures, hormones and chromosomes. Even then there can be questions and the doctors can get it wrong.

The truth is that, in reality, there is very little difference physically between a male child and a female child and there are enough possible variations between the two to call into question that child's possible gender assignment. In fact the assignment of male or female at birth is more a societal assignment rather than a medical definition. Until very recently doctors would make a conscious decision on the gender of the child on the basis of the information available and, if necessary to make the child conform to that decision, would carry out surgery on the child to correct any ambiguities that called the assigned gender into question. The results were often frightful leaving the child scarred and mutilated and out of kilter with its own gender identity. Thankfully these days a more enlightened approach is being advocated by some doctors who argue that doctors should not be so ready with surgical intervention upon a child who after all is too young to make that decision for itself and is going to have to have to grow up with the consequences of the doctor's decision. In effect they're saying that we should let the child determine which gender he or she is most comfortable with when old enough to know their own mind."

Jacqueline frowned uncertainly. "Yes I think I've heard about such cases Danny but it doesn't apply in Chrissie's case. There was no question about his sex when he was born. He was a perfectly formed little boy and no reason to doubt otherwise."

Daniela raised a finger theatrically. "Until now Jackie... until now."

"You mean he's changing somehow?"

"No I don't think so. I think he's always been this way. It was only after he became older that the ambiguity became manifest. Tell me what do you know of Gender Identity Disorder?"

"I've never heard of it."

"Well it's a horrible name. It implies some terrible malady or disability which isn't necessarily the case. There is some tendency to use more sensitive terms to describe the condition these days and, while accepting that it is something that must be addressed, there is less prevalence among the medical community to regard it as some sort of debilitating dysfunction. The most enlightened authorities simply consider it as a perfectly acceptable variation of the human condition that, with proper therapy, does not preclude a person from having a fulfilled and happy life. I won't say an ordinary life because such people are extraordinary by their very nature but certainly a life that need be no less satisfying

459

and complete than anybody else's. Admittedly life may be much more challenging to people who are born this way but that's more because of the society we live in rather than the condition itself."

"Yes but what *is* it?"

"Well I've already said that many children at birth have ambiguous sexual characteristics. These characteristics are most usually first identified with ambiguous genitalia. Actually the genitalia of a male or female are essentially made up of the same material. All foetuses start life as female. The sexual organs can develop one way or the other dependent upon the hormones generated by the body according to whether it has XX or XY chromosomes. Thus with male hormones the organ becomes a penis or with female it becomes a clitoris. Likewise the sac of the scrotum forms from what otherwise would have been the labia majora, the gonads become either testicles or ovaries and so on. The point is that the differences are actually superficial changes that are triggered by the actions of hormones while the child is still in the womb.

Well we know that all sorts of things can go wrong with such chemical changes to the body and hence it's not always possible to tell immediately which gender the child is from a physical examination. What some medical scientists now believe is that these hormonal changes go even deeper than was once thought. It is thought by some now that the hormones affect not only the development of the sexual organs but also the brain; imprinting, if you like, a gender identity on the very thought processes of the person. This can be fairly mild to extreme depending on just how much imbalance of the hormones there is. You can get the whole spectrum of severity in other words. In mild cases people may find themselves tending somewhat towards the opposite gender from which they are assigned. You may get rather masculine girls or effeminate boys or simply some people who can empathise better with the opposite sex because of some characteristics they share with them in their own brains. In extreme cases, however, the person has a gender identity so firmly imprinted on their brains that it simply doesn't match with their assigned sex. They experience the overwhelming feeling that there has been some terrible mistake. They have been literally born inside the wrong body. Their outward appearance says that they are one sex but inside they are completely convinced that they are the opposite. This is what is called Gender Identity Disorder."

Jacqueline bit her lip. "Oh God! I think I see what you mean. Chrissie often says to me that he thinks God had made a mistake by making him a boy."

Daniela nodded. "That's absolutely characteristic Jackie. As far as Chrissie is concerned he, or rather she, *is* a girl. Everything you've told me and everything I've observed about *her* tells me that that is the truth. I am not at all surprised to learn that Chrissie has had emotional and behavioural problems. Anybody would who has been raised all their life as the wrong gender. Imagine how *you* would feel if you were brought up being told all day and every day that you were a boy and you knew inside yourself that it wasn't true. Everything about Chrissie's life is a lie and she's baffled and hurt about it. Jackie I think your little boy is in fact a little girl and she's been trying to tell you that all her life. Maybe you should ignore that blasted quack of a doctor you've been taking her to and try listening to *her* instead."

"Are you telling me that Chrissie will grow up to be a transvestite or something?"

Daniela shook her head. "The correct term is transgender Jackie although there is endless discussion about the exact meaning of the words transgender or transsexual. Transvestites are people who simply dress up as the opposite sex. Many of them of course are transgender to some extent or another but transvestism is

461

really descriptive of an act not an identity. If an actor dresses up as the opposite sex in a theatrical role then they are transvestite although it has nothing to do with their own gender identity. It's just something they're doing. Of course many transgender people will dress up in the clothes that they feel more readily fits the gender they feel themselves to be but even that isn't an absolute. It is not uncommon for transgender people to so suppress their inner conviction of their gender as to go through life conforming to their so-called biological gender assignment and living lives of pretence and concealment. Sadly such people frequently live miserable frustrated lives and the suicide rate among them is shockingly high."

Jacqueline turned pale. "Oh God! Suicide?"

Daniela nodded seriously. "Yes Jackie. I'm sorry. There's no way to tell you this gently but I'm afraid that the suicide rate among young transgender people is one of the highest among any particular societal grouping. Some studies suggest that the rate is several times higher even than the rate among gay teenagers who are already as much as seven or eight times more likely to commit suicide than straight people. You can understand why. It is hard enough for gay people to deal with the guilt and shame that comes as a result of society's ostracism of their sexuality. Imagine how much harder it is going to be for a young person growing up trying to hide the very fact of their own gender; expected to fit into roles that every fibre of their bodies scream at them are wrong. Our gender is so fundamental to us; so central to how we perceive ourselves. Imagine having to live in denial of it every waking moment of your life. It's a very, very lonely place to be Jackie. Ideally there will one day come a time when society will accept all the variations in a person's sexuality or gender without the cruel bigotry that it currently imposes on those who don't fit its comfortable assumptions and such people will be able to grow up without fear. Until that time comes though, people like your Chrissie need and deserve all the help and compassion we can give them."

Jacqueline squeezed her fists in anguish. "Well what should I do?"

Daniela smiled. "Plenty I think Jackie. You know, as an active supporter of LGBT rights, I've come across quite a few transgender people now. I can tell you that there's a lot of heartbreak and sadness in many of their stories. Of course transgender people gravitate towards the gay community because it's one of the few safe havens for them in society; the one place where they are accepted. There's a fuzzy line between being transgender and being gay in many cases and I suspect that a lot of people who identify as gay are in fact transgender. There is a subtle difference. Transgender refers to a state where you identify as the sex opposite to that which you have been assigned. Being gay, means that you are attracted to people of your own gender. The two things are not the same. I have no doubts about my own gender and neither does Sarah. I think most people would unambiguously recognise us as very female. Yet we are both gay. A transgender person might be gay or straight."

Jacqueline looked puzzled. "Excuse me? What do you mean?"

"I mean that your sexual identity depends upon your gender identity. If you're a man and you are attracted to men then you are gay but if you're attracted to women then you're straight more or less. But your gender is what you consider it to be. Thus if a person is transgender then their sexual orientation should correctly be associated with their gender *identity*. If somebody is born male but is transgender to female then, should she be attracted to men, she is straight, not gay, in spite of the fact that, from a gross biological point of view, her original gender was male. If she discovers she prefers females then she's lesbian. What I said earlier is relevant. Most people don't actually work out what their sexual preferences are until they reach puberty at least and start becoming sexually interested. Gender though is something that comes much earlier. It is characteristic of transgender children that they know from a very early age whether they're a boy or a girl. Everybody does that. I'm sure that I was certain that I was a girl long before I ever knew that I was attracted to them as well. Most transgender kids know pretty much from the age they are capable of thinking about such things that there's something wrong with their bodies."

"We seem to have got off the subject Danny." Jacqueline noted. "I asked what I was supposed to do."

"Yes I'm sorry. I transgressed a little. I said plenty and I think that is the case. As I've already said I've met a lot of transgender people though my contacts in the LGBT community and there are some pretty horrific tales. With Chrissie though, I'm rather optimistic. I think she's got something rather good going for her."

"What's that?"

"She's got a loving, understanding and supportive mother who, instead of being appalled and railing against the unfairness of the hand she's been dealt, is determined to help, support and love her child whatever might be. All this time I've talked to you I have never found any evidence to suggest otherwise. You have my profound respect and admiration Jackie. Chrissie will have many difficulties to face in life but she is lucky indeed to have a mother like you to help her." Daniela paused to take a sip from her coffee. "But Jackie you shouldn't have to help her alone. If you are going to be working with us then we... and I'm sure I speak for Sarah as well... we would like to offer all the help and support that we can."

"Yes absolutely." declared Sarah. "I agree with every word Danny has said."

Jacqueline nodded gratefully. "I... I would value

your support a great deal ladies. God knows that you're the first people I've ever met who are so understanding. I... I'm just trying to get my head around all this. I mean if Chrissie is transgender as you say then what am I supposed to do to help him, or her as you say? I mean obviously I'll continue to love him and support him but is there anything specific I should be doing?"

Daniela nodded. "Well for one thing you can dump the bloody doctor you've been seeing. I was appalled when you told me that he was telling you to penalise Chrissie for being female. What a prick. The very last thing Chrissie needs is to be punished further for something she can't help. God knows what damage it will do to her to be constantly bullied into being something that she isn't. Not only that, but the bloody quack had the temerity to even suggest it was partly *your* fault for being a single mother. How dare he? Tell him to take his tincture of bat's vomit and other quack remedies and bugger off back into the dark ages where he belongs. We'll find you a proper specialist for Chrissie."

"But where?"

"Well as it happens I know a qualified paediatrician and child psychologist who specialises in transgender children. She's one of the leading specialists in her field Jackie and well respected. She has her clinic in Zurich and before this afternoon is out we're going to make an appointment for you to take Chrissie along to see her. That's the first step."

"Er I'm not sure I can afford a specialist Danny."

"Who said you had to Jackie? Haven't you been listening? I said you don't have to do this alone. We're here to help. We'll pick up the consultation fees. All you have to do is to get yourself and Chrissie to the clinic at the appointed hour and we'll see what Dr Marcie has to say."

"Dr Marcie?"

"Dr Marcella Poillette.... she's an old friend of

465

mine. I call her Doc Marcie. She's a lovely lady and fantastic with kids. You couldn't wish for a better person to counsel you on this Jackie. She's not only top notch in her field but she also cares passionately about the kids that come under her care. For the first time you'll be getting properly qualified advice from a person who knows the subject inside out and back to front."

"Will it be difficult to get an appointment Danny? I mean if she's that well known won't she be pretty full up or something?"

Daniela shook her head with a laugh. "Not at all. Oh she's a busy lady all right but we can pull a few strings in this case. She's not only a friend of mine but I'm also the patron of the charity that helps to support her clinic financially. I've made some personal contributions myself and...well let's just say that Marcie owes me a few favours. We'll get an appointment all right. You'll see."

"Well thank you Danny. I don't know what to say! What do you think she'll recommend?"

"I should imagine that she'll want to make a full diagnosis to begin with Jackie. She'll probably want to question both you and Chrissie at length and determine exactly the extent of Chrissie's transgender condition. On the basis of that she'll come up with some strategy for you to manage Chrissie's life and possible transition."

"Transition?"

Daniela regarded Jacqueline soberly. "Yes Jackie. In cases where it's called for, Dr Marcie may well advise her clients to allow their children to assume the gender role that they identify with."

"You mean allow Chrissie to be.... to be a *girl*?"

"If that is what she considers to be the healthy option for your child Jackie. If she considers that the psychological distress of being forced into the wrong gender role is harming your child then she may well recommend that you allow that child to transition into the gender they feel more at ease in. I'm sure she'll weigh up all the options but that might well be a possibility. Would that pose problems for you?"

"Oh God! I don't know. I've never even thought about that before."

"Do you think Chrissie would be happier being allowed to be a girl?"

Jacqueline nodded. "Yes he probably would but.... Oh God I don't know. It's a hell of a step. I mean what about school and things like that?"

Daniela regarded her with compassion. "Listen Jackie Dr Marcie isn't going to do anything without consulting you at every step. She's very experienced in these sort of problems. Certainly she'll be able to advise you on how to deal with school authorities and you'd have the backing of her authority if it came to asking for special requirements for your child at school. Dr Marcie's seen it all in this area Jackie. You'd do well to listen to her advice. The other thing she'll be able to do is put you in contact with help groups of people in the same boat as you. You and Chrissie are not alone out there you know. You are going to be amazed at how many transgender people there are and how many parents of transgender kids are going through exactly the same thing as you are. This condition is far more prevalent than you would have given credit for. Slowly, painfully slowly perhaps, society is changing Jackie. Things like this don't carry the same stigma they once had. There's new hope and understanding." Daniela paused to smile. "You know in many ancient societies and still in some extant societies to this day transgender people were perfectly accepted within society and even sometimes revered; almost as a third gender, celebrated for the diversity they brought to the community. Maybe one day we'll get back to that level of tolerance and understanding and come to respect people for what they are and not how we expect them to be."

Jacqueline was wringing her hands in uncertainty. "Yes ok I could let Chrissie be a girl but what about... I mean what about when he grows up and all that."

Daniela waved a hand dismissively. "That's *way* down the line Jackie. You don't have to worry about that just yet. If it is indicated then, later, Chrissie may be prescribed hormones to block puberty and prevent masculinisation at puberty. That's always a critical period. It's devastating to a transgender person when their body starts to take on adult characteristics of the opposite gender to that which they identify with so their counsellor might refer them to an endocrinologist to give them the treatment to delay puberty and allow the growing child time to decide if they want to complete the transition. Afterwards they may well be prescribed hormone treatment to feminise or masculinise their body according to their gender identity. Later, much later, they may well choose to undergo reassignment surgery to change their physical appearance. They may also choose cosmetic surgery to more align themselves with their gender; girls might have breast enhancement, bodily hair depilation or have their Adam's apple reduced and so forth. But all that's way in the future yet Jackie. What's important now is Chrissie's happiness for the moment. Right now I'm guessing that Chrissie is a very unhappy little child. That's not your fault Jackie but I think you have to give him/her every chance to find happiness now. The future can look after itself and we can look at it when it comes."

Jacqueline rubbed her hands against her temples. "Oh God! I just don't know what to think. This is a whole new set of concepts for me."

"I'm sorry Jackie. I didn't want to concern you too much."

"Please Danny it's all right. I was already concerned. In fact I was desperate. This is the first time

468

anybody has really talked any sense to me about Chrissie."

"I might be wrong Jackie."

Jacqueline shook her head. "No I don't think you are. Everything you've said makes sense. It's just that I've never looked at it this way before. I've never even heard of that gender... what did you call it?"

"Gender Identity Disorder."

"Yes that. Do you think Chrissie really fits that?"

"Well of course I'm not a professional Jackie. Dr Marcie will be able to give you a properly professional expert diagnosis on that. However from my experience and having seen Chrissie and talked to you I'd say as a layman that Chrissie seems like a classic case. Have you got internet access at home?"

"Yes."

"Well I'll give you the links to some websites on the subject. There's a lot of stuff you can be reading and there are a lot of documentaries on transgender people and transgender children on-line as well. There are several good items on You Tube if you want to look them up. There's a lot more information out there than you might think."

I was watching something the other day on You Tube you might be interested in Jackie." Sarah volunteered. "It was a couple of interviews with a young German girl who's transgender. She's a singer and apparently one of the youngest ever people to undergo gender reassignment surgery. I can't remember her name though."

"She's called Kim Petras Sarah." Daniela told her. "She's a very pretty and talented teenager. She's quite a media hit in Germany and on-line. I know a bit about her. Apparently she's insisted from the age of two that she was a girl and she's more or less been brought up that way. She was counselled by a Dr Bernd Meyenberger at Frankfurt University who's a close

469

associate of Dr Marcie."

"She seems very bright." Sarah noted.

"Oh she is. She speaks fantastic English and she's a gifted musician. There're no flies on that girl. She had her first recording contract by the time she was fourteen which is more than I managed to do."

"And this boy.... I mean this girl.... oh hell how do you describe them..." Jacqueline petered out in confusion.

"You should refer to them as the gender and grammatical person appropriate to the gender they identify as Jackie." Daniela told her. "Thus correctly Kim Petras is a girl regardless of her assigned gender at birth."

"Ok then... this *girl*.... you say she was raised as a girl?"

"Yes at her own insistence apparently. I think her parents resisted the notion to begin with but they were faced with a very determined child and a clear cut case of transgender."

"And they let her dress as a girl and everything?"

"Once they had accepted her condition yes."

"But won't it become noticeable that she's not a girl when she grows up?"

"I doubt it Jackie. She's a teenager now and there is absolutely no difference on the outside between her and any other very pretty teenage girl. Obviously she's had surgery to reassign her genitalia and she continues to take female hormones to maintain her feminine appearance but you certainly couldn't tell her from any other very girly girl. She was lucky in that she made the transition very young. It's much easier to make the transition successfully if you begin before puberty leaves you with body changes that you're stuck with and might require major cosmetic surgery to correct. Kim was lucky to have supportive parents and a progressive doctor."

470

"But don't other kids at school pick on children like that."

"Of course they do.... some of them. There are bullies in every school sadly. A lot of kids are actually a lot more tolerant than many grown ups are or give them credit for, on the other hand. A transgender child has to have certain special requirements at school naturally. That might mean some arrangements for the use of toilets or changing facilities and a considerable degree of understanding by the teachers and staff. Handled correctly there is no reason why a transgender child should stand out too much. At least they shouldn't stand out as long as they are in the gender role they feel they belong to. A kid who is forced to be the wrong gender is going to stand out like a sore thumb and attract all sorts of unwanted attention."

Jacqueline nodded. "Well that's been the problem so far with Chrissie."

"Well then you've already been down that route. Perhaps if Chrissie had simply gone to school as a girl then she might simply have blended in and been accepted."

"The school authorities would have to be very cooperative though wouldn't they?"

"Oh yes but you'll have an ally on that one Jackie. My daughter Elizabeth is coming to live with us here in Switzerland."

"Yes Sarah told me."

"Well Lizzie's a year older or perhaps a bit more than your Chrissie and I have to place her in school as well. They'll both be starting in a new primary school so you and I can go along and tackle the school together. If the school isn't ok with your Chrissie then I shan't be placing my daughter there either. After all she is the daughter of a gay woman and, not only that, she is the daughter of a publicly well-known gay woman. I shall require very firm assurances from the school that my

471

daughter's safety and privacy are assured."

"Do you think she might be bullied?"

"Oh no. Elizabeth is a pretty strong minded girl Jackie. Anybody who tries to bully her does so at their own peril. I'm more concerned about unwanted media attention and all the nuts that come with the price of fame."

"Yes I can see why you would be concerned there."

"Well then I need a school which is not only tolerant but also prepared to make special provisions to assure my child's safety. In some respects then we have similar needs Jackie. We'll go along to the school together. If they don't satisfy us that our kids' special needs are going to be met then we'll find somewhere else and it'll be their loss because our kids are something special."

"Oh God! Would you do that? I mean would you help me find somewhere safe for Chrissie?"

"Certainly. We can help each other in many ways Jackie. We're two families. All of us are going to need the inevitable babysitters and so on with our working obligations. I think we can support each other in all sorts of ways. There's another thing too. You say that Chrissie has never made any friends. Well I can say for certain that there is one person who will befriend her. Elizabeth is very precocious and she's perfectly aware of the meaning of transgender. It wouldn't worry her for a second. She naturally takes more vulnerable kids under her wing. It's her nature. She's always popular at school and something of an opinion leader. If I ask her to look after your Chrissie then it'll be a very brave bully (and there is no such thing) that gives your Chrissie a hard time. Lizzie would eat them for breakfast and then dance on the bones. She hates bullies with a passion."

"You mean your daughter would accept Chrissie for what he is?"

"I'd be prepared to bet money on it. My daughter

472

has a gay mother and she's been brought up to be tolerant and to understand how cruel people can be to those that are different. I think she'll empathise and bond with your daughter immediately."

"Oh God! That would be wonderful. Poor Chrissie's never been able to make friends properly."

"I think she's not the only one who needs some friends Jackie. I think you could do with some friends as well."

Jacqueline nodded solemnly. "You're not wrong there Danny. It seems like it's been me and Chrissie against the world for a long time."

"Well that must change Jackie." Daniela glanced at the clock. "Look before it gets any later let me try and phone Doc Marcie and see about that appointment."

Daniela rose to walk across the room to take the house phone and, after looking up the number on her mobile, dialled. Sarah poured some more coffee out for Jacqueline. "Whereabouts are you living now then Jackie?" she asked.

"We've got a little flat in Lisighaus Sarah but it's a bit too small for us I'm afraid. I looked at a ground floor flat in one of those newer houses in Schwendi the other day which would be better. The rent's a bit more expensive but if I'm working we should be able to cope."

"Schwendi huh? We'd almost be neighbours!"

"Yes it's just around the hillside."

An idea suddenly came to Sarah. "Hey if you're thinking of moving over to Schwendi there's a little cottage you might be interested in there."

"Really?"

"Yes it belongs to my boss and her girlfriend at the Hotel Toggenburg. They've used it previously as housing for the hotel's foreign staff in the winter season but Elke told me that they didn't need it as staff housing this winter. She was talking about renting it out for

473

skiing parties."

Jacqueline frowned. "It sounds like it might be beyond my budget Sarah. I mean she could probably charge far more to tourists."

"Not necessarily. She might be quite interested in having a longer term tenant with a reliable source of income. I don't think she'd put the rent astronomically high. She's a good friend of ours and I think she'd be sympathetic. It's worth trying in any case. It's a lovely little cottage. I think you'll like it."

"Well I could take a look certainly. I suppose there's no harm in asking."

"Great. I'll take you over to the hotel and introduce you."

"What about school and all that? I mean Schwendi's nice but it's a bit out of the way. The nearest primary school is in Wildhaus."

"Well it looks like both Chrissie and Elizabeth will be attending the same school Jackie so we can share the school runs if you like. Failing that there's a little mini bus that picks up the kids from the outlying farms and hamlets for school during term time."

"Oh that'll be handy. Does Schwendi get cut off much when it snows?"

"Only rarely. They keep the road down to Unterwasser pretty clear in the winter. We're not St Moritz or Davos here but this is a winter ski resort and the valley's well geared up to deal with snow in the winter."

It seemed as if Daniela had succeeded in reaching the clinic in Zurich for she suddenly spoke into the phone. "Oh hello. This is Daniela Devin speaking. I was wondering if Doctor Poillette is available. I mean is she busy at the moment? I can call back later if you wish... Oh really? Well may I speak to her please? Thank you." After a short pause Daniela was connected. "Hi Marcie! Danny Devin here. How are you keeping?" There followed a couple of minutes of exchanged courtesies before Daniela came to the point of her call. "Listen Marcie I need a favour. Do you have any slots available for consultations over the next couple of weeks or so? I know you're very busy but there's someone I'd like you to see if you can fit them in.... What's that? ... Oh well she's a lady who's a friend of mine with a young trans girl about eight years old.... Sorry... oh yes I think so....Well obviously that's up to you to decide professionally but I don't think I've ever seen a clearer case.... Oh could you? You're a sweetheart... Yes I think that will be fine. I'll have to ask of course but I don't think there'll be any problem. Thank you very much Marcie. I do appreciate it." There were a few more formalities before Daniela replaced the handset in triumph and turned to Jacqueline. "Sorted. You and Chrissie have an appointment with Doctor Poillette next Wednesday Jackie if that's all right with you."

"Of course it is. Thank you so much Danny. I don't know how to thank you enough."

"Please don't mention it. It's my pleasure."

"How do I find this clinic?"

"Ah well I was about to come to that. I have to spend most of next week in Zurich myself rehearsing with the band so you and Chrissie could drive through with me if you like and I can drop you off at the clinic and pick you up later somewhere."

"I've got a better idea." Sarah interposed. "If you're going to be practising all day Danny, then Jackie will be left to her own devices, with a young child, in Zurich for the day. If I drive you both through then I can spend the time with Jackie until you're finished. I need to go to town in any case to buy some things for Elizabeth's room. I was going to go to Winterthur but I can just as easily find what I need in Zurich and it'll be company for Jackie. I should imagine it'll be quite a difficult day for her and she might need someone to hold her hand."

Daniela smiled in agreement. "I think that's a fine idea Sarah."

Jacqueline looked overwhelmed. "Oh really. I can't ask the two of you to go to so much trouble."

"Nonsense." declared Sarah firmly. "It will be a pleasure." She turned to Daniela. "While you were on the phone Danny, Jackie was saying she's looking for a new place for her and Chrissie. I thought about that little cottage of Elke and Angelica's."

Daniela beamed hugely. "Brilliant. That would be perfect. You're a genius Sarah."

"Well we'll have to talk with Elke and Angelica."

"They'll go for it I'm sure. The bloody place has been stood empty since spring. I'm sure we can negotiate a reasonable rent and if Jackie wants to earn a little extra cash I'm sure Elke can always do with extra help in the hotel on occasion, assuming Jackie's not too busy in the pub and we're available for babysitting. I mean it's only a couple of minutes away."

Jacqueline shook her head in bewilderment. "Why are you two doing all this for me?" she asked in confusion.

"Because we *care* Jackie." Daniela told her. "I think your story and Chrissie's has touched our hearts. It sounds as if you've had too many bad breaks. I think you deserve better."

"Yes." agreed Sarah. "It's our pleasure to help out. That's what friends are for. I know we've only just met but I'd like you to consider yourself our friend. If you like I can take you around to meet Elke early this evening. Are you doing anything for the rest of the day?"

Jacqueline shook her head. "I didn't have any specific plans no."

"Well them why don't you stay for dinner and we can drive over to the hotel afterwards and I'll introduce you. There's another person we want you to meet as well. Our friend Nicole is coming over sometime or

476

other." Sarah glanced at the clock with a frown. "I don't know where the hell she's got to though. She was supposed to be here by now. She's going to be working at the pub as well. I'll give her a ring in a few minutes and see what's keeping her. Anyway, how about it?"

"Thank you Sarah. I would love to stay for dinner if it's not too much trouble."

"None at all." Sarah rose to clear the coffee cups and pot away. "I'll take these back to the kitchen unless anybody wants more coffee."

"Why don't you break out a bottle of wine Sarah?" suggested Daniela.

"Ok, Would you like a glass of wine Jackie?"

"Well perhaps just the one glass Sarah. I'd best not drink more than that because I'm driving."

"If you're staying for dinner one glass won't hurt you."

"Are you cooking Sarah?" asked Daniela.

"Well something simple perhaps. I'll have a look and see what we've got in. I'd best wait until I find out what Nicky's doing before I make a decision though. She might need feeding as well; and Charlie too, come to that. It would be just like the pair of them to forget to eat."

In the kitchen Sarah discovered a domestic crisis in progress. Chrissie, it appeared, had contrived to adorn himself with a substantial proportion of his blueberry tart and ice cream. Elrika was frantically endeavouring to repair the damage with a couple of tea towels and a notable lack of success. Sarah laughed and marched the penitent young child back into the living room to confront his mother; *her* mother, Sarah corrected herself. Jacqueline stared at him in astonishment. Chrissie was normally fastidiously delicate and careful while eating. "Chrissie!" she exclaimed. "What the hell have you been doing? Look at the state of you."

Sarah was embarrassed and apologetic. "It wasn't

Chrissie's fault Jackie." she explained. "I'm sorry but one of our cats is to blame. Lady Gaga decided that Chrissie couldn't possibly be expected to eat all that ice cream without help and so she jumped up to render assistance and managed only to knock the whole bowl all over Chrissie. I *am* sorry Jackie. I've banished Lady out into the garden as punishment."

Jacqueline groaned. "Oh God! And after all the trouble I went to dress him up nicely today. Who'd be a mother? I've got nothing with me to change him into either."

Daniela laughed. "Well since it's one of our moggies who's responsible Jackie we'll certainly pay for the cleaning."

Jacqueline waved a hand dismissively. "Oh please. There's no need. I'll just shove his clothes in the washer at home. Maybe I'd better pop back home and get him some clean clothes though. He can't stay for dinner in that state."

Daniela rubbed her chin thoughtfully. "Er I might have some clean clothes here that would fit Chrissie Jackie."

Jacqueline looked surprised. "You have kids' clothes?"

"Oh yes. I always have clothes for the occasions my daughter visits from America. I bought her loads of stuff when she was here last year and there was too much for her to carry back home. She'll have outgrown most of it by now but it should still fit Chrissie."

Jacqueline looked uncertain. "You mean... girl's clothes?"

"Well yes although there are some T-shirts and jeans and things that a boy might wear but..." Daniela hesitated coyly. "But why not let Chrissie wear something a bit girly?"

Jacqueline bit her lip in uncertainty. "I... I don't know... I mean do you think it would be all right?"

Chrissie intervened decisively. The little child's eyes lit up in hope. "Can I wear some girl's clothes mam? Please mam?"

Jacqueline surrendered with reservations. "Well all right if Miss Devin here has something er... suitable."

Daniela jumped up enthusiastically. "Oh I'm sure we can do that. Come with me Chrissie and let's see what we can find." Sarah hid a smile. She guessed that Daniela had been dying to put some girl's clothes on Chrissie. "Why don't you go and break out that wine you promised us Sarah?" Daniela continued. "You and Jackie can have a drink while Chrissie and I have a rummage about in the wardrobe?" She grasped Chrissie's hand and led the child eagerly upstairs.

Jacqueline watched them go with a haunted look on her face. "Oh God! I hope I'm doing the right thing." she murmured. "Do you think she's going to dress Chrissie up in something really girly Sarah?"

Sarah pulled a face. "I'd say there was a pretty good chance of it Jackie. Danny loves dressing people up. She got me to dress up like a girl after all and *that* took some doing. Before I met Danny I think I could have counted the number of times I wore a dress since I left school on the fingers of one hand. These days if I can get away with pulling a pair of jeans on for one day it's a result."

Jacqueline laughed. If she were to have any misgivings then Sarah was just the person to ameliorate them. Jacqueline was quite taken by the beautiful, warm hearted and sensible girl. In fact Jacqueline felt more at ease than she had in many a long day. She had felt somewhat intimidated at the prospect of being interviewed by the famous Daniela Devin but Daniela's gentle charm had quite disarmed her and Sarah's natural friendliness had completely won her over. She'd come looking for a job and found friendship and support where she had least expected it. Jacqueline felt her life had reached a turning point. She hadn't had the best of luck the last few years. Maybe that was about to change.

Sarah picked up her mobile phone. "I'd better give Nicky a buzz." she remarked before keying the number. When Nicole answered Sarah was in the mood to give her a piece of her mind. "Where the bloody hell *are* you?" she demanded indignantly. "The lady that's going to be working at the pub is here to meet you and you should have been here ages ago."

"Sorry Foxy. We're just on our way. We lost track of the time."

"Well get your arses over here pronto. It's rude to keep the lady waiting."

"We're on our way. See you soon."

"Wait a minute Nicky. Have you and Charlie eaten yet?"

"No not yet. Why?"

"Well do you want to stop for tea? I'm just about to start preparing for Danny, myself and our guests. I can just as easily cook for you and Charlie as well."

"That'd be great Sarah. I've got nothing in the house. Charlie and I were going to eat out."

"Ok then I'll see if I can rustle up a couple of extra stale crusts for you two. See you when you get here." Sarah signed off and turned to Jacqueline. "I'm sorry about that Jackie. It's too bad of Nicole not to be here on time. She's a lovely girl but she can be a right scatterbrain sometimes."

"Please it's nothing. Listen, if you're about to start preparing food, could you do with some help?"

"Oh there's no need really."

"But I'd love to help Sarah. I can't let you start to cook for six people without any help. I'm a dab hand in a kitchen anyway."

Sarah grinned. "Well ok come along then. At least we can have a glass of wine in the kitchen while I run through an inventory of my food stocks."

Daniela found the pair of them in the kitchen a few

minutes later; gossiping away with Elrika over a glass of wine as if they'd known each other for years. It was a touchingly domestic scene. Sarah was rummaging about in the cupboards looking for spices with a frown having extracted a couple of packs of chicken breasts from the fridge. Jacqueline had borrowed a pinafore and was sat at the kitchen table peeling potatoes while Elrika was washing a head of lettuce in the sink. Daniela grinned and, with the air of a magician pulling a rabbit from a hat, she gently ushered Chrissie through the door.

Sarah stopped what she was doing and gaped in astonishment. Chrissie was smiling shyly but her eyes were radiant with happiness even while she seemed a little apprehensive about her mother's reaction. Daniela had found her a beautiful pale pink ruffled dress and even a pair of girly slippers to match. She'd tied the dress at the waist with a bright pink sash and she'd found a string of red and white beads and a matching wrist bangle to accessorise the outfit. She'd even fixed Chrissie's hair and adorned it with a ribbon and an artificial rose. The result was astonishing. Any doubt that Sarah might have retained concerning Daniela's diagnosis of Chrissie's gender identity vanished instantly. Chrissie was transformed. The awkward, uncomfortable and unhappy little boy had disappeared to be replaced by a happy and extraordinarily pretty little girl completely at home in her best party frock. "Well what do you think?" asked Daniela, delighted with the affect her transformation had produced on the company.

"Why you're *beautiful*!" Sarah told Chrissie in wonderment. "You look just lovely."

Jacqueline shook her head in amazement. "My word!" she breathed at last. "I... I don't believe it. You're so *pretty* Chrissie." Chrissie grinned in sheer happiness as her mother so complemented her.

Possibly the funniest reaction came from Elrika. She nodded with satisfaction. "Ja! That's better." She declared firmly. "She looks very pretty Fräulein. She looks a lot nicer when you let her wear a dress." Daniela, Sarah and Jacqueline exchanged glances and suppressed their smiles. It was evident that Elrika had taken Chrissie for a girl all along whose mother had inexplicably dressed up as a boy.

Chrissie dashed to her mother. "Do I really look pretty mam?" she asked excitedly.

Jacqueline stared at her newly transformed child and Sarah could see that she was fighting the tears that threatened to overwhelm her. It was rare these days to see Chrissie looking so happy. It almost broke her heart. Jacqueline reached out and stroked Chrissie's hair fondly. "Yes. Yes you do."

Chrissie span around joyfully. "Can I wear this at home mam?" she asked hopefully.

Jacqueline fingered the material of the little dress uncertainly. "Well it doesn't really belong to us Chrissie." she told her. "Danny just leant us it for the afternoon honey and make sure you look after it because it's an expensive dress."

"Oh she can have it Jackie." Daniela told her. "It's too small for Lizzie now in any case. In fact I've got a lot of stuff Chrissie can have. Lizzie's grown out of most of them and there's no point in them gathering dust in the wardrobes."

"Oh really Danny..." Jacqueline protested. "I can't accept that."

"Of course you can. Elizabeth doesn't need the stuff anymore and I've got the feeling that Chrissie is going to need a new wardrobe."

"I... I don't know how to thank you."

Daniela smiled warmly. "The look in Chrissie's eyes when she saw that dress is all the thanks I need Jackie. It's an old party dress of Elizabeth's and Chrissie fell in love with it as soon as she saw it. So I thought we'd make this a little party day for Chrissie. Doesn't she look nice?"

"Yes.... yes he...I mean she does. I... I hardly recognised..." Jacqueline stumbled over the object pronoun, "*her*." Chrissie grinned from ear to ear to hear her gender so acknowledged by her mother. It made her happiness complete.

A noise from the front of the house caught Sarah's attention. "Ah that sounds like Nicky and Charlie at last. I'll go tell them we're in the kitchen." A few seconds later Sarah ushered Nicole and Charmaine in and introduced them. "Jackie this is Danny's new bass player Charmaine; we call her Charlie, and this is Nicole, our friend and Charlie's girlfriend. Nicky will be working with you at the pub."

Jacqueline held out her hand politely. "I'm pleased to meet you ladies."

Charmaine took the proffered hand. "We're pleased to meet you too." He eyes drifted to the pretty little girl hiding behind her mother. "And who's this little princess then?"

Sarah stepped in smoothly. "This is Jackie's daughter Charlie. This is Christine."

Chapter Twenty-Seven

At the weekend Jessica finally made her move although the action was not without a degree of domestic tension or unaccompanied by a certain amount of marital resistance. Her husband Damien had been quite frankly horrified by her plans at first; had put his foot down and firmly refused to countenance the whole mad scheme. Damien was an easy going man, usually quite content to allow his strong minded wife to dominate their relationship and to have her own way. Now, however, the dynamics had changed and his latent masculinity had asserted itself and demanded to be obeyed. When Jessica had announced that she intended to drive all the way down to Ticino in the south of Switzerland to confront her parents he had stood up and strongly forbidden her to do any such thing.

Jessica had been rather taken aback by this uncharacteristic resolution on the part of her husband, although she had been rather touched by his assertive protectiveness at the same time. Faced with such steadfast obduracy, Jessica had had to resort to feminine wheedling and cajoling to break down her husband's resistance. It had not been an easy task and, in the end, she had been forced to compromise. Under no circumstances whatsoever would Damien allow her to drive to Ticino alone. If she insisted upon going to Ticino then *he* would drive her there. He was not prepared to let her out of his sight for an instance. Thus, on Saturday morning, they loaded an overnight bag into the car and set off on the long drive south.

It promised to be an even longer journey than usual in fact. Jessica, ignominiously consigned to the passenger seat, tapped her foot in frustration. "For God's sake Damien honey." she moaned. "Can't you go a bit faster? There's a queue of traffic piling up behind us."

"I am *not* driving any faster." insisted Damien forcefully. "We'll get there in all good time and we'll get there *safely.*"

Jessica sighed. There was just no reasoning with men when their hormones were dictating their logic. She took a deep breath and resigned herself to their painfully slow progress. They took the E35 motorway skirting the shores of Lake Luzern to the small town of Altdorf at the southern tip of the lake before penetrating into the mountains to the south, climbing steadily towards the pass through the Adula Alps, where they formed the great divide between the temperate northern climes and the more Mediterranean climate of the southern, Italian speaking Canton of Ticino.

As they passed Andermatt and approached Goschenen, Jessica suggested, half-heartedly, that they take the high road over the pass for it was a spectacular route, bordered by the imposing peaks of the Pizzo Lucendro and the Pizzo Centrale, towering up to nearly three thousand metres and the road wound around the mountains crossing deep gorges, by way of dizzyingly high bridges, and skirting little alpine lakes. Damien vetoed the notion immediately. The weather was poor, with drizzling rain and sleet, and the pass climbed to over two thousand one hundred metres. Doubtless the sleet would turn to snow and ice on the narrow road over the pass and he refused to have anything to do with it or to imperil his cosseted wife's health and safety. Instead Jessica was forced to endure the long misery of the seventeen kilometre Gotthard road tunnel which arrowed as straight as a die through the middle of the mountains before emerging into a surprising burst of sunshine in the south.

This dramatic climatic change was characteristic of this journey. A cold and miserable day on the northern slopes of the mountains would often be transformed into

485

bright sunshine and Mediterranean warmth once one had passed through the barriers of the mountains into the south. It was well into the autumn yet the temperature as they dropped down into the valley of the River Ticino was still over twenty degrees and warm enough to lure guests into the gardens of the restaurants and grottoes of the innumerable charming stone villages of the Canton. Ticino was Switzerland but its culture and atmosphere was markedly Italian. Everything from the food to the architecture and from the language to the mentality of the inhabitants was infused with the culture of Italy. Even the flora became more Mediterranean in aspect and there were palm trees planted along the shores of the great deep lakes on the Italian borders of the Canton.

Jessica's parents lived alongside one of these great lakes. Their villa was perched on the side of a hill called the Monte Verita, "Hill of Truth" above the lakeside town of Ascona which nestled along the shore of the huge Lago Maggiore. It was a strange place to be a sanctuary for her parents' archaic homophobic intolerance Jessica thought to herself. It certainly wasn't in the traditions of the Monte Verita. Starting in the very first years of the twentieth century, the hill had a slightly scandalous history of libertarian anarchy and Bohemian progressiveness that had raised many an eyebrow in the conservatively Catholic Canton.

A man called Henry Oedenkoven from Antwerp had purchased the hill in 1900 and established a colony based on a form of primitive socialism. The colony had eschewed all personal property; rejected all notions of nationalism or party and religious dogma and held to their own rigid codes of morality. Even more startling the colony had enforced a strict code of behaviour and lifestyle among its members. Normal conventions of marriage had been rejected and vegetarianism and nudism had been obligatory. They had championed women's rights, non-nationalistic societies, the arts,

486

dance and music and even dabbled in mystic freemasonry. If the other inhabitants of the Canton had looked somewhat askance at this eccentric collection of free thinkers occupying the hill they had nevertheless attracted many other like-minded characters to the colony and it had become a haven for writers, artists, anarchists and radical philosophers. It had boasted such luminaries as Herman Hesse and Carl Jung among the visitors to the colony among numerous others. Even Daphne Du Maurier, who wrote a short story based on the colony and was reputedly not averse to the attractions of her own sex herself, probably visited there. The colony had petered out in the middle of the century but its legacy had remained and it seemed an altogether unlikely place to find conservative bigotry of the type that Sarah's parents had apparently embraced.

After driving through the attractive small town of Locarno and the outskirts of the even more attractive town of Ascona, Jessica and Damien mounted the hill and finally pulled into the driveway of Jessica's parents' villa. Jessica felt a slightly fearful and excited twinge at the sight of the big villa and its large garden. The last time she had been here was the occasion of the fateful party her parents had thrown to announce Sarah's engagement in the summer. That party had ended in unmitigated disaster after Sarah had been publicly shanghaied into having an engagement ring thrust onto her finger without her consent. It had been a disgraceful exhibition and the general consensus among the guests had been that the Fuchs' had sold their daughter off to the highest bidder to further her father's business dealings and her mother's social ambitions. Many had been sympathetic but expected the compliant Sarah to accede to her parents' wishes and marry the son of the wealthy Herr Berger. It had shocked the inner core of Ticino society, to which her mother belonged, when Sarah had broken the engagement the very next day and fled back to her valley in the north of Switzerland in complete defiance of her parents. Sarah's estrangement from her parents was now common knowledge and the subject of much local gossip and speculation. Jessica wondered just how much of the truth the gossip mongers really knew.

The villa seemed deserted and her mother's car was not in the drive. Jessica wondered if perhaps she should have called in advance to announce her arrival. Encouragingly, however her father's BMW was present and when she tried the front door it proved to be unlocked. She stepped into the house and called out. Her father emerged from his study and gazed at her in delighted astonishment. "Jessica!" he thundered. "What a wonderful surprise. And Damien too. What on earth brings you two down here?"

Jessica stepped forward to accept her father's embrace with a laugh. "Just a flying visit dad. How are you?"

"Fine... just fine. My God! Let me look at you. You're a sight for sore eyes. How long are you staying?"

"Just for tonight dad. We're driving home tomorrow."

"Good, good. You'll be staying here of course."

"Oh Dad we didn't want to put you and mum to any trouble. We can just as easily take a hotel room for the night."

"Nonsense! I won't hear of it. We've plenty of room here for you. Your mother wouldn't dream of letting you stay at a hotel."

"Well all right dad. Where is mum anyway?"

"Just gone out to the shops. She'll be back shortly I should think. Come along it's a lovely day so let's go out into the garden and have a drink."

"You're not too busy are you dad? You looked as if you were working in your study."

"Nothing that can't wait Jess. I'm not so busy I

can't find time for my own daughter. Come on I've got a fine bottle of wine to open."

Jessica caught Damien's eye flashing a warning at her. "Er not for me dad." she apologised hastily. "I'd better stick to mineral water or a fruit juice if you can squeeze its tail for that. You and Damien go ahead though."

Mr Fuchs frowned but didn't press her. "Very well then. I'm sure we've got some pineapple juice somewhere. Have you two eaten?"

"Well I was about to come to that dad. If you and mum are not too busy tonight we'd like to take you out for dinner in Ascona this evening somewhere."

"We'd love to join you for dinner Jess but you're our guests. Dinner will be on us."

Jessica shook her head firmly. "No dad. Not this time. This time we insist on paying for dinner. This is our treat."

Mr Fuchs looked uncertain. "Are you sure Jess?"

"Of course I'm sure dad. We're not impoverished you know. Treating my parents to dinner isn't going to break the bank. Anyway it's a special occasion. We've got news for you."

"What sort of news?"

"We'll wait until mum gets back. It's a surprise!"

Out in the garden they gathered around a garden table and Mr Fuchs opened a bottle of Chianti Classico Riserva for Damien and himself whilst Jessica nursed a glass of pineapple juice. Jessica let her father talk on animatedly. He seemed upbeat and delighted to see her but Jessica suspected that all was not well. He was reticent about talking of his business and, reading between the lines, Jessica detected the hint that things were not too rosy on that front. The clash over Sarah's engagement had had repercussions in that it had caused a breach between her father and Herr Berger's business consortium with the subsequent loss of Herr Berger's financial input and patronage. Her father was fighting a desperate rearguard action to repair the damage but there was no doubt that he had taken a considerable financial hit and was having to trim back. There was a mood of austerity in the air. On a positive note, Mr Fuchs seemed to have some chance of securing a deal with certain American businesses by which he hoped to salvage some of the wreckage from the Berger débâcle. He was hoping to fly out to America in December to finalise the details.

Damien discussed his own projects with his father in law and Mr Fuchs seemed interested and questioned him closely. For her part, Jessica was content to let the two men discuss business and bided her time. Finally, as the two men began to run out of steam, she casually changed the conversation. "Have you heard from Sarah at all dad?" she inquired innocently.

Jessica observed the wince of pain that crossed her father's face. He took a deep breath to compose himself. "No Jess... not a word. I was rather hoping you might have heard from her."

Jessica shook her head. "I've not talked to her personally for a couple of weeks dad. I was going to run over to the Toggenburg one of these days to see her but I'm not sure where she's living now. She's moved out of the cottage in the Alpli of course. I suppose I could phone her up to ask her new address or, failing that, Nicole will probably know where she's living. I'm a bit reluctant to do that however because she seems a bit cagey about her personal details for the moment and I'm not sure she'll appreciate somebody barging in on her private life. She's a tad defensive about this girlfriend of hers and she's apt to become prickly when somebody starts snooping around her."

Mr Fuchs frowned. "I really can't understand her anymore. I never had any reason, before this summer, to believe that she was so deceitful and or that she ever withheld secrets from us. Now it's just one long string of deception."

Jessica sighed theatrically. "Oh Dad! You can't say that. Half her life has been a deception for heaven's sake. I think being gay and not mentioning the fact until this summer counts as a pretty important withheld secret don't you think? But you can't blame her for that. You only have to look at the evidence of you and mum's reaction to her telling the truth to realise that she had every good reason for concealing it from you. You can hardly berate her for not telling the truth when you more or less cast her out into the wilderness when she does do."

Mr Fuchs mastered his irritation. "We haven't cast her out Jessica. If she's in the wilderness it's a wilderness of her own making. She's welcome back in this house whenever she wants."

"Under whose terms dad? Is she welcome back as your gay daughter or as the obedient little Sarah who always did what mummy and daddy told her to and had to hide the fact that she was gay?"

Mr Fuchs took a deep breath. "What I mean Jessica is that at least she could come and talk to us. She refuses even to answer your mother's messages. She won't tell me who this woman she's having a relationship with is and she won't even tell us where she's living for God's sake. It's intolerable that I don't even know where my youngest daughter is living. I've been worried to death about her. What's she living on for heaven's sake? She hasn't got that much money in the bank and working in a hotel isn't going to pay a great deal. It's out of season, anyway, in the Toggenburg right now so God only knows if she's got any work at all. I'm not trying to judge her here but I need to know that she's all right. If she's short of money I'm sure we can arrange something. I'm not so bankrupt yet that I'll let a child of mine go hungry, whatever has happened between us."

Jessica hid a smile. "I suppose you'd want

491

reassurances that any money you forked out to keep your poor destitute daughter from having to beg on the streets wouldn't be squandered on her girlfriend of course."

"Well naturally. I can hardly be expected to support this other woman as well. I don't even know who she is since Sarah chooses not to reveal her identity."

Jessica laughed. "Well dad I don't think you can blame her for that. Sarah has a pretty solid grounding in knowing people's homophobic reactions to their being gay. I don't know the full story but I'd guess that, for some reason or other, her girlfriend doesn't want it to become public knowledge that she's gay. For all we know her family might have just as negative an opinion on the subject as Sarah's and Sarah will doubtless sympathise with her desire to keep it quiet. Or it may be that Sarah wants to protect her girlfriend from her own family and their associates. After all this summer you were talking about confronting this scarlet woman you believed had corrupted your precious daughter and the Bergers were downright threatening towards her."

"I only want to know her identity Jessica. Surely I have the right to know who my daughter is seeing. This woman could be anyone. She could be exploiting Sarah. I have the right to know that no harm is coming to my daughter."

Jessica shook her head bemusedly. "You and mum are something else dad. One minute you want nothing to do with Sarah's girlfriend and the next you're demanding your parental rights to know everything about her. I wish you'd make up your minds."

"I just want to know that my daughter is all right Jessica."

Jessica grinned and reached into her handbag for her mobile phone. "Well I think I might be able to reassure you on that point dad. I haven't seen Sarah for some time but Maria has. Sarah went through to Appenzell to see her." Jessica opened the screen on her phone and fiddled for a minute or so before the image she was looking for appeared on the screen. "This is a picture Maria asked one of her friends to take of her and Sarah on her mobile dad. She sent me the photo. Here.... take a look. Take a look at your miserably impoverished daughter."

Mr Fuchs took the apparatus from Jessica and stared at the image in disbelief. It was the photo that the waitress had taken of Maria and Sarah resting on the front of Daniela's Ferrari in the car park of the restaurant in Wasseraun. "My God!" breathed Mr Fuchs. "Whose car is that?"

"Sarah's girlfriend's apparently dad. Sarah borrowed it for the day to drive through to Appenzell. Sharp set of wheels for somebody on the breadline right?"

"My God! It's a Ferrari 430 Spider convertible." gasped Mr Fuchs who was a bit of an enthusiast for automobiles. "That's a very expensive car."

"Yep so I'd keep your money in your pocket if I was you dad. It doesn't look like Sarah needs it right now. Being male, of course, you only noticed the car. If you take a closer look at Sarah though you'll see she's wearing one expensive designer frock not to mention some serious bling. Maria had the chance for a good look at Sarah's costume jewellery and yes those *are* real rubies on that necklace and her earrings. Now I may be wrong but Sarah does not have the impression of somebody in desperate need of a handout dad. In fact if you're in need of some finances to bail out the business, I'd seriously consider going along, cap in hand, to your daughter's household if I was you."

"Is this woman rich then Jess or is her money from her family?"

"I've no idea dad. It makes you think though doesn't it? I mean if this girl's being supported in luxury by her parents it might explain why she and Sarah are going to such lengths to conceal the fact that they're shacked up in a lesbian relationship together mightn't it? If her parents disapproved they might pull the plug on her."

"Did Sarah say anything to Maria about where this woman's money comes from?"

"Very little dad. She mentioned something about her being a business woman but, if Sarah is to be believed, she seems a bit young. She's only a few years older than Sarah."

Mr Fuchs frowned. "I don't like it. There's something rotten here. I don't like the idea of Sarah being supported by the wealth of this woman's family."

"Why ever not dad? You were perfectly willing to see her supported by Alan's family's wealth."

"That's different."

"Why?"

Mr Fuchs had to think about that one. Finally he seemed to find some distinguishing factor. "Well for one thing Jess Alan's family were aware of the relationship between Alan and Sarah."

Jessica snorted contemptuously. "Hmmph! As far as I can see there *was* no relationship. There was an *arrangement*. Alan was abroad most of the time and Sarah was gay and couldn't care less whether he was home or not in any case. Hardly sounds like a relationship to me. Anyway we're only speculating whether or not this girl's parents know anything about Sarah. For all we know they might have taken her into the bosom of the family like a long lost daughter and Sarah's got quite different reasons for hiding her girlfriend from view."

Mr Fuchs looked thoughtful. "Hmm...possibly." He bit his lip and cogitated for a moment. "Do you really think there was no relationship between Sarah and Alan?"

"Of course there wasn't dad. How could there be?

Whenever I met Sarah she hardly ever used to even talk about Alan and if she did mention him it was only in passing and not with any great enthusiasm. She didn't exactly appear love struck. I think she could take him or leave him. To be honest I think she found him mildly irritating if anything. I know for a fact that they hardly ever slept together and it didn't bother Sarah in the least. I thought she was sexless. Well now I know better."

Mr Fuchs looked unconvinced. "She always seemed perfectly happy about him to me."

Jessica shook her head firmly. "No dad. She was happy because *you* were happy. That was what it was about all along. That's why she stayed so long in a sham relationship with a man she didn't love. It was because it made *you* happy; made *you* proud of her. All her life she wanted to make you happy with her and proud of her and she couldn't bear to tell you that the relationship you'd engineered for her and had such high hopes for was a meaningless charade. She just went through the motions. She went through the motions until you set the date for her marriage and she finally woke up to the realisation that her marriage was supposed to be about what made *her* happy."

"Do you think she's happy now Jess?"

Jessica regarded her father with surprise. "It's taken you a long time to ask that question dad."

"Nonsense. I've been concerned about her welfare all along."

"Her welfare perhaps, her financial security probably, but not simply if she's happy or not. You're finally asking the right question."

"Well are you going to damn well answer it?"

Jessica nodded slowly. "Yes dad. Yes I think she is happy. I don't know all the problems Sarah has with this girlfriend of hers and I suspect there might be some but I think she's happy in spite of that. I think this is the first time in her life that she's really been in love with

495

someone. I know she must be in love simply because of the sacrifice she made for this girl, whoever she might be. She risked the most important thing in her life for this girl; her family. I know that the afternoon I drove her to the station in Bellinzona, after she handed Alan back his ring and left you that infamous letter, she was in bits; convinced that she'd lost her family for good. It didn't deter her from her course however. All she wanted to do, right then, was to fly back to her Toggenburg and the woman she loved. I've never seen such single minded determination in her. I'd say it was the single most important thing in her life. That's the action of a woman in love. Sure she's happy."

Mr Fuchs picked up Jessica's phone once more and looked at the image frozen on the screen. He had to admit that Sarah looked stunning in her red dress but there was more. She looked radiant. She had that same look about her he fondly remembered from the days they spent together hiking in the mountains; that same look of unfettered joy and pleasure in the wonder of life. There was another thing as well. The red dress on her was bold; startlingly so, but Sarah carried it with grace and ease. He'd never expected to see his little Sarah so boldly dressed and exuding such confidence. But this wasn't his little Sarah anymore. This was a grown woman, confident and assured with her own mind and life to live. His little girl was gone for good. He felt a lump in the back of his throat. There came an aching grief in his soul. "What... what was Sarah doing with Maria in Appenzell anyway?" he croaked at last.

"They were discussing the wedding dad. Specifically they were discussing the guest list."

Mr Fuchs took a breath. "I see."

"Yes dad. Maria wanted to officially invite Sarah to her wedding...." Jessica paused dramatically. "with her girlfriend."

Mr Fuchs placed Jessica's phone back on the table

with deliberate carefulness and composed himself. "Your mother will never agree to that Jessica."

Jessica raised her eyebrow. "So what's she going to do dad; boycott her only son's wedding?"

"Of course not. She wouldn't dream of missing John's wedding. What I mean is that she will never agree to Sarah bringing her girlfriend."

"Well fortunately it's not up to her dad. She's not organising this wedding and she sure as hell doesn't have veto powers over the sodding guest list. It's Maria's big day and if she wants to invite Sarah's girlfriend then mum will just have to lump it."

Mr Fuchs ran a hand through his hair agitatedly. "We already knew that John and Maria wanted Sarah to bring her girlfriend Jess although it wasn't official as yet. Your mother is quite adamant about the matter I'm afraid. She refuses to entertain the idea of Sarah bringing her girlfriend along. We have to find some way to persuade Sarah to leave the girl at home. Surely she can be made to see reason on this."

"Why should she?"

"Well just to maintain decency and harmony on the day and not risk ruining John and Maria's wedding day with an unpleasant confrontation."

"The only thing risking that dad is mum's unreasoning homophobia. If you want to maintain decency and harmony, I suggest you persuade mum to leave her *bigotry* at home."

"Be reasonable Jess. Your mother's not keen on the idea of Sarah coming to the wedding at all let alone with her girlfriend. It will take a good deal of persuading her to even be seen with Sarah in public at the moment. We'll never sell her on the idea of this girlfriend of Sarah's as well. I'm sure this girl Sarah's seeing doesn't know John and Maria so she's hardly going to be put out at not being invited to their wedding. Surely Sarah's willing to be flexible on this point."

"Oh yes dad. Sarah's willing to flexible all right. She's so willing to be flexible that she's prepared to stay away from the wedding altogether if her mother finds her so embarrassing to be seen with."

Mr Fuchs squirmed visibly. "Well I'm sure there's no need for her to go to that extreme Jess. I think your mother could be persuaded to be civil to her for one day as long as Sarah is alone and prepared not to make any public scandal."

"That is not an option dad. Sarah would have to tell the woman she loves that she is not allowed to accompany her because her family finds her presence offensive. She is not prepared to do that and I can fully understand why. In preference to that she would far rather stay away. Naturally she would love to be there at the wedding but from a misguided notion of noble sacrifice she considers it better that she avoids any risk of scandal ruining John and Maria's wedding and is willing to absent herself from proceedings."

Mr Fuchs looked sad. "Well it seems a shame for Sarah not to be at her brother's wedding but perhaps it is best after all."

"Sarah will be at that wedding dad."

"But you just said..."

Jessica's temper had been simmering for some time but now she lost patience. "For Christ's sake dad! Haven't you been listening? Sarah *will* be at that wedding. John would be *outraged* if his kid sister felt that she was unwelcome at his wedding because of our mother's blasted medieval narrow mindedness. So would Maria. They both insist that Sarah comes and furthermore they are adamant that her girlfriend is welcome too. That means that you and mum will either have to put up with that or boycott your own son's wedding. Now I realise that you've got a bit of previous when it comes to shunning your offspring's nuptials..."

Damien had held his peace until this moment but

now he intervened hastily. "There's no need to bring that up now Jess."

"I think there's every bloody need. You and mum deliberately and premeditatedly refused to attend my wedding dad and thus soured the happiest day of my life. You cut me and Damien off; ostracised us; tossed us out into the wilderness just because you haughtily disapproved of my choice of husband."

Mr Fuchs waved his hands palms down in a conciliatory gesture. "Now, now Jess. We've made our apologies for that long ago. We were wrong and...."

"Shut up dad! I haven't finished. Right now your apologies are *not* accepted. You and mum cut Damien and I out of your lives and right now you're doing exactly the same thing to Sarah. You didn't even turn up for her graduation. Have you any idea how devastating that must have been for her? All through her university studies the thing that kept her going was the thought that she wanted to make you proud of her. She worked her ass off to that end throughout university and as a result finished top in her entire year group with a first class degree. She was so happy at the thought that you would be proud of her and then what happened? You dismissed all her hard work at university as irrelevant since she would be marrying Alan and had no need of a university degree and then, since it turns out she's gay and isn't going to marry Alan after all, you turn your noses up in disapproval and don't even bother to show up for her graduation. Bang! Three years of hard work and dedication thrown down the toilet and her big day is ruined just as my wedding day was.

"Now you're threatening to do the same to John's big day. How the hell would John be able to explain to people why his kid sister wasn't at the wedding? Or, if Sarah is there, why his parents feel unable to attend? What kind of family are we supposed to appear before Maria's family and relations? What will Maria's parents think about their daughter marrying into a family that just throws its children out into the cold because they happen to fall in love with somebody they don't approve of? Whatever happened to notions of unconditional parental love? Well I've had enough of it and so has John. This rift has to end and it has to end now."

Mr Fuchs wrung his hands in agitation. His eldest daughter with her dander up was a formidable opponent. "Jessica, Jessica. Nobody regrets the situation more than I do but you've got to try and understand your mother's point of view. There have been developments since we last spoke. It seems as if the true story of Alan and Sarah's break up has become known among our friends and acquaintances."

Jessica groaned. "Oh Christ! I'll bet a barrel of gold against a bucket of pig shit that the Bergers are behind that."

Mr Fuchs nodded. "I don't think you're far wrong Jess. Certainly your mother and I have not divulged that information and the only other person who saw Sarah's letter outside of our family was Alan. Doubtless he's told his parents and they've spread it about. Presumably they were only too eager to disseminate the information that Sarah is gay since the alternative explanation (which was commonly rumoured by the way) that Sarah broke up with Alan because she felt herself being pressurised into an arranged marriage, reflected badly on them. I suppose it was their way of regaining the moral high ground."

Jessica snorted contemptuously. "Hmmph! Moral high ground my arse. Low life muck raking is more like it."

"Well whatever their motivations it seems as if they've pretty much exposed Sarah as a lesbian."

"Well so what? So the whole of Ticino society now knows that Sarah's gay. Big deal. Who gives a shit?"

"Well your mother for one Jessica. She's mortified. All her friends are talking about it, it seems. Naturally your mother thinks it reflects badly on her."

"Oh for crying out loud! This is her *daughter* for fuck's sake. Are you truly telling me that the opinion of a bunch of small minded, shallow, gossiping socialite bimbos is more important to her than her own daughter? I wouldn't give them the time of day personally. They're fucking hypocrites; all of them. Tell the lot of them to go to hell."

"I don't think she'll see it in that light Jessica. Your mother has always been conscious of her social standing."

"Well she's going to have to grow up and start understanding what's really important in life dad. I intend to tell her that."

"Really Jessica I don't think this is the best time to talk to her about this."

Jessica shook her head firmly. "No dad. I disagree. This has gone too far. I haven't driven all the way down to Ticino just to pander to mum's bloody prejudices and social ambitions. I refuse to sit back and watch my family self-destruct any longer. I mean to have it out with her."

Chapter Twenty-Eight

When Mrs Fuchs finally arrived back at the villa, she was delighted to find her eldest daughter and Damien present but her pleasure was somewhat dampened by the obvious undercurrents surrounding the familial reunion. Jessica had a look of steely determination about her that boded ill for any thought of family harmony and Damien and Mr Fuchs were squirming uncomfortably. Even a superficial analysis was sufficient to suggest that there was a monumental row in the making. Nevertheless Jessica was civil to her mother and, in accordance with the original plan, insisted upon treating her parents out to dinner. Being less familiar with the Ticino Jessica surrendered the choice of restaurant to her father. Mr Fuchs was somewhat relieved by this. He was able to choose a small rustic restaurant at Intragna; a lovely little village in the Centovalli a few kilometres from Ascona. The restaurant served excellent food but its prime attraction, as far as Mr Fuchs was concerned, was that it was out of the way, quiet and very private. He had no wish to air the family skeletons with a confrontation in one of the busier, more public locations in Ascona.

In spite of the rather rustic nature of her husband's choice, Mrs Fuchs still insisted upon dressing for dinner. Mrs Fuchs was the kind of woman to whom it was unthinkable to be seen in public not looking her very best even if the public appearance consisted of a cosy family dinner in an obscure country restaurant where the chances of being seen by the higher echelons of Ticino society were negligible. As a result her long suffering family had to endure a seemingly interminable wait whilst Mrs Fuchs perfected her appearance in the privacy of her boudoir. Jessica tapped her foot in impatience. She rather suspected that her mother had ulterior motives for her lengthy preparations. She was probably aware, by now, that there was some sort of battle looming in the offing and doubtless she wanted to be fully power dressed for the coming show down. Gucci, Prada and Versace were essential weapons to have about your person when entering a combat zone in Mrs Fuchs' opinion.

Jessica was in an equally combative mood however and, once her mother was fully decked in her finery, Jessica overruled Damien's objections and insisted upon taking the wheel of the car to drive to Intragna. In truth Damien didn't put up too much resistance for both he and Mr Fuchs had already drunk a couple of glasses of wine. The next round went to Jessica's mother however for she insisted that they take Mr Fuchs car. The car that Jessica and Damien had driven to Ticino in was a perfectly functional, reliable automobile but even Jessica was bound to concede that it had seen better days. Damien had been talking about buying a new car for some time but they already had two cars and Jessica had considered it an unnecessary expense. Be that as it may, Mrs Fuchs was adamant that they could not roll up to some restaurant behind the wheel of a vehicle that, in her opinion, was better suited to the social graces of the demolition derby at the stock car races. Jessica conceded the point to her mother without too much objection. She rarely got the chance to drive her father's expensive BMW and she relished the chance to get her hands on it even if her enjoyment of it was rather suppressed by the nagging of no less than three back seat drivers all bleating at her to slow down.

Discussions of serious matter were suspended for the course of the meal. The lovely little restaurant was lit by candle light and warmed by a log fire. The food it must be said was superb. They started with antipasto of roasted vegetables and sun dried tomatoes in olive oil accompanied by olives and slivers of cured meats. There was a delicious Bocconcini salad of chicory, celery, rocket, green pepper and cherry tomatoes topped with bite sized balls of mozzarella cheese in a lemon and olive oil dressing and, for a main course, they ate tender chicken breasts stuffed with parmesan cheese and wrapped in prosciutto ham on a bed of regional saffron risotto. The excellence of the food, the fine wine Mr Fuchs ordered and the cosy environment all helped to pacify the underlying tension and Mr Fuchs was beginning to hope that the evening might pass without hostilities breaking out. It was a forlorn hope. Jessica was in no mood to take prisoners.

At the conclusion of the meal they ordered espressos. To be more precise, Damien and Jessica's parents ordered espressos. Jessica, to her disgust, received such a withering look of disapproval from her husband that she felt duty bound to settle for a cup of camomile tea instead. To compound her irritation Jessica also had to forego the customary cigarette which she habitually enjoyed at the end of a meal. In spite of these minor annoyances, however, Jessica was by no means in a bad humour. In fact she was feeling serenely confident. She had had many battles with her strong willed mother over the years and they were usually exhausting. In point of fact, although both women would have scoffed at the notion, any neutral observer would have quickly discerned that they were remarkably alike in some respects. They were both possessed of the same single minded obstinacy and steely determination. They were, under normal circumstances, a formidable match for each other. But these were *not* normal circumstances. For once, all the cards were in Jessica's hands and she had a decisive ace up the sleeve.

Jessica bided her time as the rest of the party sipped coffee. The tension was growing by the instance. Her father, in some vain hope of defusing the forthcoming explosion, ordered a round of grappa; strong Italian style pomace brandy often drunk as an after dinner digestif. Jessica, as designated driver, had a good excuse to decline and merely waited, content in the knowledge that her father had already hastily consulted with her mother over the matter of the discussion on the table. The battle lines were drawn and she only had to conduct herself with patience for her mother to make the first move.

Finally, unable to contain herself any longer, her mother swung onto the offensive. "Your father told me, before we left the house, Jessie, that you'd discussed John's wedding while you were waiting for me."

"Yes," agreed Jessica airily, "We did touch upon the subject briefly."

Mrs Fuchs glared at her daughter. "Is it true what your father has told me Jessica?"

"Er I could do with some specifics here mum. I have no idea what dad's been telling you."

"He says that you told him that Sarah was going to be at the wedding."

Jessica affected a look of puzzlement. "I would hardly have thought that was new information mum. Sarah's is John's kid sister who he loves very much. I would have thought it patently obvious that she would be invited to the wedding."

Mrs Fuchs took a deep breath. "Why was I not consulted?"

"Er... possibly because it's none of your damn business who John and Maria decide to invite to their wedding. You're not on the organising committee you know. You're just a guest albeit an honoured one. You don't have veto rights over the invitation list."

"I think at least that John should have asked me."

"Do you? Well I don't. John and Maria will have their friends and loved ones to their wedding irrespective of whether you approve of them or not. I'm sure that there are going to be people at that wedding that I can't

505

stand the sight of but I'm not about to be presumptuous enough to think I have the right to take issue over it."

"It's not the same thing Jessica."

"No you're right. Me disapproving of one of Maria's dodgy uncles isn't in the same league as the groom's mother turning her nose up at his sister and her own daughter."

"I am not turning my nose up at her."

"Then why do you feel that there is any reason that you should have been consulted about it?"

"Don't be obtuse Jessica. You know damn well why."

"No. I'm afraid that I don't. It all seems very straightforward to me. John is getting married and therefore he will want all his family present on his big day. Sarah is his youngest sister and therefore, quite naturally, will be on the guest list. All seems pretty cut and dried from where I am."

"It is nothing of the sort. Your father tells me that she intends to bring this woman she's having an affair with to the wedding."

"It's not how I would describe it mum. "Having an affair" implies some sort of casual, possibly clandestine, fling. Since Sarah now shares a house together with her partner I think we can consider the affair settled. Nevertheless, your premise is more or less correct... Sarah will be accompanied by her girlfriend."

"Absolutely out of the question!"

"You're right. There's no question about it at all. Sarah will be at John and Maria's wedding and so will her girlfriend. The discussion is at an end."

"I cannot permit it."

"You're not in a position to do anything else mother dearest. It's not *your* wedding. You could choose who the hell you wanted if it was you who was getting married but it isn't and you have no rights to forbid the presence of anyone you disapprove of."

"I shall have words with John...."

"I'd suggest that you have words with Maria while you're at it?"

"What's Maria got to do with it?"

"A considerable amount I would have thought. She's the bloody bride for heaven's sake. This is going to be her big day. All John has to do is comb his hair, brush his teeth, climb into his tux and turn up at the church on time. Maria's the girl calling the shots and she has personally, and formally, invited Sarah and her girlfriend. If you want to argue the toss with her then good luck on that one. Personally, I wouldn't relish the thought of taking Maria to task over something she's set her mind on. She's not a girl noted for taking prisoners."

"This is absurd Jessica. We can't allow this to happen."

"At the risk of repeating myself, "we" have no say in the matter. Maria has made her mind up so we just put our best frocks on and try not to disgrace our family name in front of the bride's family."

"Surely Maria can be made to see sense."

"The person not making any sense right now is you mother. When you were writing the invitations for Sarah's wedding you included Maria as the girlfriend of Sarah's brother. There is absolutely no difference in this instance. Maria would consider it downright rude not to invite Sarah's partner as well."

"I shall have to speak with Maria's family. Surely they can dissuade her from this lunacy."

Jessica's temper flared. She rapped sharply on the table. "You'll do no such damn thing! There's enough disgrace hanging over our family as it is without you adding to it by going to the bride's family to persuade them to ostracise your own daughter."

Mrs Fuchs reeled under the assault. "I'm not the one bringing the disgrace...."

"Yes you damn well are! You are disgracing this

507

family with your homophobia. You're disgracing this family by cutting off your own daughter at the very time she needs your love and support the most."

Jessica's father jumped in hastily. "That will do Jessie. We're not going to solve anything by losing our tempers."

Jessica turned on him. "There is nothing to *solve* dad. There is no problem other than my mother's pig headed bigotry. Everybody, including Maria's family, is perfectly in agreement that Sarah should be accompanied to the wedding by her girlfriend with the exception of the groom's mother. She's the only problem there is. Everyone else is "hello... welcome to the 21st century". Only mum is still stuck back in the dark ages thinking that her youngest daughter is somehow a blight on the family name just because she happens to be gay. Well I'm sick of it do you hear? I will not have my family shamed in front of all the wedding guests because of my mother's archaic prejudice. Sarah and her girlfriend will be honoured guests at that wedding mum so you'd better start shaping up and dealing with it."

Mrs Fuchs flushed bright red. "You can't expect me to be associated with this woman Sarah is seeing."

Jessica regarded her coolly. "So what are you going to do mum? Not turn up at your own son's wedding? Becoming a bit of a pattern this isn't it... missing the wedding days of your children I mean?"

Mrs Fuchs blushed and lowered her eyes. "Of course I... I want to come."

Jessica softened her voice. "Then come mum and be welcome, and, while you're at it, try to be civil to the girl that your daughter is in love with. I know you can do it. You're the most charming hostess I've ever known when you set your mind to it."

"You can't expect me to talk to this woman."

"Oh but I can. In fact I insist upon it. You are currently the matriarch of this family and I expect you to set a good example of family unity and leadership. We all love you very much mum and we value your love in return. We don't expect that love to come with conditions attached. We can all go to John's wedding a united family or we can go terminally dysfunctional and divided for all the world to see. The choice is yours and yours alone."

"But... but what will people think..."

"They will think that we are a loving family and that Maria is marrying into a clan who will love her and cherish her come what may. That's what they'll think. We have to set an example in front of all the guests and there's another guest coming to that wedding that I haven't mentioned yet."

Mrs Fuchs raised an eyebrow. "What other guest? Surely Sarah's not bringing somebody else."

"Not Sarah. I'm bringing somebody."

"Do we know them?"

"Unlikely since I've only just made their acquaintance myself."

"Well who is it?"

"One of the company present of course. One of the five people at this table."

Mr Fuchs sat bolt upright. "One of the *five* people? Jessie! You can't mean...."

"Yes dad. I can!"

"Oh my God!"

Mrs Fuchs was floundering. "What... what do you mean?"

Jessica grinned. "What I mean mum is that the newest member of the family is sat right opposite you and trying to persuade me that a big jar of pickled gherkins and smoked kippers would be a suitable late night supper before bedtime. You're going to be a grandmother/"

Mr Fuchs rose from his seat with a roar of delight and hugged his daughter to him in a great bear hug. "My

God Jessie! This is wonderful news."

His wife sat stunned for a moment before, to everybody's astonishment, bursting into tears; tears of sudden joy. She rose unsteadily to her feet to grasp Jessica in her turn. "But this is marvellous. Oh Jessica! Why didn't you *tell* us?"

"We *are* telling you. Why do you think we've driven all the way down to Ascona? We came to tell you in person."

Mr Fuchs was pumping Damien's hand. "Congratulations! The pair of you. This is the best news we've had since John announced his engagement. I wondered why the devil you were not drinking Jess."

"Or smoking for that matter." conceded Jessica ruefully. "I could kill a cigarette right now but hubbie dearest would start foaming at the mouth if I so much as thought about having one."

"Quite right too." declared Mr Fuchs pompously.

Jessica raised a finger. "But!" she said feelingly, "I'm not the only person called upon to make sacrifices for the future generation of this family."

Mr Fuchs narrowed his eyes in puzzlement. "In what respect Jessica?"

"It is simple dad. I am bringing a new person into the world; a person who I will cherish and protect above all else. I expect my family to do the same. I want my child to grow up within a loving, caring family. I want them to feel cocooned within an extended family of loving aunts, uncles and doting grandparents who will spoil them rotten. I want them to grow up believing that love is continual, absolute and unconditional. So, for the benefit of an as yet unborn new generation, this family has to now shape up. I do *not* want to explain to my child why Auntie Sarah is not welcome in grandma's house..."

"That's unfair Jessie..." Mrs Fuchs began.

"I haven't finished mum. I've come all this way

today over the paternal protests of my overly worried husband to have my say and I mean to do so. I'm the one on the hormone driven, emotional roller coaster at the moment and I demand to be indulged. Right now I, and the little jelly bean within me, are the most important members of this family; important because we represent its future. Therefore I have every right to make demands right now; make demands on behalf of that future and my child's well-being. I strongly suggest that you listen to them and be aware that you will thwart me at your peril."

Mr Fuchs frowned, "What demands Jessie?"

"A very simple one dad. I ask only a simple question. Do you love your daughter Sarah?"

"Well of course I do...."

"Thank you. And you mum?"

Mrs Fuchs blushed. "She... she's my daughter whatever she's done. Of course I can't approve of..."

"A simple yes or no is required, mum, not a list of conditional clauses."

"Yes I love her. Of course I do. How could you think otherwise?"

"Good. I'm delighted to hear it because I love my sister too. So does John, so does Damien, so does Maria and, I fully expect, so will the child growing inside me. Well now it's time for us to prove it because, right now, we're not doing a very good job of loving her. My kid sister has been cast out into the wilderness at the very time she needed the love and support of her family the most. Her family was always the most important thing in the world to Sarah. She was always the most vulnerable of us; the one who needed to know that her family loved her and were proud of her the most. Now look what we've done to her. She's going through a terrible change in her life when she's had to face up to her own sexuality. I know society is evolving and there is not the same stigma attached as there once was but it's still a painful

511

process and not one that a person should be expected to pass through in lonely isolation and cast out from her own family; the very people whose responsibility it is to nurture and cherish her."

Mrs Fuchs bit her lip. "I... I had no intention to cast her out...."

"But nevertheless you did mum. We all did. None of us are blameless. Immediately we knew what Sarah was going through we should have rallied around and given her every support we could offer. Instead, not one of us has had the sodding decency to even pay her a visit to let her know that she is still loved and thought of. To our shame, it took Maria, the newest member of our family, to reach out to Sarah. It took Maria to tell Sarah that she was welcome amidst her family and so was her girlfriend. It took Maria to do the decent thing and she's set an example to every last one of us up by doing so. We've been a crap family to Sarah and it ends right now."

Jessica paused to tap a finger on the table imperiously. "Tomorrow Damien and I are driving back via the Toggenburg. We are going to tell her that she has all the support of Damien and I as well as John and Maria. I intend to tell her and her girlfriend too that we expect to see them at John's wedding and also, since I intend to rope her into being godmother, that we expect to see them at the christening of my child too. So, mum and dad, here's the deal. The younger generation of the family has made the collective decision to ensure that Sarah and her girlfriend are at that wedding as honoured guests and that they are both welcome within our family. That is non-negotiable so you're just going to have to lump it. Now of course you might decide that social reputation and bigotry is more important to you than your love for your family and boycott the wedding. In that case it will not be a matter of casting Sarah out of the family but of you casting yourselves out of your own family. John will have Sarah and her significant other at his wedding and I will have them at my child's christening; celebrations and perpetuations of our family. Whether you decide to be a part of that or not is entirely up to you."

Mr Fuchs swallowed. "Is this an ultimatum Jessica?"

"I'm afraid it is dad. I do not wish to bring my new-born child into a family that has forgotten the duties and responsibilities of unconditional love. So here is what is going to happen. The pair of you will turn up at John's wedding, suited and booted and, once there, you will stand united with the rest of us. You will warmly embrace your estranged daughter and ask her forgiveness. You will furthermore extend a hand of friendship and invitation to Sarah's girlfriend. You will do this in the name of your grandchildren and because I, as the carrier of the first of these, demand it. This is not a matter open to negotiation or procrastination. It is not a matter that deserves any further discussion. If you wish an active participant role in the future of your children and grandchildren then this is exactly what you will do. These are my final demands.

Chapter Twenty-Nine

It was late at night and Jessica, feeling strangely awake, had wandered out into the garden of her parent's villa on the hillside overlooking the town of Ascona and the great lake, Lago Maggiore, nestling between the mountains in the south of Switzerland. The night air was cool but her vigil was rewarded by the sparkling of lights along the lake front below her and the pale iridescence of the moon shining in the still waters of the lake. She felt a great calm now that she had thrown the gauntlet down before her parents. It felt almost as if she had grasped the mantle of leadership from her mother and father; relegating them to the past whereas she and the child within her represented the future. It had almost been a tangible assumption of power and recognised as such immediately. Her parents had seen her adamant emergence and had seemed almost frightened of this new and resolute daughter of theirs; the daughter who was through with their petty bickering and commanded their obedience to the imperatives of biology.

It was all about family after all. Families, however, were not static entities but rather dynamic evolving threads. The older generation must inevitably pass the baton to the new. No generation owned the family; they merely acted as custodians and, when their day was done, their custody would pass to their children and theirs to their own children in turn. There could be no slavery to the morals and attitudes of the past for the new age demanded its own set of rules. It was the younger generation that determined those new rules and the elders must bend to them or lose any relevancy they had. It was hard perhaps but it was the way it had always been. It was the way it had to be.

There was a boat out on the lake, its navigation

lights twinkling as it picked across the great body of water in curious isolation. Jessica watched it with pleasure and placed her arms protectively across her belly; a gesture she had found herself doing a lot in the past few days since learning of the life within. An owl hooted from a copse of trees a hundred metres away. Jessica smiled at the sound for it made her think of Sarah. Her singular little sister had always loved to hear the owls hooting by night in their childhood in the Toggenburg. She'd been able to identify what sort of owl it was by their call and she'd imitated them perfectly; leaning out of her bedroom window by night to hoot back at them and becoming excited if they responded to her. Jessica had loved her for those silly little quirks of hers.

She heard footsteps in the garden behind her and smiled once more. She did not need light to know who approached her in the dark. She would recognise her husband's step anywhere. "Jessica?" he called softly and hesitantly.

"I'm over here by the tamarisk honey."

He padded up behind her and folded his arms about her. She snuggled contentedly into the warmth of his embrace. "What the hell are you doing wandering out into the garden on your own?" he wanted to know.

"I just wanted a breath of air sweetheart. Don't worry... I wasn't slipping out for a crafty cigarette or anything."

"But it's cold Jess and you're not wearing a jacket. You've got to take care of yourself."

"Oh stop being all male and protective. It's not that cold and I'm not going to miscarry just because the temperature drops into single figures." She ameliorated her scolding by reaching over her shoulder to caress his face affectionately. For all her grumbling about it, she was oddly touched by his concern for her. "Have mum and dad gone to bed?"

515

He nodded. "Yes. They were still looking a little shell shocked though. Do you think you might have been a bit harsh with them?"

She shook her head. "No honey I don't. We don't have time to mess about any more, There are biological clocks ticking and I want this stupidity resolving. If it takes a shock to bring them around then so be it."

"This is important to you isn't it Jess. Bringing your family back together I mean."

"Yes. Yes it is. Becoming pregnant has brought it all into focus. It made me understand the things that are really important and right now..." she took his hand and moved it to her belly, "this is what is important; important for all my family."

He kissed her gently on the neck. "I love you Jess."

"I love you too."

"I'm scared Jess."

"Of what?"

"I don't know... the future.... becoming a father and all the things that go with it."

"Don't worry hun. You'll be a fine father and the future will take care of itself." She sighed in deep contentment. "Just think of all the things we have to look forward to. The future starts tomorrow but then it always does. Tomorrow though will be an exciting day. I'm going to call John and Maria in the morning and see it they can come through to the Toggenburg to meet up with us and Sarah. Then we can tell everybody about my pregnancy together and form a coalition of the new generation my parents will never dare to defy. I'm dying to see their reaction. Then again perhaps we can finally get to meet this enigmatic girlfriend of my sister's. Won't that be fun?"

"Yes... yes it will. God! I love you."

"Well that's what it's all about when all is said and done. The future's a cold dark place without it." She stared out over the lake. "With love though we can all face the future together."

****

To be continued...